A
NEW
SEASON

Enjoy

Irene H. Jones

A NEW SEASON

IRENE H. POUGH

YorkshirePublishing
www.yorkshirepublishing.com
Write Now.

ISBN: 978-1-942747-35-2
A New Season
Copyright © 2015 by Irene H. Pough

Yorkshire Publishing
3207 South Norwood Avenue
Tulsa, Oklahoma 74135
www.YorkshirePublishing.com
918.394.2665

Dedication

In loving honor of Mother, and in loving memory of Dad (1921-2014). Your love for each other, family and God has been an inspiration and guiding force in my life. Your marriage—an amazing love story no one can duplicate.

Acknowledgment

Dear Readers,

A New Season is the sequel to Demons of the Great Sacandaga Lake. This story came about while I was working on another idea for my Lake Series characters. When talking with my mother about my story idea, she suggested I write Summer's story instead of what I was working on. Low and behold A New Season came to life. While this is Summer's story, many of the characters from my first story reappear and add to the twist and turns along the way. Of course, we get to meet some new people as Summer's story evolves.

I'd like to thank the Greene County Sheriff Deputy who allowed me to pick his brain for ideas on which branches of law enforcement should be a part of Summer's story.

I hope you enjoy reading A New Season as much as I enjoyed writing it for you. Connecting with people is important to me, so please feel free to find me on Facebook at www.facebook.com/Author.Irene.H.Pough or contact me through my email at irenehpough@gmail.com.

Enjoy,
Irene Pough

1

Great Sacandaga Lake Community, New York

Summer Newman covered her mouth to hide another yawn as she sat quietly in the county courtroom. Two men whom Summer did not know, or care to know for that matter, were on trial for raping two women as well as acts of sexual harassment toward other women from the community. Her mother, Amanda Newman, having had her own encounters with the two men many years ago and the past winter, was there to be the prosecution's star witness against them. Summer fought to listen to the women give their testimony, as fatigue and jet lag from the long trip from Denver, Colorado, to Albany, New York, and the long drive to the county courthouse was rapidly seeking to overtake her.

───※───

Summer had originally planned to arrive in New York on the previous night in order to have adequate time to travel from Albany to the Great Sac Community. Once there, she would visit with her mother, meet her extended family, and have a good night's rest. However, a late spring storm in the Rockies that produced five inches of wet snow had delayed Summer's flight in departing from Denver. Then, when she reached Saint Louis to change flights, Summer encountered frustrated travelers who had been delayed from their departures by turbulent thunderstorms in the region. She had to scramble along with the hordes of people in the airport to find a connecting flight to Albany. What a mess! Summer finally reached Albany at four thirty in the morning. As promised, she called her mother, who was now staying at their grandmother's cabin in the Great Sac Community. A smile brushed her lips as she recalled hearing her mother's sleepy voice on her cell phone.

"Summer." The gosh awful noise coming through the phone sounded to Summer as though her mother was stretching, yawning, and goodness knows what else while greeting her.

"Hi, Mom." At that moment, it struck Summer of how tense she had been during her arduous journey. Hearing her mother's comforting voice was just what she needed.

"Oh, honey, thank goodness you finally called. You don't know how happy and relieved I am to hear from you."

Summer grimaced, as she realized just how tired her mother must be at that early hour in the morning. "Mom, I'm sorry to have awakened you."

"Oh, precious, do you honestly think I was sleeping?"

"No."

"That's right. I tried to sleep, but I was afraid I'd toss and turn Kevin right out of the bed." Summer could imagine her mother lying in bed while restlessly waiting to hear from her. Darn storms and delays. How many nights when Summer was still living at home had she come in during the early morning hours to find her mother still awake? When Mom saw that she was home, she'd simply smile at her and say good night. No words of chastisement, simply the smile and good night. Summer smiled as she listened to her mother continue on. "So, I got up and came out here where I've been curled up here in the chair by the fire to quietly think and worry about you. I'm surprised Gram didn't hear me and come out to investigate. At any rate, where are you?"

"Mom, I'm pleased to say that you no longer have to worry. I'm okay. I'm here in New York. Yes. I'm at the airport heading out to pick up my rental. Yes. I requested one with GPS. Yes. I will pull over and call you if I don't think the GPS directions match what you have already told me." Summer chuckled. "Oh, Mom, you know, you sitting up and waiting for my call reminds me of how you used to wait up for me when I was younger." They laughed together, then Summer added, "At least you worrying about me is one thing that hasn't changed in our lives since the beginning of this year."

"My Summer Sunshine, you are right about that. As your mother, I will always be concerned for you. I love you, Summer. This is going to be a tough day for both of us." Summer heard her voice drift off. It sounded as though she might be sniffling. At that moment, she wished she was there in the cabin with her mother to give her a hug, rather than being at least two hours away.

"I love you too, Mom. You've always been my hero. I know that you are nervous, and with good reason. Just remember what you always have told me."

"And what might that be?"

"That no matter what happens, we'll get through this together." Summer giggled at her mother's sleepy response. "Yes, I do sound like you. Go rest and I'll see you soon."

Summer returned her focus on the court proceedings. She was pleased that the session was moving along quickly. The courtroom was packed with people there for the trial of Junior McGrath and Shannon Green. While the defendants were on trial for sexual assault against two local women, Summer had to wonder how many people were there to simply hear what her mother had to say against them. She yawned. For the morning session, Summer was seated with her extended family, in the row behind her mother, Kevin, and their friends. She sat and looked at the silhouette of her mom, whose dark hair with slivers of gray hung down loosely on her shoulders.

As Summer sat there and watched her mother, she attempted to imagine what she must be feeling at that moment in time. Summer wondered if she would ever have as much courage as her mother, who was once again confronting more demons of her past. For thirty years she lived far away from here, in Baltimore, Maryland. Now, everything was different. Issues that unfolded during her mother's winter vacation with Andrew and Cassie had brought to light the truth about her past. Those demons that had driven Amanda away from the Great Sac Community had inadvertently left a lasting impact on Summer's life.

Summer watched her mother rise from her seat to take the stand. For one brief moment, she turned ever so slightly so that their eyes met. Summer knew that look. There was strength and determination in her mother's eyes. Amanda Newman was on a mission. *Only my mother, after thirty years of avoiding the scum who had raped and impregnated her, would have the courage to step up and help other women whom the two men had also violated. Hopefully now, Mom will find the justice that has eluded her for all of these years.* Summer sighed these thoughts to herself.

When her mother turned around to take the oath to tell the truth, before being seated, Summer saw her look at Dr. Kevin Wentzel of Baltimore, Maryland. Mom had met him at their dear family friends' cabin, Cassie and Andrew Phillips, the previous winter during the week of their vacation. Summer smiled to herself as she recalled the phone call she received after her mother returned home. She had simply said, "Thanks to Cassie and Andrew and their scheming, I'm in love. I almost died. I've been reunited with your Uncle Jim and some old friends. Plus, I could have been, but wasn't arrested for slugging two men who are no better than pond scum."

That abridged version of the week set the tone for the rest of their conversation. Summer laughed and cried as her mother provided in-depth details of the week's adventures. She was thrilled to hear that after all those years spent alone, Mom was ready to take a chance at love, with Dr. Kevin Wentzel, the director of Trauma Medicine at one of Maryland's finest medical centers. Summer knew from their countless conversations that followed that Mom was genuinely happy. She also was happy for her and the positive turn of events in her life. Summer had wanted to fly to Baltimore to see Mom and Kevin together; however, life did not allow that to happen for her back then. Lo and behold, Summer received a call from her mother stating that she and Kevin would be able to take a mini vacation for Valentine's Day. If a visit was acceptable with her and Mitchel, they were planning to fly out to Denver to see them. A smile touched the corners of Summer's lips as she recalled how much she had enjoyed meeting Kevin, and how from the first moment she laid her eyes on him, that she approved of him being in Mom's life. The smile didn't further develop on Summer's lips as she remembered how her mother was on "high-alert mother" mode and had watched the interactions between her and Mitchel. While Amanda had kept her feelings to herself, Summer knew how to read her mother's expressions. After five years of her marriage with Mitch, her mother did not exactly express warm affection toward him. It was as if she was waiting for Mitch to disclose his true self. Perhaps that came from her mother working with abused women, watching for signs of flaws in a relationship. Perhaps it was just Mom being Mom loving and worrying about her. Summer recalled that when she was growing up, her mother always saw things before she did. That eagle-eye trait of hers had annoyed Summer at one time in her life. Now, she understood it to be wisdom that does not come with book learning. Her wisdom is a gift from the Great Spirit. Summer knew that this morning, the trial and the private court session that was to follow had her mother's undivided attention. However, after the dust settled and they were together, Summer had a feeling Mom would take one look at her and know what was happening in her miserable life. The way things had been left back in Denver with Mitchel, Summer was actually glad for the break in her life's drama to be here for her mom. Maybe she needed this time away from Mitchel to sort out her feelings toward him. Maybe she did need to share her grief with her mother.

This morning, Summer's emotions were all over the place. Thanks to travel delays, Summer had not met her extended family as planned. Shortly before court began, she was introduced by Mom to her Uncle Jim, Aunt Melissa, and Samantha, one of her five cousins. There had been no real time for them to begin to get to know one another, just the initial "Pleased to meet you." It was a bit awkward and overwhelming for Summer to have this instant family, and be sitting here in court with them. Yet in the few minutes of interaction with her Uncle Jim, and listening to Mom and him speak with one other, Summer could tell that he was her mother's brother, from his smile to the same dark expressive eyes, and that drawing together of the brows—scary to see their likeness in each other.

Summer was content to sit in the second row on the aisle alongside her cousin Samantha, whom she looked forward to getting further acquainted with later in the day. From the vantage point where Summer was seated, she was able to glance over to the section of seats on the west side of the courtroom. She noticed a rather large man dressed in a red-and-blue plaid flannel shirt with the sleeves rolled up to just below the elbows and a thermal top, or as her mother would say, long johns covering his arms. Well-worn blue jeans covered his bottom half, and dirty work boots were on his feet. His legs were stretched out in front of him with his ankles crossed. Summer noticed his expression was grim. His eyes were intently focused on her mother, especially when she began to answer the assistant DA's questions. A shiver of uneasiness crept through Summer. She had to wonder. Was this man her mother's friend, or foe?

Summer watched and listened to her mother respond to the assistant DA's questions. She spoke with poise and clarity about the incident that had occurred between her, Junior, and Shannon on New Year's Eve at the bait shop pavilion, where the community party was held. Looking at the two defendants and hearing what they were doing to her mother, Summer could not blame her one bit for slugging and kneeing them. In her opinion, they deserved that and more. A smile touched Summer's lips. Oh yes, she was Amanda Newman's daughter, and she quickly decided it was probably for the best that she would never have contact with either man. Summer winced as she thought about her mom, and what encountering them on New Year's Eve had done to her. These were the two mystery men whom she had heard about in one, and only one, carefully worded conversation by Mom about her past and her biological father, who had raped Mom so long ago. At that moment, Summer did not know if she really wanted to hear the rest of her mother's testimony. Knowing that her mother was raped and hearing details of what had happened were two entirely different things. Summer would soon find out if she had the strength to hear what Mom lived through. But that would have to wait. It was the defense attorney's turn to cross-examine her about New Year's Eve. Summer watched her mother. Her heart almost broke as she saw the distress in her mother's eyes, and heard it in her voice. Still, Mom held it together to the point of effectively silencing Vanessa White, attorney for the defense.

Assistant District Attorney David Donaldson, much to Summer's relief, apologized for the inconsiderate behavior of Attorney White. In Summer's mind, the hoity-toity attorney with a chip on her shoulder should have apologized on her own. She listened to her mother, who clearly understood that her testimony for the prosecution was only for collaborating information, regarding the long-standing sexually violent behavior of the defendants.

It was thirty years ago, but with poise and unwavering voice, Amanda Newman told the heinous events that transpired and perpetrated against her, as if it had happened yesterday. Summer felt sick. She wanted to vomit right there in the courtroom when she heard Attorney White cross-examine and attack the strongest and most caring woman Summer had ever known. Summer was holding back the floodgates of her tears as she listened to Mom calmly respond. Now, everyone knew all the sordid details of that fateful day. Then, Ms. White made her final statement and asked the question that put the court into an uproar. "So, Amanda, thirty years after your alleged rape—"

Alleged rape! Summer could not believe what she was hearing. Did that woman honestly think her mother was acting? Hadn't the woman heard her testimony? Summer shook her head in disbelief. She now fully understood why her mother had left the mountains and had gone to live in Baltimore. No wonder Mom never wanted to talk about life up here in the Great Sac Community. The people who were supposed to care for her had abandoned her in her time of need! Many people appeared to be as stunned as Summer. They gasped and drew their hands to their mouths. At that moment, Summer felt something warm on her right arm. She looked down and found much to her surprise that Samantha had reached over in an attempt to console her. After brief eye contact and mouthing the words *thank you*, Summer returned her attention to the courtroom to observe the reactions of others. It was the man sitting across the aisle, whom she had observed earlier in the day and who had been watching Mom, who again drew her attention. His grim expression continued. His jaw was clenched. Now, she noticed that his hands were drawn into fists as they rested on his upper thigh. Summer had to wonder whom, or what, he wanted to punch. She hoped not her mother, because that man looked like he could be a force to be reckoned with.

———◦◦◦———

Summer was glad when the judge recessed court for lunch. She stood and stretched her tired body.

"Wow," Samantha quietly exclaimed, as she stood and looked at Summer. Her eyes were shimmering with wetness as she said, "Aunt Amanda sure is something. I can't believe how much courage she has had to live with those memories for all of these years."

"Yes, she is a courageous woman, plus strong and loving." Summer studied her cousin. It was obvious to her that there was definitely a family resemblance between them. "Samantha, I want to thank you for supporting me and Mom, especially when things got a bit dicey in there."

"You are very welcome. After all, we're family, and that's what our family does—we care for one another; especially when life gets tough."

"I suppose you learned that from your mother." Summer saw something pass over Samantha's eyes. "Sorry, I shouldn't have said that to you. Unfortunately, being my mother's daughter, I have a tendency to speak without censoring my thoughts. As a result, I sometimes inadvertently hurt others with my words."

"Apology accepted, with no hard feelings. You know, Summer, today is a bit awkward for me as well." Summer raised a brow in the same manner Mom would. She remained quiet to encourage Samantha to continue. "I mean meeting Aunt Amanda and you, and hearing what she went through in her life."

Summer nodded as a half smile formed on her lips. "Awkward is one way of putting it, I suppose."

"My dad has always shared stories with us about your mom and him growing up together, but whenever we would ask about her leaving in the summer of '79, he would make like a clam and close up. We all would see him go someplace deep within himself. Even after Aunt Amanda and Dad were reunited last winter, he still would not tell us everything that happened between them."

"I can understand that." Summer sighed. "Your father has had to come to terms with his past actions and how he has hurt Mom. He and some other men betrayed my mother's trust and abandoned her when she needed them most in her life. I don't blame her one bit for leaving here and not telling anyone other than Great-gram where she was." Summer gently placed her hand on Samantha's arm. "Now, you and everyone who was sitting here in court know the truth for why she left—why we left thirty years ago. One of those two lousy defendants is my father. Talk about awkward. Somehow, I have to reconcile all of this for myself and my future."

"Summer."

Even though Summer was appreciating her cousin reaching out to her, she was glad to hear the familiar voice calling out to her at that moment. She looked past Samantha and smiled.

"Yes, Mom." Summer attempted to sound upbeat as she saw the weariness in her mother's eyes. The morning had taken a major emotional toll on her.

"Honey, your Uncle Jim has recommended that we all head over to the diner for a quick bite to eat before coming back for the afternoon session." Amanda held her gaze on Summer. "Do you want to join us?"

"Sure. I'm famished!"

"Great. We'll be heading over in a few minutes."

<hr/>

Summer was standing out in the hall looking out onto the busy street while waiting for everyone else to finish using the restroom. She smelled a touch of roses as she felt an arm circle her shoulders. While inhaling a breath, she looked over to find her mother standing next to her. Summer turned and, without a spoken word, wrapped her arms around her mother's waist.

"Oh, Mom, I didn't tell you before that I am so proud of you." Summer sniffled, as she felt her mother's embrace tighten. Then Summer felt Mom's breath and gentle kiss on her hair, as she had done countless times before in her life.

"And I'm proud of you for making the choice to be here to support me, as well as to find out which slug is your father." Her mother's voice was intentionally quiet for only them to hear. "You know, honey, as much as I draw strength from Kevin, Cassie, Andrew, and your Uncle Jim, you are the one who means the most to me. I love you, my Summer Sunshine. You brighten my day, as you have since the moment you took your first breath. It's you and me kiddo, and together we'll get through this afternoon, just as we have encountered every other cumbersome mountain in our lives."

—⊸◊⊶—

As Summer and Amanda exited the courthouse with the others, she saw that man again. He was standing out on the sidewalk conversing with a small group of people. It seemed to only take a moment for him to sense their presence, turn his head, and watch them head down the steps, and onto the sidewalk to make their way across the street. There was something about that man that had worked its way under her skin, and Summer instinctively didn't like him, or at least the way he watched her mother.

—⊸◊⊶—

The afternoon court session was brought to order by Judge Van Talen, who would then gave her ruling on the rape case. Summer was once again seated behind her mother. She was well aware of her mom's nervousness. Would justice finally be served for the violence that had been inflicted on her so long ago? Summer drew in a deep breath as she listened to the judge.

"Mr. McGrath, Mr. Green, both of you men were wise in not requesting a jury trial. This is perhaps the smartest thing you both have done in your lifetime. With the testimony and evidence provided by the district attorney's office and your attorney's lack of substantial evidence to repudiate the prosecution, I have no choice but to find you both guilty—on two counts of sexual assault. You both will serve five-teen years for your crimes. I will add a personal note that you both are fortunate that the statute of limitations is up for Ms. Newman to file rape charges against the both of you. Trust me when I say, if, I could convict you both for your shameful acts against Ms. Newman, well, be thankful I am confined to abide by the law."

Summer smiled as her eyes met Samantha's and was pleasantly surprised to find she was also smiling. Justice had been served. Summer's father, whichever one that might be, was going to prison. Now, Mom and she would be able to slay the rest of that demon that had been haunting them for all these years.

Much to Summer and most everyone else's surprise, Junior asked to have a few words with Amanda before being removed from court. Summer drew in a breath as her gaze fell on her mother. Oh, yes, Mom was now sitting a bit straighter in the seat intently listening as Junior turned and looked straight at her. Summer watched him and listened. She was surprised by the sincere apology he gave to her mother. Mom had been his friend who had stood up for him when others had bullied him about his disability. Summer saw her mother raise her hand and use a tissue to dab her eyes. She heard Mom sniffle as she nodded and continued to listen to Junior. He did not stop speaking until he received Amanda's forgiveness. Summer was stunned by this request.

Then, Summer watched as her mother slowly rose from her seat. "Your honor, may I approach Junior?" her mother's voice was as cool and refreshing as a cold drink in the heat of midsummer. Having grown up as Amanda Newman's child, Summer knew to expect the unexpected from Mom. She had a feeling that this was going to be one of those times. Summer watched and prepared herself for whatever might happen next. With Judge Van Talen's permission, Amanda walked up to the defendant's table where she stood facing Junior. Her words were sincere as she commended him for taking accountability for his actions and his memories of their shared history. Summer felt a tear well up in her eyes as her mother accepted Junior's request for forgiveness. Then without fail, her mother brought humor and a touch of lightness into the moment when she too confessed her guilt of inflicting pain on Junior, by asking for his forgiveness. Summer smiled. At that moment, sheer pride radiated from Summer as she looked at her mother, a woman of incredible strength, who in the pursuit of justice had taught a valuable lesson to everyone present in the art of forgiveness and reconciliation.

The break passed by too quickly for Summer. She felt the butterflies filling her stomach as she walked back into the courtroom. Her mother was now wedged between Kevin and her Uncle Jim. That was too bad, for Summer needed Mom's strength to get through this session. Summer was prepared to once again sit in the row behind them when her Uncle Jim intercepted her.

"Summer, since this next part of the proceedings involves you, how about giving me the honor of caring for you along with my sister? Come on up here and sit next to me." With only brief encounters with him earlier in the day, his expression was difficult to read. Summer turned her gaze to find Mom watching their interaction. Her mother's nod and slight smile was all Summer needed to make her decision.

"I would like that, Uncle Jim. Thank you." A tear suddenly made its presence known and escaped down Summer's cheek.

"Hey now, us Callisons—or in your case since your mother changed her name to one of our ancestors—us Newmans are tough," Jim quietly spoke as he pulled his handkerchief out of his back pants pocket. He handed it to Summer and said with a smile, "It's clean, feel free to use it during court."

Summer sniffled. When she finished wiping her nose, she found her uncle still watching her.

"Summer, you look like you could use a hug." He slightly smiled. His eyes had that twinkle she had noticed earlier in the day. "I happen to have one just for you, if you want it." Summer nodded. She leaned into her uncle's embrace.

When Judge Van Talen was settled on the bench, Summer sat with the rest of the people that were allowed to be in the court for the final proceedings. She was not surprised that when the judge addressed her mother, she really seemed to care. Then Judge Van Talen spoke directly to her.

"Summer, regardless of what you hear in the next few minutes, remember, child, that above all else, your mother loves you. The choices she made thirty years ago, and has made over the years since then, were the right decisions for you both at the time when they were made."

With those words, Summer turned to look past her uncle to her mother. She was already looking toward Summer and nodded. In a moment, they would know the truth about the identity of Summer's biological father.

"The DNA of Junior McGrath and Summer Newman is not a match."

Summer gasped. How could that be? Something had to be wrong. Summer was confused as she looked over at her mother. The judge addressed Amanda; then, she spoke to Summer who turned her gaze from her mother to the judge.

"Summer, this is obviously a shock for you as well. I'm sorry, my dear, that you have to wait to find out the identity of your biological father."

Summer nodded, then turned to look at Mom, who was sniffling. It was her mother's brittle voice that drew Summer's concern.

"Your Honor."

"Yes, Amanda?"

"There's no possibility that the test is wrong. Is there?"

Summer saw the signs. Her mother was on the precipice of a panic. She leaned forward in an attempt to make eye contact with Kevin. Fortunately, he saw Summer look toward him and readily understood her concern. He nodded. Summer sat back in her seat and released an anxious breath of her own.

At that moment, her Uncle Jim raised his arm behind her and drew her close to him. Totally surprised by his reaching out to her, Summer immediately tightened. Then, she felt his gentle squeeze on her shoulder and she began to relax. *So this is what it's like to have extended family. I might be able to get used to this,* Summer thought, then listened to the judge respond to her mother's question.

"No, Amanda. There is no mistake. Junior's blood is O, and Summer's—"

"Is AB+."

Summer remained in her uncle's embrace as she reached her hand over his lap toward her mother, in hopes that she would see it and grab a hold. Tears were streaming down both mother's and daughter's cheeks. Jim fortunately intervened for Summer and placed Amanda's hand on Summer's hand. Without a word spoken, they laced fingers as their hands came to rest on Jim's lap. Then Summer felt her uncle's large calloused hand gently close around their hands. Summer breathed out a quiet sigh. She looked up at her Uncle Jim who was now watching her. His eyes spoke of love and concern. This morning, he had been a mere stranger to her; now they were family. How blessed she felt at this moment to have this man in her life.

Summer was still in shock as court was adjourned. She felt lightheaded and sat back down in the seat she had occupied. Jim placed his hand on Summer's shoulder. She looked into his caring understanding eyes. He quietly spoke to her, then excused himself to give Summer and her mother a moment alone. Kevin, who had been attending to Amanda, had also stood and moved slightly away from them to give some privacy. This was their moment to be family and come to terms with the unexpected results. Mom slid over to sit next to Summer. She opened her arms and invited Summer into her embrace. Summer didn't move. She simply looked at her mother, as if for the first time in her life—not sure of who she was.

"Summer, please. I need to hold you as we move on to sort through this mess." With that said, Summer understood that her mother's distress was equal to hers. She wasted no time in moving into her arms.

"Oh, Mom," Summer whispered. "Have you really known all of this time, who my real father is, and didn't tell me?"

Amanda sniffled back her emotions. "Summer, honey, please believe me when I tell you that I honestly believed Junior, or with a slight chance Shannon, might be your father. They raped me, and then nine months later, you were born. At that time and throughout your life, I never considered any other possibility. Obviously you were a late arrival, and your father and I never knew—until today. Oh goodness." Amanda released a deflated breath.

"Mom, do you mean to tell me that my father was here in court with us?"

"Yes, Summer." Amanda looked past Summer to Kevin and Jim, who continued to stand next to the row they were seated in, as if on protective detail. She released a breath laden with fatigue. "And he is looking at me, as if he were looking through his scope on his rifle ready to shoot me dead. Oh gosh, all hemlock I wish—I don't know what I wish, I guess just that things had been different for us." She reached over and touched Summer's cheek. "Honey, I am obviously going to have to address this with your father—sooner rather than later. Of course you will have an opportunity to meet him. Since this will not be easy for any of us, how do you want to handle meeting him?"

"First, I want to give you a hug." Summer didn't wait for her mother to respond. She leaned over and wrapped her arms protectively around her. "I love you so much, my amazing mom. Before we discuss my meeting my father, or perhaps not meeting him just yet, I need to ask you something." She felt her mother tighten her hold, and sniffle. "Is my father going to hurt you for not realizing that you were pregnant with me before you were raped?"

"My precious Summer Sunshine, that's a good question. Knowing the man as I do, his words will hurt." Summer sucked in a breath as her mother continued to speak with her I-mean-business tone of voice. "Honey, you can trust me when I say he knows better than to touch me. I'll deck him, and heaven help him if ever he hurts you!" A slight grin formed at the corners of Amanda's lips.

"Oh, Mom." Summer was now smiling while shaking her head. "I have no doubt that you will do what you must to protect us. So, about my meeting him."

"Yes."

"I suggest that we not put off the inevitable and get it over with." Amanda nodded in agreement. "So, Mom, is he still here, or has he left?" Summer and her mother eased out of their embrace. She watched her mother's eyes gaze over the people who remained in the court; then her eyes seemed to fix on one man in particular. Summer had never in her life seen this type of look appear in Mom's eyes before today. It was as if her mother had suddenly become another person. Then she spoke.

"Oh yes. He's still here, and as you said, we might as well get this over with."

With that, Summer and her mother stood. Amanda quietly spoke to Kevin and then Jim, who reached over and gave Summer a quick hug and reassurance that everything would turn out okay. She was glad that Uncle Jim was so positive. She sure wasn't, and her poor mother—well, she may appear to be okay; however,

Summer knew that inside, Mom was a mess. Summer walked slowly toward the courtroom door with her mother. As they approached the door, Amanda slid her hand around Summer's elbow and gently squeezed as she paused in front of four people. Summer watched her mother narrow her gaze onto one specific person. Her look was intense.

"Come with us," was all Mom said before ushering Summer out into the hall. They walked over to a quiet area by the one large window looking out onto the street below. Summer remained quiet as she watched Mom for cues. Her mother drew in a deep breath as a large man approached them.

"Amanda," his voice was curt.

Summer gasped as she looked at this rough-looking man, ready to kill his prey: her mother. His eyes seemed to be spitting out sparks of fire toward her mother, who appeared to not have any fear of him. Amanda, while remaining quiet, was speaking clearly through her eyes. She looked dangerous. Their silent interaction was a bit disconcerting for Summer, who could only watch.

"Don't say another word." Summer had heard that sharp tone from Mom many times before in her life. Fortunately, this afternoon, the tone was not being projected toward her. She watched her mother draw in another breath. Her brows continued to draw closer together while looking at the man. Then, she turned her gaze onto her daughter.

"Summer, this is your biological—" she paused, drew in a breath, and continued. "This is your father, Stephen Johnson." Summer thought she heard a slight softening in her mother's tone as she continued. "He is also the father of your sister Rose."

"Stephen Johnson," Summer repeated to her mother and added with a touch of sarcasm, "gee, Mom, aren't I lucky! Today, I get to meet Rose's and my daddy. No more half sister. The family secrets are out."

"That is correct." Amanda breathed out while tenderly looking at Summer. She knew how difficult this must be for her. Then as she turned to meet Stephen's glare, without warning, it was as if a blast of cold air swept over Mom turning her frigid. There was a chill in her voice as she spoke, "Stephen, this is our daughter, Summer Brooke Newman, who I might add is the only good that came out of '79."

"Summer." Stephen breathed out as he looked intently at his daughter.

"Hello." Summer's voice was equally cool to match her mother's.

At that precise moment, Summer felt her mother's arm come protectively around her. She was glad, because her father turned out to be the man whom she had been watching throughout the day. He was the rather large man dressed in a red-and-blue plaid flannel shirt with the sleeves rolled up to just below the elbows, and long johns covering his arms. Well-worn blue jeans covered his bottom half, and dirty work boots were on his feet.

2

Summer was well aware of the silent exchange between her mother and this man she had been introduced to as her father. Their eyes were communicating words only the two of them were privileged to know. There was one thing Summer was certain of at that precise moment in time. Her mother's stance and expression informed Summer that Mom had more to say to him. So Summer stood next to her and quietly watched and listened to the interaction that followed between her parents. Oh yes, her mother was on a roll.

"Johnson."

Wow! Mom called him by his last name, not his given name. Then there was Mom's tone—not good. She noticed the change in her expression. Mom's eyes seemed to take on a darker hue, and her jaw had tightened. Summer chuckled to herself. *Poor man*, she thought. *You're dead where you stand!*

"Mister, I see that look in your eyes. If you are going to act like a jerk and say things that hurt, then I recommend that you say them to me, and only me when we are in private."

Oh yes. Summer knew Mom meant every word coming from her mouth. She stood quietly, watching and listening to her mother as she verbally blasted her father.

"Johnson, I warn you. Don't you dare say anything that will hurt Summer. She is the innocent one in all of these turn of events here and now, and in our lives thirty years ago." Summer saw the man wince at her mother's words laced with venom. "I'll be danged if I'll tolerate you mistreating Summer on account of me heading out of here after *you*," Amanda made sure she emphasized the *you* for effect, "betrayed me. This is an over-the-top emotional day for all of us. I swear on Rosie's grave, if you hurt her—"Tears were streaming down her cheeks. Her breathing was growing increasingly shallow. Summer knew the signs in her mother: anger and panic.

"Amanda," Stephen beckoned.

Summer did not like what she saw unfolding. She protectively slid her arm around her mother's waist. Without realizing it, Summer tucked her chin while raising one brow. Her warm chocolate-brown eyes radiated the suggestion that hot embers lie out of sight. There she stood in solidarity with her mother.

"Mom, please take a deep breath. While you do, I have something of my own to say to my father, Mr. Johnson." Summer clearly spoke his name with an edge to her voice. She felt her mother's hand encasing her shoulder increasing in pressure. It was a warning for her to choose her words carefully. However, Summer chose to ignore the reminder for now. "My mother," and just like her mother, Summer emphasized her own important words. "My mother taught me to respect my elders. Even though you are my biological father, as of now, we are still strangers meeting for the first time. First, allow me to say I do not appreciate how you have spoken to Mom and cast a holier-than-thou attitude toward her while we were in court. Secondly, I waited my lifetime to find out the identity of my father. Like my mother, with what she shared with me when I was old enough to understand what happened to her, I believed that my father was one of her rapists. I will admit that I am relieved with the results."

"I'm sure you are." Stephen watched his daughter with the same intensity as when he had watched Amanda when they were in court.

"Hmm, interesting that you say that to me, and with a tone of self-righteousness." Stephen raised a brow as he watched and listened to his daughter, a spitfire like her mother. It was questionable as to who was more surprised when Summer completed her thought. "I don't consider an untrustworthy betrayer to be much better than a rapist. You all violated my mother."

"Summer." Amanda gasped, as she looked pleadingly at her daughter. "Please. We have a chance to start over."

"No, Amanda. Summer's right. I deserved that." Hurt resonated in Stephen's voice as he looked at his daughter standing before him. She was right. They were strangers; however, when he looked at her and listened to the vinegar in her voice, he heard echoes of him and Amanda when they were younger than her. Pain and hurt, rejection and the need for reconciliation, would it ever end for them? Stephen heard Amanda sniffling. His heart was breaking as he held his gaze on Amanda. Stephen longed to reach out and gently pull her into his embrace. He longed to make up for all his past transgressions. Knowing just how precarious this moment was for all of them, Stephen remained silent and listened to Summer continue speaking.

"Mom"—Summer turned slightly to look into her shimmering eyes—"I love you and am here for you. Right now, I need to state what I am feeling toward this man, who is my father."

Amanda held Summer's gaze as she slowly nodded. She knew her daughter, who was stubborn as she would not be satisfied until she had spoken her piece.

"Go ahead, Summer. I am listening." Stephen watched mother and daughter standing together as a united front.

"Mr. Johnson, the trial against Mom's rapists has ended. Praise be! However, your trial to determine if you are worthy to be known by me as my father has just begun, and I am both judge and jury who will either condemn, or exonerate you."

"Oh, Summer, no," Amanda wept out, as tears streamed down her cheeks. "Please, don't be bullheaded like your father and me. Oh please, my Summer Sunshine, I taught you better than that."

"Mom, like it or not"—Summer smiled warmly at her mother—"as you have known for years, and too often chose to ignore, I too am bullheaded. I also have something else that I feel I must say to Mr. Johnson." Amanda nodded, then drew in a deep breath as Summer returned her attention to Stephen, who stood close enough to feel the energy while quietly watching the interaction between mother and daughter.

"Mom has told me about her encounter with you during this past winter and how you two have already reconciled many of your differences. Obviously, my being your daughter is another unforeseen glitch in your relationship." Summer saw Stephen wince at her words and heard her mother suck in air. "For now, all I ask, Mr. Johnson, is that you give me time to process what has happened in our lives. My concern is not only for myself, but also for Mom and what this revelation is doing to her."

Summer heard her mother continue to sniffle. She saw something in her father's eyes as his gaze turned to her mother. Could it be love and desire for the past they once shared? Summer had no idea.

"Mr. Johnson, like you, there are other people in Mom's life. I believe that you are aware of the special relationship Mom has with Dr. Wentzel." He nodded. "Earlier this year, I had the pleasure of meeting Kevin, when they came out to Denver to visit Mitchel and me. Right from our first evening together, I knew that he is someone special and important in Mom's life. He makes her smile and laugh as I've never seen before. He understands her panic and is amazingly gentle when he helps her work through one. They converse about any topic and show respect for one another's viewpoint, even if they disagree—not that I saw much of that."

Summer smiled and giggled. She noticed the touch of a smile on the corners of her mother's lips as she added, "when Mom looks at him, I see her love and something else that cannot be put into words. Needless to say, I fully approve of their relationship. Even if I didn't, I know Mom is happy, and that is all that matters to me. Just so you know, Mr. Johnson, I hopefully look forward to the day when Mom and Kevin decide to marry and he becomes my stepdad. So please, knowing how I feel toward Mom and her relationship with Kevin, don't expect me to suddenly feel all warm and fuzzy toward you, and have an instant relationship with you, and please don't expect me to immediately say, 'I love you,' when I don't know you as a person."

Summer was aware of her mother's sniffles and her gasps while she spoke what was on her heart. She was also aware of the silent words spoken as her parents' looked at each other. It amazed Summer to find that after thirty years of being separated, they still had a deep connection. Unsure of what to make of that realization, Summer turned to her mother.

"Mom, I'm sorry if you are offended in any way by what I have said in the past few minutes. You have always taught me to speak my mind, and that is what I've done." Summer gently hugged her mother, then added, "I need some air. Will you excuse me?"

"Of course, Summer."

"Mr. Johnson," Summer slightly nodded toward Stephen before stepping away from him and Mom. Her expression was unreadable; however, Stephen had a pretty good idea from what she had previously said that she did not have a very high opinion of him. Why should she at this point in their lives?

Amanda watched Summer walk over to join Kevin, Cassie, Andrew, and their family. Summer said something to Kevin, who then gave her a gentle hug. At that moment, Amanda glanced over to see that Stephen was intently watching their daughter. She could only wonder what Johnson must be feeling as he watched Summer speak with Samantha. They laughed and walked together to the stairs, where they made their descent and disappeared from sight. Stephen, who had been intently watching their daughter and the others, turned his attention to focus on Amanda. His eyes penetrated deep into her, as if he was intending on opening every door into the deepest depths of her soul.

"Stephen, this is a difficult day for all of us." Without hesitation, Amanda slid her hand onto his arm. She felt his muscles in his arm tighten at her touch. Instinctively she pulled her hand away. "Sorry. Old habit." Silence hung between them for a moment until Amanda regained her voice. "Stephen, please listen and hear what I have to say to you." A renegade tear slid down her cheek. She wiped it away as she continued. "I am truly sorry that Summer was not very receptive of you as her father, or as a part of her life. Please, give her time." Stephen rolled his eyes. "Honestly, she really is an amazing young woman. Granted she has inherited most of my traits that we know are not all terrific, but honestly—" Stephen made a grunting sound while Amanda sighed. A tear fell from her reddened eyes. "If only, if only things had been different for us, perhaps—" She sighed. "We can't change the past. So all I can do is to ask you to do the right thing. Please, give Summer the time she has asked for to process what has happened in our lives."

"Amanda," Stephen's tone was cool as the lake in late spring. "For now, I will respect our daughter's wishes. However, once again our past has come back like a hungry mosquito sucking blood from us."

"I know," Amanda breathed out with exhaustion.

"Even though by now, all of Great Sac Community undoubtedly knows our business. We probably should go someplace more private, or perhaps more comfortable, to finish our conversation about everything that has happened here today, and revisit the events of thirty years ago."

"I agree, most of the community probably knows about us by now, and we do need to talk." Amanda really didn't want to talk. She simply wanted to disappear from the courthouse, and sit by the lake with Kevin's arms securely around her. Still, she knew she owed Stephen some private time for them to discuss their past and present.

"Looks like we will have to wait. Your knight in shining armor is headed our way."

"Stephen, please," Amanda sighed out, as Kevin approached them. "Kevin is a good man. I love him and trust him with all of my life. If it were not for Kevin and his support, I would not have had the strength to make it through today."

Stephen sighed, as he ran his fingers through his hair. "It's obvious that he loves you as well." Stephen allowed a faint chuckle to escape from him.

"What's so funny?" Amanda raised a brow, as she turned from watching Kevin to see what was causing Stephen to chuckle.

"Oh, just that, Doc, being a city man and all, he has the demeanor of a man, or male animal ready to lay stake on his claim." Stephen half smiled as he bumped his shoulder into Amanda. "That would be you, Calli," calling her by his old nickname for her. "You're his gal. He's coming to let me know I've lost you to him."

"Johnson," she sighed out while shaking her head at his analogy.

"Amanda," Kevin's expression and voice was filled with concern, as Amanda slipped into his embrace. "Honey, you're looking exhausted. Are you about ready to go?"

"I am tired. However—" Amanda raised a brow as her gaze met Stephen's. She dared him to say something. For the moment, he remained quiet. "Kevin, before you came over here to join us, Stephen and I were discussing the need to go someplace more private to further discuss our latest life-changing revelation about our past."

"That is understandable." Kevin's gaze and quiet voice was just what Amanda needed. "Honey, are you sure you feel up to continuing this discussion right now?"

"No, I don't feel up to this. However, I want to get this conversation finished." Amanda sighed. Stephen saw how drained she was. He was about to speak when Amanda said to Kevin, "Would you, Cassie, and Andrew be acceptable to Stephen and me going over to the diner to have a few more minutes alone for us to finish talking about him being Summer's father?"

"Of course, sweetheart." With that, Kevin leaned in to give Amanda a simple kiss. It was one for effect, to inform Stephen that he and Amanda were a couple. "We'll walk downstairs with you and be outside in the park waiting for your return." He then drew his arm protectively around Amanda's waist and escorted her from the courthouse.

"Oh, Samantha, it is so beautiful outside. Too bad we had to waste most of it being inside for the majority of today." Summer felt the warm sun shining down on her, as she walked with her cousin down the courthouse steps.

"Yes, it is beautiful. Let's consider it a gift for all you had to endure throughout this day."

"Mmm. I'll accept the gift."

Samantha drew in a deep breath, then slowly exhaled. "Great day to go hiking—not too hot, not to cool, just right."

"I agree. Being a park ranger, I get to spend plenty of time out on the trails in the Rockies. When I'm out on the trails, I get to interact with park visitors. Mostly, I enjoy being out communing with nature. Mom says it's our heritage from our great-grandma."

"It sounds like an awesome job. Do you have many people getting injured while they are hiking?"

"There's always one or two people during a season who do get hurt from a minor accident. It's because they do dumb things when they're on the trails. So many injuries could be avoided if they just used common sense. The critical accidents are heart-stoppers. Fortunately, we haven't had a major one in about six years. Then, I have the wildlife, and their safety, to be concerned about as well. Again, people do dumb things, and far too often, it is the innocent animals that get blamed for humanity's stupidity."

"Wow! Summer, you sound so much like my dad, and what he says about people who don't respect the mountains and its natural inhabitants around here."

Summer beamed as she took in her cousin's words. "I guess that makes sense since we are family." Both women smiled and nodded. Then Summer added, "Family. I like that. I'm hoping to come back here this summer and spend some time with your family and check out some of the local hiking trails."

"It's the best." Samantha's smile increased with a hint of pride. She looked around. Summer turned her gaze to see what, or whom, Samantha was looking at. Her eyes focused in on her Uncle Jim and Aunt Melissa as they spoke with Cassie, Andrew, and Kevin. Her mother had disappeared across the street to the diner to have a private conversation with her father. Summer didn't want to think about him. She returned her focus back to what Samantha was saying.

"Even though my dad thinks that the Adirondacks are the greatest mountain range, I would enjoy going out to Colorado and checking out the Rockies."

"Goodness, your dad sounds so much like Mom. You should have heard her comments about the Rockies when she came out with Kevin to visit me in February."

"Is that the first time she was out to visit you?"

"Oh, no." Summer laughed. "Mom loves to find any excuse to come out and visit me. Actually, I think she likes to come west not for me, but for the Rockies. Two years ago we did some light hiking and camping in the back country. There were times when I could barely keep up with her. Still, as much as she enjoyed herself, Mom is convinced that the Rockies don't hold a candle to the Adirondacks. Samantha, even though our parents obviously have their feelings about these old mountains being superior to other mountain ranges, you are welcome to come visit me anytime."

"Thanks, Summer. I just might have to take you up on that offer. Knowing my dad, I better tell him about the trip after I return home so he can worry after the fact."

"Your dad, my mom." Summer sighed. "I can't believe how similar they are."

"Scary, don't you think?"

"I don't know." Summer glanced back over at her family and friends, then added, "I am beginning to like this family of ours."

"I'm glad to hear that, because I already like having you as my cousin."

Summer and Samantha allowed companionable silence to fall between them as they walked over to the bench and sat down together. A bird cheerfully sang out from a nearby maple tree, as they sat silently together while taking in the moment.

"Summer," Samantha kept her voice quiet. "You and your mother certainly had a shock with the DNA results."

"That's for sure."

"You know, I saw your father's—" Summer drew in a sharp breath. Samantha quickly continued upon realizing that Summer was not ready to call Stephen her father, "Sorry, *Stephen's* initial reaction as your mother and the judge discussed your blood type. Summer, I've known Stephen my entire life, and I have never seen the expression that he had on his face as he too processed your mother's words, or unspoken words." Samantha studied Summer for a moment then added, "With the time you and your mom spent with him outside of the courtroom, you obviously have met him, so I am curious to know, what are your first impressions of your father?"

"My first impressions...well," Summer slowly began while exhaling, "it was awkward, to say the least. My mother in her typical fashion laced him out in lavender, and then I was not much nicer."

"Oh, Summer. I am so sorry to hear that. Dad and Stephen graduated from high school together. Since my parents and

Stephen are good friends, he comes over to our house all of the time, or Mom and Dad go over to the bait shop or to Stephen's cabin to hang out. You know—they're friends. Please, try to believe me when I tell you that Stephen is one of the kindest and honest men I know. He would do anything for anyone and not expect anything in return."

"Kind? Honest? Do anything for anyone? Samantha, you were sitting in the courtroom with me. Remember, we sat together. Didn't you hear what my mother said in her testimony? If it hadn't been for the wonderful Stephen Johnson fighting with her, she never would have been at the lake that night where she encountered those two losers." Without warning, tears began to stream down Summer's cheeks. "Maybe you like him. But in my eyes, my father is just as guilty as the two rapists. He betrayed my mother's trust. If he had been a man, as he should have been, we probably would have stayed up here."

"Summer, I'm sorry for your pain. None of us can change the past. From conversations I've had with my parents, what I know of Stephen, and the amazing phone conversations I've been having while getting to know your mom, I am certain that both of your parents are well aware of the mistakes that they both made in their relationship. Speaking in defense of your father, I will say that I firmly believe that if Stephen knew your mother was pregnant that August of '79, he would have done everything in his power to protect her and resolve their differences. He loved your mother. Summer, in all fairness to Stephen, you need to remember that it is your mother who made the choice to walk away. If I were you, I'd hold out any judgment on him and his and your mother's past until you've been able to get to know him for the man he is today." Samantha glanced at her wristwatch, then over to Summer who was dabbing her eyes. "I have to get going so I'm not late for my shift at the nursing home. Summer, I hope I wasn't too out of line with you and that you will not hold my words against me. I just think your father deserves a fair chance."

Summer sniffled as she held Samantha's gaze. Her cousin had been brutally honest and given Summer much to consider. "Samantha"—Summer swallowed the copious amount of wetness collecting in her mouth—"I appreciate your honesty. Have a good evening at work."

⸺⬤⸺

Summer was glad to be alone as she sat in quiet solitude. First, she watched her cousin leave; then she watched the blur of people passing by on foot and in their vehicles. It felt good to not have to think about anything, especially her family. The sound of clicking heels drew Summer's attention. She looked up to see Cassie approaching her. A slight smile came to her lips. This woman was her mother's best friend, and boss. Through the years, Cassie had taken on a role of aunt in Summer's life, and been known to be a trusted confidant. As a result of Cassie and Andrew being family friends, she had grown up with their two sons, Nathan and Ryan—sometimes royal pains and other times best friends. Now, as adults, while having traveled down different roads, Summer continued to keep in touch with her two dear childhood friends. Later, she just might have to call Nathan and lean on him for support as she sorts through her feelings.

Click-click-click. Cassie's heels sounded on the pavement. Summer smiled. Now, having been through three court sessions in one day, as well as her conversation with Samantha, Summer felt as though she had just jumped overboard from a sinking ship. Cassie was the life preserver that she would cling to at this moment. In true Cassie style, she did not wait for Summer to invite her to sit. She saw the need in her eyes now flooding with tears. Cassie quietly sat down and placed her hand on Summer's leg. Summer sniffled as she leaned her head on Cassie's shoulder.

"Summer, I know that you are in shock with the news you have received." She handed Summer a tissue, unaware she still had her uncle's handkerchief.

"Thanks." Summer sniffled then wiped her eyes and nose. She looked over at Cassie with sadness. "Aunt Cassie, I can't believe what Mom endured, the secrets she has carried with her all these years, and now the truth about my father."

Cassie removed her hand from Summer's leg and drew her arm around the younger woman. Summer clung to her.

"Summer, we all are in shock with the latest revelation in your mother's and your lives. You're correct in that your mom has held much of herself locked away for thirty years. Safety and trust are huge issues for her."

"But, I thought she did trust you."

"She did, and she does. Summer, it's important to understand that your mom only trusts to the point where she would not become totally vulnerable and exposing her shame and betrayal, and that's okay. Only this year—along with you, Andrew, and Kevin—have I learned who she really is. In fact, every day I learn more of who my friend is as a person. Summer, your mom is very special to me. Knowing the truth about her past does not alter my feelings for her. If anything, the truth has drawn us closer. I admire her for her courage and strength."

"I'm glad to hear that, Aunt Cassie." Summer hugged her and sighed. "I just can't believe that somewhere in her mind, or heart, she didn't have an idea that Mr. Johnson might be my father."

"Oh, Summer," Cassie spoke with a calm, soothing voice. "One thing I am absolutely sure of is that until today, your mother did not have any idea that Stephen Johnson was your biological father."

Summer sighed as she looked down at the ground. She slid her foot back and forth on the pavement, as she had done as a child when considering something of great importance. "First, Samantha was defending Mr. Johnson, now you're defending Mom. I'm so confused."

Cassie drew Summer closer to her. "It's okay to be confused. All I ask of you is that you remember one thing for me."

"What's that?"

"Remember, Summer, that no matter what your mother has done or not done, the one thing that has remained consistent in your life is that she loves you."

"Thanks, Aunt Cassie. You always know what I need to hear."

The sound of voices approaching caused both Summer and Cassie to look up. Summer immediately saw that Andrew and Kevin were walking in the lead, with Jim and Melissa walking behind them on the sidewalk. The mood was subdued. Summer was glad that they were all here with her, and her mother—when she returned from her meeting with Mr. Johnson. As they came closer, Summer noticed that her uncle was not focusing on Aunt Melissa or the other men, nor was he looking toward her or Cassie. His eyes were focused on the diner across the street.

"Uncle Jim, are you okay?"

With that, the others turned their attention toward Jim, who had looked over at Summer. His smile was slight, as if for show. Summer noticed something in his eyes.

"I'll be better when your mother and Johnson finish their conversation." Jim drew his brow together as he added, "And I see them emerge from the diner without the diner being damaged, and neither of them needing medical attention."

"Jim," Mel cautioned, well aware of Jim's concern and seeing what his response was doing to Summer. "You're upsetting Summer."

"Sorry, kiddo." Jim winked at Summer.

She gave him a nod and touch of a smile as her lower lip slightly lifted at the corners. In only knowing one another for a few hours, Jim had already claimed his niece as one of his girls. Summer had no idea of just what that meant, other than that he intended on loving her and, if need be, protecting her should a situation rise to warrant his attention.

"Honey, Summer asked if I am okay. I honestly answered her."

"Yes, you did, Uncle Jim." At that moment, Summer felt the need to stand. She stepped over to stand by her uncle as she spoke, "Thank you for not coddling me, for being honest and sharing your concern. Actually, with knowing Mom's temper and her panic, I too am concerned not so much for Mom, but for what she might do to Mr. Johnson."

"I see we are thinking similar possibilities of what might be happening over there."

"I don't think either of you need to worry," Kevin added, after glancing across the street.

"Oh?" they both asked.

"Amanda is emotionally and physically drained. All she is probably wanting to do is go to either her grandmother's cabin or Cassie and Andrew's cabin by the lake."

"Kevin's right," Cassie added. By now she had stood up and stepped over to stand next to Andrew.

"My concern is for Amanda and the fact that she has fought off panic attacks all day. Eventually, her body is going to give in, and her attack will come on hard. Having witnessed Amanda defending herself against Junior and Shannon last New Year's Eve, and not being able to get through the crowd to assist her, I do understand your concern. Before Amanda and Stephen left to have their private conversation, Amanda assured me that all she plans on doing is conversing with him. I trust her to keep her word."

"Kevin, you made a good point. Still," Summer now turned her gaze to her uncle and asked, "Uncle Jim, do you think we should go over and order something to drink to enable us to spy on them?"

"Summer, with the information Kevin has shared with us, and knowing your mother as I do, I believe that at this moment it is in our best interest to stay here and wait for her return."

"On that note," Cassie interjected with the hope of changing the subject to give Summer an emotional break, "perhaps we should decide on what we all are going to do about dinner for this evening. Shall we all dine together?" Cassie turned her gaze to Melissa.

"That would be lovely." Melissa turned to Jim and asked, "Don't you agree?"

Jim realized that he had everyone's eyes on him. He gave a slight uplift to the left corner of his lips. Summer chuckled, as she noticed he did the same quirky thing her mother often did when considering her answer.

"Uncle Jim, you better say yes." Summer's eyes sparkled as she spoke with a familiar tone Jim had heard countless times before in his life.

"Summer, no offense, but, little girl, you sound an awful lot like your mother." Everyone laughed, including Summer. "So, since you women have decided for us that we are dining together, when and where do we want to have dinner?"

"Well, since Amanda and Kevin are spending the night at our cabin, and we know that Amanda is exhausted and will need to rest, or perhaps take a stroll by the lake to decompress, I suggest we dine at our cabin." Cassie looked directly at Andrew and then at Kevin. Both men wisely nodded in agreement. "Melissa and Jim, how about you plan on joining us at the cabin, let's say, around six. We'll barbeque."

"Wonderful idea! What is already on the menu, and what would you like for us to bring to add to dinner?"

"We have crab on ice, Amanda's favorite, steak, and fresh asparagus. So we'll need a salad or baked potatoes." Melissa and Cassie continued to quietly kick around ideas for dinner, excluding the others for the moment.

"So, sis has gone to crab over lake trout." Jim shook his head, and listened to Kevin and Andrew share the story of Amanda trying sushi and her dislike of raw fish. A picture of the moment and what it must have been like came to Jim's mind with ease. He chuckled, then turned to Summer. "What about you, Summer, what's your favorite fish to eat?"

"Lobster, but if it helps to ease your mind, I do enjoy salmon, largemouth bass, and venison over beef."

"Really now. Venison you say." Jim smiled. His eyes seemed to dance with delight. "When did you acquire a taste for deer meat?"

"Mom used to take a road trip out to Western Maryland to a place where she was able to buy venison. Since the meat had not gone through government inspection, I'm not sure how legal her buying the meat was, but we did have fun on our secret road trips, and the venison was awesome to eat." Jim had a twinkle in his eye and a very slight smile as he listened to Summer. She noticed, and cleared her throat. "Anyway, living out in the Rockies, I do have friends who hunt. Plus, Uncle Jim, I enjoy big game hunting. How about I come home with you and Aunt Melissa to help with food preparation for later and tell you about some of my hunting adventures? I'd also enjoy hearing about hunting in these parts."

"Has your mother ever told you any stories about us hunting?"

"No," Summer said with a touch of hesitancy. She saw something in her uncle's eyes. He had stories, and Summer was certain that with her mother involved, they were going to be doozies.

Jim did not wait to start sharing stories. People passing on the sidewalk turned their attention to the frivolity of the group. Summer found herself to be lost in the moment, laughing to the point that new tears were streaming down her cheeks.

"Great! The old storyteller is at it again. I certainly hope he is not retelling the worn-out story of me and the moose on the lake."

Summer jumped when she heard her mother's quiet voice coming from behind her. Apparently no one in the group had noticed Amanda approaching them. Summer squealed. With the noise she made, everyone turned their attention to her. Amanda stepped around Summer and slid into Kevin's arms.

"So, Mom, how did it go?" Summer quietly asked.

"It went." Amanda sighed. "I came close to a full-blown panic." She felt Kevin's hand slowly begin to move on her back, as he always did when she panicked. Even now it was a comfort. "I guess it could have gone better, but then again, it could have been a whole lot worse for us. Our past is like a nor'easter. Every time we think we've begun to dig out of the storm, more trauma blows in and is piled on top of the snowbanks of unresolved issues. I told Stephen I'm sorry for the pain I've caused him." Amanda looked tenderly at her daughter. "Summer, I also told your father that I'm sorry for the pain I've caused you."

"Me?"

"Yes, honey, you. Thanks to me, you have not had the privilege of knowing your father. Even though Johnson and I have our moments"—Amanda sniffled. She felt Kevin's hand slightly move on her back. She drew in a deep breath—"your father is not a bad person. Yes, he and I made mistakes. It's our past. You both deserve a chance to get to know one another as adults."

"Mom."

"Summer, allow me to finish. I told Stephen that if he wants to contact you and try to build a relationship with you before you leave at the end of this week, that he should contact either Cassie"—Amanda glanced over to Cassie who nodded, then returned her gaze to Summer and added—"or your Uncle Jim to help him set things up." Amanda paused and turned her gaze to her brother. "Did you get that, Callison, I offered your services for you."

"I heard you, sis."

"Good, because right now, I need some distance from Johnson. Jim, I need for you to step up as my brother and take care of my daughter for me. After all, Johnson is your best bud." Everyone noticed the slight sting in her voice. Then Amanda sighed. "I'm tired and more than ready to get out of here." She was looking directly at Kevin, who nodded in agreement.

"Mom," Summer called out, concerned for her mother, who was leaning into Kevin for strength. "We have begun planning dinner for this evening. I'm going home with Aunt Melissa and Uncle Jim to assist Aunt Melissa with their contribution for our dinner."

"Oh, that sounds nice." Amanda yawned. "Oh, excuse me."

"Amanda, we're taking you to our cabin to rest, then picnic with us by the lake," Cassie added. "Melissa, Jim, Summer, we'll see you all around six, or a little before."

Summer hugged Mom, Kevin, Cassie, and Andrew. She stood on the street with her Uncle Jim and Aunt Melissa for a brief moment, watching the others slowly walk toward Kevin's rental. Then the three turned and headed in the opposite direction.

3

Melissa stood at the kitchen sink peeling potatoes to be boiled for a traditional potato salad, and scalloped potatoes with fresh chives and sharp cheddar cheese. An assortment of fresh vegetables was placed on the counter by the sink. Movement from outside the window caught her attention. Pausing from her work, Mel watched Summer slowly walk toward the path that Jim, the children, and she had made years ago leading into the woods. Summer had her phone to her ear and appeared to be deeply engrossed in a conversation. A smile brushed over Mel's lips as she watched her niece.

"My goodness, Mellie, what has captured your undivided attention?" Jim asked as he entered the kitchen and walked over to stand next to Melissa. He opened the drawer where Melissa kept the paring knives and removed the one he preferred to use. Without a word, Jim picked up a potato and began to peel alongside her. As they worked together, she turned on the faucet and washed off the potatoes. As Melissa carefully placed the potatoes in the old aluminum kettle to be filled with water and then on the stove to boil and cook, she glanced up at Jim and softly spoke with concern in her voice.

"Summer is outback walking on the path into the woods. She has her cell phone to her ear. Seeing her out there reminds me of our girls when they lived here at home. Countless times, when they wanted privacy during their conversation, they each took the portable phone out there with them."

"So our niece has caused you to take a trip down memory lane." Jim paused with his peeling and glanced over at Mel. "Is that a good thing or a bad thing?"

"Good thing, although I am concerned for Summer."

"Me too, Mellie. Tell me, what worries you?"

"Jim, remember the shock we experienced when we all found out that Amanda had come back here and then went missing out on the lake?"

"Do I remember? I will never forget that night."

Melissa stopped peeling the potato she was holding and laid the knife on the counter. She wiped her hands before allowing her gaze to fully meet Jim's. "Honey, we know how we felt with regards to Amanda, and how we responded."

"Why do I feel a *but* coming on?" Jim could see the invisible wheels turning in his wife's head.

"That's right, there's a *but* in all of this."

"Tell me what you are thinking, Mellie. Knowing you as well as I do, I will not doubt you are right in whatever is concerning you."

Mel softly smiled at Jim, then glanced out the window before returning her attention to Jim. "Our family has been through so much emotional pain over the years; especially the end of last year and the beginning of this year. You and I know how we are feeling about Amanda and everything that has happened, and I have a fairly good idea of how Amanda might be feeling." Mel saw Jim's slight turn of his head. "Well, perhaps I don't, considering Stephen is directly involved."

"Honey, with those two, anything is apt to happen."

"True. But, Jim, we know that somehow they will figure this out, and what Summer being their daughter will mean for their lives from this day forward. What we don't know and what concerns me is how Summer is feeling with hearing about her mother's past, and now knowing who her father is. One part of me says leave her alone to sort through her feelings."

"And the other part of you wants to be her loving, caring, meddling aunt and offer to be a confidant for Summer."

Mel smiled. She leaned over and gently kissed her husband on the cheek. "Callison, you are so smart. That is exactly what I am thinking. So, since I am stepping away from the last of the potatoes, please finish them for me. Then please fill the kettle with water just to the top of the potatoes and get them going on the stove to boil and cook."

"Anything else, madam?" he teasingly asked.

"Well, now that you mention it"—Mel's eye sparkled to match her smile—"if you feel like it, you could prepare the vegetables for me as well."

"I could," Jim responded with a hint of laughter in his voice, as he nodded toward the window facing the sunny backyard. "Go on outside and check on Summer. I'll man the kitchen."

—◦◦◦◦◦—

A cool gentle breeze rustled the leaves of the hardwoods tucked in among the evergreens. In a tree nearby, a cardinal whistled out to his mate. The sound of weeping caused Melissa to hasten her step as she walked farther into the woods. Melissa walked with quiet steps toward the mournful sounds, her eyes searching the area for Summer. As Melissa came around the bend past a cedar tree, the sound of weeping grew louder. Mel paused when she saw Summer sitting on a fallen pine tree. Summer had obviously ended her call. She sat there on the log with her knees drawn up against her chest. Her feet rested on the tree. Her head was tucked into her arms and on her knees. She wept.

"Summer," Mel intentionally kept her voice quiet as she slowly approached Summer. Her heart ached for her niece. "Summer, what's wrong?" Mel asked, as she stood only a few steps away from her niece.

It was then that Summer looked up. Her eyes were puffy and red. Her cheeks were wet and rosy from the tears. Melissa rushed over to her and sat down on the fallen tree next to her.

"Oh, you precious child, come here," Melissa said as she wrapped her arms around Summer. "Goodness, Summer. You look as though your world has fallen part." Mel felt Summer tighten her arms around her. Years of experience cautioned Mel to tread lightly at this point. She intentionally kept her voice quiet as she spoke. "Summer, I'm here for you. You go right ahead and cry some more, if that will help you to feel better. Or, we could talk. Whatever you want or need from me, you tell me." Melissa did not utter another word. She simply held on to her niece as she wept.

Summer sniffled as she continued to lay her head against her aunt's shoulder. "Thank you, Aunt Melissa."

"Oh, Summer, sweetie, you don't need to thank me for sharing my shoulder with you to cry on. My arms were intended to care for sad or injured ones, whether they be my own children, strangers I meet while on an EMS call, or you, my niece. Summer, you and your mother are my family. I will always be here for you and your mom."

Summer eased from her aunt's embrace, pulled the handkerchief from her pocket that her uncle Jim had handed her while in court, and wiped her nose. She looked at the handkerchief and softly chuckled. "I guess it's a good thing Uncle Jim let me borrow this."

"That it is." Mel softly smiled. Her heart ached for Summer and the turmoil she appeared to be in. "So, is there anything you would like to talk about, or did my hug do the trick?"

"Your hug was greatly appreciated. Thank you." Summer sniffled. "Oh, Aunt Melissa, my life is such a mess." She sighed. "I need to talk with Mom about some stuff happening in my life out in Colorado, but now with everything that has erupted with my father—my father, the one and only Stephen Johnson! Can you believe it?" Summer shook her head as if to clear herself of the fog she felt had engulfed her. "Mom told me a few stories about Mr. Johnson when I was younger."

"Mr. Johnson?"

"Yes, Aunt Melissa, Mr. Johnson. At this point, that's about as far as I can go with acknowledging him as a part of my life." Summer sighed. "Aunt Melissa, it was so awkward to stand there in the hall of the courthouse with Mom and look at my father for the first time in my life. I had noticed him during the court proceedings glowering at Mom, and took an initial dislike toward him. How dare he act that way toward her! Mom went through heck because of him."

"Oh, dear." Sorrow filled Mel's body as she listened to her niece continue.

"After court was adjourned, and we were in the hall together for the first time as a family, it was not good. The electrical current rippling between Mom and him could light up the whole east coast. It was intense, and then I added my own electrical charge to it." Melissa remained quiet, observing the intensity of the expressions that took form on Summer's face as she spoke. "My poor mom, she's exhausted, no doubt heading for a panic—if it hasn't happened yet, and well, you heard her."

"Yes, I did, Summer." Mel gently rested her hand on Summer's shoulder. "I trust that when and if she panics, Kevin, who loves her deeply, and your mom's friends will assist her through her crisis."

"You're right." Summer attempted to smile.

"Summer, you are so blessed to have Amanda as your mother. She loves you and would bring down the world if it meant protecting you and making you happy." This brought a slight smile to Summer's lips, and a chuckle. "Her life experiences have taught her valuable lessons. As your mother, she is able to see the big picture for all of you."

"The big picture?"

"Yes, Summer, the coloring and landscape of the picture of your life has changed. Stephen is now woven into your mother's and your life, whether you care to acknowledge him as your father or not. What I heard your mother say to you is that Stephen's and her past is just that—their past. Their colors are vibrant reds, greens, blues, and the terrain is rocky and rough with some quiet streams occasionally thrown in to the picture for moments of peace and tranquility. Right now, with today's DNA results, your mother needs her own space and time to process everything that has happened—and changed—in all of your lives. In the midst of all of this, your mom loves you, and even though she is now in a relationship with Kevin, she still cares about Stephen. Summer, Stephen's not the same man your mom left thirty years ago. Your mother longs for you to know your father for who he is as an older man. She is right. Stephen is a good man. Summer, I believe that you should listen to your mother and find the time to speak with your father before you head west."

Summer sighed out heavily, as if the weight of the world was on her shoulders. She sniffled, gazed around the forest, then allowed her eyes to once again meet her aunt's.

"Thanks for listening to me and for your words of wisdom. I certainly have more to consider."

"Glad I could help." Mel stretched her legs out in front of her, and then went back to sitting position. "Is there anything else you'd like to talk about?"

"Not right now." Summer glanced at her wristwatch, then over at her aunt. "Oh goodness. It's getting late. I'm sorry, Aunt Melissa. I came here to help you and Uncle Jim, and here I sit in the woods blubbering like a baby."

"Don't worry about it, Summer. Your Uncle Jim is on potato salad and scalloped potato detail as we speak."

"Uncle Jim?"

"Why, certainly." Mel's eye twinkled with a hint of mischievousness. "After twenty-nine years of marriage, I have him just about trained."

"You're kidding, right?"

"Perhaps you should ask Jim if I'm kidding." Melissa patted Summer's leg, then stood and stretched. "You take as long as you need out here. I'm going to the house to see how your uncle is coming along with the salad."

Summer watched her aunt make her way along the path toward the house. Her family continued to surprise her with kindness and love. Still, as much as Summer was enjoying this new relationship, she felt the need for the familiar voice of an old friend. Sliding her hand into her front pocket of her slacks, Summer pulled out her phone and selected her contacts. Scrolling down her list of actual names and code names to hide certain identities from the wandering eyes of her husband, Summer stopped when she reached business contact NPAAL, also known as Nathan Phillips, Attorney-at-Law. Plus, Nathan happened to be Cassie and Andrew's oldest son and her best friend. She waited. Unfortunately, Summer reached Nathan's private voice mail.

"Hi, it's me Sum. I'm here in the Adirondacks with Mom and your parents, well, right now I'm with my aunt and uncle. But anyway, I really need to talk with you. Please give me a call A-S-A-P. Thanks. Bye."

Summer sat for a moment with her phone in hand listening to the birds. She was just about to call her boss to check in with him when her phone rang. Releasing a sigh of relief, Summer answered the call.

"Hey, Nate, thanks for returning my call so quickly."

"Hello, Summer. I'm sorry I missed your call. Mom had my ear. From what she said and your voice on my voice mail, court was quite stressful for all of you."

"It sure was. Did your mom tell you that I met my father?"

"She did." Nathan paused. He understood Summer's moods perhaps better than most people—with the exception of Summer's mother. When Summer remained quiet, Nathan quietly continued. "So your father is your mother's old lover, and not a convict. That's good news, right?"

"I guess when you put it that way, it isn't quite so bad." Summer sighed. "But, Nate, that's not why I called you. Well, not totally."

"Oh. So tell me what's going on." Silence. "Sum, we've been friends since our diaper days. You know you can tell me anything, and unless you give me permission to share our conversation, I will hold your confidence as if you were my client. My lips are sealed. So talk to me, Summer."

"Nate." Summer drew in a deep breath. She then slowly released the breath knowing that she had to state what was on her mind before she lost her courage. "Nate, I need you to be my lawyer. I'll pay your fees, of course, and I think I need you to find a private detective to look into some things for me." There, she said it. Summer drew in a cleansing breath and waited for Nate to respond.

"You're serious."

"Yes. I am dead serious." Summer sniffled.

"Okay, then I need to know why you want me to be your attorney. Is now a convenient time for you to talk privately with me? You're laughing. That's a good sign."

"I believe that sitting by myself here in the forest behind my aunt and uncle's home with only the woodland creatures lurking about and birds in the air is about as private as I can get."

"I have to agree with you." Nathan chuckled. "You in nature, why am I not surprised?"

"You know me well. That's why I need you on my side."

"Summer, you have me worried." Nathan paused then quietly added, "Tell me what has you so upset."

That was all Nathan needed to say, and for the next half hour, Summer shared her concerns regarding her marriage. He asked questions, Summer responded. "Well," Nathan sighed. "From what you have shared with me about the changes you've seen for the past nine months with Mitchel and his evasive response to your call earlier this afternoon, I believe you have a right to be suspicious of him. Since I am practicing law in Maryland, I am not familiar with Colorado divorce law. However, before you go into a panic on me, allow me to say, I do happen to have some friends who live in Colorado Springs. Nikki and Alex are both attorneys who also happen to be married and have a private detective on their staff. If you will agree to having them take lead on your case, representing you with me, and doing the legwork out there, I will be pleased to corepresent you. Plus, at key times, I will make trips out to Colorado to be in court with you."

"Oh, Nate, really?"

"Yes, and, Summer, I was committed to helping you when you first said that you need me to be your lawyer. You are my best friend."

"And you my best bud." Summer sniffled as she swiped away the tears that had pooled in her eyes and were now trickling down her cheeks.

"Now," Nathan's voice remained quiet, while his tone became very serious, "about my fee."

"How much?" Summer felt a pang of dread knowing that Nathan's attorney fee was probably going to be more than she could afford. Plus she had agreed to have his friends represent her.

"Since you are my best friend, and at times like a sister I never had, I will not charge you for my services."

"Nate!"

"Summer, I'm doing this for you pro bono. I'll see what I can negotiate with Nikki and Alex for an acceptable fee for their services. Regardless of what they say, you are not to worry about the financial cost." Nathan listened for a moment. "Summer, are you crying?"

"Yes. But, Nate, this time they are tears of happiness. I know with you helping me, everything is eventually going to be okay."

"Yes, it is, Summer. I promise you that as your friend and as your attorney. Thank you for trusting me to take care of this for you. Sum, unfortunately, I need to end our call as I have a client waiting for his appointment with me."

"I'm sorry to have detained you. But thanks again, Nate, for everything. Good-bye."

"Bye, Summer. We'll talk again soon." She heard the clicking sound in her ear. Nathan was gone for now to help someone else. Summer pressed End on her phone. It was time to rejoin her family.

—————

Just as Summer stepped from the path into Jim and Mel's backyard, she saw her mother and Kevin, both dressed in casual clothes; they were standing with Jim and Mel by the picnic table. An older woman with a wrinkled, elongated face, dark eyes, stringy white hair, and similar build to her mother, was sitting in one of the cushioned lawn chairs. When the older woman smiled at something Uncle Jim had said, Summer knew in her heart who was sitting in the chair: her great-grandmother. Finally, she was going to meet the woman who was so special to her mother.

It was Jim who first noticed, and he drew the others' attention to Summer approaching them. Amanda turned her gaze to her daughter. In one fluid motion, Amanda unlaced her fingers with Kevin, then stepped away from the others and walked toward Summer. Her eyes observed everything about her daughter. Fatigue. Bewilderment. Something else that caused Amanda to go on high "Mom alert." Neither one spoke as Summer melted into her mother's arms. Summer breathed in the familiar scent of her body, along with the smell of wood smoke on her clothes, and in her hair mingled with the scent of lavender shampoo. Her mother's arms were drawn protectively around her, as if to shield her from the world. If only she knew everything that was going on in her life. Now was not the time to broach the subject and add to her worry.

"Mel told me you and she had a good conversation."

"We did." Summer nuzzled closer to her mother. "Mmm. I've missed your hugs."

"I like hearing that, and having this time to give you a hug. This has been a rough day."

"That it has." Summer released a long slow heavy sigh.

"I have a feeling being in court, and discovering that Johnson was your father, was only part of your rough day."

Summer raised her chin to look at her mother. She sighed, then quietly asked, "How do you do it?"

Amanda held her daughter's gaze. Summer had grown and matured into a remarkable woman. Yet right at that moment, age didn't matter. Summer was Amanda's little girl who needed her mommy.

"In a couple of weeks, I will have had thirty years of practice in learning all of your moods and expressions and how to interpret them. You, my precious child, are in pain." Summer sniffled as her mother continued to quietly speak to her. "For some reason, you feel you need to protect me from whatever is going on in your world. Honey, while Johnson is enough of an issue on his own, I can handle more than one crisis at a time. When you're ready, I have a shoulder reserved for you."

"Oh, Mom. I love you." Summer sniffled.

"I love you too. Now, since everyone is probably watching us having our mother-daughter moment, let's go join them. Then, I may introduce you to your great-grandmother, Gentle Spirit."

Summer knelt down next to the chair so her great-grandmother, Mary Freeman, did not have to strain to look up and see her. The aged woman smiled with warmth, while revealing a few gaping wholes where teeth should be. Then Summer noticed her wrinkled hands. When the older woman touched Summer's hand, she felt a gentle tenderness in her touch.

"Gram, it is so nice to finally meet you. Mom has told me many wonderful stories about you." Summer felt the tear escape her eyelid and slide down her cheek.

"What's this? Oh for land's sakes! Child, are you a crier like your dear mother?"

Summer glanced up at her mother who had her hand over her mouth to hide her smile. She slightly raised her brow, then winked before returning her attention to the family matriarch. "Yes, Gram. Unfortunately, like Mom, I'm a crier along with being stubborn, occasionally threaten to string people up for bear bait—"

"Oh great," Jim mumbled under his breath. Unfortunately, both Amanda and Mary heard him.

"James, that will be enough of your comments about our Summer. I'm pleased to hear that Summer has enough gumption to stand up for herself. She obviously learned that from our Amanda." The old woman nodded for good measure. Pride radiated from her eyes as she looked at her family.

"There you go, James," Amanda was softly laughing as she teasingly spoke. "My daughter has gumption, and Gram's right, she learned it from me, James Callison."

"Amanda," Jim's voice was tight, as he was forcing himself to not say what was foremost on his mind at that moment.

Mary burst into laughter as she listened to her grandchildren. She saw Summer's gaze pass between her mother and uncle. The older woman reached over and patted Summer's arm. "Child, in time you'll get used to those two, and how they pick on each other. I'm just glad I lived to see them put aside their differences and be family once again, and now you are here with me as well. I don't think life could be much better than this."

4

The cool air of evening by the lake, the gentle lapping of water against the shoreline, and the softly darkening sky was the calm, peaceful ending everyone gathered at the cabin needed—to bring an end to a rather trying day. Empty meat and fish trays and dishes once filled with salads and vegetables remained on the picnic table, as everyone sat back in the Adirondack chairs in front of the porch in a semicircle to enjoy coffee, or more wine and conversation under the pines with a perfect view of the lake.

Mary Freeman sat in a sturdy cushioned lawn chair with Jim's jacket around her shoulders to ward off the evening chill. One of Cassie's throw blankets covered her legs. Of course, the older woman had initially protested all the attention until Amanda stepped in and spoke to her in Mary's language of their people, the Mohawk. Mary had taught Amanda to speak this language when Amanda was a young child. Jim, being a busy little boy with plenty of ideas to occupy his mind, had not bothered to learn his grandmother's language. He had thought it was a silly game for them to play—learn the strange language. Years later, this alternate means of communication had proved to be a blessing for Mary and Amanda. Many times during the past thirty years, they had used this language to speak privately on the phone.

Summer, along with everyone else, watched and listened to the two women converse. She was mesmerized by their voices as they spoke and laughed with ease.

"Wow, Mom, besides this being rude for you both to speak in a language we can't understand." Jim added a comment supporting Summer's observation. Amanda remained quiet, although she rolled her eyes at Jim for what he had said as Summer continued, "This is amazing to finally hear you and Gram speaking this language together. I have to say, when I was growing up, it was a bit unnerving to only hear your side, especially when I didn't understand you, not that I understand either of you here and now. I remember that it was weird to listen to you and watch your expressions as you spoke. I always suspected that the two of you were talking about me." Summer allowed her questioning gaze to pass between them. Both women softly smiled and chuckled.

"Sometimes we were," her great-grandmother responded. Then she turned her aged eyes—nearly the same coloring as Amanda's and Summer's—to Jim, who was intently observing the women of his family. "Other times your mother and I were discussing her unresolved issues with your uncle. More than once over the years, James would show up at my door while we were chatting. He'd make himself comfortable and sit right there at my kitchen table sipping his cup of coffee while we talked about him."

"That was rude," Summer responded while looking sympathetically at her uncle.

"I agree," Jim added in solidarity with Summer.

"Neither one of you needs to encourage the other, thank you." Amanda huffed.

"Summer," Mary's voice took on a soft, yet commanding tone as she spoke. "You may think we were being rude, if you like. In reality, it was our way of staying in contact with each other, and keeping my Amanda safe. I was the only one who had believed her"—Mary shot Jim a quick chastising glare—"and the only one who stood up for her, not that it did any good around here. But as we all know, that is the past. Now, thanks to my Amanda's bungled secret return, my intervention last winter, and today's verdict in court, after tonight, we no longer need to have that secrecy between us."

"I'll drink to that," Amanda said, as she raised her nearly empty coffee cup to toast her family. Others joined in with the toast. Laughter and conversation filled the air.

"Mmm." Summer sighed out with contentment. She drew in a deep breath as she looked at the landscape before her. "This is awesome being here in the lower Adirondacks with all of you. Mom and Uncle Jim, I'm glad that Gram got you to talk things out between you. For all of my life, Cassie and Andrew have been my adopted aunt and uncle. Their sons and I have been close as we grew up together, in a way like siblings or cousins." Summer turned to look in Cassie's and Andrew's direction. "Please don't interpret what I'm about to say as dissing you and not appreciative of everything that you have done for me over the years."

"Summer, as you said, we've known you all of your life. We know you too well and would never think that of you."

"Cassie is right, Summer. You have a special place all of your own in our hearts."

"Thank you, Cassie, Andrew. I do love you both."

"We know, Summer, and we love you."

Summer then turned her gaze to her family. "Aunt Melissa, Uncle Jim, it is nice to have spent time with you and getting to know you as family. Now, you both are also special people in my life, rather than as family members Mom and I are estranged to. While I still love Cassie and Andrew, well—"

"Summer." Her Aunt Melissa sniffled. "I believe we all understand what you are trying to say to us. We love you as well."

"Thanks, Aunt Melissa." Summer stretched. "I didn't mean to get to sappy on all of you." There was mutual consent of all gathered there that Summer had been fine in expressing her feelings. "Will everyone please excuse me? I do believe I'd like to take a walk down by the lake before it gets too dark for me to see where I'm going." Summer turned her gaze to her mother. Amanda smiled warmly at her and nodded. She understood her daughter's need to be alone with her private thoughts.

"Don't worry, Summer," Jim spoke up. His voice seemed to echo in the night. "If it gets too dark and you can't see, you give us a holler. We'll send your mother for you. She still has eyes like a hawk, whether it be day or night."

Summer noticed that Jim winked at his sister. Amanda smiled and shook her head as she gazed at her brother. In that moment, their eyes communicated a private conversation no one else was privileged to know.

Her family. Summer's thought immediately turned to the new addition in her family: her father, Stephen Johnson. Even though they now had to deal with Johnson being part of their lives, and what role he might play in Summer's future, so much good was happening in their family to offset the unresolved issues confronting them. Her mom and uncle are reunited.

"Even though your uncle was teasing with you, and me with his remark, be careful walking down there on the rocks by the water's edge. With the loss of light, you may easily slip and turn your ankle."

"Yes, Mom. I'll be careful." Summer took one step, then paused and turned back to look at her mother. "You know, Mom, you really don't need to worry about me."

"Oh?"

Summer held her mother's gaze. Her mother looked exhausted from the day's emotional demands. Summer was glad that Amanda was surrounded by people who loved and cared for her well-being. She glanced around while beaming with joy at the people in her midst.

"Think about it. We have Aunt Melissa who is a nurse here with us. Kevin is a trauma specialist, and Andrew a pediatric cardiac specialist, not that I'm a child anymore, but I'm sure you get my point. They, along with you and Great-Gram, are here to look after me if I should get hurt."

"Point taken, thank you." Amanda smiled as she added, "Go on and enjoy your walk."

"I will. Love you, Mom."

"I love you too, Summer, be—" Amanda grinned. Her weary eyes seemed to twinkle with happiness from deep within. "I know, you'll be careful."

With that said, Summer turned toward the path. Amanda listened to the conversation that resumed while she watched her daughter make her way to the lake using the same path she had walked on during the past winter. Last winter, Amanda had walked over packed snow blanketing the earth. Now, the path was dry with old, dead pine needles blanketing the ground. Amanda knew the scent of pine, and the sound of the water on the lakeshore was sure to be soothing to Summer's troubled soul.

Kerr-plunk. The noise of a fish jumping in the lake caused Summer to pause and look out at the ripples. *It must have been a big one,* Summer said to herself. *Maybe I should get a one-day fishing license and try to see what I can catch. I wonder if Uncle Jim would let me borrow a rod and lures? I suppose I could always check out the bait shop I passed by to come up here to the cabin.* Summer stood for another moment watching smaller movement and ripples on the lake. Then, she continued on toward the water. The sight of a large rock looked enticing for Summer. She carefully walked over to it and studied its form with her eyes and hands. Perfect. In no time flat, she had scaled the rock and was perched on top of it, looking out over the lake toward the eastern shore. Summer drew in a deep breath while allowing her mind to mull over the events of the day.

Lost in thought, she did not know how long she had been sitting on the rock. One thing was certain, the sky was growing increasingly dark as night was falling. The sound of a rock shifting by the water's edge drew Summer's attention to the shore near the rock where she was sitting. Summer saw the figure of a man quietly approaching.

"Kevin? Is that you?"

"Yes, Summer, I too felt the need for a walk and some time for quiet reflection. Seeing you sitting up there, I wonder, if perhaps together we could reflect on some things that involve both of us. May I join you on the rock?"

Summer glanced down at him. She wasn't too sure if he could climb up the rock or not. Then she remembered earlier this year, when her mother and Kevin had visited her in Colorado. They had gone to do some light hiking on one of Summer's favorite trails in the Rockies. On that day, with a light snow packed under their boots, Kevin had proven to be agile and more athletic than she had first assumed. He also had attentively cared for her mother—major act of approval in Summer's eyes. Summer smiled down at him while realizing that it was best to not assume anything about this man. His eyes were bluer than the lake, and seemed to radiate fondness and concern. A touch of gray over Kevin's ears was just enough to make him appealing to a woman's eye. Summer smiled to herself as she thought of her mother's first description of Kevin. Her mother was correct. Kevin was some nice eye candy, and the best part for Summer was that Kevin was her mother's eye candy—finally sweetness for Mom.

"Well, Kevin, if you would like to join me on my perch, then by all means climb up." Summer's smile seemed to move to her eyes as she teasingly added, "Do you need my help?"

Kevin paused to chuckle. "Summer, if you aren't something! With your expression and your tone of voice, there is no doubt in my mind that you are Amanda's daughter." Kevin climbed up onto the rock while Summer laughed and commented about her mother's fine attributes. "You know, Summer, last winter on the morning your mother and I met, she had a panic attack."

"I'm not surprised. Speaking of panic, Mom's been evasive with me about how she was feeling about court and everything. Has she had her meltdown yet?"

"Yes, Summer, when we got back here this afternoon, she had a major panic attack. It was the panic where she was crying hysterically—hyperventilating. I needed to hold on to her so she felt safe."

"Wow!" Summer was surprised to hear how her mother's panic had changed from when she was living at home and Mom would panic. "I'm glad to hear that you know what to do to care for Mom." Her voice had grown quiet.

"Summer, I care more than you'll ever know. Attending to and alleviating pain from physical trauma is second nature to me. The human brain, on the other hand, is well protected by skin and the skull. We may use technology to see when something physical happens to the brain. However, a person's mental health is another world all of its own. Your mother's panic, her mental health, is important for me to understand—if I am to love her and care for her as a whole person. Believe it or not, your mother is helping me to be a better trauma specialist."

"Really?"

"Yes. She is my teacher, helping me to be more sensitive to my patients' needs and to take into account that the person lying on the trauma table may have emotional trauma beyond what we are able to immediately recognize. I'm learning her physical and verbal cues and possible panic situations that may trigger a panic."

"Wow! I guess growing up with Mom, I took a lot of stuff for granted."

"Summer, she's your mother, and you accepted her for who she is." Summer softly smiled and nodded while Kevin continued to speak. "Acceptance is important for anyone, especially for someone with a mental health illness that we may not readily see, or understand. Your mother and I have come so far from the first day we were together and she panicked." Kevin drew in a deep breath and slowly exhaled. Summer remained quiet. She wanted to hear about how Kevin had helped her mother with her panic. "That day, as soon as your mother stood, I could see something was wrong with her. She was like a frightened bird taking flight from the porch. It took every ounce of restraint in me, not to mention Cassie warning me, to remain on the porch and not immediately follow her down here. When I did follow her path, I found her sitting on this rock. At that moment, as strong as your mother is, she seemed so fragile, as if a gust of wind could break her into small bits of being. Summer, you and I don't know one another very well. However, you remind me of her with your own strength and fragility."

"Hmm." Summer looked intently into Kevin's eyes as she spoke. "Strength and fragility, that is an interesting observation you've made about Mom and me. In light of our conversation, I don't think you see us this way simply because you are a doctor, who is trained to observe and diagnose." Kevin remained silent, listening. "I believe that most people immediately see our strength and fail to recognize that we too, like most everyone else, have our insecurities, or as you prefaced it, our fragility." Kevin nodded in agreement with Summer. "You know, Kevin, I'm not at all surprised by how well you already know Mom. When you both visited me in February, I was blown away by how the two of you click. It's as if you've been together forever, rather than a few months. You're good together. Mom is most assuredly happy being with you. But, Kevin, the fact that you have managed to see, or perhaps understand, me on a deeper level than even my closest friends is a bit disconcerting for me."

"Summer, it was never my intention to put you ill at ease."

"Somehow, I already know that, and I am certainly not uncomfortable with you. It is obvious that you care about Mom and me. Thanks." Silence replaced their conversation as both sat and looked out over the lake. Then Summer chuckled and asked,

"Kevin, when you first came to talk with me, you mentioned this rock. I'm wondering, is this the rock that the two of you were snuggled together on when JJ and Peter caught you kissing?"

"Oh yes, this is the rock where—" Kevin's slight turn of his mouth and his eyes informed Summer that he had gone to the memory of the first day he had shared with her mother. Kevin cleared his throat and then continued, "Actually, Summer, it may have been a good thing that your cousins came along when they did."

"Please, say no more!" Summer felt her cheeks warming at the thought of her mother and Kevin getting it on. "Even though I'm happy for you and Mom, there are some things I don't think I want to know about Mom and your relationship."

Kevin chuckled along with Summer's giggling. They grew quiet again.

"Kevin, I'm glad we're having this time alone to talk and get to know one another. Sitting here and listening to you, I definitely understand why you and Mom click."

"What do you understand about our relationship?"

"I'm really pleased to hear about how you care for Mom and her panic. But it's more than that. When Mom first told me that she was in love with you, I think it was the first week after you both returned home, and she called me to tell me about her adventures."

"Adventure is one way of putting it."

"That's what life is with Mom, an adventure." Summer laughed as memories soared through her mind like a warm breeze. "Anyway, when she said she loved you, I had my doubts that it could happen so fast. I thought she was being reckless. Then when you were visiting me in February, I saw that you two click, but being my mom's protective daughter and not wanting her to be hurt by you, or any man for that matter, I still had my doubts. Today, you were Mom's rock to stand on. I'm pleased to see my worries were for nothing. Now, it is obvious to me that you deeply love Mom and she definitely loves you." Summer's voice was soft, yet filled with emotion while simply stating the fact.

"Summer, I am proud of you and how protective you are of your mother. You are very observant and correct. Your mother and I do love each other. When my divorce from Meg is final, we plan on marrying and intend on spending the rest of our lives together. I tend to be a bit old-fashioned in my thinking. Since you and I are talking about your mother's and my relationship, do you approve of us marrying?"

Summer sat for a moment looking out over the lake before turning her gaze to meet Kevin's gaze. Her expression was a contradiction of happiness and sadness. "Kevin, are you asking me for my permission to marry Mom?"

"Not your permission, but your blessing."

"Thank you for thinking of me. Oh yes, Kevin." Summer sniffled. This surprised Kevin. "Oh, yes, I approve of you marrying Mom. You know, Mom has waited her whole life for you, so have I."

"Hmm." Kevin had an idea of what Summer had meant by her words; however, he needed to hear them from her so they could continue this conversation. "Would you care to elaborate on what you mean when you say that you, as well as your mother, have waited for me?"

"Sure." Summer sniffled again and wiped the wetness from her eyes with the back of her hand. "I have never shared this with Mom because I knew it would make her sad."

"And you wanted to protect her from being hurt."

"That's correct." Summer exhaled. "When I was a little girl, I was jealous of my friends who had both their mom and dad in their lives. It didn't matter if their parents were married or divorced. My friends had a family that was complete with both parents. Even though Mom and I are our own unique family, loving and caring for each other, it was obvious that Mom and I were missing the link we needed to make us like everyone else."

"That must have been difficult for you."

"Sometimes, it was excruciating. Especially when Mom had her motorcycle accident. Even though I was nineteen when Mom had the accident, she almost died. For the first time in my life, I realized how alone in the world we had been and were. I know that if she had died, I would have turned to Cassie and Andrew as my adopted family, and they would have loved me. Still, it would not have been the same."

"I know you said you had not shared any of your childhood feelings with your mom, and I understand why. Summer, have you ever shared your trauma of your mother's accident with her?"

"No, Kevin. I knew it would upset her to know how deeply she had scared me, and well, you know, I love her."

"Yes, I do know."

Summer allowed herself to giggle, pause, and draw in a deep breath. "You know, Kevin, there is something else I never told Mom about the father thing."

"Oh?"

"Yes," Summer smiled. "When I felt lonely, longing for a dad, I would pretend that Uncle Andrew was my father."

Kevin chuckled. "Makes sense."

"I guess it does. Still, even though he walked me down the aisle when I got married, something, or someone, was missing." Summer fell silent. She quietly brushed away another tear.

"I'm not surprised that you asked Andrew to step in on your wedding day as your father. I happen to know that he loves you very much. Still, it is understandable that you felt a void in your life."

"You get it!" Summer gave Kevin a smile of approval. "I did have a void. But that is no longer the case. Now, on the brink of turning thirty years old, I have you in my tattered life as my soon-to-be stepdad." Overcome by emotions, Summer began to weep. Kevin shifted his weight from his one hip onto the other to allow him access to his back pocket. He pulled out a small packet of tissues and handed one to Summer. She raised a questioning brow at his preparedness.

"I keep stocked up on tissues for your mother." Summer giggled as she regained her composure and dabbed her eyes and nose.

"You know her well."

"Yes, I do. Now, back to our conversation that has about puffed up my ego to the outer reaches of the universe. If we're not careful, we might need to call in your mother to bring us back to Earth." Summer giggled again. Kevin liked hearing Summer let down her guard. Her giggle made her come alive, and he hoped to hear more laughter from her in the days ahead. "Thank you, Summer, for wanting me to be a part of your life."

"Why wouldn't I?"

"Well, I'm far from perfect and have three estranged children who would be more than pleased to share their opinions of me with you, especially my daughter, Nicole."

"Mom has told me briefly that you and your children have had some issues with your divorce." Summer's voice had grown softer as she spoke with concern. "Do you think things will get better between you and them after the divorce is final?"

"At this point in my life, I have no idea of what is to become of my children and me. I suppose time will only tell." Kevin grew quiet.

"I guess that old saying is appropriate for me as well with discovering who my father is."

"That it is. You know, Summer, I've been giving considerable thought to all of us, including you and your father. In light of everything that has occurred in your mother's and your life today, I see some similarities with your father and what I'm experiencing with my family."

"Oh, will you please share your thoughts with me?"

"Certainly. Since my children were born, I have had a relationship with each of them. We were a family. At one time we all truly loved each other. We built some wonderful memories together. But along the way, we also unintentionally and intentionally hurt each other and grew apart. Bitterness, resentment, and anger replaced the love we once shared. With the separation and divorce, Kyle, Nicole, and Brian chose their allegiance to their mother."

"I'm sorry." Summer breathed out.

"So am I. Summer, it is quite obvious to me that besides your protective nature, you have a strong allegiance to your mother, and I don't blame you one bit for loving her. She is mighty special." Summer agreed. "Today, you and your father met for the first time in your lives. It obviously has been a shock for both of you. What grieves my heart for you is that both you and your father missed out on what my children and I had, a lifetime of memories. However, there is hope for the two of you."

"Hope?"

"Yes, Summer. Hope. Now, you and your father have an opportunity to create a meaningful life together as parent and child, granted you are both adults, but if you both want a relationship, you can build it together. I'd give anything to have an opportunity to rebuild my relationship with any one of my children."

"Kevin, Summer, where are you two?" Amanda's voice carried down to the lake from under the pines. "Jim and Mel are getting ready to take Gram home."

"We're finishing our conversation and coming along," Kevin called out. He turned to Summer and quietly spoke. "Summer, I'm glad we've had this time to talk. I hope it's the first of many that I get to share with you as my stepdaughter. We best return to the cabin and bid farewell to your, or should I say, *our* family."

"Our family. I like hearing that." With that, Summer slid down the face of the rock. She took a few steps, then waited for Kevin who took his time to ensure that he didn't fall. "Kevin, thanks for listening to me and for sharing that with me—you know, about your family."

"You're welcome." They continued on up the path in companionable silence to where Amanda stood waiting for them. Then Kevin slid his arm around Amanda's waist, leaned over to brush his lips against her jaw, and lightly kissed her. Summer smiled.

"Mom, now I see why you and Kevin chose to sit on the rock."

"The rock?" Amanda knew Summer and Kevin had been perched there like a pair of birds while deep in conversation. She looked up at Kevin and could see his smile in the growing darkness of night.

"Yuuup! The one and only rock! There I was sitting on the rock lost in thought, and Kevin found me. He listened to me, and I must say, Kevin gave me some good stepdad advice."

"Stepdad?" Amanda's gaze had shifted between Kevin and Summer.

"Yes, Mom, stepdad! He's a keeper." Summer leaned over and brushed a kiss on her mother's cheek. She stepped back and released a breath of contentment. "Mmm. Essence of Mom. Love that softness and smell. I'm heading on up to say my good-byes." With that, Summer hastened away from them toward the cabin.

"Thank you," Amanda breathed out.

"You are welcome." Kevin could feel the calm in Amanda's body as he held her in his arms. He was glad that the tension and panic storm had passed.

Amanda laid her head on Kevin's chest. "I don't need to know what was said between you and Summer. It was your time on the rock. Whatever you said, it obviously helped her. So thank you."

Kevin moved his hand from Amanda's back to touch her chin with his pointer finger. He gently moved her chin up and lowered his lips onto hers. As their kiss intensified, Kevin slid his hand to Amanda's back, firmly holding her against him. Amanda slid her arms up Kevin's chest to bring her hands around his neck.

"Amanda," Jim called out.

Amanda and Kevin drew apart as Amanda huffed out, "Good grief, first his son interrupts us last December when we were on the rock, and now my brother interrupts while we're here on the path by the lake. Tell me they aren't related."

5

The small clock illuminating the dark bedroom in the cabin indicated it was three o'clock in the morning. Once again, Summer was awake. She had said her good-night to her mother, Kevin, Cassie, and Andrew around eleven and prepared for sleep. Before she turned in, she placed a call to Mitchel. That had been a mistake.

After three rings on the house phone, Mitchel had answered Summer's call. It was only a little past nine in the evening in Denver. Still, Summer knew by the sound of Mitchel's voice that he was annoyed by her interruption. He claimed to be grading papers and did not appreciate her waiting until that time of night to finally call him. Summer ran her fingers through her hair by her left ear, something she had done for years when stressed. She drew in a breath, and then as calmly as her mind would allow, she said, "Well, if you had listened to your voice mail I left you this afternoon and returned my call earlier this evening, I would not be interrupting you from your paperwork, or whatever else you are doing."

Summer was annoyed with herself for the last statement she had made. Nathan had warned her to not let on that she had suspicions. But Summer had, and she could not take her words back. Fortunately, Mitchel chose to ignore her dig and defended his actions earlier in the day.

"I was in a meeting that ran longer than I had expected. By the time I was out, received my messages from my answering service, and listened to my voice mails, I realized that given the time difference, you had probably gone for dinner with your mother."

"You still could have called." Summer knew she sounded mulish. She felt it.

"And have the barracuda take a bite out of me! No way."

"Mitchel, that wasn't necessary," Summer snapped in anger. "Mom has already had her day in court. You do not need to add your testimony regarding how much you dislike her. Sorry to have bothered you."

"Summer, I didn't mean to attack your mother."

"Yes, you did. You know how much I love her, and by ridiculing her, you indirectly hurt me. I get it, Mitchel. Don't worry. I won't call you anymore this week, and heaven forbid interrupt your important life that obviously no longer includes me." Summer hung up her phone. She grabbed a tissue from the box on the nightstand by the bed, then cried her heart out. Soft tapping sounded on the door. Summer sniffled back her tears.

"Summer, may I come in?"

"Yes." Summer realized that her sweatshirt had wet spots from her tears that had fallen from her eyes. She wiped her moist hands on her jeans. The door opened, and her mother walked in. She paused and quietly closed the door behind her before coming over to the bed. Summer noticed that she was ready for bed. In the midst of Summer's crying jag, she had not heard anyone come upstairs. She wondered how many others had heard her crying.

Amanda knew her daughter was in pain. Why, was yet to be determined. Mother's intuition told her that Summer's tears were far more than Johnson. She had a feeling that Stephen had nothing to do with these tears. Something or someone was hurting her daughter, and this did not bode well with her.

"You look like you need a hug." She sat down next to Summer and drew her daughter into her embrace. "My Summer Sunshine, a turbulent cloud—that I have a feeling is beyond my control or ability to do anything about—has formed over you."

"You're right, Mom. Since my tears are over my life in Colorado, you can't fix this problem."

"And you don't want to talk about it." Summer shook her head as she remained cradled in her mother's arms. Amanda's heart ached for her daughter. "I respect that. You know I can do something to ease your pain while we're here together."

"What's that?" Summer sniffled.

"Since I've been back up here, Gram gave me a stash of her tea. How about while you get yourself ready for bed, I go back down to the kitchen and make you a cup of Gram's herbal tea for calming your nerves."

"Thanks, Mom." Summer sighed. "I appreciate you not pushing me about sharing my troubles with you. We'll talk soon. Right now I just need time to think. Gram's tea sounds interesting. It might be what I need."

"Good. I'll be back with tea in hand."

<hr />

The tea had tasted good and did help to calm Summer's tattered nerves. After a time of tossing and turning, Summer had succumbed to a fitful sleep. Now, she was awake and decided to get up. She slipped from her nightgown into her sweatpants and a sweatshirt for warmth and comfort. The cool planks of the floor under her feet caused Summer to rummage through her suitcase for a pair of socks. Summer stepped over to the door and opened it, only to have the hinges squeak. She paused and listened. The cabin remained quiet as Summer carefully made her way downstairs and into the great room.

Summer walked over and knelt before the hearth. She placed her hands above the coals. There was one spot that felt slightly warm.

Taking the poker in her right hand, Summer stirred the coals and found live embers. She added newspaper and kindling, then gently blew. A flame suddenly danced before her eyes. Summer added more wood and walked back to the couch to curl up under one of Cassie's afghans to watch the fire and think about her life.

Sometime later, the sound of a squeaking floorboard informed Summer that she was no longer alone. She looked over toward the door to see her mother dressed in a similar fashion to her entering the great room.

"Mom, I'm sorry to have awakened you. I thought I was quiet when I came down here."

"Summer, honey, you were quiet. I was still awake and heard you tiptoeing through the hall and down the stairs. Kevin, on the other hand, is sleeping soundly for both of us." Amanda continued on into the room and sat down on the couch next to Summer, who changed her position to curl up next to her and pulled the afghan around them. So many days and nights during Summer's childhood they had shared a moment like this, snuggling together, as they chased away the worries in their minds. "You built a nice little fire. This reminds me of when Kevin and I were here with Andrew and Cassie last winter. It was late at night like this when we sat by the fire and talked."

"Just talked, like when you sat together on the rock?"

"The rock, hmm. I may need to interrogate Kevin about what he said to you about our day after all." Amanda giggled, then added, "Sunshine, just so you know, Cassie joined us here by the fire."

"Mom, you're blushing."

"Perhaps I am."

"I get it. You kissed and nothing else happened because Aunt Cassie joined the two of you. Wow, you are full of surprises. I'm glad."

Summer snuggled in next to her Mother, who gently hugged her. Companionable silence fell between them as they watched the fire. It was Amanda who broke the silence.

"Fires are soothing. I find that when I focus on the flames, I enter into a quiet place of meditation and am able to find clarity as I sort through my muddled-up thoughts." Amanda intentionally kept her voice quiet as she spoke. "Summer, earlier today, we broached the subject of your father." She felt her daughter tighten in her arms. "We're not going to discuss him tonight, unless you want to." Amanda searched her daughter's eyes. "Hmm. I'm right. No Johnson. You have been thinking about whatever was troubling you earlier today, then tonight, when you were in tears and were not wanting to dump on me. Perhaps, now that everyone is asleep, and we're here together, it is time for us to have the conversation you've been avoiding."

Summer released a very heavy breath. She pulled a tissue from her sweatshirt pocket and blew her nose. Amanda sat next to her and patiently waited for Summer to complete her rituals before she unloaded her heart on her. Summer returned the used tissue to her pocket and then snuggled back against Amanda while drawing the blanket closer to her.

"Mom," at that moment, Summer's voice sounded so young. Amanda felt the pit of her stomach dropping out. Her daughter was in tremendous pain, and she still didn't know what was wrong. "You've been through so much today. Please, don't try to shush me and tell me that you can handle what is going on. I know you can. I just feel like I should give you a break."

"Oh, my Sunshine, you are so compassionate, so caring, simply amazing. Honey, I've had a break with the time I spent with Gram this afternoon and tonight, as well as with the wonderful meal and evening we shared with our family and friends. Summer, we are so blessed. The love and support we give to each other is what makes the trials easier to bear. It's like the old song. We lean on each other for the strength we need to help get us through our problems."

"Mmm. The old song 'Lean on Me.' I remember you singing that to me when I was younger. You taught me to create my group of 'go-to people' to lean on to help me through different situations in my life."

"So am I to assume you have decided to lean on someone other than me? If so, that is okay, as long as the one you lean on is truly there for you in your time of need."

"Mom, I do need you, and will need you in my corner as things progress." Summer no longer was able to will the tears to remain in her eyelids.

"Tell me, Summer. What is so wrong in your world—your life," Amanda was now fighting to keep her own tears in check as she softly spoke to Summer, "to cause all these tears—this pain?"

"This afternoon while I was at Aunt Melissa and Uncle Jim's, I called Nathan and talked with him." Amanda smiled. She fully approved of Summer's choice of confidants. "Mom," tears were streaming down her cheeks as she quietly wept out, "I need Nate's legal assistance."

"Legal assistance, oh goodness," Amanda gasped. Legal assistance from Nathan could mean one of two things: divorce or criminal defense. Neither option was good. "As in divorce?" she quietly asked.

"Yes," Summer openly cried out. With that, Amanda drew her daughter into her arms.

"Oh, my Sunshine, my precious Summer Sunshine, no wonder you were crying with the intensity of a severe tropical rainstorm earlier tonight. Tell me, Summer," Amanda's voice carried warning for Summer to tell the truth, and her eyes conveyed her concern as she spoke, "has he abused you?" Amanda was speaking from her own experience and from years of counseling battered women and children. She shuddered at the thought of her own child being emotionally, physically, and/or sexually violated by her husband. "If he has abused you, have you reported it? I don't care if it was only one time. You know one time is one time too many. Is there official documentation of the abuse, and not simply his word against yours? We both know how that goes."

"Mom"—Summer saw the fire in her mother's eyes. Her mother was fierce as a wildfire when it came to protecting those whom she loved and cared for and the women at the crisis center. At that very moment, Summer realized how fortunate she was to have her mother in her corner. Summer knew that with Mom and Nathan on her side, she was going to make it through this crisis in her life. She sighed out—"in some ways, I almost wish it were as simple as abuse."

"Simple." Her mother's eyes sent out sparks of concern that conveyed her passion for any victim of abuse. "Honey, abuse isn't simple. It's devastating."

"I know, Mom. I know you are speaking from experience." Summer sighed. "Let me see if I can clarify what I'm trying to say."

"Please do." Amanda's heart was grieving for her daughter. She wanted to magically make Summer's pain disappear, but she couldn't.

"I guess by saying 'abuse would be simple,' I mean, if Mitch had beaten me or done something sexually violent against me, I would have been out of our home in Colorado in a heartbeat and at your door in Baltimore."

"I'm glad to know that," Amanda quietly stated, while her heart was racing with concern like a thoroughbred on the final stretch at Saratoga going for the win. Falling into a combination of overprotective mom and counselor, Amanda gently smiled at her daughter while stating, "So apparently, all of my years of harping at you about abuse actually has sunk in."

"Yes, Mom. You did well in teaching me to take care of myself. That's why since there is no abuse, it has been so difficult for me to make this decision."

Amanda studied her daughter. She believed Summer when she said that Mitchel had not physically or sexually abused her. While physical and sexual abuse leaves telltale signs that victims do their best to hide, psychological abuse is not so readily seen or identifiable, especially for the victim. Amanda had her concerns. For now, she would wait for further information from Summer before making a judgment call on that particular abuse. With a little nudging, Summer began telling her story.

"It all began last September, shortly after the new term at the university had begun."

"Classes began in August, so the changes didn't begin right away?" Amanda asked for clarity.

"Yes, that is correct. At first I didn't notice anything was amiss in our relationship. You know, we both live busy professional lives. Sometimes one of us or both of us would have work commitments that caused us to have to cancel or postpone our evening or weekend plans." Summer pulled the afghan closer to her as she spoke. "Until last fall, Mitchel and I would always intentionally do something special together to make up for the work time we had taken out of our personal-relationship time. It could be as simple as going for a long walk, ordering pizza and watching a movie, out for a romantic dinner, dancing—you get the drift." Amanda nodded, while observing Summer as she continued. "So, when Mitch said he had department meetings for a couple of weeks in a row, I didn't think too much of it and expected that we would plan something special in the near future."

"But, it never happened."

"No." Summer sniffled. She wiped her reddened eyes.

Amanda felt the aura of the pain in Summer's body as they sat together on the couch. She gently encouraged Summer to share more details. The holidays, beginning with Thanksgiving at Mitchel's parents' home, were a tumultuous time for them. Summer had a cold coming on and did not feel her best. Mitchel accused her of planning to get sick to draw attention to herself and spoil the day for his mother, who had put such tremendous effort into making the holiday perfect for them.

Amanda recognized the signs—the words—psychological abuse was taking shape. For now, she kept her professional observations to herself and listened to her daughter. Christmas began with brittle normalcy that involved breakfast together and the exchange of their gifts. In years past after opening their gifts, Summer and Mitchel usually found themselves back in bed, where they would share their love for each other. This past year, there was no intimacy. In its place was an argument and Mitch packing a bag in haste and walking out "to cool down," as he prefaced it. After Mitchel had stormed out of the house, he had called once during that week to inform Summer that he would return when, and only when, he was ready. Summer was alone on New Year's Eve feeling like her world was crumbling before her. She had no idea where Mitchel was; however, her suspicions were mounting.

Summer and Amanda clung to each other and wept in companionable solidarity. To know what Summer had endured in her marriage thus far just about ripped Amanda apart. Right at that moment, she longed to lace Mitchel out in lavender and then string him up for bear bait. Knowing how she felt, Amanda decided it was for the best that Mitchel was in Denver doing goodness knows what and that she and Summer were in upstate New York. As the new batch of tears subsided, they both agreed that they needed a brief break in Summer's story. Summer made hot tea for both of them while Amanda stoked the fire. By the time Amanda was done, the fire was ablaze and would probably still be burning at dawn.

Settled back on the couch together with tea in hand, Amanda resumed their conversation. "The fall and winter were an extremely difficult time for you. Summer, honey, I'm wondering why the pretense that everything was all right in your marriage when Kevin and I visited you?"

Summer was no longer able to look at her mother. She sighed and took a sip of tea rather than immediately responding to her pointed question. The warmth from the tea and the fire blazing in the hearth warming the room felt good. Finally, she looked at Mom, who was quietly waiting for her to speak. Her mother's dark eyes filled with love warmed her as well.

"It's simple. I saw how happy you were with Kevin, and I did not want to ruin your time with me by telling you what was going on in my marriage."

Amanda leaned over and placed her cup of tea on the table in front of the sofa. She then reached over and took Summer's cup from her hand and placed it on the table alongside her cup.

"Come here you," Amanda quietly said while opening her arms. Summer immediately snuggled into her embrace. "Oh, my child. I do love you so, especially for wanting to shield me from your pain. However, as your mother, I detected the marital strain between you and Mitchel. He's a lousy actor and best not give up his day job."

This statement laced with sarcasm caused Summer to chuckle. Mom always seemed to know just when to add humor to a stressful situation. Summer nuzzled into her, as she had done when a baby. She felt safe as she listened to her mother's calm, soothing voice.

"I saw the pain you were desperately attempting to hide from me. Sunshine, Kevin saw it as well. You and your well-being was our primary conversation as we sat on the flights traveling back east. Honey, you need to know that we respect your right to privacy, so that is why I did not call you and interrogate you."

"Thanks, Mom."

"You are welcome." Amanda gently placed her head on Summer's head. The simple act brought comfort to both of them. "You should know that your situation has drawn Kevin and me closer in some unexpected ways."

"How so?"

"While neither of us are active churchgoers at this point in our lives, we do believe in the power of prayer. So, knowing that there was nothing we could do for you until you were ready to confide in us, we have been praying for you. I have been asking the Great Spirit to help you." Summer smiled. She knew her mother grew up in the church; however, she had chosen to weave together the spirituality of the Christian faith and her grandmother's religion.

"Honey, I've directed my prayers to the Great Spirit beseeching the Spirit to send someone to help you, to guide you through this wilderness journey that you are on, and bring you from pain to joy."

"Wow!" Summer paused to give herself time to absorb what her mother had just said. "Mom, you need to know that Mitchel and I have been trying to reconcile our differences. It's not going well. In my heart, I knew I needed to make a decision about my future. I've been torn between staying or separating while we are in counseling. When you called to tell me about the trial, and that the DNA results would be disclosed for us, I believed that this was a sign to get me out of Colorado for more than the trial and discovering the identity of my father. Until yesterday, I had no clarity for what I was going to do in regards to my faltering marriage. Sitting out in the forest, talking with Aunt Melissa about my father, then sitting alone and meditating on my marriage, this powerful spiritual force seemed to come over me. It's hard to put the moment into words." Amanda smiled softly, and nodded in agreement. "I remembered being a little girl and going to Sunday school, and the times we went to church, something weird would happen to me during the time of prayer. Since then, prayer has always fascinated me."

"Fascinated?"

"I don't know how else to put it. Yesterday, I prayed for the first time in a very long time. Then, I called Nathan."

"I'm not surprised that you chose to lean on Nathan. You need him, and most likely someday in months or years to come, he will need to lean on you for support. That's how love and true friendship works."

"I'm glad you're not mad at me for talking with Nathan before I told you what was going on." Summer yawned. Fatigue was suddenly sweeping over her.

"Sunshine, I'm not mad that you waited until now to share your pain with me. If you had told me over the phone or earlier today, we probably would not be snuggling together here on the couch with a beautiful fire burning in the hearth. How about you lean on me and close your eyes for a little while. Then, when you feel you want to go to bed, we both can head upstairs."

———

Kevin awakened not long after daybreak. He looked over at the side of the bed where he had expected to find Amanda sound asleep. The other side of the bed was empty. He felt the sheets. Cold. Amanda had obviously been up for a while. Kevin sat up and proceeded to dress for the day. Life with Amanda has taught him to be prepared. Given that they were staying in a cabin by a lake in mountains, a hike may well be added to their day. It didn't take long before Kevin was descending the stairs. As he peered into the great room, he saw the remnants of a fire in the hearth. Memories flooded over him from when he had fallen asleep on the couch with Amanda cradled in his arms. When he came closer to the couch, he saw Amanda in the sitting position with her legs extended on the coffee table. An afghan was over her legs. Kevin smiled. That couldn't possibly be comfortable. Then, he saw Summer curled up on the couch with her head on her mother's lap. They both looked so peaceful. Kevin didn't have the heart to wake either of them. He quietly moved out into the kitchen and began to make coffee for all of them to enjoy later on.

———

Amanda smelled the coffee in her sleep. Her eyes slowly opened. She yawned, as she looked around the great room, and found Kevin sitting in an oversized chair sipping his morning coffee.

"Good morning," Amanda whispered.

"Good morning," Kevin said while getting up from the chair. He walked over to the couch and leaned down to place his lips onto Amanda's. She smelled and tasted the toothpaste, along with the coffee. *Minty fresh coffee. Yum!*

"No fair," she whispered. "You brushed your teeth, and you are drinking coffee without me."

"You looked so peaceful. I didn't want to wake you. I'll get you some coffee." Kevin quietly said, as a smile grew on his lips.

"Kevin, please wait on the coffee, and help me lift Summer's head, so I can put a pillow under her head and then get up."

"Of course." Kevin seized the moment and leaned in for another quick kiss before assisting Amanda with Summer.

Amanda circled through the great room to check on Summer as she made her way from the bathroom to the kitchen. Her daughter lay on the couch in the fetal position with the afghan Amanda had tucked around her still in place. Summer slept. They never made it upstairs to the beds Cassie had prepared for both of them. Amanda missed not having spent the night with Kevin. She reconciled her sadness of not sleeping in bed with Kevin with the fact that her daughter needed her. Summer was in pain and needed her to be a source of comfort. Amanda was glad to have had that special time with Summer. As she looked at her beautiful daughter asleep, oblivious to the world around her, she had to wonder how long it had been for her daughter to have a peaceful night's rest. "Sleep, my child. Your mother is here. I will protect you," Amanda quietly breathed out her words to Summer. She touched her fingers to her lips then reached down and placed her fingers on Summer's head, as she had done so long ago to kiss Summer as she slept.

Kevin was seated at the table when Amanda joined him in the kitchen. Two mugs were filled with steaming coffee, and cream—no sugar. Amanda stretched. As she did, her sweatshirt drew upward leaving a space of bare skin between the shirt and her sweatpants. Kevin noticed everything about Amanda, from her rumpled hair to her soft skin on her abdomen, and even her bare feet. She made him smile.

"See something you like?" Amanda quietly teased, as she sat down in the chair next to Kevin. His hand slid over onto her shoulder to pull her closer to him.

"I certainly do. Unfortunately, for now, I'm afraid that all I can do is look, and give you another kiss."

"Mmm. I'm so sorry I never got back upstairs last night. I'll gladly take the kiss you offer me."

"Honey, you obviously were needed down here."

Kevin glanced toward the great room, then back at Amanda. Her warm moist pink lips beckoned Kevin to touch and taste her sweetness. Just as their mouths touched, Kevin's cell phone indicated that he had a text message. They drew apart. No kiss. Amanda sighed. She looked at her steaming cup of coffee, picked up the cup to take a sip. As Amanda swallowed her first delightful sip of coffee, sending warmth, and the anticipated jolt of caffeine into her body, her eyes met Kevin's eyes. Something was out of kilter in their world.

"Kevin, what is it?"

"Amanda, honey, that was my lawyer. I have to call him."

"Right now?" Amanda had a very bad feeling that began in her toes and ran all the way up her spine to the top of her head.

Summer awakened to the sound of the front door of the cabin quietly closing, the sound of a car motor, and the crunching of tires against the crushed gravel leaving the drive. She lay on the couch and listened to the quiet voices she heard coming from the hallway by the door. Summer immediately sensed that something was wrong. She sprang up from the couch and hastily made her way to the hall.

"Oh, Summer, good morning." Cassie smiled tenderly at her, while Andrew added his morning greeting.

"Good morning, did I hear Mom and Kevin leaving?" Summer glanced around the quiet cabin.

"Yes. We didn't mean to wake you up," Cassie said as Andrew handed Summer a handwritten note. "Your Mom and Kevin have a two-hour drive to Albany to get Kevin to the airport for his flight to Baltimore."

"So she says in her note, amongst other things." Summer smiled as she drew the note to her chest, as if to will the words on the paper into her body. "Mom is too much!" Summer yawned.

"You look like you could use a cup of coffee," Andrew suggested.

"Sounds good." Summer made her way to the kitchen with Cassie and Andrew. As she stepped into the kitchen, the sun reflecting on the lake out in front of the cabin caught her eye. It looked like a beautiful day outside. Summer took her place at the table, while Cassie placed a plate of almond and cinnamon pastries on the table and Andrew filled three mugs with coffee. He slid one mug over to Summer before taking his seat.

"Mom said that Kevin's lawyer contacted him earlier this morning, something about his divorce, and that's why he is making this hasty return to Baltimore." She looked to both Cassie and Andrew for confirmation. Summer shook her head, then added, "I wish Kevin's ex-wife would sign off on the divorce so they may move on with their life together."

"So do we."

Companionable silence followed by quiet conversation fell among the three as they sipped their coffee and ate their pastry. Summer wiped her mouth and stretched. She immediately noticed that two sets of eyes were lovingly watching her.

"Thank you for breakfast. I do believe I'm going to excuse myself and get dressed for the day. Then, I'm going to take Mom's advice that she gave me in her note. It's a beautiful day, and even though our plans have been altered, I'm going to make the best of it."

"What might those plans include?" Andrew asked Summer.

"Mom was going to take me to the bait shop so I could see my father's place of business, and where she had her altercation with the two parasites. I actually was looking forward to going there. She also was going to rent a canoe for us to use out on the lake." Summer paused, then added, "I think I just might venture over there by myself and go out on the lake."

"That might be a good idea—just be careful."

"Of course, Uncle Andrew." Summer smiled and stood. She picked up her plate and cup, then turned and walked over to the sink. After placing them on the counter, she quietly made her way upstairs to get ready for her day's adventures.

6

Wednesday morning at the bait shop in early May had traditionally been a fairly slow time for the owners, Stephen Johnson and Wesley Jones. Most local folks who come to the shop purchase bait, perhaps a new lure or two, exchange local gossip, and drop their own canoes, kayaks, or rowboats into the lake. At this time of year, both Stephen and Wesley were confident that boat rentals would increase with the onslaught of late spring and summer vacationers. On this particular day, Stephen was down by the lakeshore inspecting the last row of the rowboats for damage they might have sustained from a recent storm. So far, all the rowboats, canoes, and kayaks had fared the storm without damage.

Wesley was in the shop attending to merchandise, taking calls for boat rentals, as well as renting the pavilion for spring weddings and the local high school prom. Today, among other things, it was Wesley's responsibility to be checking the lists of inventory against the products that they had in stock on the shelves. He was counting the packages of fishhooks they had out when the bell on the door began to jingle. Fully expecting Stephen to be coming in for a long overdue coffee break, Wesley didn't look up from his work as the door slowly opened. There was no loud male voice and heavy footsteps. Then, the door closed considerably quieter than Wes had expected. This was not the norm at the bait shop.

"Excuse me."

The soft female voice surprised Wesley. He looked up from his clipboard to see Summer standing by the door. She was dressed in casual attire appropriate for life in the mountain lake community. Wesley smiled as he read the football logo on her sweatshirt. Denver. He had an idea of what Stephen would have to say about her team choice. Wes laughed to himself as his eyes perused over the rest of her clothes. Summer wore faded jeans and hiking boots on her feet. Her dark hair was pulled back into a ponytail. She wore no makeup. Her high cheekbones and warm dark brown eyes that seemed to sparkle with gold flecks reminded Wesley of her mother, when they were younger. Looking at Summer, his adult niece standing there in the bait shop, Wesley could only imagine what Amanda had looked like at age thirty. Beautiful.

"Good morning. Welcome to the Bait and Tackle Shop." Wes greeted Summer with a smile. He knew Summer was probably there to see Stephen, rather than to see him. With how things were left on Monday, his brother-in-law was sure in for a surprise.

"Thank you, and good morning to you." Summer smiled in return. She spoke clearly, as she took a hesitant step toward him. "I'm Summer Newman, Amanda's daughter." Wesley nodded in acknowledgment that he recognized her. "I'm sure we met on Monday at the courthouse during Mom's numerous introductions. It was a rather overwhelming day for me, so I do apologize for not remembering your name."

"Summer, no apology is necessary for not remembering my name. You have had many people to meet this week." Wesley moved toward her. He extended his hand to greet her. "I'm your Uncle Wesley Jones, or Wes, as most people call me. You may call me by either name."

Summer liked how warm and friendly he was, without being pushy. She reached out her hand to shake Wes's hand. "I'm pleased to meet you, Uncle Wesley. Over the years, Mom did tell me some stories about growing up here in the mountains. If I remember correctly from her stories, and she and Uncle Jim talking about people on Monday night, you and Mom were in school together."

"That is correct." Wes was nodding, smiling and wondering. Amanda, like everyone else who had grown up during the '60s–'70s era in the Great Sac Community had an arsenal of stories about life in this community. He could only imagine what stories Amanda may have shared with Summer about him, and the rest of the Great Sac crew, as they had called themselves.

After hearing Amanda's testimony in court on Monday, Wes would not have blamed Summer for not wanting anything to do with the people who had betrayed her mother. Still, here she stood in the bait shop wanting to get to know him. Wes suddenly felt in some ways honored, and in other ways humbled by this action on Summer's part. He felt certain he knew whom she had inherited that trait of reaching out to others from: her mother. For a moment, Wesley's words seemed to stick in his throat. Then he said, "Your mother graduated two years after your Uncle Jim, your—" He saw something sweep over Summer's eyes and immediately realized he needed to be cautious in speaking about her father. So he simply stated, "Ah, Stephen and me."

"Okay." She nodded and smiled with gratitude for his astuteness regarding how she felt toward her father. "You know, Mom has been telling me who is who, so hopefully as I make my rounds to introduce myself, I won't be totally lost with meeting everyone in my family. It helps to put names and faces together."

"I'm sure it does." Wesley cleared his throat. "That sounds like your mother wanting to make things easier for you by telling you who everyone is, and probably a story or two about us as well." Summer nodded. "Yes, indeed"—he smiled—"she's looking out for you."

"You know her well."

"I used too. When she was here last winter, I didn't get a chance to really talk with her. I hope she hasn't changed too much over the years." Wesley looked at Summer with warmth in his eyes. "Amanda always was the caregiver of our band of friends. She was full of life, the one you wanted to have join in an activity, especially if it was winter and we were playing hockey. Your mother was he—" Wesley's cheeks took on a tinge of pink as he held back his words and corrected his language. "I mean heck on skates." Summer smiled warmly as she listened to her uncle's perspective on her mother as a person. "Summer, your mother was—I mean, *is* special." Summer noticed the word her uncle placed his emphasis on. She nodded as she continued to listen to him speak with admiration for her mother. "Amanda could see things the rest of us took for granted. She was always trying to make right a wrong. You were there on Monday. You heard Junior remind many of us about how kind your mother had been toward him when we were kids."

"Uncle Wesley, Mom still advocates for those who are victimized by others. She works to bring about positive change for the voiceless battered women of Baltimore City and Baltimore County. I now have to add upstate New York to where Mom engages in her acts of social justice." Wesley nodded. Then Summer asked, "So, Uncle Wesley, with how our conversation is going about Mom, I'm curious."

"About what?"

"Were you one of the guys whom she turned to back in '79 and didn't believe her?" There was a sting in Summer's voice. It was clear to Wesley that Summer had inherited some of her mother's forthrightness, and attitude—as well as her kindness. He didn't blame her in wanting to know about her mother's and her past. "Unfortunately, Summer, when everything happened that August in '79, I wasn't here. I was out of town visiting my cousins who live in Boston. I will never forget Becky calling me with the news. She was weeping as she told me what happened to your mother and what rumors were being smeared around our town about her. I couldn't believe it when Becky told me your father—" Wesley saw the look in Summer's eyes at the mention of father. "I mean, Stephen"—Summer nodded—"and your Uncle Jim had not believed her. As Becky shared the story with me, I literally became physically ill with knowing what had happened to your mother. Then, I also wept." Summer held his gaze as Wes added, "Summer, I imagine from your expression that you are surprised to hear that I will admit that I cried." Summer nodded. "I did. Your Mom—no woman for that matter deserved what happened to her." Wes slightly shook his head as he called to mind the memory of August '79. "By the time I got back here to the Great Sac Community, your mother and"—his expression softened as he looked at Summer, then said—"and you were gone. Her absence left a deep void in our lives, especially for Becky. For many months after she left, when Becky was not at work at the Lakeside Coffee Shop, where she worked back then, I was the only man she would speak to here in our community."

"When you say Becky, do you mean as in my Aunt Becky, who is my father's younger sister?" Wes nodded. "And she was sitting between you and him in court, then standing with you both at the courthouse," Summer added while piecing together people in her mind.

"That is correct. Their brother Phil is the middle child in their family. I apologize for not making that family connection for you earlier in our conversation," Wes added.

"Not a problem."

"Thank you, Summer. Now, where was I?"

"Aunt Becky."

"Oh, yes! Your Aunt Becky and your mother were like sisters when we were growing up. For thirty years, Becky never gave up hope and prayers that someday she would return, or that somehow we would find out where she was living and go to see her. Those two women had a special bond, and when their brothers betrayed Amanda—your mother, well, it was as though they had also betrayed Becky. She made Johnson's and Jim's lives pure he—I mean, *heck* for years to come. It seemed as though every chance she got, she would drive her verbal knife into them and then twist it for good measure."

"You said that Aunt Becky would not speak with the men of this community, especially Uncle Jim and my—Mr. Johnson. On Monday, after we left court, I did notice that she was speaking with her brothers. So has she forgiven them?" Summer quietly asked.

"It took time, actually about ten years, for Becky to fully accept her loss and forgive Stephen and Jim. I'll tell you what, it was mighty tough being married to Becky, being brother-in-law, friend, and co-owner of this business with Stephen, and friends with Jim. You have no idea how much my life improved when Becky reconciled with those two men." Summer giggled. "It's not funny." Wesley added. He was not smiling.

"I'm sure it was not funny. However, listening to you describe Aunt Becky and knowing Mom, I could picture Aunt Becky while she was in her snit with all of you men—well, Uncle Jim and Mr. Johnson. Mom and Aunt Becky must have been something when they were growing up together as kids."

Just as Wesley was ready to respond, the door seemed to blow open. Both Wes and Summer looked at the door as it nearly hit the back wall. In the doorway stood no other than Stephen Johnson. He was dressed almost the same as when he had sat in court earlier that week. Now, he had a ball cap on his head, red flannel shirt covering his body with a long john top sticking out of his rolled-up flannel shirt sleeves, blue jeans dirty from working outside covered his bottom and legs, and scuffed-up muddy work boots were on his feet. Summer visually inspected him from head to toe. Her deadpan expression did not reveal her thoughts. Still, it was safe to say that they had not improved much from the other day.

"Summer," Stephen blurted out. He was overcome by shock in seeing her standing there with Wesley. Stephen began swallowing a copious amount of saliva, which had suddenly formed in his mouth. No other words came from him as he stood there staring at his daughter. Apparently his legs and feet had also temporarily forgotten how to move. Finally, Johnson found his voice. "This is a surprise." Stephen glanced around the shop to see where Amanda might be lurking about. He didn't see her anywhere.

"I'm sure it is a surprise for you to find me here. I've been enjoying getting acquainted with Uncle Wesley." Stephen nodded with approval. Summer remained standing by her uncle and watched her father as he continued to stand in the open doorway. She had noticed his eyes searching like a predator hunting its prey. "If you're looking for Mom, don't bother." Summer kept her voice calm and even as she spoke. "She's not here. I came alone."

"Alone, is good." Stephen finally got around to closing the door. He could not remember when he had last felt so awkward when speaking with a woman. Oh yes. He remembered. New Year's Eve when he was talking with Amanda and dancing with her; that was before he knew who she was. *This is your daughter, for cryin' out loud. Get a grip, man!* The lecture he gave to himself did not help to calm his nerves any, especially after their initial meeting on Monday afternoon. In all honesty, Stephen had not expected Summer to seek him out like this. He figured she really did not want to get to know him as anything other than—how had Amanda prefaced it? Oh yes—*"one of the mighty men of the lake who provided the sperm"* that had created her. Yes, Johnson was befuddled by this turn of events. Summer, by her own volition, was at the bait shop. When he turned back around, he could not stop looking at her. Everything about Summer—from her grooming to the clothes she wore, her posture, and the slight raise of her brow as she watched him—reminded Stephen of Amanda. Silence hung between them. Their breathing was labored with anticipation. Who would make the next move? Finally, Stephen took a hesitant step toward Summer and Wesley.

Wesley saw the intensity in Stephen's gaze. His face was a quandary of mixed emotions. Wesley then glanced over to look at Summer. He realized that Summer was equally as intense as she sized up her father. They remained silent. Wesley suddenly felt like an intruder in this awkward family reunion. Neither one noticed as he slipped away from where they stood.

"So, this is the infamous bait shop Mom has told me about."

"I don't know about infamous," Stephen could not help but allow his lips to turn upward. "However, this is Wes's and my bait and tackle shop." Stephen could usually carry on a conversation with anyone, but not now. He actually felt nervous. "I know it doesn't look like much." He shrugged. "Wes and I are proud of what we've accomplished here over the years. When we bought the old shop, it was half this size, no boat rentals, no pavilion to rent out, or community gatherings offered. Feel free to look around."

"Thank you, I think I will."

Summer took a step and stopped in front of a display advertised as environmentally friendly bait. Rubber worms. She began to softly chuckle. Her melodious sound took Stephen by surprise. It was so sweet and reminded him of two women he had loved in his life: his mother and Amanda. Stephen continued to watch Summer as she reached out and took a hold of a package of worms. She then looked up at him. Her warm chocolate eyes were filled with sparks of energy that danced in the fluorescent-lit room. He noticed the slight raise of her right brow and the subtle lift of the right corner of her lips. His daughter. Amanda's daughter. Alive, not dead like their other daughter, Rose. Summer had sought him out on her own. Why? Stephen had no idea. That does not matter. Here is his chance to have a relationship with her. He knew as Amanda had warned: he had best not blow it.

"Seriously, Mr. Johnson, rubber worms?"

Summer's formality of calling him Mr. Johnson stung. At that moment, he had to wonder if they would ever get to the place where Summer felt comfortable to call him her father. Or would he always be an acquaintance to her? He'd consider that at another time. For now, his daughter was there with him. It was their moment in time. Stephen had a feeling Summer had more to say, and she did.

"Eco-friendly? Please." Summer rolled her eyes. Stephen could not believe it. This was the same spot where Amanda had stood with her friends when she went into her whole long defense and benefits of fishing with real worms instead of rubber worms.

"Goodness, you certainly do have strong feelings about rubber worms. I can appreciate that." He watched her eyes as he spoke. "Summer, while most folks around here prefer real worms and minnows, some people prefer rubber worms rather than having to deal with touching real worms."

Now, Stephen was defending using rubber worms, when he would not be caught dead fishing with them. What in tarnation was going on with him? Stephen watched Summer as she glanced down at the package she held in her hands. He noticed the shape of her fingers, long and beautiful like her mother's. The one noticeable difference with their hands was that Summer did not wear nail polish like her mother. Her nails were short and clean. Interesting difference. Stephen decided to tuck that information away in his mind. Their eyes met as Summer lifted her chin. Self-assurance oozed from her as she studied him. Stephen knew exactly whom she had inherited that trait from.

"People are so strange," Summer stated matter-of-factly. "They think rubber worms—that are manufactured in an unregulated factory somewhere in the global community, that puts all sort of pollutants into the air, and inevitably in our water supply—are good for the environment."

Stephen noticed her stance as he listened to her speak with clarity. Granted, he's not a fan of rubber worms, but they are liked by many avid fishermen and are in the bait shop for a person's fishing enjoyment. Now, Summer has just presented an environmental conservation argument for why he should pull every package from their shelves and stop selling rubber worms. It was obvious his daughter was speaking from an educated perspective and not simply from opinion. Johnson was drawn in by her passion and listened to her speak.

"People are so self-centered. They don't consider the ramifications for their actions. Do you know how many of these things get lost off of a hook and end up in the bottom of a stream, river, lake, or the ocean? They are rubber and do not disintegrate, and reenter the food chain as a deadly source of food." Stephen did not respond. He was mesmerized by the fire in her dark eyes as she spoke. "They are harmful. So tell me how they are environmentally friendly?"

"Well, Summer, I have to admit I am unaware of how many rubber worms are lost on an annual basis around the world's water supply. Honestly, I do admire your passion for the environment, and have been known to take up my own causes over the years. So, since this is such a vital concern of yours, Wes and I will discuss our position on rubber worms and see if it warrants our pulling the worms from our shelves."

"Are you patronizing me?" Summer was now scowling.

"No. I'm not." Stephen actually was feeling a sense of pride for his intelligent, articulate daughter. "I'm actually pleasantly surprised, and proud of how defensive you are about the environment."

"Thank you." Summer's expression softened. "I do care about our world. I work hard to protect our natural resources and its inhabitants."

"That is quite obvious." Stephen nodded with approval. Perhaps with their mutual love of nature, they might find a common ground for a relationship. "Summer, you may rest assured that the folks who do fish our lake and use rubber worms are careful when they fish. Having fished the lake for all of my life, I can also say I've never gutted a fish and found a rubber worm, or part of one, in its belly."

"I'm glad to hear it." Summer nodded in approval. "Sorry if I seemed to be a bit over the edge about the environment. I guess since I know what you do for a living, and since I am so defensive of the environment, I should tell you that I'm a national park ranger out in Colorado. My passion in my work is in maintaining the balance between conservation and humanity."

"Really. That is wonderful. I'd like to hear more about your work, if you feel you want to share it with me."

"Sure. I'm used to talking about my job, fielding questions from visitors to the park I work in." Summer saw something pass through Stephen's eyes. "I...um..." She paused for a brief moment then added, "I didn't mean to sound as though your desire to know about my work is going to be told to you as a rote speech I might give to tourists."

"Somehow I never got that impression." Stephen gave Summer a slight nod, as he removed the cap from his head, ran his fingers through his hair, and replaced the cap on his head. Summer watched him move his fingers through his graying hair. She noticed the fine lines by the corners of his eyes. He had a small scar on his cheek. She had to admit to herself, given his age, he's rather handsome. "Summer," her father's voice brought her back to the present as he asked, "how about we continue our conversation while I give you the nickel tour of this place?"

"I'd like that." Summer realized that she really meant her words. Seeing how much he enjoyed his work at the bait shop, and obviously enjoyed spending time in the outdoors, Summer felt as though perhaps this could be a safe way for them to begin to form a relationship. She wanted to get to know him. When had her attitude changed?

Stephen gently took the package of worms from Summer's hand and replaced them on the shelf. "Let's head outside. We'll stop down in the pavilion so you can see where your mother took out Junior and Shannon, then we'll continue on down by the lake." His eyes held Summer's. He watched a smile form on her lips as she nodded. "Wes," Stephen called out.

"I can hear you and see you both just fine." Wesley had to smile as he heard the excitement in Stephen's voice and saw the look in his eyes. Happiness radiated from him.

"Summer and I are going out for a walk."

"Take your time. And, Summer," Wes called out, as he watched them head to the door.

Summer paused and turned to look toward the counter where Wesley quietly stood watching them. "Yes, Uncle Wesley?" she responded, curious to know what was on his mind.

"If your fa—I mean, Johnson steps out of line, and you're close enough to the water's edge, you have my permission to shove him into the lake."

Summer began to giggle. Tilting her chin up, she found Stephen watching her. He was not smiling. Summer noticed his one brow was raised as he spoke.

"Hey, Wes, you do remember who Summer's mother happens to be."

Wes chuckled. "Of course."

"Exactly. So, I'd appreciate it, if you would keep your ideas to yourself."

Summer cleared her throat causing Stephen to return his gaze to her. Her eyes sparkled with anticipation. "I gather you are concerned that I might actually dump you in the lake?"

"Something like that."

"And you aren't telling me what that something is, so I guess I will have to ask Mom if she might know."

"She knows all right." Stephen exhaled. Summer chuckled, while easing into a smile. With that, Stephen, taken in by the moment, also chuckled. He knew in his heart that his life was never again going to be dull, now that he had both Amanda and Summer in his life. "Let's go before your uncle gives you any more ideas." Stephen stepped to the side of Summer and opened the door. Standing there, he allowed her to walk out the door in front of him.

––––~⚬~––––

There was a touch of coolness in the spring air in the lower Adirondacks. Hardwood trees were budding and leafing out against the backdrop of the Evergreens. In many ways, being by the lake reminded Summer of home in Colorado. Home. Mitchel. Their problems. She had not thought of Mitchel for most of the morning, and did not want to start going down that path while spending this time with her father. Summer drew in a deep breath for cleansing and calming her nerves.

A chickadee chirped from a nearby oak tree and then took flight. Summer paused in her step to watch the small bird land on an overturned canoe. *Chick-a-dee-dee-dee*, the friendly bird greeted them. Summer softly chuckled as she watched the bird. Stephen, in turn, paused to look at the bird and Summer. For one brief moment, he allowed himself to imagine what it would have been like to have stood in that same spot with Summer when she was a child. He imagined her hair, her style of dress probably would have been similar to how she dressed today. Johnson figured she would have been precocious, full of life, and keeping him on his toes every step of the way. Standing there with Summer and seeing her abandoned appreciation for a simple little bird touched his heart. He allowed his smile to fully form on his lips as he watched her.

"Looks like you've been officially welcomed."

"It looks that way." Summer's expression and tone of voice revealed her appreciation for nature. "Hello, little chickadee."

Stephen watched. The bird seemed to dance around on the canoe at the sound of her voice. It called out, *Chick-a-dee-dee-dee*, then flew the short distance to the overturned rowboat that happened to be closer to where Stephen and Summer stood. They chuckled together, amused by the fearless bird encountering them. For Summer, this was a nearly perfect moment, at one with nature.

Summer drew in a deep breath, then slowly exhaled. She looked out over the lake imagining what it must have been like for her mother and father to have grown up in the community together. She found herself wondering what it must have been like for her parents to have fallen in and out of love. Summer glanced up to find her father watching her. She tentatively smiled. This man and her mother had given her life, and her love of nature. At that moment, Summer knew in her heart that Kevin had been right in advising her to spend time to get to know her father.

"It is so beautiful here by the lake." Summer breathed out, as if to whisper in harmony with the slight breeze. Stephen nodded in agreement as Summer continued with her thoughts. "I can understand why Mom came to the lake that night to think about her life—about you." Pregnant silence hung between them. Then, it happened. Summer asked, "Was the spot near here?" The question had come, and Stephen knew what spot she meant.

"It is," Stephen swallowed back his emotions. "It's about a half mile up the lake on the west shoreline. Today a cabin sits where we used to party, swim, skate in the winter, and where it happened." Stephen grew quiet.

"Uncle Wes told me that he was out of town the night it happened to Mom." Summer couldn't bring herself to say that her mother had been raped. She could see the pain in her father's eyes, and intentionally kept her voice quiet as she spoke.

"He was." Stephen sighed, as he looked out over the lake to the east shoreline. He did not—could not—look at his daughter.

"But you were here."

"Yes. I was." Again, Stephen fell silent. The full impact of that night, the ripple effect it continued to have on people was disconcerting for him. Because of that night, he had lost a lifetime with Amanda and his daughter Summer.

"I, ah-um," Summer stammered. She could not remember the last time she had been so at a loss for words. Not the way she wanted this first private meeting, and conversation with her father that had begun fairly well, to be going at this point.

Stephen hooked his thumbs in his back pockets. His eyes once again held Summer's probing eyes. He conveyed his own understanding of how difficult this moment was for her. "Take your time, Summer. I'm not going any place."

"That's good, because it may take me awhile to articulate what I'm trying to ask and say." She drew in a breath. "Let me begin by saying thank-you for showing me around the bait shop. Seeing the spot where Mom had her altercation with the two men, knowing her side of the story, and hearing your version has provided me with a clear picture of the event."

"It was my pleasure to show you around inside, and now out here."

"I do want to further discuss life here in the Adirondacks, conservation and economic growth, hiking—that sort of stuff, but for now, there is something more pressing on my mind."

"So, I gather from your inquiry about the night and spot where your mother was raped, and mentioning this past New Year's Eve." Stephen waited for Summer to continue. He could see her struggling to find the right words.

"On Monday afternoon, when I spoke with you, I was rather opinionated and defensive of Mom." Stephen slightly nodded in agreement as she spoke to him. "I now realize that it was unkind of me to declare that I was your judge and jury, especially since I do not know anything about you, except from hearsay. Mom has always taught me to be careful of making hasty judgments about others." Stephen allowed himself to smile while listening to Summer speak. "Since I met you on Monday, I've had a chance to talk with Mom and a few people about how I feel about us being related."

"I'm sure you have." Stephen said no more. He was curious to see where his daughter was going with this conversation.

"My cousin Samantha is one of your biggest fans. She thinks I'd be crazy to not want you to be in my life."

Stephen chuckled. "I am not surprised. Samantha Callison is mighty special to me. You see, your Aunt Melissa and Uncle Jim have given me the honor of being Samantha's godfather. The older girls have Melissa's cousins as their godfathers. I guess, since I was without your sister Rose in my life, or you"—Summer noticed the hurt in his eyes. As quickly as it came, it disappeared. Stephen swallowed the wetness in his mouth and then continued—"I probably did go a bit overboard on embellishing Samantha with gifts and my undivided attention through the years."

"Could be." Summer suddenly felt a wave of jealousy. Now where had that come from? Why be jealous of a relationship that her father and her cousin had over the years? Why? Because it should have been hers.

"According to Samantha, and what she knows of yours and Mom's past, she believes that you loved Mom, and if you had known Mom was pregnant with me that August, you would have done things differently. Samantha also pointed out that Mom was the one who was wrong in walking away from you," Summer paused then added, "from here."

Stephen had not expected their conversation to get this deep between them, so quickly. This was the time for him to be honest with Summer and, more than that, with himself.

"Summer, Samantha's opinions have been formed from our relationship and from overhearing adult conversations through the years. Unfortunately, in many ways she's right. I did love your mother. Summer, if I had been given the chance, I would have fought for us to be a family."

"That's what I don't understand. Mom told me that your father was the minister in this community. If you went to church and learned all about God and love and if you loved Mom as you say you did, then why didn't you fight for her to be in your life? Why didn't you believe her after she was raped? Why didn't you love her enough to care for her when she needed you most?"

Stephen was speechless. The old saying goes, "out of the mouth of babes," well, his daughter had just said it all in a nutshell. He saw the tears pooling and escaping from Summer's lids. She swiped them away with the back of her hand. Stephen felt his own tears sliding down his cheeks.

"Why didn't I?" Stephen sighed out. "Because I was being self-centered. I didn't love God and others before myself. I was focused on my pain of losing your sister, and didn't know how to reach out to your mother to love and support her emotionally, and share my pain with her, so we could heal together." Summer was mesmerized by his blunt honesty. She had not anticipated this. "The way I treated your mother from the time we lost Rose, until she was raped and fled from here is shameful. Not the type of behavior you would expect from a minister's son. Because of my actions, I was just as guilty as Shannon and Junior in forcing Amanda to believe she had no choice, but to leave here. It broke my heart when she left. However, now I fully understand why she did it, and I do not blame her one bit. Your mother and I accept that we cannot change the past. In forgiving each other and closing that door of our past, we are now able to fully move on with our lives."

Stephen saw that Summer was intently listening to him. "Summer, if it helps you with processing your mother's and my relationship, I will tell you, that in many ways, I still love your mother. She was the first one who reached out to me and accepted me as a part of the community when my family moved here. I was nine, she was seven. Your Uncle Jim and the other children were not as welcoming as Amanda. I fell in love with her that day, and she fell in love with me." Summer was unable to hide her surprise by this lakeside confession. "Through the years I tried to convince myself that I hated your mother for leaving me. But my love for her was stronger than my hate. Now, God has given us a second chance at having a loving relationship."

"But, Mom's with Kevin now. She loves him."

"Yes, I know that they love each other." Stephen softly smiled at his daughter. He could see her love and concern for her mother. It made him proud. "I am grateful that Kevin has found his way into your mother's life, and she is able to trust him to not hurt her as I once did. Summer, I am not going to intrude on their relationship. Love is an amazing fragile gift that we are all given by God to share with other people."

"What do you mean that love is fragile?"

"Love is not simply saying the words. It's about nurturing the relationship we have with the other person, accepting them for who they are and not trying to change them into being who we think they should be. When we don't treat love as a fragile gift, it often breaks, and unfortunately, many times may not be repaired, and relationships end."

"Wow." Summer sighed. "You still love Mom, but you are willing to let her go."

"That's right. But, Summer, even though we know that our past is just that—our past, there is still hope for your mother and me. Yes, our romantic love for one another is like a burned-out fire. Our old passion from our youth will never again be ignited. But our love based on friendship forged between us as children is intact. Through forgiveness and reconciliation, we have looked deep within ourselves and found that our love has matured to accept our past, and embrace the present and future as friends, and more importantly as your parents."

"Parents."

"Yes. We are your parents. I am your father, whether you care to acknowledge me as such or not. I hope that in time, we will be able to develop a meaningful respectful relationship, perhaps only as friends, but still able to acknowledge each other as parent and adult child. Summer, we have been handed a beautiful gift. What happens with our gift, only time will tell."

"Actually," Summer hesitated.

Stephen saw a dramatic change in Summer's expression. "Yes?" he responded with hopes that she would continue to share her feelings.

"I…um." Summer sighed. "Oh…gee, this is hard."

"Take your time, Summer." Stephen watched her eyes, her mouth, her body slightly moving as she fought to find her words.

"Okay, I can do this." She drew in a deep breath then said, "I want to apologize to you for my actions on Monday. I was out of line with you."

"I didn't see it that way." His voice was quiet.

"You didn't?" Summer was confused.

"No." Stephen gave her his classic warm smile. "Summer, I saw a young woman who's world had been turned upside down, and she was attempting to find some control and stability within the chaos. Granted, there were moments when you could have passed as a dead ringer for your mother." He winked and gave Summer his quirky half smile. Summer in turn blurted out a ghastly sound—perhaps a chuckle. "Summer, you were honest with me, and I respect you for that."

Summer sniffled. "Wow! I didn't see that coming. Thank you for letting me off the hook. But you know you didn't need to be that easy on me."

"I know I didn't. But you know that four letter word—*love*—has a way of making us do strange things sometimes."

"Okay, with you stating it that way, it must be some kind of love that is making me stand here, and ask for a second chance to prove to you that I am worthy of being your daughter."

Stephen felt his emotions churning within. He swallowed hard as he gazed into Summer's moist eyes. "Summer, you don't have to prove anything to me. You already have by being here, and having a candid conversation with me. I am proud of you."

"Thank you."

"Now that we know where we stand with each other, how about I treat us to lunch?" His smile and his eyes were inviting and hopeful.

"I'd like that, and just for kicks, I'd like to try something."

"What's that?"

"I'd like to try calling you *Dad*."

Stephen felt his heart do a flip-flop. She had called him Dad. His eyes sparkled with joy. "Feel free to try it out as much as you like."

"Okay, Dad." Summer gave him a shy smile. This was new territory for her. "How about during lunch, you enlighten me about the Adirondacks?" He nodded. "Good, and I just might have a story or two to share with you about the Rockies."

As they turned to head back up the incline to the bait shop, Summer paused. Stephen also paused and looked over at her. "Is something wrong?"

"No, Dad. It's just that, since we're trying new things together, I was just wondering what it might feel like to have my father give me a hug."

Stephen opened his arms. "Come find out." With that, Summer stepped into her father's arms. Unbeknownst to them, Wesley had happened to look out the window at that moment to see where they might be. He watched them embrace, and as they did, he felt a tear trickle down his cheek.

7

Summer could not remember the last time she had laughed as much as she had during lunch with her father. His stories about life in the Adirondacks gave her a clear picture of him, as a young boy struggling to find his identity as a minister's son and as his own person. She was amazed to discover he was caring, humorous, intuitive, a smart man who had a unique blend of conservationist and businessman running through his veins. Perhaps one of the most amazing things for Summer to discover about her father was, how many of their views on conservation, politics, and religion were in alignment with each other?

Then, there were the stories Stephen had shared with her about his past relationship with her mother. She saw the way his eyes lit up when he talked about their past. At one point, Summer had to wonder how much truth there was to the stories she was hearing. Summer smiled to herself as she unlocked the door of her rental car. She turned around to face her father, who was leaning against the side of his pickup truck. His arm rested on the rim of the bed. He looked so at ease as he stood there.

"Dad, thank you for allowing me to interrupt your day, for showing me around here, for lunch, and especially for your stories about you and Mom."

For thirty years, Stephen had gone to the cemetery to have one-sided conversations with his dead daughter, Rose. Here and now, his daughter Summer, who was alive and full of life, had thought she was an interruption. Stephen knew in his heart that she was the best interruption he could ever have had that Wednesday morning. He reached out and gently took Summer's soft slender hands into his rough, calloused large hands. Then he drew her hands to his lips and placed a soft kiss on them. "My Summer Princess." Now, where had that corny juvenile name of princess come from? Stephen had no idea. He could not imagine Summer as a child running around with a tiara on her head.

Summer giggled. Her eyes became moist with emotion. "Princess." She looked down at her clothing that covered her body. She smiled. "While I certainly am not dressed as a princess, I like that as your special name for me," she said with wistfulness in her voice. "Thank you for picking something totally different from Mom's nickname of Sunshine."

"Sunshine, you say."

"Yes, and why do I feel as though you have another story about Mom?"

Stephen chuckled. "Because I do. Your mother loved a day that was filled with sunshine. It didn't matter if it was the middle of winter, the thermometer registered zero, and the wind was whipping through the valley. If the sun was shining, Amanda was happy."

"My mom. Goodness, she hasn't changed too much through the years."

"Back in the day, there was a singer by the name of John—"

"Let me guess." Summer smiled. "John Denver, and the song was 'Sunshine on My Shoulders.'"

"That's the one." Stephen watched Summer's eyes. *They were dark and expressive, very similar to her mother's expressive eyes.* "I take it you are familiar with the song."

"Oh yes." She chuckled. "Mom used to sing that song to me when I was little. Oh. My. Gosh." Summer paused as she studied her father. "Now I get it. That was a special song for you and Mom." Stephen nodded. "So as her Summer Sunshine, as she has called me, I bet I reminded Mom of her good memories with you."

"Perhaps."

"You don't think so?" Summer attentively watched him. "Knowing Amanda, I have a feeling she sang that song to you because she loves you, and you remind her of everything that was good in her corner of the world. The goodness doesn't necessarily have anything to do with the life she once lived up here in the Great Sac Community. Summer, you are your mother's sunshine. Like the sun shining in the sky, you bring happiness into her life."

"Wow! Thanks for sharing that with me." Summer beamed. At that moment, Summer's cell phone indicated she had a text message. "Excuse me. I need to take this."

Stephen stood quietly next to his daughter. He watched her expression as she read her text. He saw the lines on her forehead draw together with concern. Something was amiss.

"Apparently, I missed an earlier text from Mom."

"That's not good."

"Mom will be okay, when I tell her about our visit. Even though you two have your issues to work through, you should know that Mom is your best cheerleader. She wants us to have a relationship." Stephen was unable to speak as emotions swept through him. He simply nodded in agreement with Summer as she spoke. "I'm sure you need to get back to work, and I need to attend to some matters."

"I do have more work to do before the days end. However, as one of the owners, I can occasionally skip out from work. After all, how often do I get to spend time with my daughter?"

"Until now, you didn't. Visiting my sister's grave doesn't count." Summer saw something almost dark pass over Stephen's eyes. "I'm so sorry. I was out of line." Stephen nodded. "Dad, before I leave here today, I have one more question for you."

"Ask away."

Summer felt the tears forming. She didn't want to cry. Then, she saw her father stand up straight and reach over to gently place his hands on her shoulders. She stepped into his embrace.

"Before I return to Denver on Monday morning, can we spend more time together? I'd like to talk with you about some things going on in my life. I'd like your perspective," then she added while forcing back her tears, "as a man, and as my father."

"Of course, Summer. I'll do whatever I can to help you." Stephen saw the tears Summer was attempting to hide. His daughter was hurting. Perhaps this was his chance to redeem himself for bungling up his relationship with her mother so long ago. "Let me give you my cell phone number, and my house number—oh heck, you might as well have the number for here at the bait shop, as well." They chuckled at Stephen's willingness to allow Summer full access to his life. She did the same.

With the numbers in Summer's phone, she slid the phone back into her pocket. Summer sighed as she watched her father step around her and open the driver's door of the rental car.

"Thank you, Dad, for a wonderful day."

"You're welcome, Princess." He gave her his smile and nod that meant he genuinely felt what he said. "And, Summer," his words caused her to pause, as she was placing her right foot onto the floorboard. "Whatever is going on in your life, I'll be more than happy to listen and help you in any way that I can." Summer sniffled, nodded, and slid into the car as he added, "You be careful driving around on these roads. Moose occasionally have a way of wandering down onto the road and are not as easy to see as deer."

"Thanks, Dad." Summer softly chuckled and smiled at him. "You sound like Mom."

He commented, as she had expected. Summer allowed her father to close her door, securing her into the vehicle. She knew he was standing in the same spot next to his pickup watching her as she drove off.

Laughter greeted Summer when she opened the door of the cabin and stepped out onto the front porch overlooking the lake. Her mother sat with her hip positioned on the rail and her back leaning against the post. Summer noticed how relaxed she looked. Another person had joined the group and was sitting with their back to Summer as she took a step toward them.

"Hello, everyone," happiness flowed from her voice. She moved toward her mother to take her place by her. Greetings came from all around the small circle. Her mother was smiling while observing her.

"Welcome back, Sunshine. Cassie and Andrew mentioned that you went out on an adventure."

"I did."

Amanda noticed the slight movement of Summer's body, averting eye contact, and an unwillingness to offer more details about her adventure. Something had happened that Summer was not yet willing to reveal to her. She had an ominous feeling as she observed her daughter and spoke.

"I'm glad to hear that you have been exploring the area on your own." Again, Summer's body language betrayed her. Interesting. Amanda continued, "I tried to reach you. When your call went to voice mail, I figured you were hiking in a spot with poor reception."

Summer shifted her weight from one leg to the other. Then she glanced out over the lake. Bingo. Now, Amanda was certain her daughter was withholding something, and it was important.

"Mom, I wasn't hiking." Summer turned to look directly at her mother. "I was with Dad."

"Dad?" Amanda's world had just shifted on its axis. No more Mr. Johnson. Summer was now calling her father *Dad*.

Summer watched her mother as she continued, "Yes, Dad. This morning after you left for Albany with Kevin, I went over to the bait shop and spent time getting to know him."

"Oh. I see." Amanda grew quiet.

"After Dad showed me around the bait shop, we went out for lunch." Summer continued to regale them with her adventures. Amanda remained silent. "Mom." Summer was now concerned. She did not know how to interpret her mother's silence, nor her expression. "Are you upset with me for seeing him without giving you a heads-up?"

Amanda's face remained void of any indication of her emotions as she spoke. "Did you take the initiative to contact your father, or did Johnson contact you?"

"I took the initiative." All of a sudden, Summer was concerned that her mother appeared to be retreating into herself. "Mom, are you okay?"

"Yes, Summer, I am. Surprised, but okay." Amanda released a slow breath, then added, "I'm glad that it was a good experience for both of you."

"But?" Summer heard the familiar tone in her mother's voice. She may say she's glad; however, Summer knew her mother was guarding her tongue from saying what she truly felt.

"There is no *but* about your father and you. I'm glad for you. Let's just leave it at that." Amanda's voice and expression remained deadpan. She was not revealing anything about her true feelings to Summer. "Perhaps, now that you are finally here, you'd like to see your surprise I brought back with me for you from Albany."

Summer turned to look in the area where her mother was now gazing. At that moment, the man who had been quietly sitting in the chair stood.

"Nathan!" Summer exclaimed as she lunged into her friend's arms. Laughter erupted from everyone on the porch.

"Hey, Sum."

Nathan hugged her tightly to his body. Their parents excused themselves, leaving them alone on the porch, while Summer clutched onto Nathan's black sports jacket and wept.

"Go ahead and cry, Summer. I'm here. We'll get through this together, just as I promised you when we spoke on the phone." Nathan intentionally kept his voice quiet, soothing for Summer while she cried and he consoled her. He handed her a tissue, which seemed to appear from nowhere.

"Thanks."

"Anything for a friend. Let's go sit down, and then we may talk about anything you want."

Summer nodded, and allowed Nathan to guide her to one of the Adirondack chairs his parents had previously been occupying. "When did your parents and my mother vacate the porch?"

"When you were plastered against my chest and sobbing your eyes out." Nathan teasingly smiled at his dear friend. Summer noticed the wet blotches on Nathan's light blue oxford shirt.

"Sorry about carrying on so, it's just that, well," Summer paused. Nathan watched her eyes as she spoke. So many emotions. "Nathan, who's idea was it for you to come up here? What about your practice, your clients, and court appearances?"

Summer noticed that his blue eyes sparkled like sunshine reflecting off the Chesapeake Bay on a hot summer's day. The top button of his shirt was open to reveal wisps of light brown hair that matted his chest. His jeans and brown loafers gave Nathan the casual urban look.

"Would you care to tell me what you find so humorous?"

"You don't miss a beat, do you?" Summer now allowed herself to smile, while realizing that something about her expression must have tipped Nathan off to what she was feeling.

"Remember, I'm a lawyer. I read people—assess them as they speak. You, my friend, are fun to read. So, tell me what you were smiling to yourself about, and then I'll tell you why I'm here."

"I was thinking about us as friends, how we both are dressed for the day, and how urban you still look." Summer giggled.

"What can I say, guilty as charged, the city is in my blood. But you, my friend, are an eclectic mix of urban and country. I could invite you to go out to a fine restaurant down in the Inner Harbor of Baltimore, and you would look exquisite in a stylish dress. Here you stand in your casual attire and look totally comfortable, as if you belong here. I hope that quality of being comfortable in your own skin, no matter what the setting may be, never changes in you." He paused and tenderly smiled at her. "You also are hurting. Then, there are our parents who have been in contact with me regarding their concerns for you. Summer, it's one thing for you to call me in tears. But, my friend, your mom calling me in tears, my dad turning to me for advice on how he might help you, well, I had to clear my calendar and get up here to see you, as your friend and as your attorney."

"I'm glad you did." With that said, Summer and Nathan settled in on the porch for a long conversation about her crumbling marriage. After a half hour of Nathan jotting down notes during their conversation, Nathan pulled out his phone from his jacket pocket. He hit speed dial number 20 and waited.

"Hello, Melinda. Nate Phillips here. Yes, it has been a while. I am hoping to catch either one or both of your bosses in between appointments, or court." Nathan smiled at Summer who was sitting still as a mouse, watching and listening to him. He mouthed "smile" as a muffled voice could be heard coming from his phone. "Hey, Alex. Thanks for taking my call. Right." Nathan chuckled, as he reached over and gently rubbed Summer's hand. He felt the tension in her body. His heart grieved for her and the pain she was enduring. "Listen, I am sitting here at my parents' cabin in the Adirondacks with my good friend Summer, whom I've told you and Nikki about. Yes. Sure, let me Skype you in on my tablet. In the meantime, I'm going to hand my phone to Summer so she may introduce herself to you." Nathan did not wait for Summer to respond. He simply placed his phone in her hand and set to work on his tablet.

"Hello, Summer," Nikki's face appeared, and her voice sounded from the tablet.

Summer tentatively smiled at the tablet, said "hello, Nikki," then turned to Nathan.

"My Colorado lawyers?" she questioned; her legal team laughed in unison.

"That they are, Summer. Nikki and Alex Blards, attorneys-at-law specializing in divorce and criminal defense. Nikki, Alex, my dear friend Summer Newman."

With the introductions out of the way, Nathan immediately got down to business with Summer's team. She listened to Nathan provide information from the notes he had taken while speaking with her. It amazed Summer to discover that the Blards team had already been doing their own digging into Mitchel's behavior since Monday afternoon, when Nathan had made contact with them. Summer gasped as she watched and listened to Alex read from his own notes.

"Summer, our PI Paul Seetley has already found some interesting information about your husband's finances. Are you aware that Dr. Brown has at least two separate bank accounts from your joint bank account?"

"I figured he probably had one separate account, as I have my own account, and bank security box where I keep my annuity, bonds, and emergency cash, as well as some jewelry. The joint account is for our household expenses."

"That's good to know. When you get back to Colorado, we will need for you to provide us with a full financial disclosure."

"Of course. I have nothing to hide."

"We're glad to hear that. For now, let's not worry about your personal finances. We'll have time for that as we proceed with your divorce. At this point, even though I believe I already know the answer, are you aware that one of Mitchel's separate accounts is an offshore bank account in Jamaica?"

"No." Everyone saw her expression, and heard the shock in her voice. Nathan reached over to take Summer's hand.

"We're not surprised, Summer," Nikki's voice was quiet, consoling. "Mitchel is not the first spouse to do this, and is probably going to try to explain it as being his nest egg for you both to retire on."

"It would appear that your husband has also been incurring a large financial debt through gambling."

"Gambling." Summer shook her head in disbelief. The rest of the conversation was like a swarm of bees buzzing in Summer's ears. All she heard was the noise. She felt the fear of impending sticks from more painful stingers. The next thing Summer knew, she was saying good-bye and that she would contact Nikki and Alex next Tuesday when she was back in Denver.

———

Amanda found Summer by the lake, sitting on a pine tree that had been brought down during one of the winter storms. She stood back a ways from the lakeshore watching her daughter, who had disappeared after she and Nathan had completed their call. Nathan had shared with Amanda that Summer had requested some time alone to think. Amanda had given her a half hour—long enough. She saw the way Summer was sitting on the felled tree with rounded shoulders, her legs drawn up, and her arms wrapped around her legs. At that moment, Amanda felt her eyes moistening. Summer reminded Amanda of when she was a child no more than ten years old. Summer always would sit hugging her legs when she was hurting. Comfort. Now, as an adult, her daughter was hurting.

"Summer." Amanda stepped forward. Her quiet voice matched her silent steps. Summer sniffled and turned to look in the direction from where her mother had called to her. She tentatively smiled, knowing her mother was observing and assessing her, as only she did.

"Mom," Summer sighed out. She looked exhausted. Her eyes were puffy and red from crying.

"You picked a beautiful spot to come for meditation, contemplation—for renewal."

"It is pretty." Summer sighed out. She did not invite her mother to sit with her. She simply returned to gazing out over the lake. Gentle soothing waves lapped against the rocky shoreline.

"Honey, I wanted to let you know that I am going up to Gram's."

"That's nice," Summer's voice trailed off. It was obvious to Amanda that her child was only half listening to her. She understood how it was to be hurting so deeply within.

"I'll see you tomorrow." With that, Amanda turned and began her quiet retreat to the cabin.

"Mom," Summer called out.

"Yes, Summer," Amanda quietly spoke, as she paused in her step.

"What do you mean that you will see me tomorrow?"

"Summer, honey, with Nathan visiting and staying overnight, there is not room for all of us to sleep here. Since I'm in the room that had been his, or should I say *is* his, I'm vacating for tonight and perhaps tomorrow night, and am going to spend time with Gram."

"Oh." Amanda saw the sadness in Summer's eyes and body.

"Summer, if you need to talk with me during the night, or during the day when I'm up at Gram's, you know you may call me."

"Okay," Summer sighed with relief.

Amanda smiled tenderly at her daughter. "Just so you know, tomorrow I'm planning on doing some easy hiking up in the mountain so that I may have some time alone to think."

"Thanks for telling me." Silence. "Mom."

"Yes, Summer." Amanda watched Summer slide off the fallen tree and step toward her. Without a word spoken, Amanda opened her arms, and Summer stepped in to her mother's embrace.

"I love you, Mom."

"And I love you, Summer." With that, the two women separated. Amanda turned and slowly walked back to the cabin. Summer returned to her spot by the lake to think for a while longer.

8

Denver, Colorado

Summer slowly breathed out a sigh of relief as she walked through the door of the baggage claim area with her small carry-on bag and duffel bag. All around her, travelers were greeted by family and friends waiting for their arrival. There was no one to greet Summer. Mitchel was in Boulder, at the university, or goodness knows where. At that moment, a pang of sadness swept through her. Two years ago, Mitchel would have been at the airport smiling and hugging her to welcome her home. Not today. Life had radically changed between them. Love, the fragile gift, her father had told her about, had been broken. Summer sniffled. Her love for Mitchel had been ravaged, damaged, and was slowly dying. Her love for her father was now growing as a young fragile plant filled with hope as it reaches for the sun and gentle rains to nurture its future life. Summer's trip to New York had turned out far better than she had ever expected. A slight smile found its way to the corners of her mouth as she walked on. Her mother, the star witness for the prosecution in the trial, reminded Summer that standing up for oneself is never easy—no matter how long ago one encountered the pain. A person must draw upon their inner strength, as well as select a few people whom they may trust to assist them, as they endure life's challenges. Trust. Mitchel had most assuredly broken Summer's trust. *His loss*, she breathed out to herself. *I have Mom, Dad, Nathan, my lawyers and colleagues, my extended family and friends.* She named many of them to herself. *Goodness, look at all of the people whom I may turn to, and when push comes to shove, I know that I could even turn to Kevin. After all, he's to be my stepdad, and the one who shared some of his own pain with me and got me to reconsider my attitude toward Dad.*

Summer sniffled. She realized she was moving a bit slower than normal for her and felt stiff from having sat for too long on two different flights. Her jeans, which usually fit like a soft well-broken-in leather glove, now were plastered against her tired body, rubbing in uncomfortable places. Not fun. Summer's feet were sweaty and tired from being bound in her hiking boots for too long. Her zip-up sweatshirt hung on her like a wrinkled old rag. At that moment, Summer blew through her lips to hopefully remove a piece of hair that was hanging down in her right eye. She didn't want to stop her walk toward her Jeep simply to corral her unruly hair.

Despite how exhausted Summer was feeling, the long flight home from New York had gone relatively smoothly for Summer. While sitting on the planes, and while waiting for her connecting flight to Denver, Summer had reflected on the conversations she had with Nathan and her father. Her thoughts returned to these two men as she walked through the airport to the parking lot. There's a lot to be said for first impressions. Sometimes they are wrong. Summer chuckled to herself. Stephen Johnson was a prime example of a wrong first impression. Her father had turned out to be totally different from the man whom Summer first thought him to be, when she observed him sitting in the courtroom intently watching her mother. After spending time together last Wednesday, along with their pleasant phone conversations, Summers found herself at the bait shop early Saturday morning with a temporary fishing license and all the gear she needed, as well as minnows and live earthworms to fish with. Having her father as one of the owners of the bait shop had saved Summer a considerable amount of money for rental equipment, license fees, and bait. Of course, Johnson had refused to take any money from her. His treat. Summer smiled as she recalled how she had sat on the lake in the canoe with her dad at his favorite fishing spot. They quietly talked and chuckled as they cast their lines and reeled in their fish. Together they had caught a couple of nice trout, which they cleaned together, put on ice at the shop, and then shared at Stephen's home that evening. During their time together that evening, Summer had shared her pain of the demise of her marriage. Stephen had listened, didn't cast judgment on her, or Mitchel. All he did was offer her an ear, a shoulder to cry on, and a place to stay, if she needed to get out of Colorado in a hurry or simply needed a place to retreat to for rest and renewal. Perhaps what surprised Summer most was her father's sincerity and willingness to come out to Denver to be with her should things get overwhelming for her. He promised that having learned from his mistakes with her mother, that he would be there for her, no matter what. "After all," he had said with a twinkle in his eyes that were spilling over with love and concern, "you are my princess."

Summer felt moisture forming in her eyes. She blinked away the moisture and sniffled as her thoughts turned to Nathan. Once again, Nathan, Summer's oldest and dearest friend, was coming to her rescue. Goodness knows that the two of them had been through so much drama together in their younger days. Summer had to wonder if there would ever be a time in her life when she did not inevitably turn to Nathan for comfort and help. What would happen to their relationship if Nathan ever got married? Would his wife accept Summer, as Nathan's friend? At that thought, Summer stopped midstep. She said to herself, *Nate and I are so similar to Mom and Dad, minus the thirty-year impasse. Now Mom has Kevin in her life, yet with everything that happened in Mom and Dad's life, she is still seeking to be friends with Dad. I can only hope that if the day ever comes when Nate gets serious with a woman, that she will accept me as an asset, and not a threat.* An unexpected tear fell from her eye. Summer sniffled as she stepped closer to the door leading outside. She simply had to get a grip on her emotions. Crying at the drop of a hat was not going to change anything. Summer drew in a deep breath for courage, that she did not feel, then took a step toward the walkway for long-term parking. Lost in thought, Summer walked on.

————

Summer found herself smiling as she walked toward her muddy green older-model Jeep parked between two pristine clean vehicles. Without warning, laughter erupted from her. She stopped midstep, lowered her bag, then pulled her phone from her pocket. After snapping a picture of her vehicle parked between the Audi and Nissan, she sent the picture with a brief comment to her mother. As she placed the key into the lock on the door, her phone beeped. After throwing her bags onto the passenger seat and climbing in the driver's side, Summer checked her message.

> That's my girl! We sure are a messy pair! LOL. Glad you
> arrived safely. :) Love you.

"Love you too, Mom," Summer breathed out, as if her mother who was now in Baltimore, Maryland, could hear her. Somehow in an unexplainable way, Summer was certain her mother had heard her. Love. The love Summer shared with her mother certainly was different from that which was being forged with her father. Still it's love, their love—indestructible and indescribable. "Thanks for getting me to smile just when I need it." Summer knew in her heart that somehow she was going to get through this crisis, and knowing the support system she now had in place, made the present not quite so daunting. It was—is—time to go home and deal with life.

———◆———

Summer pulled her Jeep into the drive, alongside the ranch-style home that she and Mitchel had purchased three years ago. The carport Mitchel had promised to fix during his summer break from teaching still was unusable and, in Summer's opinion, should simply be torn down before a winter or summer storm took it down for them. Depending on what happened with their marriage, and if she stayed here, Summer just might take it upon herself to tear the eyesore down by herself. As expected, Mitchel's car was not in the drive. Her wave of sadness continued as thoughts of the information her lawyers had shared with her began to bubble deep within. Hidden money—gambling. Summer was certain it was only the tip of the iceberg. She opened the driver's-side door and slid out from behind the wheel. Home. She needed time to unwind and collect herself before seeing Mitchel.

Upon entering the side door of the house and into the small mudroom off the kitchen, Summer drew in a breath to see what lingering smells were still present to greet her. She smelled the scent of laundry having been dried within the past two days. Apparently, the weather had not allowed for Mitch to hang his wash outside on the clothesline, or he was simply too lazy to be environmentally conscientious and chose to use the dryer. Since Summer was in the mudroom with a weeks' worth of soiled clothes in her bag, there was no time like the present to get a jump on doing her wash. With bag in hand, she walked over to the washing machine and lifted the lid, then commenced to put her load of dirty clothes into the machine. As Summer reached up onto the shelf to take down the laundry soap, she noticed a new brand of soap had been purchased and was on the shelf next to their partially used bottled of liquid soap. A sickening feeling hit her stomach. Was Summer paranoid, wanting to find things wrong in her home that she could use to blame Mitchel for the collapse of their relationship? Looking closely, without touching the new bottle, Summer could see evidence of soap having trickled down the outside of the bottle. She was certain that there was a story behind the new container of soap and had an ominous feeling the story was going to grow like an unwanted weed in a vegetable garden.

With the wash begun, Summer took her phone from her pocket and began to take photos of the laundry room. Then she opened the dryer and found clothes still inside. As Summer began removing Mitchel's clothes, it was obvious that he, or someone else, had purchased a new wardrobe for him. A part of Summer simply wanted to leave Mitch's clothes in a heap on the floor. But as sad and as rejected as Summer felt, she couldn't do that. So Summer began folding his clothes, that is, until she found the petite black cotton sweater and black lace bra. Summer gasped as she dropped the sweater and tangled bra from her grasp, as if they were a deadly spider. They certainly were not a part of her wardrobe. Summer's initial sadness was replaced with anger at Mitchel's boldness, flaunting his indiscretions in front of her. Without hesitation, Summer picked up her phone and dialed Nikki and Alex's number.

"Summer, how nice to hear from you. How was your flight home?"

"Nikki, the flight home was uneventful." Summer sniffled. She suddenly felt exhausted. A part of her wanted to go back to the airport and return to New York; after all, her father had invited her to come back anytime she wanted. No. Running from the problem would not solve it, any more than her mother running thirty years ago had solved her problems. *Thanks, Mom, for that valuable life lesson*, Summer thought. Then, she said to Nikki, "I'm sending you some photos I just took while in the mudroom of my house. Mitchel apparently has a girlfriend, and had the audacity to have her here in our home, while I was in New York." Now, Summer began to whimper. She was struggling to hold back the deluge of tears threatening to break through the invisible dam in her eyes.

"Oh, Summer, I'm so sorry to hear this." Nikki spoke quietly, full of compassion for her client. Summer quietly listened to Nikki's words of encouragement. "I just got your pictures. Hmm. Looks like Dr. Brown is definitely a naughty naughty man. Our PI has brought in his son, Paul Junior, his part-time assistant, to also work on your case. PJ just happens to be a student at the school of law at Boulder. Having a PI who is also a student will help us gather information we might not otherwise have been able to get on Mitchel, and his life as a professor. It will be interesting to discover what else Mitchel has been up to before and during your absence."

"Nikki, I'm so angry, I could slug him for what he's done."

"Summer, you have a right to be upset with Mitchel. He has betrayed your trust."

"That's for sure! There no longer is any trust between us, or at least for me. You know, Nikki, I am beginning to understand how Mom's anger caused her to wail on those two slugs last winter. More than that, even though we have different situations, I'm beginning to understand just how helpless Mom may have felt after she was raped. I feel violated by Mitchel."

"Summer, it's good that you are able to process your anger. You have a right to be angry at Mitchel for what he has done to you. I know you are an avid outdoors person, and go hunting, hiking, etc., so the temptation may be for you to strike out—if he pushes you too far."

"How do you know? Oh wait—Nate told you."

"Yes, he did. Summer, Nathan cares about you and is very concerned for your well-being. Why else would he have called Alex and me to help you? Right. As your lawyer, I suggest that any weapons you might have in the house, you keep them locked up. Summer, we will bring Mitchel down. However, you're not going down with him."

"I'll do my best to play nice."

"I'm sure you will. Anything else that you find as evidence of his indiscretions, send to us. Alex and I will certainly incorporate this into our motions on your behalf." Silence. "And, Summer…"

"Yes?"

"Make sure that you intentionally take time to do something that brings you joy. Throughout this ordeal, you need to work at maintaining balance in your life."

"Thanks, Nikki. I'll do my best."

"I know you will, Summer. We'll talk soon."

Summer was so glad that she called Nikki. Before their conversation ended, she had an appointment scheduled to go down to Colorado Springs to meet with Nikki and Alex, in the privacy of their office. She also had her to-do list to complete before the meeting. Summer sighed as she removed the teakettle from the hot burner. She poured the boiling water over the tea leaves that she had placed in her cup. The soothing aroma of her great-grandmother's herbs filled the air. Summer could not wait to taste the tea her mother claimed could cure whatever ails you. Mmm. The hot beverage with a spoon of honey added for sweetness felt good as it slid down her throat. As Summer sipped her tea, she moved about assessing the kitchen for further evidence of Mitchel's other woman having intruded on her territory.

Opening the refrigerator door, Summer found a bottle of pinot noir and an open bottle of some fancy-named white wine Summer knew had not been in the refrigerator before she went east. Picture time. Opening the vegetable tray, Summer found a container of tofu, portobello mushrooms, sliced carrots, onions, snow peas, as well as other vegetables she knew had arrived in the house after she had departed. Opening the freezer, Summer found that the venison she had hunted and killed last season, and pork she had bought was still there. Good thing. A smile brushed her lips as she removed a package of venison steaks to thaw. After she completed the work she had planned for the remainder of the day, her meat and the vegetables that she had found in the refrigerator were going to taste mighty fine. She might even help herself to a glass of *their* wine. After all, the items were in her home.

As Summer walked through the kitchen into the living room, nothing appeared to be out of the ordinary. She sat down in her favorite chair and removed her hiking boots. With the work she had ahead of her, Summer needed to be comfortable. That means no shoes. Leaving the overripe-smelling shoes out on the back porch, Summer walked back into the living room and over to the television. She turned it on to her favorite music station. When Summer was younger and she was summoned to help her mother with a major cleaning or work project, they always jammed out to classic rock and roll. Mom always said good music made the work seem not so bad. She had been right, and at this moment, Summer needed all the "not so bad" that she could get.

With vacuum in hand, Summer walked into what should have been the formal dining room, which they used as an office and area for guests to sleep on the daybed. Summer removed the cover and linens from the bed. She carried them out to the laundry and began her next load. Then, Summer returned to the small room and commenced to take down the bed. The whole time she worked, she sang along with the songs blaring out of the television speakers. In no time, the room was empty.

Next, Summer headed into their bedroom. She looked at the carelessly made bed and ripped the covers and blankets off the bed. It was rather difficult for Summer to get the queen-size mattress off the box spring by herself, and through the doorways and hall. Still, she did it, and by now was sputtering under her breath. It was truly best that she was alone with her anger, as she returned to the bedroom for the box spring and bed frame. When the box spring was off the frame, Summer noticed something lying on the carpet under the bed. Picture time once again. Summer snapped a shot of the underwear that certainly was not hers. Oh, it was going to be interesting to hear Mitchel's reason for the underwear. Summer walked out to the kitchen where she got her rubber gloves, a ziplock bag for her evidence and returned to the bedroom. Another picture was taken of the underwear now in the bag, and then added to the collection of the other woman's clothing, now placed on the top shelf in the front-hall closet.

While Summer was taking the bed frame apart, she found something small wedged between the bed and the side table. A used condom. Summer felt numb. It was obvious that Mitchel either didn't care that she might find the evidence, or he was doing this on purpose. Neither one bode well with her. Sadly, it was "picture, rubber gloves, and ziplock bag" time once again.

Sweat was pouring off Summer as she took apart the bed frame and then set it up in the den. With box spring and mattress on the bed, Summer dumped the dirty linens and blankets in a heap on the bed. Mitchel was in for a rude awakening when he returned home, and discovered their new sleeping arrangements. Summer looked at the mess and actually began to feel better. She was no longer going to allow him to pretend as though they were a happy couple. Their change in sleeping arrangements was only the beginning. Returning to the master bedroom, Summer set to work on getting the daybed into her room and set up for her to sleep on.

—⁓⁓—

At six thirty in the evening, Summer sat out on the back porch with a hot cup of coffee in her hand. Her empty dinner plate sat on the small table alongside the chair she sat in. She had enjoyed her meal of venison and their vegetables. Now, she sat listening to the familiar sounds of suburbia on the west side of Denver. Off beyond the back of the property in the trees, birds were singing and squirrels were scurrying about. The city was so different from being by the lake with family and friends in the Adirondacks. The peace and tranquility was gone. Summer felt very much alone.

Just as Summer was ready to hit her speed dial number for her father, she heard a vehicle pull into the driveway. She recognized the sound of the car motor. Mitchel was home. Summer took another sip of coffee as she listened to the car motor go silent. Then, there was the sound of the car door slamming. Summer remained on the porch listening to the sounds in her home. The front door opened and closed. There was no calling out to Summer, no welcome home. She listened.

"What in the blue tarnations is going on here!" Mitchel yelled, as he came storming through the house and out onto the porch. "Summer, have you lost your mind?"

"Nice to see you too, Mitchel. My trip? Fine. Thanks so much for asking." Summer snarled. Her darkening eyes shone with anger as she stood. She picked up her plate and took a step toward Mitchel, who continued to stand in the doorway. "I take it you have seen your new sleeping arrangements. Since you were obviously someplace else this afternoon, and not here with me, I have made the executive decision that we are no longer sleeping together. I'm not in the mood to further discuss these changes with you. I'm exhausted, and I am going to my room to get ready for bed, so please move out of my way." Summer glared at Mitchel, who stood in the doorway with his mouth hanging open in shock.

Mitchel stepped aside to allow Summer to move past him. As she started past Mitchel, he forcefully took a hold of her forearm.

"Summer," he said with pleading in his voice. She raised a brow as she glanced down at Mitchel's hand and then back to see his expression. "You can't mean this. I know that for the past few months, I've not been as involved in our marriage as you would like."

"Really, I hadn't noticed." Sarcasm dripped from Summer's voice.

"Honey, baby, while you were gone, I had a lot of time to think about us. I'm here now, and I am hoping we can start over."

"Don't honey or baby me." Summer's eyebrows were growing increasingly closer together. Her scowl deepened. "Mitchel, you obviously didn't think hard enough. *If* you cared about me, you would have taken time to talk with me when I called you while I was in New York. *If* you cared as much as you say you do, you would have been at the airport to greet me. *If* not at the airport, you would have been here to greet me. *If* you cared, you would have at least called me to make sure I arrived home safely. More than that, you would have been home to share dinner with me."

"Dinner." Mitchel glanced over at the kitchen door.

"Yes, dinner, and yes, I did cook up the vegetables you and your sweetheart left in the refrigerator. You can take the tofu to her. I'd rather eat meat."

"Summer, I…" Mitchel swallowed hard.

"Don't even try to dignify what we both know is true with a lame answer. Now, take your slimy adulterous hand off of me. You had best pray to your maker that your hand does not leave marks on me, or else."

Mitchel released his hold on Summer. They both looked at her arm, pink from his pressure, but no lasting indentation from his fingers. Their eyes met. Summer's dark eyes were as threatening as a storm rocking and rolling through the mountains.

"Oh, Summer, you have to believe me. I would never abuse you."

"You already have." Shock resonated all over Mitchel's face as Summer added, "Remember, my mother works with abused women. She's taught me well to know the signs. I am going to bed. Sleep well in your new room." With that, Summer began to turn away from Mitchel.

"I'm sorry," he whispered. "I never meant to hurt you."

"I know." A tear fell from Summer's eye as she turned from Mitchel and quietly walked to the bedroom. Mitchel remained standing in the doorway, numb from what had just happened between them.

Mitchel finally found the strength to move from the doorway. He locked up the house and walked into the den to begin the daunting task of making his bed for the night. The den. Summer had banished him from their bed. Mitchel's mind raced through everything that had been said between them. What else, besides the food had she found, would have tipped her off to him having had company in their home while she was gone? What made Summer believe his company had been female? He could have had a gathering with some of his graduate students. Something had made her suspect a woman had been in their home.

Mitchel drew in a deep breath. As he loosened and removed his tie, he began to retrace the activities during his week. All of a sudden, Mitchel remembered the day it had rained, and what they had done together. Mitch bolted through the den to the kitchen and into the mudroom. He flipped on the light. There on the shelf next to the laundry soap Summer had purchased and used, like a beacon shining from a lighthouse identifying treacherous rocks in the waters at night, sat their container of laundry soap. Looking at the two containers, Mitchel felt no cheer. He was in a boat that had hit a rock and was slowly taking on water. Mitchel sighed as he opened the dryer door and found a load of Summer's clothes. Forget *slowly* taking on water! Mitchel had just capsized. He raked his fingers through his hair as he recalled the rainy day when they had done a load of wash together, besides other things. It was the one time he had been bold enough to bring her to their home. Mitchel never expected Summer to find out. They had been careful, or so he thought. What had Summer found in the wash?

Mitchel felt sick to his stomach as he walked over to the door and looked out into the dark backyard. He pulled his phone from his pocket and dialed the number he knew by heart.

"Hello," a sleepy young female voice spoke into the phone.

"Jesslyn."

"Mitch, what's wrong?"

"Everything. Remember the day we did the load of laundry together?"

"Yes. It was a wonderful day. Actually, I'm glad that you mentioned that day. I was going to ask you to see if I left my black sweater and my black lace bra at your house in the dryer with your clothes."

Mitch gasped for a breath as his phone slipped from his hand, fell to the slate floor, and shattered into pieces. He knelt down and slowly began picking up the pieces of his phone that is now destroyed. Looking at the shattered phone that he now held in the palm of his hands, Mitchel thought how ironic that his phone represented his life. Broken.

9

The week quickly fell into some sense of normalcy for Summer. Rising a half hour earlier than what had been her normal time of six o'clock, Summer was able to shower, grab a cup of coffee, and eat her breakfast without encountering Mitchel. Then, she would head out the door and drive down to work at the rangers station in the National Forest. Toward the end of the first week, when Summer glanced into the den, she found Mitch's bed was empty. No big surprise. At least now, with Mitch staying away, he was no longer pretending to love her and care about her feelings.

Summer was glad that she had taken the time on Friday afternoon to drive down to Colorado Springs to meet with Nikki and Alex. So far, their PI's investigation had disclosed that Mitch had actually been gambling before they had been married. She was shocked to know that Mitchel had hidden his addiction from her so well. Paul had also discovered from his sources that two years ago, Mitchel had become involved with some less-than-reputable people with his betting. Danger was sure to follow.

Then, there was the issue of a woman by the name of Jesslyn. Paul Junior had been efficient with his surveillance and investigation of her and Dr. Mitchel Brown. Jesslyn had taken numerous undergraduate courses taught by Mitch. She had already participated in two of the geological sciences field studies Mitchel had led. Now, she was a graduate student with Mitchel as her adviser, as well as his teaching assistant and his mistress. Talk about unethical and reprehensible behavior. This news of Mitchel and his lover was what brought Summer to unwanted tears. The black lace bra and sweater and the bedroom scene flashed through Summer's mind. The blatant proof of Mitchel's affair made Summer feel sick to her stomach. She knew in her heart that if Mitchel had been only guilty of gambling, she would have clung to hope and fought for their marriage. But infidelity, breaking Summer's trust on such an intimate level was unforgivable. Given what they now knew of Mitchel, his illegal activities and his relationship with Jesslyn, Nikki and Alex had drawn up Summer's petition for separation, as well as an order of protection, and were ready for Summer to sign the petition. It would be filed with the court in Denver first thing Monday morning. Summer sniffled, wiped her nose, regained her composure, and without hesitation, picked up the pen and signed the petition.

⊸⊶⊷⊶⊶

A warm late afternoon breeze filtered through the screens on the porch. Summer had taken her time driving home from Colorado Springs. By signing the papers, Summer had consciously chosen the road that she and Mitchel would be traveling down from here on out. There was no turning back. Mitchel had forced Summer to play her hand. Her ace was out, and she would no longer be made a fool of by Mitchel.

Summer sat in her favorite chair with a glass of iced tea on the side table and a new novel in hand. She had stopped in a small bookstore on her way out of Colorado Springs, and purchased the book as a treat. As Summer opened the cover of her book, written by one of her favorite authors, her cell phone rang. A smile immediately took shape on her lips as she listened to the ringtone. Placing the book on her lap, Summer drew in a deep breath as she reached over to the table and picked up her phone.

"Hi, Nate. To what do I owe this call from you?"

"Hello, Sum. I just spoke with Alex. He told me that you had been in to file your petition for separation, as well as an order of protection."

"I did. Nate, did Alex tell you what Paul has discovered about Mitchel and his secret life?"

"Yes, and knowing how devastating this is for you, wishing I could be there to give you a hug, I decided to call you."

Summer felt the tear form and trickle down her cheek. It didn't surprise her that Nathan was concerned about her well-being. Although Summer initially felt that she did not want to talk with anyone this afternoon, or tonight, she was glad to hear her friend's voice on the other end of the line. With Nathan, Summer could open up and share what she was truly feeling—good, bad, indifferent. When her mother or father called to check up on her, Summer tended to guard her words to not concern them more than they already were toward her well-being. Summer actually smiled as she listened to Nathan speak to her with tenderness. With her family and friends by her side, she knew she would survive this storm in her life. Granted, it may turn out to be like that of an F5 Tornado before the divorce was through; however, Summer Newman would survive, and have a story to tell in the end.

"Nathan, it's Friday evening in Baltimore. You should be focused on a date—you know, a love life, and not checking in on me." Nathan chuckled and made a comment that brought a tentative smile to Summer's lips. "Hmm. If my love life wasn't in the tank, I'd give you some advice. However, right now—"

"Hey now, Sum, no beating yourself up! I do value your judgment right up there with my parents."

Summer sniffled. "Well, thank you, Nate, for your vote of confidence in me. I'm honored to know I rank up there with your parents. So, since you don't need my advice on dating, have you called to check on me as my lawyer or as my friend?"

"Well, Sum, I'm guilty on both accounts. As your lawyer, I'm glad to know what Nikki and Alex are doing for you thus far. I knew they would be a good match for you. Having said that, my real motive for calling is, I'm first and foremost concerned about you as my friend. Plus, I have to admit that I'm being a spy for my parents."

"Your parents?" Summer felt warmth engulf her as Nathan shared Cassie and Andrew's concern for her emotional well-being. As if worrying about her wasn't enough, they were seeking to assist her with her legal fees. "Oh, Nate, you can't be serious."

"Oh, but I am!"

"Nate," Summer was desperately sniffling back her emotions, "I love your parents. However, I don't need them to pay my legal fees for me, any more than I need Mom and Kevin or my Dad to help me out financially. Please assure them that I am financially able to retain Nikki, Alex, and you as my legal team."

"Summer, I hear your anxiety. If you aren't careful, you are going to levitate right off your chair. So, please do us both a huge favor and take a deep breath."

He heard Summer mumble under her breath. Nathan knew she had to grumble to herself before they could continue their conversation. Some things, or friends, in life never changed. Nathan was glad.

"Nathan Phillips, stop smiling at me and silently laughing at me," Summer whined.

"Sum, I am smiling. However, not laughing—not today. Right now, your emotions are a train wreck waiting to happen. The last thing I want is you getting hysterical on me. In all of my years in practice, I have not seen one person no matter how strong or determined they are come through their divorce unscathed, and without some emotional pain. My parents are simply trying to help to alleviate some of your pain by helping you the only way they know how: financially. You and I both know that when Andrew and Cassie devise a plan to do something for someone that they care about, there is no stopping them."

Summer sniffled and wiped her eyes with the back of her hand. She had to smile as she heard Nathan refer to his parents by their given name. Summer knew for a fact that out of sheer respect for them, he would never call them anything but Mom and Dad to their face, or to anyone else. Only with her did he take the liberty of being less than proper. Summer knew that because she occasionally did the same when she spoke with Nate and referred to her mother as Amanda. It had been a private joke of theirs for years—too many to count.

"So, Sum, don't be surprised if you receive a generous monetary birthday gift from my parents."

"Nate, you know I always appreciate them remembering me on my birthday. However, please do your best to convince them to not send me more money, than perhaps to go out for dinner and a movie." Summer felt the tears coming like water cascading over a waterfall high up in the mountains. These were not tears of sadness but tears of joy—humility knowing that she was thought of so highly by his parents.

"Sum, I'll do my best." Then he softly added, "You know Mom and Dad love you."

"I know, but." Summer sighed. "Oh, Nathan, what will my mom say if your parents send me money for my legal—"

"Sum, FYI, your mom and Kevin have already been discussing this issue with my parents. They, along with me, have warned Mom and Dad that you will not approve of their gift. Regardless of what we have said, there is no stopping them." Summer sighed as she listened to Nathan. She was overwhelmed by her friend's generosity. "Besides, Sum, in Mom and Dad's minds, this is the only way for them to reach out to you and help you in your time of need. I gently suggest that you, my dear friend, put aside your pride. Please don't get in a dander by my saying that about your pride and graciously accept their gift. Please, Sum, if for nothing else, please do this for me." Summer smiled as she heard the pleading in Nathan's voice. How many times had he used that same tone while they were growing up together? "Believe me when I say that I have been reigning my parents and your mother in since you have told them this week about your plans for filing for your separation. Actually, I've had to reign in Kevin as well."

"Kevin?"

"Uh-huh." Summer could tell Nathan was smiling once again. It was the smile of near gloating, which had always driven her nuts when he had one up on her. She didn't want to but found herself smiling with Nate as he continued. "Your soon-to-be stepdad would like nothing more than to come out to Denver, pack you up, and bring you to Baltimore to stay with your mother and him. He told us it would be worth it to be arrested for kidnapping to know that you are safe."

"Oh goodness, Nate, what is it with that older generation wanting to rescue me? This past week when I spoke with Dad, I discovered that he too wants to come out here, pack me up, and bring me back to New York to stay with him so he can make sure I'm safe. He said he is putting out feelers for state jobs I would be qualified to apply for." She heard a chuckle. "Nate, be honest and tell me, am I missing something? Have they all forgotten that we're adults? Go ahead and laugh. But you and I both know it's not funny."

"No, Summer, it's not funny. But, Sum, think from their perspective for a moment. Parents, friends, whether we want them to or not, they love us and worry about us." Worry. Summer found her mind do an instant replay of the conversation she had with her mother not long ago in the wee hours of the morning when they were in New York.

"You're right."

"Yes, I am, my friend, and think about this. Our parents are considerably older than us. Heaven knows they are not ready for rocking chairs." Summer snickered. "Our mothers would have my head for saying that, so don't you tell on me either. This stays between us." Summer agreed. "The point is, our parents have been through situations that have shaken their worlds. Because they love us, they want to protect us from the pain we have to endure in order to move on with our lives."

Just as Summer was ready to respond, she heard the familiar sound of Mitchel's car pulling in to the drive. "Nate, I don't believe it. Mitchel is here. I need to go."

"I hear dread in your voice. Call me later so we may finish our conversation."

"I will, Nate." Summer ended her call. She replaced her phone to the table and picked up her glass of iced tea to take a sip.

Last year this time, Summer would have risen from her chair and greeted Mitch as he came through the door. Not now. She remained on the porch and listened. It wasn't long before Summer heard Mitchel walk into the kitchen. He paused at the counter by the refrigerator, opened the top cupboard, and took out a wineglass. She heard Mitchel firmly place the glass on the counter, then open the refrigerator door and remove the bottle of wine, which had been left from his dinner with his lover. Summer remained in her chair on the porch listening to him move about, while looking out toward the tree line behind the house. A part of her wished that he would go on into the den or the living room and leave her to her solitude. His steps on the tile floor informed Summer that Mitchel was heading to the porch.

Summer felt his presence as he stepped through the door. She glanced over to see that Mitchel had loosened his tie and rolled up the sleeves of his white shirt. His footsteps were heavy against the cement floor as he took two steps and then paused. Their eyes met. Summer saw something different in Mitchel's eyes—pain, regret, perhaps sorrow. Any other day, Summer would have felt compassion toward Mitchel. Not today. She continued to quietly observe him.

"Summer, since Monday night, we've been like two ships passing in the night. May I join you, or am I banished from here as well?"

"This is neutral territory. Mitchel, you know perfectly well that you banished yourself from our bed by your scandalous actions."

"I deserved that." Mitchel's Adam's apple jumped as he swallowed. His gaze fell away from Summer.

"Yes, you did," Summer snarled. "Why you suddenly want to sit with me is beyond my comprehension. Why tonight, Mitchel? It's Friday night, why aren't you off with your sweetheart? What's the matter, is she unable to be your lover tonight, so you come slithering back here like an old tomcat?"

Summer knew her words were mean, and that was what she felt. Mean. She wanted Mitchel to hurt right along with her. Mitchel did not respond as he stepped over to the other chair and sat down. He looked out into the backyard. Silence hung between them. The gentle breeze that had been blowing outside was becoming stronger. Low-hanging clouds were moving in and taking shape in the sky.

"I don't appreciate being compared to a tomcat, and Jesslyn's bodily functions are none of your business." Summer was surprised by how softly Mitchel had spoken the other woman's name. How long had it been since he had last spoken her name with tenderness? Summer couldn't remember. She glanced over at him to find that his eyes were fixed on the outdoors, as if searching for something unreachable.

"I guess the weather forecast is going to prove to be right after all." Mitchel breathed out.

"It's not only going to be stormy outside, but in here as well." Mitchel sighed, then took a sip of wine. "Summer, I came here this evening in hopes that we could sit together and have an honest conversation."

"Honest, you say?" Summer looked at Mitchel with total surprise. "You wouldn't know honesty if it bit you in the backsides. Beside that, I've found that if you want honesty, you need to spend time in the outdoors because nature doesn't lie, only humanity lies."

"All humanity, or just me?" Now, Mitchel turned to look at Summer. Her eyes seemed to have a faraway look in them. "Many people choose to lie and betray another person's trust. Sadly, Mitchel, you are no different." Sadness oozed from Summer's expression. "Since you said that you want to have an honest conversation, answer this question for me. When did you stop loving me? Or should I say, stop finding me desirable?"

"Summer, don't do this to yourself." There was no tenderness in his voice. His tone was that of an educator prepared to lecture a student. "You are a very desirable woman."

"Just not to you."

"I…" Mitchel could not bear to look into Summer's glistening eyes. "Oh crap. Summer, you are a very desirable woman. You are smart, articulate, compassionate, a warrior for nature. Do you have any idea how hard it is to be married to you and feeling like I never quite measure up to your expectations?" Mitchel's words hurt, as if he had slapped her across the face.

"So let me see if I heard you correctly. You say that you still find me desirable. However, because I have such a high standard of living for myself, you find yourself less than me, so in order to compensate for your shortcomings, you sought love and devotion from one of your students to provide for…for what we no longer have between us. Mitchel, you're pathetic to sit there and think that I am gullible enough to allow you to let me take all of the blame for our broken marriage. I feel sorry for you, Mitchel."

"You feel sorry for me?"

"Yes, you. I asked you to be honest and tell me when you stopped loving me. You still haven't answered my question. Then again, it really doesn't matter anymore because I'm through participating in this one-sided relationship. I suggest you pack a bag and go to your lover's home for the weekend."

Mitchel looked at Summer in disbelief. She was kicking him out of their home. Had that been his motive all along when he had driven over there? Had he gone there seeking to have Summer's permission to leave and not feel guilty? Whatever the reason may have been, their conversation was finished for tonight.

"If that is what you want, Summer." Mitchel did not wait for Summer to respond. He stood and, without hesitation, walked into the house.

Summer remained on the porch. When she heard the front door open and close, she stood. It was then that Summer walked into the house. Making her way through the quiet rooms, she came to her bedroom, flopped down on her bed, and cried her heart out.

10

Summer was out on a trail with a breathtaking view of the valley when her cell phone rang. She paused near a large rock and leaned against it as she pulled her phone from her pocket. Having programmed both Nikki's and Alex's numbers in with the song "We Are the Champions," she knew her caller was one of her lawyers.

"Hello, Summer, I hope this is a good time for me to call you," Alex asked.

"Perfect. I'm out here on the trail heading to a primitive campsite to see the condition that it was left in by the last campers. What can I do for you on this beautiful day?"

"Thank you for reminding me that it is a beautiful day. Perhaps I can convince Nikki to take a long lunch with me, or even cut out from work early." He laughed at Summer's response. She was right; Nikki would not leave work simply because it was a pleasant day to be outdoors. "Well, Summer, if one of us is to enjoy this day, then I'm glad to hear you are the fortunate one. You deserve it! Now, I hope my news will add to your joy."

"Hmm. You are calling me envying that I work outdoors most days, and now you tell me you have news that you hope will add to my joy. So, I imagine the news has to do with my separation from Mitchel."

"Yes, it does, and Nikki told me I had to call you right away—"

"Alex, I know that you are enjoying yourself, but your suspense is killing me here."

A blast of laughter coming through the phone caused Summer to smile. "Oh, all right. Summer, teasing you is such fun." Summer cleared her throat and smiled. Sometimes, like right now, she couldn't believe how much Alex reminded her of Nate. She decided that was a good thing—a very good thing, as she listened to Alex. "I just received a call from Ashley Prime."

"Ashley Prime, who's that?" Summer's curiosity was piqued.

"Well, Summer, she introduced herself to me as Mitchel's lawyer. She's from Boulder and will be representing him during your separation and divorce."

Summer swiped the beads of moisture from her forehead with the back of her hand. She pulled out her water bottle and took a sip. Her voice was tight and filled with annoyance as she spoke. "Figures he got a woman to be his legal representation. I bet she is petite, blond—"

"Summer, in all honesty, I've never seen or heard of the woman before we spoke this morning, so I can't answer what she looks like for you. But I will tell you that Mitchel has received his papers and has agreed to your separation. It would appear that he does not want to cause you any more unnecessary pain. According to Ms. Prime, Mitchel is willing to move out of the house as early as this weekend."

"This weekend—wow! Oh, how fortunate am I to have such a caring, not-soon-enough-to-be ex-husband." Sarcasm dripped from Summer's words. "I wonder if this is his birthday present for me. Then again, knowing Mitchel, he probably doesn't remember that Saturday is my thirtieth birthday. Summer pulled her cloth handkerchief from her backpack and wiped her head.

"Oh, Summer, I'm sorry for this timing with your birthday. We can make him wait if you would like."

"Alex, thank you for caring. But you know this may just be the birthday present I need. Many people dread their thirtieth birthday. Not me. This is a time for celebrating—starting over, or starting out new—a year filled with possibilities for new life."

"I like your attitude, and so will Nikki. Knowing my wife, she will want to go out and celebrate with you." With that comment, an idea began to take shape in Alex's mind. If he could pull it off, Summer was in for a surprise.

Summer chuckled. "I like that idea of partying with the two of you. So, Alex, back to Mitch, how will this work? Will I be able to keep certain items, or does he get to come into the house and plunder it?"

"That is a good question. No. Mitchel does not have the right to simply walk into the house and take what he wants. For now, he will remove his personal items. All shared property will be negotiated as we move along with your divorce."

"Thanks for clarifying that for me. Here are my next questions. How do we make sure that Mitchel plays by the rules? Do I have to be there?"

"No, Summer. Nikki and I have discussed your situation with Nathan. Some divorcing couples are able to separate property together. Given the tension between you and Mitchel, you will not be at the house when he comes to pick up his things."

"I'm glad to know that. But, Alex, I don't trust him. He might do something to the house, or to my personal belongings out of spite."

"Summer, we will not allow Mitchel to destroy anything or take what is not his. Nikki and I plan on driving up to Denver early Saturday morning. We will be at the house to do a walk-through with you. Then, you will leave. We will be there as your friends when Mitchel arrives. Then, we will call you when Mitchel has left the house."

"Okay." Summer breathed a sigh of relief. She wouldn't have to see Mitchel on her birthday. "Alex, will he leave his keys with you?"

"Of course, and we will have a locksmith scheduled to change your locks later that afternoon."

"Wow, you and Nikki think of everything. Thank you, Alex."

"Summer, you don't need to thank me. My job is to look out for your best interest. Besides, Nathan would have my head if I didn't go the extra mile for you." With that, Summer not only smiled, she laughed. "Good to hear you laugh. We'll talk soon."

Summer ended the call and returned the phone to her pocket. Break time was over, and she had a campsite to investigate. Taking a deep breath, Summer drew in the fresh smells of nature. She loved her job. The vacationers she met during the summer months were usually appreciative of her knowledge and fun to get to talk with about the area. Summer really liked to learn where the vacationers called home and what had motivated them to visit the Rocky Mountains.

A ways up the trail, as she came around the bend, Summer heard and saw movement in the thicket. She stopped and watched. There it was for a brief second—a small brown nose. The leaves rustled. Then she saw the big brown eyes peering out at her. Summer took a cautious step closer. As she did, the fawn moved back into the thickness of the brush. She heard movement, and once again caught sight of the fawn. It sounded like a larger animal, perhaps the doe was there with the fawn. If that was the case, then why hadn't the mother protectively sought refuge for herself and her young away from Summer? This troubled her. There could be only one explanation. Summer quietly peered through the leaves. There lying on the moss-covered ground was the doe. Her breathing was labored. Her tongue hanging out of her mouth. This doe was in distress. Summer was preparing to make her call for help when she saw that the left hind leg was bloody. The deer had an open wound obviously from an encounter with a predator that rendered her unable to move. A tear slipped down Summer's cheek. She sniffled.

"Little Momma, don't you and your baby worry or be afraid," she kept her voice quiet. The doe attempted to lift her head, then heavily dropped it to the ground. "It's okay. I promise. Summer's here now. If it is the will of the Great Spirit, I will save you both."

Summer slowly and quietly moved back out onto the trail. She pulled out her phone and hit speed dial for the rangers station. While Summer waited for Cathy Long to answer the phone, she breathed out a prayer. Finally, in what seemed to Summer like an eternity, Cathy answered the phone.

"Rangers Station."

"Cathy, it's me Summer." There was urgency in her voice. She needed to get Cathy to understand immediately that this is no social call, to simply gloat about being out on the trail on a gorgeous late May day.

"What's wrong, Summer?" Cathy had an affinity for her fellow ranger, who was now going through her marital separation and divorce. She was five years older than Summer, been through a horrific divorce that had left her bitter of men, and loved to spend her time working with nature. More importantly, Cathy shared a sense of connection with Summer, as she too had Native American roots: Cheyenne. Summer told Cathy what she had found along the trail, gave her coordinates, and as senior ranger over Cathy, instructed her on getting help from the wildlife sanctuary and anyone else she could think of. Time was of the essence in saving the doe and her fawn.

Summer kept her vigil checking on the deer, then returning to her spot on the trail to wait for help. Ten minutes after making her first call to Cathy, Summer's phone rang. Good news. Help was on its way. The only thing was that it would take at least an hour for help to arrive.

"Cathy, I don't know if the doe will last that long."

"We'll hope for the best, my friend. The Great Spirit led you up there today for a reason. I believe you were sent there to save those animals."

"I hope you're right."

Summer heard a loud noise in the sky. She looked out toward the east. "Oh no, Cathy, there's a helicopter heading this way. That is sure to scare the deer." Summer saw the helicopter fly over. She saw the letters and logo on the side of the helicopter. "Great, just what we don't need. The local television station is flying over us."

"Wow! Who would have thought you rescuing a doe and her fawn would make the news!" "I really don't think that the deer care if the world knows that we are saving them."

"Well, the world does care, and you are going to be deemed a hero. It's about time we got recognition for the good work we do."

"Cathy, I'm not doing this job to get my name in the news." She sighed, as she glanced up at the helicopter that was making another circle in the sky.

"I know. Your humility is one of the things I admire about you."

"Thanks." Summer breathed out a sigh of relief. "I see Wayne and Bill from the wildlife sanctuary, along with some other men with state and fed logos on their shirts are here. Oh goodie, now I get to play with the big boys."

"And you will quickly remind them that you are equally, if not more qualified than them to call the shots."

Summer took a long slow sip of water as she watched the men approach. As they got closer to Summer, Wayne smiled and raised his hand in a friendly wave. She returned a smile and wave. Then, she glanced back at her watch. It had been exactly an hour from when her initial call had been made to Cathy.

"Welcome, gentlemen, glad you could make it." Summer winked at Wayne, who immediately understood her attitude.

Only Wayne and her boss knew of Summer's passion for her work. When it came to wildlife and conservation, Summer could run circles around any of them.

"Bill, good to see you again." Summer reached out her hand to welcome the newest team member working at the wildlife preserve.

"Good to be here to help."

Summer had a sneaky suspicion that Bill had ulterior motives for being there, like how good the rescue would look on his resume. She sighed to herself. This cynical attitude toward men, thanks to Mitchel, was not conducive for a good working relationship with other men.

"I recommend that we move closer to the doe and her fawn. However, due to the weakened vulnerable state of the doe and her skittish fawn, I suggest that Wayne and I approach them first."

"Now hold on," Tim, from the state environmental protection agency, piped up. "You're just a ranger, we're—"

Summer turned her gaze on the man who was speaking. Her right eyebrow shot up as her lips grew thin. She swallowed as she fought back an immediate response. George Davidson, Park Ranger, who also happened to be Summer's boss, saw the fire in Summer's eyes. She was hot and angry, reminding George of one of the sulfur pools bubbling up at Yellowstone. If you went too close, you could, or would, be severely burned. George also knew that if his pompous colleagues were not careful, Summer Newman would blow right on time, just like Old Faithful.

"Tim," George's tone was stern. "It is in your best interest to refrain from making any further comments about Summer's ability to handle this situation. She's not just a ranger, as you say. Summer is our colleague and the one who I am turning to for her expertise with this situation." George turned his eyes from Tim to Summer. "Now, boss, how about you tell us how you want to handle this situation."

Summer appreciated George referring to her as boss. It was their private joke since Summer had higher credentials than

George, been to Congress to fight for conservation, and mediated conflict resolution with landowners while working in Wyoming. She just didn't have the paid years' experience on the job. With George's direction, everyone listened to Summer's assessment of the situation. Her idea was dangerous to say the least. However, given the severity of the situation, and time being of the essence, George, Wayne, and Bill agreed.

"I can't believe George is letting her go into the brush. That woman could be hurt while trying to attend to the wounded deer. The animal should be put down. It's the most humane thing to do in this situation," Tim muttered under his breath.

"Perhaps you think it's humane, but we agree with Summer. Look at her," Bill whispered.

Tim and the others stood in awe as Summer, a few paces ahead of Wayne and George, crept toward the doe and her fawn. She slowly held up her hand to inform the men to stay back. They listened. Summer inched forward then stopped.

"It's okay, little momma. I'm here to help you just as I promised. I'm sorry it's taken so long." Summer's voice was barely audible as she crept toward the wounded animal. "I had to get help. Just like you have to wait around for your buck to get his act together, I had to wait on my bucks." The animal stirred. "Shh, it's okay, little momma, stay put. Summer won't hurt you. I'm your friend." Summer softly continued to coax the deer to trust her. Big brown eyes blinked; however, they did not waver from watching Summer. By now, Summer was sitting on the ground next to the deer. No one moved as Summer attended to the injured deer. It was questionable as to which man was more shocked when Summer managed to get water from her bottle onto the deer's tongue, only to have the deer snort and throw saliva and water toward her. "It's okay, little one," she softly mewed, "have a little more," and this time, the deer did her best to lap up the liquid. The men were mesmerized by Summer's interaction with the deer. Perhaps the most surprising was when Summer began to gently stroke the deer's neck. Again, Summer quietly spoke to the deer; it was as if no one else was there with them. "Now, little sweetheart, we're going to give you a shot so you will sleep for a little while, then we'll take you and your baby to safety so you can heal from your wounds."

"Unbelievable," Tim breathed out. "What is she, some kind of animal whisperer?"

"No. Summer simply has gifts that neither you nor I possess," Bill quietly spoke with a touch of pride. "In the nine months that I've known her, I have learned amazing things about wildlife." Bill watched Summer with awe as he added, "She sure is something."

———◦◦◦———

Finally, the doe was tranquilized and being brought out to the all-terrain vehicle that was waiting a half mile down the trail from where Summer had found the injured deer. The fawn, too big to be carried, was led down the trail on a leash of vines with leaves—hastily made by Summer, who encouraged it to follow its mother. Why vines? Summer wanted the fawn to smell the familiar and hopefully not be as traumatized by the intrusion in its life. The television helicopter remained on the scene filming, following Summer and the others as they made their descent from the mountain with the doe and fawn. Back at the rangers station, after the doe and fawn were on their way to the wildlife refuge, Summer was surrounded by the media. She was being deemed a hero.

"Really, I'm not the hero in this. I'm part of the team that rescued the doe and her fawn. Each one of us played an intricate role here today. It's because we worked together that we have a happy ending. Thank you for your interest in the well-being of these precious animals. I suggest that in a few days, people visit the wildlife refuge to see how they are doing. You will be surprised to discover how many other animals call the place home. Again, thank you, now if you will excuse me, I have work to attend to." With that, the interview was over.

"Live at Five—amazing rescue of a doe and fawn in the National Forest. Park Ranger deemed animal whisperer for her part in the heroic rescue."

Mitchel had just entered his hotel room, which he had rented for the week, and turned on the television to hear the sound bite before the newscast went to commercial break.

"Great," Mitchel sighed out as he loosened his tie, kicked off his shoes, and walked over to the small refrigerator. He opened the door and took out a cold beer. "A park ranger rescued a deer. I wonder if Summer was involved?"

Mitchel sat heavily in the chair by the window and turned his attention to the broadcast. The pictures from the helicopter zoomed in to show most of the rescue. He could not believe what he was seeing. Right there in the middle of it was Summer. His wife—his estranged wife—had rescued the deer. He should be at their house, listening to her tell what had transpired up on that mountainside earlier in the day. Mitchel could imagine how animated Summer's expression would be as she regaled him with the unfolding of the rescue. Her eyes would shine with joy from helping the deer.

Then, as Mitchel watched and sighed, the newscast picked up the story at the rangers station. Summer looked amazing to him in her rumpled uniform. Smudges of dirt were on her face and globs of something on her shirt. Still, she was breathtaking as she stood there in her element. She gave credit to everyone who had been part of the team. *How like her to think of others rather than herself*, Mitchel thought. Guilt swept through Mitchel as he took a sip of beer. *How many times during our marriage did Summer give, never expecting anything in return, and I simply took while expecting her to continue to give without question?* Mitchel moaned as he looked around the typical, boring hotel room. Tonight, looking at Summer on television, it was as if Mitchel was seeing her for the first time; his wife, the woman whom he was now separated from. He would give anything to change his past, to not have hurt Summer, and be at home with her. But Mitchel knew he could neither undo what he had done nor change the course his life was now on. Summer deserved better than him, and on Saturday, he'll go to their home and remove all his clothes and personal items.

———

Saturday morning came quickly for Summer. She was up at six o' clock, showered, dressed, had breakfast, and had cleaned through the entire house by eight o'clock. Satisfied with her work, Summer threw on a sweatshirt she had just received from her father as a birthday present. On the front of the sweatshirt was the logo for the bait shop. The size was too large for her build; however, for Summer, it was perfect. After all, it is her first birthday gift she has ever received from Dad. Summer smiled as she walked out the front door. With the busy schedules she and Mitchel had, free time was always given to relaxing together, going some place, not spending time on improving the exterior of the house. So Summer decided that while she still lived there, she would do something about curb appeal, but what?

The sound of a car slowing down and stopping in front of the house caused Summer to look toward the street. Nikki and Alex had arrived. Summer smiled and waved, while her insides were turning like dryer set on high speed.

"Good morning."

"Good morning, Summer."

"What a lovely street you chose to live on," Nikki said as she stepped closer to Summer.

"Thank you. I was just walking around trying to decide what I should do to give the place some curb appeal."

The three walked around the outside of the house to the back porch. Together, they explored possibilities of how Summer could create a space enjoyable for her while she lived there. Once inside the house, the walk-through didn't take too long. Then, it was time for Summer to leave before Mitchel arrived to gather his belongings.

———⸙———

Summer arrived back at the house with the back of her Jeep loaded with new work gloves, gardening tools, potting soil, flowers for sun, flowers for shade, potted plants to be placed on the porch, a bird bath for the backyard, bird feeders and seed. Alex came out of the side door to greet Summer as she got out of the Jeep.

"Hi, Alex, where's Nikki?"

"She went out to pick up lunch for us and to make a couple of stops along the way. With my wife, there's no telling when she will be back."

Summer smiled as she listened to Alex speak. She knew that he deeply loved Nikki and teasingly was acting as if he had a problem with Nikki being gone. As they walked back into the house and quietly talked, Summer visually scanned each room for what Mitchel took. Sadness weighed heavy on her heart. It was real. Mitchel was gone for good. Summer and Alex had returned to the kitchen, where Summer was in the process of making a fresh pot of coffee for them to enjoy, when Alex's cell phone rang.

"Excuse me," he said as he placed his phone to his ear. "Hello, honey." Alex proceeded to walk out the mudroom door and onto the porch for more privacy. Summer wondered what that was all about; however, she knew their personal life was none of her business. In less than two minutes, Alex returned to the kitchen. "Well, Summer, according to my wife, she has lunch and a surprise for you."

"A surprise," Summer looked at Alex with curiosity.

"Yes, after all, it is your birthday." Alex smiled. "Now, before you start in that 'we should not have done anything for you.'" Summer giggled. Her lawyers were getting to know her too well too soon. Plus, they were becoming amazing friends. "Just wait until you see what we have for you. If you do not like what Nikki is bringing you, we can return your present for something else."

"You have me worried." Summer looked deep into Alex's eyes and realized that Alex was not revealing anything by his expression. Oh, he is good. Summer could only imagine how he must be in the courtroom. At that moment, she was glad that he was on her side.

The sound of the front door opening informed Summer that Nikki was there. "Alex, where's Summer?"

"In the kitchen with me." Summer was ready to move toward the door leading into the living room, when Alex gently took ahold of her arm to stop her. Then, he blocked her way. "Oh, no, you don't, birthday girl. Nikki will let you know when you may come into the living room." He continued to quietly speak with Summer so she would not hear what Nikki was up to in the other room.

"Okay, Alex. Ready in here. Now, have Summer close her eyes, and you lead her into the living room to see her surprise."

"You heard her, Summer. No peeking on the way." Summer smiled and nodded. She sniffled, commented, and closed her eyes, as Alex led her from the kitchen into the living room. "You haven't peeked?" Alex asked, as they slowly entered the room. Summer had her head tilted down toward the floor.

"No, but your suspense is killing me." Summer giggled.

"Well, Summer," Nikki spoke up from not too far away. Sheer joy filled her voice. "You may open your eyes."

Summer raised her chin and opened her eyes. She blinked. Tears began to tumble freely as she took a step.

"Mom," Summer cried out while flinging herself into her mother's open, inviting arms. "Oh, Mom." Summer sobbed. "Oh my gosh! What are you doing here?" Summer squeezed her mother as if to make sure that she was real.

Mom hugged her back, while her own tears silently fell down her cheeks. She softly kissed Summer on the side of her head against her hair just above her ear. Then, she tenderly said, "I'm here to spend your birthday with you." Mom teasingly added, "That is, unless you don't want—"

"Mom, don't you even think about finishing that sentence. Of course I want you here. You are the best present I could ever get. Oh, Mom, this is perfect. I love you." Summer didn't care how foolish she might look. Her mother was standing in her living room on her birthday holding her.

"And I love you, my Summer Sunshine." With that, Amanda softly began to sing, "I got sunshine on a cloudy day..."

Summer sniffled, drew her head up, and gently kissed her mother on her cheek. "Thanks for being my special mom. You always know what I need and how to make me smile." Still holding on to her mother, Summer looked over at Nikki and Alex, who were now standing with their arms around each other. "And, you two," Summer exclaimed, "thank you so much for doing this for me. I want to hear all about how this surprise unfolded and who, even though I have a pretty good idea"—Summer was now smiling through some left over sniffles—"who was the instigator."

The birthday meal was finished. Dirty plates and tumblers were neatly placed on the counter by the sink where they would be washed later. Alex and Nikki had left a short while ago. Now, Summer sat on the couch in the living room with her mother holding her close. The music was lulling Summer to sleep as she felt the gentle rise and fall of her mother's chest against her cheek. Then she felt Mom's lips upon her hair on her head. The kiss reminded Summer of days long gone, when she would nap on her mother's lap. Now, as an adult, her mother's side wasn't too bad either.

11

Summer could not believe how enjoyable it had been to work into the evening with her mother, and then up at the crack of dawn to finish planting the flowers she had purchased. After a morning filled with laughter, showers to clean the dirt off them, Summer and Amanda headed out to the wildlife refuge center to see the doe and fawn that she had helped rescue. On the way to the refuge preserve, Summer explained that in time when the doe was healed of her injuries, and the fawn was stronger, the two would be taken from the clinic rehab area out onto the range with the other inhabitants. Of course, with the explanation came more questions. Summer fielded each one with poise and self-assurance. Amanda listened to her daughter with pride as well as her own deep understanding of where Summer's passion for nature had come from. Her daughter may not have grown up in the Adirondacks as Amanda had; however, her maternal heritage was evident, as she lived out her life.

———✦———

The sign for the Wildlife Refuge area indicated visitors were to park in a designated area and employees in another area. Summer turned on her directional to indicate she was turning in to the parking lot. After downshifting her Jeep, she reached over to her glove box, opened it, and grabbed out a parking permit. Amanda noticed the permit said, "National Park Ranger." She also noticed that after placing the permit on the rearview mirror, Summer did not pull in to the visitors' parking area. Instead, she went into the staff parking area. Then, Amanda saw markers by two spots designated for state and federal visitors affiliated with conservation. Summer glanced over at her mother, who was taking everything in around her.

"Kind of nice not being an ordinary visitor, don't you think?" She smiled while sliding her top teeth over her bottom lip. It was a habit Summer had developed as a child to not appear to be boasting, a trait Amanda had informed her would turn people off from wanting to be her friend. Mom would gently correct Summer by telling her, "Yes, it's okay to feel good about what you are doing with your life, just let others be the ones to tell you how good you are. No one enjoys being around one who brags for too long. You're a good person, and you, Sunshine, deserve to have many friends in your life." Summer always remembered her mother's words and practiced them in her life. She chuckled out loud.

"What has stuck you?" Amanda asked, as she looked with softness at her daughter who at that moment radiated happiness. She was glad that Summer's focus for the moment was on the animals she had helped rescue, and not focused on her crumbling marriage. There would be time for that, but not now. This was their moment to enjoy.

"Oh, I was just remembering some wisdom I received as a child from a rather smart woman."

"Goodness, you must be remembering something Cassie once shared with you."

"Mom, you know I was meaning *you*." Summer had that look. It's the one that says, "Really, you're going to be goofy with me?" She shook her head while her mother was smiling at her. "Honestly, Mom, sometimes you can be silly, and I love it. Actually, I was thinking about what you told me a long time ago about boasting, and the news interview. I had a perfect opportunity to blow my own horn about saving those animals—"

"But you didn't. You gave credit to the others who were involved in the rescue, and in doing so, you have gained respect and admiration, not only from colleagues, but from strangers as well who were watching the news and listening to you speak."

"Yes, I have, and you know, Mom, sometimes it still is difficult for me to accept when you are right." Summer softly smiled at her mother's response and added, "Mom, I do appreciate your words of wisdom."

"Compliment accepted, and on that note, how about you showing me around the refuge area? I can hardly wait to see the deer." Amanda's eyes shone with pride as she spoke, opened the door of the vehicle, and slid her feet to the ground. Summer came around the front of her Jeep and joined her. Together, with arms linked, they began their stroll through the small parking area.

As they moved toward the main building, Summer glanced over at the visitors' parking area. "Look, Mom. Look at how many cars are here in the parking lot. I can't believe how many people must have listened to the newscast, and my invitation to come see the deer and other wildlife, or heard from others about our rescuing the deer."

"Curiosity isn't always a bad thing." Amanda smiled with pride at Summer. "I for one am as curious as the others gathered here to see the precious creatures you saved."

"Mom," Summer breathed out. "We've already been through this—I didn't do it alone."

"No, you didn't, and I'm not thinking of this from a bragging point of view. Summer, that morning, you were first on the scene. I believe that the Great Spirit led you up that trail to the deer knowing that you would tap into your heritage, and your amazing gifts. The Great One knew that once you saw the need, you would open your heart and lovingly save the doe and fawn. Summer, honey, if you had not been up in that mountain with the intention of seeing the condition of the primitive campsite, the outcome of this story would probably have been totally different. Because of you, the fawn will grow up experiencing the love of its mother. Together the doe and fawn will continue on in life as family."

"Thank you, Mom." Summer sniffled. "You are a super cheerleader."

"It's easy to be your cheerleader." Amanda gently touched Summer's arm and then pulled out her phone. "Now, how about you show me these deer so we can take some selfies. Then, I can go back east and do what I have cautioned you not to do."

"And what might that be?"

"Brag of course!"

With that said, the two laughed together, linked arms, and walked into the building marked Staff Only. Soon they would see the deer that Summer had been instrumental in rescuing earlier that week.

———————

Tuesday night, Summer sat alone on her back porch. She was tired from a busy, emotionally draining weekend. With her mother surprising her on Saturday and staying until that morning, Summer had not had time to experience the difference in how the house felt, now that Mitchel and his personal things were gone. Even Nikki and Alex had been a buffer for her. Summer allowed a tired smile to creep to her lips. Family and friends had taken care of her to allow her to have a happy birthday. Summer quietly breathed out, "Even you, Dad. You knew Mom was here, still you took time to call me and wish me a happy birthday." An unwanted tear slid down Summer's cheek. "Great." She huffed. "Okay then, if my thinking about Dad is going to bring on the opening of the floodgates, I might as well hear his voice." With that, Summer picked up her phone and punched in his speed dial number on her keypad. She waited.

"Bait shop, oh wait—" There was the sound of something being knocked over. Then, a muffled string of words. "Hello."

"Hi, Dad, are you okay?"

"Super, Princess."

Summer listened to him obviously clumsily moving around. She cautiously asked, "Were you by any chance sleeping?"

"Ye-up! Guilty as charged." He yawned. "Working on the new dock down at the lake for most of the day was tiring. I was watching the baseball game. You know early season games are not usually as exciting as late-season games, when the World Series is at stake."

Summer giggled. "Say no more. The excitement lulled you to sleep. That is why I like to watch football and hockey." Summer heard her father chuckle then add a comment about her sounding eerily like her mother. "Dad, you should know that Mom is now pointing out to me some personality traits that I've inherited from you. So you had best be careful. Sometimes, what you see in me may be a reflection of yourself."

"Okay, Princess. I get your gist. Gee-whiz, you know you just sounded an awful lot like your Aunt Becky."

"We are related."

"Yes, we are. So, what is going on with you that made you decide to call me tonight?"

For the next two hours, they talked about life in the Great Sac Community, how Stephen was handling the news of Amanda and Kevin setting a date to be married, and the location. Then, when the moment was right, Stephen zeroed in on how Summer was coping with her separation. Tears freely flowed as Summer shared how she felt at this moment in her life.

"Dad."

"Yes, Summer." His voice was quiet to match Summer's mood.

"Thank you for listening, for just letting me talk out my feelings. For not judging me."

"Princess, you don't need to thank me. I should be the one thanking you for wanting me to be a part of your life." She heard him sniffle. It was easy for Summer to imagine those crystal-blue eyes holding her gaze in his. That quirky way he moved his brow and the slight twitching of his jaw. Her dad.

"Dad, with my grandfather, your father that is, being a minister, was he as good a listener as you are?"

"Do you mean, am I like him?"

"I guess that is what I'm asking."

"Your grandfather was a phenomenal man. Unfortunately in my careless youthful days, I chose not to emulate him in my life. And," his voice grew quiet, "we both know what that cost us." Summer listened to him candidly speak about his life lessons.

"Dad, I think you need to cut yourself some slack."

"Really, in what way?"

"You were young, and supposed to make mistakes. Now, you are older and have grown into being a person filled with wisdom that comes through making those mistakes. You listen and are guiding me in a way that is totally different from Mom. You can chuckle at that. But I think you know what I mean. Mom has her own wisdom that I need at certain times. Tonight, I needed you, and you rose to the occasion. I think my late grandfather, the Reverend Johnson, would be proud of how his son has turned out."

"If you don't beat all! How did I ever get so lucky to have a daughter like you?" Stephen's question was actually more for himself than for Summer.

"I think Mom would say that the Great Spirit had something to do with it."

Stephen chuckled. "Yes, she would, and I agree. God certainly has had a plan for all of us. His timing has not been ours. Summer, in the midst of everything that is going on in our lives, I believe that this is our season to grow as individuals, and as a family."

"I like that. Our season. That reminds me of a song Mom used to sing."

"I know the one you are referring to. However; before it was a song, it was scripture. 'For everything there is a season, and a time for every matter under heaven.' Ecclesiastes 3:1 in case you want to read it for yourself—and the rest of the verses that give wisdom to carry you through life."

"You never cease to amaze me. Perhaps I should call you Reverend Dad."

"Oh no," Stephen cautioned. "I'm more the prodigal son—" He did not complete his thought as a yawn escaped him. Summer found herself yawning right along with him.

"Well, Dad, I guess we had best say good-night before one of us ends up falling asleep while we're on the phone."

"I agree. I'm glad you called, Princess."

"Me too. I love you."

"I love you too. Good night. Sweet dreams."

"Good night." Summer sat in the cool still darkness of night on the porch. Still holding her phone in her hand, she hugged herself while feeling the softness and warmth of the sweatshirt her father had sent her for her birthday touch her skin. "It is a good night," Summer breathed out. "I have a father along with my mother to love me, and to love in return. Thank you, Great Spirit—God—whomever you are."

—⁂—

Days turned into weeks as the summer season progressed. Each week, Nikki and/or Alex would contact Summer regarding the separation and preparation for filing for divorce. During the most recent phone conversation, Nikki informed Summer that Mitchel's lawyer was filing for a motion to suspend divorce proceedings until Mitchel returned from his six-week geological immersion trip he was leading in Alaska.

Alaska. Mitchel was going to Alaska. Summer grumbled as she walked the trail. Of course Mitchel was heading out of town. Walking away was what he did best. No doubt he would have Jesslyn with him. Summer felt as venomous as a rattlesnake coiled and ready to strike. Surprisingly, she didn't want to strike at Mitchel. She had her sight set on the other woman. Jesslyn. Oh yes, Summer wanted to strike out at her as a snake lunging for a field mouse. She wanted—no, make that, she *needed* someone to blame, to hate, to devour for her marriage dying before her eyes. On this day, who better to blame than Jesslyn?

Summer sighed as she slowed her pace on the trail. She eased into the small cleared area with a rough cut bench and sign with information about the area. Removing her day pack from her shoulders, and placing it on the bench, Summer rummaged around in it to find an energy bar and a bottle of water. She ate the bar, rotated her shoulders, then took a long sip of cool water. Summer then walked over to the wooden box that opened to be a registration desk with a form for hikers to log in their personal information and intended destination. She was pleased to see that many people had already stopped to register. Summer listened to the people who had stopped to read the informative sign and discuss what they had learned. Then, someone exclaimed, and all eyes turned toward the sky. There overhead was a bald eagle. It appeared to not have a care in the world as it glided on the wind. Nature on display for humanity to appreciate.

Summer walked on, meeting many vacationers who were utilizing the easy-skill trail. Children bubbling over with joy, like a brook tumbling over rocks on a hot summer's day, were seen walking with their parents. Others had to be called back and reminded of the dangers of straying away from their family. Some couples walked at slower paces walking hand in hand, while others moved at a steady pace pushing each other on. In the midst of Summer's stormy feelings toward Mitchel, and his new life with Jesslyn, Summer found herself glad for the reminder that there were good people in the world, and eagles soaring above the chaos of this world.

Alaska

Mitchel breathed out a sigh of relief as the small plane landed up in the mountains of Alaska. He had come ahead of his graduate students with his team to set up the base camp for the six-week field study. Stepping out onto the near-virgin soil, relatively untouched by humanity until now, Mitchel drew in a deep breath. In the pristine beauty that surrounded him, he understood the necessity of treating the land, and its inhabitants, with gentleness. His team would do their research while leaving as few scars as possible. *Summer would be pleased,* he thought. Summer. This was the first he had thought of her since he had left Boulder two days ago. Mitchel sighed as he thought about the dreams and plans they had made to take a trip to Alaska for their tenth wedding anniversary. He shook his head and grumbled to himself.

"Professor, after we gather firewood for tonight and start the fire, any special place you want the dining all-purpose tent and sleep tents to be set up?" Mitchel looked over to where his crew was standing. He then realized that they all had been watching him and waiting for his directions.

"Well," he drew in a breath, as if to gather his strength for the tasks that lay before them. "I like the view of the mountains and the lake from here. Let's put the dining tent here so that we can enjoy the view while we are eating, or gathered for conversation, and study."

Mitchel was glad that decision was quickly made, and he was able to once again be alone with his thoughts. He stepped away from the others, took out his phone, and pressed the three numbers of the Denver-Boulder area code. Mitchel paused, then dialed the rest of the number. He waited. Voice mail. "Yeah, Summer. It's me Mitchel. You obviously know that," he cleared his throat. "Well, I am up here in Alaska and found myself thinking of you, and...well, I hope you are well. I guess we'll talk when I return home—I mean to Boulder, in early August, and we go to court. Take care." End of message. Mitchel suddenly found himself shaking, as he was overcome by emotions.

"Professor, are you okay?" someone asked as he stepped away from camp.

"Mitch," Simon, Mitchel's good friend and colleague, broke into Mitchel's thoughts. "You seem troubled from your brief phone call. Is everything all right?"

"Nothing to worry about."

Simon had been Mitchel's best man at Summer and his wedding. He knew many of Mitchel's secrets, his affair with Jesslyn, and had been one whom Mitchel had turned to after Summer filed for separation.

"Hmm. I know you too well, my friend. Your expression tells me that you have woman trouble."

"You do know me too well," Mitchel released a slow deflated breath. "Simon, you'd think that right now my thoughts would be of Jesslyn, and her impending arrival."

"But that's not the case."

"Right. I was thinking of Summer, and the dreams we had shared about coming here. Simon, I've been a fool. I played with fire and burned not only myself, but Summer as well."

"It's obvious you still love Summer."

"Of course I do," Mitchel snapped. "Simon, I've done things, more than having an affair, and made it so she no longer loves me or wants me in her life. Frankly, I don't blame her. I no longer deserve to have Summer in my life."

"This sounds serious."

"It is. However, it will have to wait, because here comes our crew with the wood for the fire. We have work to do." With that, Mitchel and Simon joined the others.

Denver, Colorado

Summer knew the missed call and voice mail were from Mitchel. After filing for her separation, Summer had changed his ringtone to something she felt was more appropriate for what she was feeling toward Mitchel these days. Her ringtone of the old country song "Your Cheatin' Heart" had been the dead giveaway that Mitchel had called. It was now early evening; she sat outside by the small water feature she had recently added to the flower garden she had recreated. Last year, the small garden had been a mess of overgrown weeds. Now, a few bees not yet ready to turn in for the night were busy going from one flower to another. Summer sat quietly and watched them. She pulled her phone from her pocket and finally called her voice mail. She listened. A tear silently tumbled down her cheek. She sniffled, and hit Delete when the message ended. Summer stood and breathed out, "Mitchel, think of me all you want. You made your choice. I've made mine. A part of me will always cherish the memory of what we had, and how we once loved each other, but I'll never trust you again. Don't even think about trying to win me back after your return from your trip to Alaska." With a nod of determination, Summer turned and walked onto the porch. She then disappeared into her home for the night.

12

By the middle of July, Summer's days had become a blur for her. When not at the park working in the office, or out on the trails monitoring visitors and protecting wildlife, she could be found at the wildlife preserve. The doe was healing nicely, and soon would be strong enough to be released out into the preserve with her fawn, where they would live with all the other refugees. It was Thursday afternoon; Summer had finished her shift and was ready to head home. Both she and Cathy had been complaining all day about the oppressive heat and the need for rain that had been forecast for the weekend. Stepping outside only confirmed the needed relief predicted for the weekend. The break in the weather could not come soon enough for her. She glanced up at the sky. Interesting. Troublesome. Spiked layered storm clouds were moving in. Perhaps the rain would come sooner rather than later. A breeze began to stir.

Summer had an ominous feeling. The weather forecasters may have missed the mark on predicting this storm. Now, Summer hoped to make it home before the early arriving storm fully blew in. She opened the door of her Jeep as her cell phone began to ring. A smile brushed her lips as she drew her phone from her pocket then slid onto her seat.

"Hello, Bill. This is a nice surprise. What's up?"

"Hey, Summer. I was wondering if you were planning on stopping by the preserve on your way home today?"

"Yes. I had planned on stopping by to spend a few minutes to check on our deer. The storm seems to be moving in rather quickly. So I won't stay too long."

"Hmm. You plan on stopping by only to check on our deer?"

Summer chuckled. There was something playful, yet caring, in Bill's voice. In the past few weeks while checking on the deer, she had begun spending more time with Bill. Through the course of their interactions, Summer discovered that her first impressions of him had been all wrong. Bill has a great sense of humor, was quick minded, intelligent, and appeared to be an all-around good guy. Even her mom had noticed Bill's good qualities in the short time she had met him. She had pointed out that he was someone she could see becoming a good solid friend for Summer. Once again, those first impressions Summer was known for making were biting her in her fanny. Summer laughed to herself. She should have learned with her first impressions of her father to hold her thoughts.

"Bill, you and I are friends. Technically, I'm still married and am not sure—" Summer abruptly stopped speaking as she fought to hold back her emotions.

"Summer. I'm sorry. My teasing went too far. I treasure you as a friend and don't want to cause you to turn away from me. Please forgive me for making you uncomfortable."

"Forgiven." Summer sniffled.

"So, you're still coming over, right?"

"Yes, Bill. I'm still stopping by." Summer felt a smile attempting to form on her lips.

"Good. I look forward to seeing you when you get here. And, Summer, be careful. In case you haven't been paying too close attention to the sky." Bill chuckled. "I know you have seen the changes in the sky at the park. Here at the preserve, the storm is moving in a heck of a lot quicker than the meteorologists had first thought. It looks like we could get some nasty weather."

"You are right. I've been watching the sky and feeling the change in temperature. I see the sky is churning. But, I haven't heard any updated forecasts. How bad is it supposed to get?"

"Tornado watch."

"About what I figured." Summer cast her eyes toward the darkening sky. "Thanks for the info. I better run back into the office. I need to let Cathy and our other staff know so they can get home or to safety here at the park, if necessary."

By the time Summer reached the preserve, her Jeep was dented from the rain and hail storm she had driven through. She parked, grabbed her purse, and bolted through the pounding rain for the door. Summer was soaked and shivered when she stepped inside. The air-conditioned room felt like a walk-in cooler compared to the outdoors.

"Hey, Summer." Bill, Wayne, and two other men she quickly identified as volunteers all greeted her with smiles.

"Hey, guys."

Greetings and smiles were exchanged as Wayne handed her a towel and a dry tee shirt. Summer remained in the room to listen to the men chat. She turned her back to them, unbuttoned her shirt, toweled off, drew one arm out of her shirt, dried, and slid her arm into the dry tee shirt. She felt a hand take a hold of the collar of her shirt as it began to fall. Summer glanced over her shoulder and smiled. Of course, Wayne, being a gentleman and friend, had stepped up to help her. Now, fully dressed, Summer turned around to face the men.

"So who's the wise guy who put in the order for nasty weather? You know a good soaking rain would have sufficed."

"Summer, we thought you were the one who requested a little excitement." Wayne grinned.

"Not me! But I do have to tell you all, I did drive through some mighty big hail—quarter- to half-dollar-size on the way over. Do you have the emergency radio on?"

Before anyone could respond to Summer, the tones went out. *Bzzzzz-bzzzzz-bzzzzzz.* Three-second pause. *Bzzzzz-bzzzzz-bzzzzz.* Then, the broadcast. They were in line for a direct hit from the tornado that had touched down.

"Oh crap."

"Holy Mother—"

"Do your prayin', cussing, whatever else you want to do, after we get into the storm shelter," Wayne announced. He calmly walked over and held the door open. His voice was low–key, yet commanding, as he hurried people to make their descent down the stairs. He shook his head in disgust when he saw that his employees had thought of themselves before Summer's safety. "Summer, we need to get down into the shelter with the others. I sure am glad that you are here with us."

"Me too, Wayne. You're right. We do need to get down with the others." Summer sighed. "Still, I worry about the animals having to fend for themselves."

"Me too. However, right now, you are at the top of my list for taking care of." Wayne winked at Summer. She gave him one of her slight brow lifts, while questioning what else he had on his mind. "You better come through this unscathed, or I'm in a heap of trouble."

"Wayne, why are you so concerned for my safety and staying out of trouble? You know I am good at fending for myself."

"I know you are, but, Summer, you need to understand. If anything were to happen to you during this tornado, I'd have to deal with your mother."

"My mother?" Summer gasped. "Yes, your mother." In the dim light provided by the emergency lantern, Summer could see what she thought was a look of worry on Wayne's brow. "Granted I only met her once, but that woman is scary where you are concerned."

"Mom's not scary—well..." Summer thought of the altercation between her mother and father at the courthouse and her testimony during the trial.

"Look, Summer, that woman loves you, as ferociously as any female animal in the wild loves its young. I do not plan on being the one to tell her that something happened to you while you were on my watch."

Summer smiled warmly. "Don't worry, Wayne. I won't let her take too big of a bite out of your hide."

"Gee, Summer. That's mighty comforting." With that said, Wayne reached over and placed his hand on the back of Summer's neck. "Wind's picking up. Get your head down."

An hour later, Summer emerged from the building with Wayne, Bill, and the others. The center as well as the barns and outer buildings with the injured and recuperating animals were undamaged. It was a miracle.

"Will you look at that!" Bill exclaimed. "The tornado took out the sign for the preserve, then jumped the road."

While the men stood in amazement discussing the close call they all had just lived through, Summer stepped away from them. She pulled out her phone, took pictures, then sent a text to her mother. It did not take more than three minutes for a response.

> Wow! Thanks for the update. So glad you are safe. Tell Wayne he did good—won't have to string him up for bear bait! LOL. Love you.

Summer burst into laughter. Tears ran down her cheeks like a torrential downpour.

"What struck you?" Wayne asked. Summer sniffled back her emotions while walking over to rejoin the others.

"I sent my Mom a text, shared pics of the tornado damage, and got a response."

"Is she worried?" Bill asked.

"No. Quite the opposite." Summer smiled at Wayne as she held out her phone toward him. "Take a look."

Summer held on to her phone for Wayne to read the text. He read it, looked at Summer, and burst into laughter.

While the tornado had jumped the road and not ravaged the wildlife preserve, the rangers station at the park had not been so fortunate. Every day while repairs were being made on the building, Summer and Cathy worked out of the open-air pavilion. Both women rose to the occasion and found that the tornado taking out the station had actually opened doors for greater communication with park visitors.

Summer was standing near the trail entrance with a family showing them how to register in the log, and sharing the importance of doing so, at the start of their outing and during their hike on the trails. The crunching of tires on the crushed gravel on the road and parking lot caused Summer to glance over as the vehicle stopped near the pavilion. Summer saw George get out of the pickup and walk over to the picnic table where Cathy was working. Summer was glad that the family was anxious to get on with their hike up into the mountains, as she too was anxious. George was there. As her boss, George could be there to see how the normal everyday things were going in the park, or he could be there to check on the reconstruction of the rangers station, or—Summer swallowed then drew in a deep breath—he could be there to tell her in person whether she gets to go back east for her mother's wedding or will have to stay here.

—⁓⁓⁓—

"Summer, Cathy has told me she can handle things around here. So how about you and I take a walk."

George had that look. Summer already knew in her heart what they would talk about. She felt the pricklies on her skin and felt the impending doom.

"Sure," she said while trying to sound upbeat. George motioned the way he wanted them to go to ensure their privacy during their conversation. They walked over to an old bench near the original path leading into the park. A sign hung there proclaiming, WARNING—DANGER, for it was known to be a daily route and feeding area of a family of black bears. They were not the most welcoming creatures. Summer released a heavy breath as she sat down. George sat down next to her and folded his arms over his chest. While appearing to be relaxed, Summer knew George was in full work mode. Still, she remained quiet and waited for him to begin the conversation they were obviously avoiding.

"This is turning into quite a summer around here." George was gazing at the busy parking area. "Wayne tells me the deer you were instrumental in saving are thriving. Looks like they will be released into the preserve next week sometime."

"Yes, they will. I'm glad their story has a happy ending," Summer paused then allowed her eyes to settle in on her boss. "George, why do I feel as though our conversation will not have a happy ending, or perhaps the happy ending I envision?"

"Summer, sometimes you are way too perceptive." He sighed, while he allowed his eyes to meet hers. The warm dark-chocolate eyes that reminded George of a delightful piece of chocolate candy had turned black as coal. He watched her eyes, the muscles in her jaw, the pulsing of her neck.

Then she quietly spoke.

"Sometimes I am too perceptive, and other times, as my mother would say, I'm dumb as a bootjack."

"A what?"

"A bootjack." Summer sighed. "Mom used to use that expression when I was a child. When I questioned what it was, she described what a bootjack looked like and what it was used for. In the past, it was used to assist a person in removing their boots from their feet. This spring, when I was at my dad and uncle's bait shop, I actually got to see one. Dad showed me how it worked. Pretty cool, if you ask me. I'm thinking of finding someone who can make me one for taking off my own boots. But that's not what you came here to discuss with me. So, boss, what is going on?"

"Summer, I can't let you have the time off for your mother's wedding." George turned his gaze back toward the forest. He couldn't bear to look into Summer's eyes.

"George, I understand." With the soft acceptance in Summer's voice, George turned to meet her gaze. He was surprised that along with her disappointment, Summer had an uncanny depth of understanding conveyed in her eyes as she spoke, "Mom and I both knew it would be a long shot for me to get the time off. I have a backup plan. My Aunts Becky and Melissa will be at the wedding, and both have promised me that they will take a gazillion pictures for me. Now, my friend"—a devious smile began to take form as she spoke—"if Mom was marrying Dad, well, I just might have thrown a temper tantrum for not getting my way."

"And you would have every right to throw that tantrum, just as you have that right to be upset for not being at this wedding. Thank you, Summer, for understanding."

"No problem, but now you owe me one."

"That I do." George stretched. He stood then held out his hand for Summer to take. "Come on you, time to get back to work."

From the onset of the trip to Alaska, things had not been going well for Mitchel. A bear along with a pack of wolves was becoming a concern for everyone. Every day and night, teams patrolled camp and the dig area in the mountain to ensure everyone's safety. Then, there was the rain, the mud, and the bad moods Mitchel had to contend with right along with his own misery.

Mitchel stood at the side of the all-purpose tent while sipping a cup of coffee. *Ping.* His cell phone sounded. He pulled out his phone to read his message, and gasped. Mitchel felt his heart rate increase as the impact of the words settled in on him. *Ping.* Another text, and this one had a picture attached.

Your ex is a beauty.

"Oh no," Mitchel moaned. It couldn't be happening. He looked over at his students. There in the midst of the group sat Jesslyn. She was safe being in Alaska with him. But Summer. "Oh, what have I done." Mitchel breathed out, as he aimlessly walked out into the lightly falling cold rain.

"I don't know. What have you done?" Simon asked, as he stepped close to Mitchel while raising an umbrella over them.

"Look at these messages."

"Man, who have you ticked off? What does Summer have to do with it?"

"Si, I've gotten involved with some people, whom you don't want to know." He waited for Simon to speak. His friend remained silent, inviting Mitchel to confess to him what he had been doing, and what may now be endangering Summer.

"Mitch, you are unbelievable. Gambling. Debt."

"I know I really have screwed up. If you had been in Vegas with me for a conference—"

"Hey, now don't hang this on me."

"You're right. It's not your fault." Mitch sighed. "Si, I have lost everything. Summer found out about the gambling, and the offshore account this summer, after she filed for our separation and her petition for divorce. I think it would have been okay if I hadn't run into some more trouble which may get one or both of us killed."

"I gather by trouble, you mean with your unsavory friends, who now have an interest in your wife." Simon looked at his friend with new eyes as he listened to Mitchel continue to confess his descent into the world of organized crime with one of the most powerful players out of Vegas. He no longer knew his friend.

Unsure of what else to do, he reached over and cuffed Mitchel on the back of his head. "Man, you are downright stupid! Gambling wasn't enough for you. Now, you're into drugs as well! Mitchel, you deserve everything that happens to you. But Summer, my goodness, man, she does not deserve this."

"I know. I never meant for her to become involved."

"You never intended? How could Summer not become involved?" Simon huffed. Sheer disappointment filled him.

"I deserved that." Mitchel felt a chill go through him as the rain continued to fall around them. Simon asked more questions, and Mitchel answered. "When Octivani's daughter applied for grad school, I was instructed to recommend her for fellowship. Of course she is here."

"Let me guess, Jesslyn."

"You guessed it. I'm sleeping with the devil's daughter."

"And if you don't do everything the devil tells you, Summer is going to be the sacrificial lamb." "Simon, I can't allow that to happen. I need to call my lawyer and come clean about everything so she can hopefully help me straighten out this mess before it's too late."

"Yes, you do." Simon pulled his hooded waterproof jacket up over his head. He handed Mitchel his umbrella, then turned to walk back to their students gathered under the all-purpose tent.

13

It was the second Saturday of August. Summer had gone through her morning routine of breakfast and then cleaning through her home. She was surprised at how quickly her task was completed, now that there was less to clean without Mitchel living there anymore. Dressed in an old tee shirt and shorts made from cut-off jeans for working around the house, she stepped through the back door onto the porch. The coolness of the cement floor felt good on her bare feet. A light breeze gently stirred the dark green and taupe drapes Summer had hung for privacy, and to keep out the late afternoon sun. She walked over to her favorite chair and placed her glass of iced coffee on the small circa 1940s table she had found at a flea market and had recently refurbished. In Summer's mind, it was a perfect find to go with her cedar Adirondack chairs and footstools and her birch-wood table lamp that her dad had sent her. She smiled as she glanced down at the throw rug she had found while shopping with her mother during her surprise visit. The blocked colors of green, taupe, burgundy, and a medium shade of blue gave the space the pop of color it needed without being intrusive. Summer walked over to the full-length screen windows and drew back the curtains to allow the sun to warm the space. She planned on sitting and reflecting on her life and this special day for her mother. If Summer was in upstate New York, which she obviously was not, thanks to scheduling problems and her personal life being in shambles, she would be—Summer glanced at her wristwatch. Ye-up! The ceremony was completed. Her mom was now married to Kevin. If Summer was there, she would be celebrating with them at Andrew and Cassie's cabin by the lake. It truly was a perfect location for a wedding. Summer brushed away a bit of moisture that had found its way to the edge of her eye. "Now, now, no pity party, Summer Newman," she lectured herself and sighed, as she looked out into her backyard. Birds were flying to the feeders she had hung, bees were busy at work in her flower beds. This scene caused her to slightly smile away her sadness.

Summer continued looking out toward the woods beyond her property's edge. Something shimmery in the trees caught her eye for a brief moment. She focused on one area in particular. Then, while releasing a long slow breath, Summer turned and stepped away from the window. As she moved away, she wondered if someone was watching her through a pair of binoculars. If she was a gambler like her "not soon enough to be ex" husband, she'd bet that whoever was watching would soon discover that she was rather boring to watch, and leave.

Ping. The bird feeder was swinging back and forth. The noise and movement caught Summer's immediate attention and momentarily froze her with fear. *Ping. Crash.* The birch-wood lamp toppled—no, it crashed to the floor. Summer gasped. She knew that sound. "Oh crap," she exclaimed as she lunged for the floor. The impact of hitting the cement floor, minimally buffered by the carpet, knocked the wind from her. Pulling her phone from her pocket, Summer dialed 911 while she slithered to the back door, which she had left open to draw the cool breeze inside the house.

Nikki and Alex arrived forty-five minutes later to find a buzz of activity around Summer's home. The street in front of Summer's house was cluttered with marked and unmarked police vehicles. A uniformed police officer stopped them as they attempted to pull into Summer's driveway. After informing the officer of who they were showing identification, they were allowed to continue on and park in Summer's drive behind her Jeep.

They gazed around the neighborhood before stepping onto the front walk. People congregated in front of their homes were being interviewed by the police detectives who had already taken Summer's statement. The detectives took notes and then moved on, knocking on neighbor's doors to see if anyone had seen anything unusual that morning, or in the past few days. Other officers were out in the woods behind Summer's home searching for evidence left by the shooter.

Summer was still shaking when she opened the front door to welcome Nikki and Alex into her home. "I'm so glad you're both here. Please do come in," she said through tears while ushering them into her home and closed the door behind them.

Nikki gently drew Summer into her embrace. As Summer's sobbing began to soften, Nikki led her to the couch where they sat together, and she held her while she sobbed.

Alex was greatly troubled knowing that someone had intentionally tried to hurt Summer. Certain that Nikki was the best for consoling Summer, at the moment, he disappeared into the kitchen. There he filled the teakettle with water and placed it on the stove to boil. With two tries of snooping in the cupboards, Alex found the teacups and Summer's selections of tea. Knowing better than to choose a flavor of tea for Summer or his wife, Alex prepared a tray with an assortment of tea bags and cups for them to choose from.

While Alex waited for the water to boil, he walked over to look out of the back door leading to the porch. Crime scene tape was secured across the door barring him from entering. From where Alex stood, he saw the shattered lamp and shards of glass on the floor. Then, his eyes turned to the window. A small hole now boldly marked showed the point of entry. Glancing over at the wall of the house, Alex saw another area marked where the bullet had been removed. It broke his heart to see what had been done to Summer. The teakettle whistled, drawing Alex back to the task at hand—helping to calm Summer's tattered nerves.

———

Detective Adam North appeared at Summer's front door as she took her first sip of peppermint tea. Summer placed her cup on the table and went over to the door to greet the detective and invite him in. After being introduced to Nikki and Alex, the detective then turned his full attention to Summer.

"Ma'am, since your home is now a crime scene, you need to leave until we have completed our investigation and we determine that it is safe for you to return."

"Of course," Summer's voice was still shaky. "Detective, do you have any idea how long I should plan on living elsewhere? I mean, so I know how many clothes to take with me."

"No, ma'am, I don't. Unfortunately, from what you and Mr. Blards have told me, there is cause to believe it may be awhile before your life is back to normal. Do you have family or someone you could stay with so that you are not alone?"

"For now, Summer will be staying with us," Nikki stated while reaching over and gently squeezing Summer's hand.

"Nikki," Summer was shaking her head no, as she spoke. "Thank you, but I can't impose on you and Alex."

"Summer, you're not imposing. We have a guest apartment over our garage intended for our family to use when they visit. Right now it sits there empty. You have a need, and as of this moment, we're adopting you as family." Summer sniffled while listening to her friend. "You will have a private entrance to your own space so you won't have to feel as though we are keeping an eye on you, although we will take precautions to ensure your safety while you are with us. After work on a hot afternoon, you can take a swim in our pool or use the hot tub to relax in before turning in for the night. If that isn't incentive enough, think about this, Summer: the distance from our home to the park where you work and the preserve where you volunteer is actually closer than from here to either place."

"Nikki's right, Summer. While she did lay out a fine opening statement for why you should take up our offer to stay with us, I'd like to add: I know that Nathan will agree with us about you staying at our place."

"Okay," Summer sighed with resignation of being defeated on many fronts. "You both have convinced me, especially you, Alex, when you played the Nathan card." Summer smiled weakly. "But," Summer lifted her finger to further make her point. "I won't freeload off of your generosity. You will allow me to pay rent."

"Hmm. Rent wasn't part of this negotiation." Alex's eyes held tenderness as he gave Summer his "trust me, everything will be okay" smile and added, "We'll figure something out." "Then it's settled." She looked over at Detective North, who was quietly observing their interaction. Summer noticed for the first time that he was dressed in a black suit, cream-colored shirt, and shades-of-gray tie, a total professional. He did not smile. That did not stop Summer from noticing his neat, groomed hair, no facial hair, an aura of self-assurance—*Stop*, she warned herself. *He's here to do his job, and you—don't go there!* "Detective, as you heard Nikki and Alex, I'll be with my friends until this nightmare is over." She stood while asking him, "Will you be the one to let me know when it is safe for me to return home?"

"That's a fair question," Adam said while not taking his eyes off her. Where Summer's eyes were warm brown, his were blue as the sky on a clear summer day. "Of course I will stay in close contact with you to update you on our progress." Then with phone in hand, he asked, "What is your cell phone number, and the address where you will be staying, so I may contact you about your case?"

Summer gave Adam her number, then excused herself to pack her suitcase.

—⊶⊷—

"Nikki, thank you so much for being here. I just don't know what I'd do if I was here alone."

"Summer, you are welcome. But you know, I have a feeling you would figure out a solution. Since you are not here alone, what may I do to help you?"

"My duffel bag has my casual and old clothes to bum around in. So that is ready to go along with my pillows. Goodness, I hate to sleep on unfamiliar pillows." Nikki smiled and nodded, while fully understanding Summer's feelings. Together they quietly talked and packed the rest of Summer's belongings she would need until the situation was resolved, into her suitcase and garment bags. Then, after one more glance around the room, they walked out into the living room where Detective North and Alex stood quietly conversing. Both men had serious expressions.

"What's wrong?" Summer moved her gaze from one man to the other. "Alex, please tell me."

"Ashley Prime has informed me that Mitchel has returned from Alaska. It appears that Mitchel and his girlfriend came home to find their place ransacked. Mitchel is accusing you of taking out your anger on him and is filing charges against you."

"He what?" Summer fell back against the door casing. She choked back a sob struggling to make itself known.

"Mrs. Brown," Detective North said.

"Detective, I'm not Mrs. Brown. I kept my name, thank goodness. When you address me, please refer to me as Summer, or Ms. Newman." At that moment, something changed in Summer's demeanor. From somewhere deep within, a touch of her mother seemed to have appeared in her stance and tone. Her darkening eyes also conveyed her anger at the absurdity of Mitchel's accusations. "Will someone help me out here with understanding how I could be responsible for Mitchel's place being vandalized? Every day I go from home to work to volunteering at the wildlife refuge preserve, and then home again. I regularly do my shopping and banking when I'm on my way home to not waste fuel. So, given my schedule, how in the heck did I have time to get up to Boulder to trash his place? I don't even know where the two lovebirds call home! Oh, he's good." Summer shook her head. "Like I have time to taunt him when I'm probably being shot at because of him and his stupidity!"

"Summer," Alex calmly responded, "we've already informed Ms. Prime that Mitchel's accusation against you is ill placed. Paul is rounding up witnesses so that we will be able to collaborate your whereabouts from the day they left Boulder until their return. Summer, we will prove that you did not strike out against Mitchel. You also need to know that I told Ms. Prime about you being shot at this morning. Our information has calmed her down—for now. From what she implied, it would appear that we have more to learn about old Casanova Mitch."

"Great." Summer suddenly felt exhausted. To make matters worse, she wanted her mother to be there to wrap her arms around her and tell her that everything would be all right. Tears were once again forming in her red puffy eyes.

"Ma'am," Detective North spoke with compassion in his voice. "There will be time to sort this all out. But for now, you need to leave the premises and go with your lawyers, your friends. When you leave here, you will have one of our officers protecting you at all times, to ensure your safety until this attempt on your life is resolved, and you can get back to having a normal life again."

"Police protection. I'll be watched. Wait a minute! Am I going to be able to go to work?" Fire was beginning to burn in Summer's eyes as a heated discussion erupted between Summer and the detective. She was fuming mad. Fortunately, before saying anything else, she realized her anger was not toward Detective North. He was simply doing his job. Mitchel was undoubtedly the cause of all this chaos in her life. Mitchel. Oh, how Summer would love to give him a piece of her mind, instead of the poor man who had just been verbally blasted by her.

Detective North held her gaze while not revealing any of his thoughts about Summer or her situation. "Ms. Newman." There was a subtle change in his voice that caused Summer to feel a rush of heat pass through her. Then Summer saw something in his eyes—concern, tenderness. She lectured herself for thinking something other than the man was doing his job. Then his slight smile about did her in. Summer could only imagine what a full smile would do to her. She instinctively knew he would hold true to his word, when he said, "I will do my best to ensure your daily schedule is not interrupted." Summer sighed. She knew that she had to pull herself together, and not think of him beyond being a police detective. She knew nothing of him. Still, there was something about him that was drawing her in. Summer knew she had to shake off these unrealistic feelings. They had only met, for goodness' sakes, and he was a cop. Besides that, she was still married. Not smart, Summer.

"Well, Detective," Summer sighed out, "as long as you try. You see, my work as a forest park ranger is important, as important as—" Summer stopped midsentence. "Oh no."

"What?" Nikki asked.

"This means I will not be able to volunteer at the preserve, doesn't it?"

"Unfortunately, for now, ma'am, it would be best if you didn't go there." Adam's voice conveyed his deep understanding.

"Say no more. I'll have to call Wayne and tell him to remove me from the volunteer schedule for a while." Summer sighed, looked round her home. She picked up her bag. It was time to leave.

—⁓—

Outside of the house, crime scene tape was placed around the perimeter to inform unauthorized people to stay out. Nikki walked with Summer over to her Jeep, helped her place her luggage in the back area, and climbed in the passenger seat. They slowly backed out of the drive and onto the now-quiet street. Neighbors were no longer lingering about to see what was happening at Summer's place. Alex remained at the house with the detective to have a private conversation before following them home.

—⁓—

Nikki and Alex sat by the pool, each of them sipping a chilled glass of White Zinfandel. Summer was swimming laps to burn off her anger. When she reached the edge of the pool, she kicked over onto her back and slowly made her way back to the stairs by the end where Nikki and Alex were seated. She stepped out of the pool.

"Feel better?" Alex asked while pouring a glass of wine for Summer.

"Perhaps a little," she said, while wrapping herself in a large towel. Summer walked over and sat down in a chair next to Alex. "Thanks." After swallowing a sip of cool wine, Summer said, "As much as I appreciate what you both are doing for me, I need to make a phone call. Since I am not going to worry Mom on her wedding day, I need to talk with my dad."

"Of course, Summer. Finish your wine or take it with you to sip on while you converse with your father. While you are chatting, I'll go ahead and make up a salad for dinner. When you have completed your call, we will meet back here. Then, we'll put the steaks on the grill and share a relaxing meal together."

—⁓—

Summer walked into her apartment that reminded her of a five-star hotel. Nikki and Alex had thought of just about any amenity a person could need while staying there. Satellite television, Wi-Fi, microwave, a coffeemaker, and more. When Nikki had first showed Summer the apartment, the small refrigerator was empty. Now, thanks to Alex stopping at the grocery store on the way home, she had cream for her coffee, wine, an assortment of fresh fruits and juice, danish, bagels, and cream cheese. She quietly closed the door behind her and then stepped farther into the coolness of the space. Having left the windows open, rather than turning on the AC, Summer felt the cool breeze against her damp skin. Quickly toweling off, Summer changed from her wet suit into her dry clothes. Then she sank into the plush dark-brown chair and called her father.

"Princess, my goodness, how did you know I was thinking of you?" His voice revealed his joy in hearing from her. Summer suddenly felt very alone, and longed for him to be there to hold her close.

"Hi, Dad. I'm glad to know that you were thinking of me. I need…" and with that, Summer burst into tears.

"Hey now, Princess, are you crying? Summer, honey, what's wrong?"

"Oh, Dad, I wish you were here. I need one of your hugs." She sobbed.

"Summer, you are breaking my heart. Princess, tell me, what's wrong? Has Mitchel done something else to hurt you?" His voice had grown quiet with concern.

With that, Summer proceeded to tell Stephen about the attempt on her life as well as Mitchel's allegations. Needless to say, he was shocked to hear that someone had attempted to kill his daughter, whom he had only been united with earlier that year. He also had much to say about Mitchel. At that moment, Summer realized it was probably a good thing the whole middle of the country separated them—well, make that separated her father and Mitchel.

"Oh, Dad, thank you for listening to me."

"You're welcome, Princess—anytime." Silence. "Summer," his voice was gentle.

"Yes, Dad?" She then drew in a deep breath, as if finally able to breathe.

"I know that today is your mother's wedding. I heard from your Aunt Becky it was mighty nice. Have you by chance spoken with your mother?"

"No, I haven't. Like you, I've also heard from Aunt Becky, along with Aunt Mel and Cassie who all have sent me pictures. The wedding looked lovely, and Mom was beautiful." Summer listened to her dad share his own view on the pictures he had seen of Amanda on her wedding day. Summer knew his heart was saddened by the fact that her mother would not share his life as his wife. However, it warmed Summer to know that he was doing his best to be supportive of Mom's choices she had made in her life. "Dad, even though I would love to hear from Mom about her special day, I'm avoiding calling her."

"Really, Summer, and why is that?"

"Because if I try and keep my voice upbeat asking her about the wedding, she will be like a bloodhound." A blast of laughter filled Summer's ear. "Go ahead and laugh," Summer actually found herself smiling, as she continued. "You know that somehow, even through the phone, Mom will pick up the scent from me that something is wrong, and despite how hard I try to act as though life is good, she'll keep at me until I give it all up to her."

"My goodness, girl, you are right! That woman could be a bloodhound. Cripes, why didn't I ever see that in her?"

"Simple. You weren't looking for it. I'd also be willing to bet that Uncle Jim never saw her as a bloodhound."

"Probably not, for Jim, your mother was more like an angry old junkyard dog."

"Dad," Summer exclaimed.

"Hey now, Princess you started this raging on your mother by calling her a bloodhound. So, don't you dare try to lay guilt at my feet."

"Guilty as charged." Summer chuckled, then sighed. "Gee, it felt good to pick on Mom, even though she wasn't here to defend herself."

"It's good to hear you sounding as though you're starting to feel better."

"Dad, you know Nikki and Alex are a blessing for me to have in my life, especially today. But, I can now smile and even laugh because of you being here for me as my dad—my special friend."

"Summer." He cleared his throat. Summer had to smile, as she was fairly certain his eyes were probably moist. One thing she quickly learned and liked about her dad was that under the guff mountain man persona, her dad's a softy, like a cuddly teddy bear.

"Yes, Dad."

"Even though we'll both probably end up in the doghouse with your mother when she discovers that there was an attempt on your life and neither of us have told her, you'll never know how much I appreciate you turning to me in your time of need."

"Dad, it was a no-brainer to call you. You're also right. When Mom finds out I was shot at, she will be more than mad at both of us for not telling her. She'll be livid, and turn in a heartbeat from bloodhound to junkyard dog, ready to rip someone's hide off of their back."

Stephen burst into laughter. Summer listened to him as he pulled himself together and asked, "Summer, does your mother know you talk about her like this?"

"Oh, heck no! Don't get me wrong. I love Mom dearly."

"I know you do."

"However; Dad, she's so much fun to pick on, and you're the only one who appreciates my humor. Think about it, Dad. Could you see Kevin teasing with me about Mom the way you and I do?"

"You have a point." With that, the two were laughing and sharing more stories about the woman they both loved. "Summer, in all seriousness, when you do decide to talk with your mother about today, she's going to have a strong reaction. If you don't want to tell her by yourself, I'd be more than happy to do a three-way conference call with you."

"Thanks, Dad. I really appreciate knowing that you have my back. But I'll be able to handle my conversation with Mom. I might call you afterwards, so you can then call Mom and calm her down." "I will do that for you."

Summer glanced at her watch. "Oh goodness. Dad, I didn't realize it was so late. Nikki and Alex are waiting for me to have dinner with them."

Hasty good-byes were exchanged. Summer made her way to the door and was feeling better as she emerged from her apartment to join her friends for dinner.

14

Summer awakened from a sound sleep to her phone ringing. She immediately recognized the ringtone. Sleepily glancing at the bedside clock, she saw the time was two thirty-four in the morning. The two-hour time difference indicated that it was four thirty-four on the east coast.

"Mom, what's wrong?" Summer anxiously asked, while orienting herself to being in a different location from her bedroom.

"I don't know, Summer, you tell me."

"Mom." Summer rubbed her eyes, then made a ghastly noise while stretching. "Do I need to remind you that it's your wedding night? You should be asleep or doing something—with your husband."

"Summer Brooke," Amanda's quiet stern voice indicated she meant business. "I know perfectly well that it is my wedding night. You needn't worry about Kevin and me enjoying it. Now, my dear child." Oh yes, Summer knew that tone all too well. "As your mother, I missed you not being here with me—with us. Besides that, I fully expected and looked forward to hearing from you at some point during the day. My dear girl, I know your habits. You not calling, or texting me is most definitely not like you. For some reason, Summer Brooke Newman, you avoided contacting me on my special day. So this leads me to suspect that something serious has happened to you during the past twenty-four hours. Why is Mitchel my primary suspect in your reason for avoiding me?"

"Mom," Summer tried to sound upbeat, as she could tell that the bloodhound, which she had teasingly talked about with her father a few hours before, was wide awake and on the hunt. "Really, you don't need to worry."

"Uh-huh." Silence. "Tell that to someone who does not know you and who will believe you at your word. First, your father was evasive with me when I called and questioned him about hearing from you, and now you are in your 'Mom, you don't need to worry' mode. Something is not right. So, Summer Brooke, no more denying, talk to me."

Summer sighed. She truly did not want to upset her mother. Still, she knew by her tone it was time to be honest with her. Well, maybe she'd try to stall her for another minute or two.

"You called Dad?" She hoped this would lead to a different direction in their conversation. "Do you think that was wise? You know, with how you two were once going to be married, and Rose and me and—"

"Nice try diverting my attention to talking about your father and our past. It isn't going to work, neither is asking me about my wedding. Summer, when I had not heard from you by five o'clock our time, and you were not returning my texts or calls, I was more than a little worried about you. I knew with Johnson not being at our wedding, that he would have had an opportunity to speak with you. So he obviously moved straight to the top of my list to interrogate after Cassie and your Aunts Becky and Melissa. They all said you were very brief with your text responses to each of them. When I contacted your father, Johnson tried to play off your conversation with him as being carefree. However, I heard the concern in his voice when he told me not to worry about you."

"Well, Mom, you are right. I was avoiding talking with you." She heard her mother gasp, then she quickly added, "Only because I didn't want to ruin your wedding day."

"Ruin my wedding day? Summer, honey, how could you possibly ruin my wedding day?"

With that, Summer curled up in her bed and shared every detail of her Saturday with her. "So, Mom, now you know. Since I didn't want to upset you, I called Dad and talked with him."

"Oh, my precious Sunshine, while I appreciate your concern for my happiness, Summer, honey, above all else, you're my child, and if you need me, I expect you to contact me regardless of how bad you think the situation is, or what day it is."

"I'm sorry for causing you to worry." Summer sniffled.

"Hey now, you have nothing to be sorry about. You did what you thought was right at the time, and you were being my sweet considerate daughter. Your father, on the other hand, has disappointed me for not telling me you had a crisis, or that he stepped up and helped you through your distress, and that your wonderful friends also helped you through it. Now that I know what is going on and that you are safe, tell me, was he as helpful as you've claimed?"

"Yes, Mom. Dad was terrific. He listened, consoled me, and then managed to get me to laugh by the end of our conversation. I think he's really getting a handle on being a dad."

"Hmm, sounds that way. Summer, I truly am glad that you called him and that he was able to be the parent you needed."

"Oh goodness, Mom. I hear the unspoken *but*. So my turn to ask, what's wrong?"

"I was just thinking about us. You. Me. Your father."

"And how Dad both is and isn't a part of our lives?"

"Something like that. Summer, even at the age of thirty, it would not be wrong for you to wonder what it would have been like for Johnson and me to get back together."

"Mom, I—"

"Please, allow me to continue. Your father and I are not the same people that we were thirty years ago. Time and experiences have changed, and define, who we are today. Stephen Johnson is a good man. I am grateful that we have been able to reconcile many of our differences, and now we are friends and share our love with you. Since we found out that Johnson is your father, I've seen a beautiful relationship begin to blossom and grow between the two of you. Having said that"—Amanda yawned—"prior to the DNA results, you were able to meet Kevin and begin to establish a relationship with him. I've even heard you call him your stepdad. I know that makes Kevin very happy, me too. Yesterday, I married Kevin, and we plan to spend the rest of our lives together—till death claims one of us. He is the man whom I love. Summer, with your new life with your father, I hope—"

"Mom, while I've wondered what it would have been like for you and Dad to have been married while I was growing up, and what it would be like now for you two to get back together, I love you and respect you. Therefore, I would never intentionally do anything to hurt you and Kevin, even though I think my dad is the hotter man of the two." Summer giggled.

"Summer Newman," Amanda feigned embarrassment, while understanding how her daughter thought. Johnson had aged nicely and still could make her heart warm. Still, Stephen was not Kevin, nor was Kevin Stephen. Both men had amazing qualities that made them uniquely special. Stephen had captured his daughter's heart, and her love. In Amanda's eyes, that's the way it should be.

"Mom," Summer yawned. "Even though I thought I was doing right by not calling you, I'm glad you called me. Do you realize that it is now six thirty your time?"

"Ye-up! The sun is coming up over Lake George. Goodness, it is simply breathtaking sitting out here on the balcony of our hotel room in the stillness of early morning. I guess I'll make some coffee and watch the sun continue to rise."

"Oh, Mom, you are sitting outside watching the sun rise. If I had called you yesterday and told you what had happened, right now you'd be in bed with Kevin."

"Not necessarily. You know that I love the quiet of morning."

"Regardless, I called you on your wedding night—morning. That's pretty unromantic."

"And how do you know I wasn't savoring in my mind and heart the romance I shared with Kevin when I called you?" There was playfulness in her voice.

"Oh-oh, Mom, you are too much." Summer giggled. "I love you."

"And I love you, Summer. Now, as your mother, I'm going to tell you to go back to bed and get some sleep."

"Yes, ma'am. Good night and good morning, and I love you and—"

"Good-bye, Summer. I'm hanging up now."

"Bye, Mom."

Summer lay back on her pillows and reflected on the conversation she had with her mother. That woman sure was something. With all of Summer's care in not wanting to spoil her mother's day, she had known something was wrong. Summer laughed as she picked up her phone. Time to send a text message to the one person who would appreciate her humor. Summer was drifting off to sleep when her phone indicated a text message was in her box. She rolled over, picked up her phone, and opened the message.

> You called it. Blood hound she is! LOL!! I should have warned you, she's also an old clucking hen who loves you. FYI, I'm an old rooster who loves you too. We'll talk soon Princess—you take care.

Summer rubbed her tired eyes. She yawned. Both her parents were up with the rising of the sun. *Better them than me,* Summer thought as she smiled to herself, snuggled under her blanket, and fell fast asleep.

Monday afternoon was quiet at the national park. There were cars and SUVs parked along the edge of the parking lot relatively close to the rangers station. Two other vehicles were parked farther down in the lot. One belonged to a couple who had signed in earlier in the day to camp in one of the primitive sites. The other belonged to the police officer providing protection for Summer.

Summer appreciated the compromises the Denver police had agreed upon to enable her to continue to work; however, she was not to go beyond the immediate area of the rangers station. Now, Cathy got to enjoy Summer's favorite part of her job, out monitoring the trails. Still, Summer would not complain because sitting at the office greeting visitors and registering campers sure did beat the alternative of sitting in Nikki and Alex's apartment, or lounging by their pool all day. That was not Summer's idea of fun! So as Summer sat with Cathy in front of the rangers station enjoying the quiet of the day in the bright warm sunshine, she breathed in the scents of pine, wild flowers, and the faint smell of a campfire drifting on the gentle breeze. The sight and sound of a familiar vehicle pulling into the parking lot drew their attention.

"Looks like you've got company."

"Cathy. Bill is just a good friend."

"Right, and I'd have to be blind to not see how he looks at you."

Summer opened her mouth to speak, then promptly clamped it shut. She intently watched Bill approach them. Concern filled her. If Cathy was correct with her assessment, and Bill was interested in her, this could be a problem—a messy problem.

"Hey, Bill," Summer called out. "What brings you up here to see us?"

"Hi, Summer." His smile was warm and playful. Then his eyes shifted to focus on Cathy. "Hello, Cathy." Summer noticed the difference in his voice. She watched her friends as they gazed at one another. Goodness. It appeared to Summer that Cathy had been wrong about whom Bill might be romantically interested in.

"Hello," was all Cathy said, before she lowered her eyes.

Momentary silence hung between the three of them until Summer spoke up. "So, Bill, what brings you up here to see us?"

Bill shifted his gaze from Cathy to Summer. He smiled. "Well, Summer, since the police are only allowing you to come to work here at the rangers station, I thought it might be good for me to check and see if you are complying with the rules. You are—right?"

"Yes, Bill, I'm behaving myself and staying close to, or in, the office."

"Glad to hear it." His smile revealed his relief. "Wayne spoke with your detective to see if it's okay for us to visit you. That's why I'm finally here."

Oh great, Adam is now thought of as my detective. Just what I don't need! Summer thought as she glanced around the parking lot. Her gaze returned to Bill. "I am glad you got permission and that you came to visit. I've missed seeing everyone. So tell me, what's going on at the preserve?" "A lot! Since you and Cathy played important roles in the saving of the deer, I offered to personally stop over and tell you both that this afternoon, we are releasing the doe and her fawn into the preserve."

"Oh, that's wonderful!" Summer exclaimed.

"Hooray!" Cathy clapped her hands together.

"I agree, it is terrific, and we want you both to come and be with us for the moment."

Summer's happiness plummeted as she listened to her friends. As part of the agreement for her to be able to work, which had been a major battle with the police captain and one detective in particular, she couldn't go to the preserve.

"Summer, I have more good news. Wayne contacted the police to see if they'd make an exception and if you could be with us for this special moment. After all, Wayne reminded them that if it weren't for you, the deer probably would have died. The captain assured Wayne that this one time, they would provide someone to accompany you."

"Bill," Summer sniffled. "I do appreciate all you and Wayne have done to make accommodations for me. However, I will not be able to attend. My lawyers and I have a meeting with Mitchel and his lawyer this afternoon to hash out some issues with our divorce, as well as another issue."

"Oh, that's too bad. We'll miss you. Cathy, will you come by yourself?"

Summer noticed a change in Bill's expression as he spoke to Cathy. She smiled to herself. It was nice to see someone interested in her friend, as perhaps more than just to have a platonic friendship. Cathy deserved to have a good man like Bill in her life, and he in turn deserved to have a terrific person like Cathy in his. She listened to Bill as his voice seemed to grow quieter while he spoke.

"After we release the deer, I'd like to show you around the preserve, you know, if you have time."

"She'd love to," Summer answered for her friend, who suddenly appeared to be like a statue and unable to speak.

Cathy weakly smiled and nodded. Her cheeks were increasing in color. "What time do I need to be there?"

"Come on over when your shift ends. If you get there before we're ready to release the deer, you can have a cold drink and relax out in our employee area." Bill glanced at his watch then back at Cathy and smiled. "I'll see you later then, Cathy."

"Yes, I'll see you later," and with that, Bill headed for his pickup to return to the preserve.

By four thirty that afternoon, it was questionable as to which park ranger was more nervous. Summer did not want to think about driving down to Colorado Springs to go to the meeting. The thought of seeing Mitchel and what he had done made Summer feel nauseated. She sat back in her chair behind the large front desk and released a slow breath. Summer was about ready to pull her bag from the bottom drawer of her desk when she heard footsteps on the small porch. It was normal for visitors to come up onto the porch area and read notices and points of interest on the bulletin board before coming inside. Summer listened to the footsteps on the seasoned pine boards, then saw the figure in the screened doorway.

"Oh my," Cathy breathed out. "Now he's something to look at."

"You have Bill," Summer quietly said as she stood. She noticed everything about Adam from his neatly combed hair to his hint of a five o'clock shadow and his dark suit, which she figured had to be uncomfortable on that warm day.

"Hmm. Is that a hands-off statement?"

"No comment." Summer smiled as he entered. "Good afternoon, Detective North."

From her initial meeting with Adam on that fateful Saturday morning, Summer had felt drawn to him. Every time they were together to discuss the progress, or lack of progress, on her case, either at the Denver precinct or at the apartment, he made her feel safe and cared for. Now, with Adam being there at the park, something didn't feel right to her. "I expected my escort to be here by now. Is everything all right?"

Summer noticed his eyes; while fixed on her, they were aware of everything around them. "Everything is fine, Summer. Frank has been relieved of duty for this afternoon."

"He has?" Summer walked over to the window and looked out into the parking lot. Sure enough. The unmarked car that had been in the lot since she had come to work was now gone. "So what am I to do about going into the city for my meeting?"

"I'm here to follow you to your apartment, where you will leave your Jeep, and then I am taking you to your meeting."

"Oh," Summer's eyes seemed to grow larger, as she comprehended what Adam had just said, and not said. Something was up, and it had Summer feeling very uneasy. "Then I guess we should be going." Adam nodded. He remained standing by the door as

Summer gathered her belongings and said her good-bye to Cathy. Summer stopped midstep and looked straight into Adam's eyes. "Good grief, you come here, and I forget my manners. Cathy, I'm sorry for being so rude. This is Detective Adam North. Adam, this is Ranger Cathy Long, my good friend and colleague."

"Nice to meet you," both exchanged greetings.

"Now, we can go."

"It was that important for you to introduce us before we left?" Adam asked as they made their way off the porch and down the steps.

"Sure was. You both are important people in my life." Summer glanced over at Adam. His lips had a slight curve to them. She weakly smiled at him and then sighed as she slowed her step and pulled her keys from her front pocket. Adam, fully attentive to Summer, adjusted his step to stay with her.

"That was a heavy sigh."

Without another word, Adam gently took hold of Summer's elbow. She wasn't surprised by his concern. His touch caused her to feel a surge of warmth sprint through her. Their eyes met. Summer saw something she had not seen before in Adam. She felt her heart do a flip-flop.

"It was heavy. Adam, you know everything that is going on, so I can be honest with you." A tear slid down Summer's cheek. He stepped closer. Their bodies touched. Then he reached over and brushed away the wetness on her cheek with his thumb.

"Of course you can be honest—I want you to be honest with me, Summer." His face was close to hers. Tenderness rippled from his voice. "Tell me what's troubling you."

"Everything. I come to work and keep up a brave confident front. When I'm around Nikki and Alex, I try not to overwhelm them with my misery—my frustration, my fears. I just want whomever tried to kill me to be caught so I can go home to my house." She sobbed. Adam gently pulled her into his embrace. "Adam, I want my life back."

"Oh, Summer. You have every right to feel frustrated. I promise you, we will find out whomever is trying to hurt you. In the meantime, I will keep you safe." He tucked his chin on her head. A gentle breeze stirred. "Summer, you're in no shape to drive. Tell you what, I'll drive you down to Colorado Springs to your lawyers, and then home afterward."

"But, Adam, my Jeep will be left here. I won't be able to get to work tomorrow morning without my wheels."

Adam smiled as he reached over and carefully placed a piece of Summer's hair behind her ear. "We'll work it out later. Right now, we need to get you to your meeting, and I am here to make sure that you are safe. So, shall we go?" Her smile and nod was all Adam needed to again take hold of Summer's arm and lead her to his car.

15

Mitchel sat in the waiting room of the law firm of Alexander and Nicole Blards with his attorney Ashley Prime. He was anxious and would like to have been most anywhere other than there for the meeting with Summer, his wife—his. Mitchel sighed.

"That was a rather heavy sigh," Ashley quietly stated as she turned her gaze to meet Mitchel's weary eyes.

"I guess." Mitchel fell silent. He glanced around the office waiting area decorated in subdued colors and abstract paintings on the wall. Cozy lamps, rather than bright overhead lights, were positioned on tables for a calming affect. It was not helping Mitchel.

"This will be the first time I've seen Summer since we separated in May. In June, before I left for Alaska, I thought about calling her and stopping over to see her. Then I remembered her Order of Protection. Knowing Summer, and how angry she is with me, she would have had me thrown in jail." Mitchel fell silent as he collected his thoughts. "I know I shouldn't have sent her the voice mail while I was in Alaska, but I just couldn't stop thinking of her. I've hurt her in ways that I never imagined I was capable of. Now, because of how I've screwed up, we're getting a divorce." Mitchel glanced around the room. "Ashley, look at this waiting room and the activity happening down that hallway. Summer's attorneys obviously are expensive."

"Yes, they do have a large staff, which comes with time of establishing oneself as a successful practicing attorney, or partnership. Mitchel, I'm curious. Are you insinuating that since I only have an administrative assistant and one paralegal working for me that perhaps I'm not as good at my job as your counsel as Summer's legal team is for her?"

"No, of course not. Since I know what Summer's salary is, I'm just wondering how she can afford to have them represent her."

"I've been wondering that myself."

At that moment, Ashley and Mitchel turned their focus on the increased activity and noise coming from down the hallway. A small group of people came toward them and stopped by the door leading out of the office. Alex and Nikki turned from the door and walked over to stand in front of Mitchel and Ashley. Power and self-confidence exuded from both of them as they stood together in the room.

"Good afternoon, I'm Alexander Blards, and this is my wife, Nicole Blards."

"Good afternoon. I'm Ashley Prime, Dr. Brown's attorney. We've spoken a few times on the phone. It is a pleasure to finally be able to put a face with the voice I've become familiar with hearing on the phone."

"Yes. We have spoken, and I agree with you, counselor, it is nice to finally meet. It would be nicer if we all had met under other circumstances. Divorce is never easy for any of us," Alex stated succinctly. He was establishing that this was strictly a professional business meeting. Of course, his navy blue suit, white tailored fine blue-striped shirt, and red tie completed his professional persona.

"Mr. and Mrs. Blards, allow me to introduce you both to Dr. Mitchel Brown." She glanced around the room. "And where is Ms. Newman?"

"Summer called me a few minutes ago to inform us that there was an accident on the freeway, so they're tied up in traffic." Nikki was a tower of composure as she stood looking at them. Her red suit with a white camisole peeking out of the top button of her jacket and red-and-white sling-back pumps stated that she, right along with Alex, was in control of the situation. "They should be here in about ten minutes. In the meantime, may we get either of you cold or hot refreshments while we wait for their arrival?"

"Nothing for me."

Mitchel looked confused. "You said *they*. You mean Summer is not coming alone?"

"No. Dr. Brown. Since there is an open investigation into the attempt on Summer's life, Summer is currently living under the protection of the Denver police department. Detective North is accompanying Summer here today."

"Do you all really think Ms. Newman is in such grave danger that she needs special attention from the police department?"

"We do." There was no warmth in Nikki's voice as she turned her gaze to meet Mitchel's eyes.

All conversation ceased as the door opened. Summer—dressed in her dark-green park ranger's uniform, hiking boots on her feet, hair pulled back into a ponytail, and no makeup on her face—stepped into the room. There was no smile on her pink full lips. Her expression was one of sheer seriousness. Right behind her, slightly to her side with his hand gently placed on the small of her back, was Detective Adam North. His demeanor indicated that he meant business. Summer would in no way be hurt while on his watch, if he could help it.

"Sorry, we're late. The accident and traffic was horrid. We heard there was one fatality."

"Oh goodness. How awful!"

"Detective, good to see you," Alex said as he moved closer to them and extended his hand in greeting. "Summer, Detective

North, allow me to introduce you both to Ms. Prime, Mitchel's attorney. Of course you both know Mitchel."

Summer and Mitchel were now silently and intently looking at each other. An unexpected tear slid from the corner of Summer's eye. Mitchel noticed it. Without a word, he reached into the inner pocket of his suit coat and removed a small packet of tissues. He handed one to Summer.

"Thank you," she quietly said, as she reached out and took the tissue. Her hand brushed Mitchel's. As she sniffled back unwanted and unexpected emotions, she felt the slight movement of Adam's hand on her back.

"Well, shall we all go into the conference room and begin our meeting?" Alex asked. He then turned to Adam. "Detective, if you don't mind waiting here and will have a seat, Mr. Seetley will be along shortly for his meeting with you."

"That will be fine, Mr. Blards." Adam gently rubbed Summer's tense lower back. His warm hand helped her find an inner calm to face the impending meeting. "Summer, if you all finish your meeting before I have concluded mine, you are by no means to leave this building by yourself."

His eyes intently held hers with a depth of concern Summer had never experienced before in her life. Summer found herself begin to nod and slightly smile. Any other man saying that would have sent Summer into a tirade about being able to care for herself. But this was Adam, and he was completely different from the type of man Summer would naturally want to have a relationship with. He was proving he cares about her, and not simply because he was a cop and she a damsel in distress. Something was clicking between them. Chemistry. Whether Summer wanted to admit it to herself or not, she was already in a new relationship—an unusual one—but still, a relationship.

"You don't need to worry about me leaving here without you, Detective." She saw the faint smile in his eyes and the corner of his mouth as she turned to go to her meeting. Her heart did a flip-flop.

━━━⟋⟍━━━

The cool air in the conference room vibrated with tension as Summer sat down in the cool high-back leather chair positioned between Nikki and Alex. Her lawyers were making a statement. In here, they were Summer's protectors. She watched as Mitchel held the chair for his lawyer, and then took his seat across from her. Once again, their eyes met. Summer saw the fatigue in Mitchel's eyes, the lines by them, and the strain on the muscles by his mouth. He too was hurting.

━━━⟋⟍━━━

While Summer and Mitchel were in conference working through the details of their divorce with their lawyers, Adam sat with Paul, in his private office down the hall, for their meeting. The two men had been working together for a few weeks, and now conversed with a sense of camaraderie. "I've been doing some nosing around into the life of one Jesslyn Octivani." Paul allowed his words to settle in on Adam. He watched the detective, who seemed to be in no hurry to ask any questions. Instead, he took a sip of his coffee that by now had cooled.

"And what might you have found?"

"The woman is not as squeaky clean as she wants everyone to believe." With that said, Paul picked up a manila file folder and slid it across the top of his well-polished hardwood desk. "Take a look."

Adam saw something in Paul's expression, his interest was piqued. He carefully picked up the folder and perused through Paul's well-documented notes and photos on his investigation thus far. "So, our girl has a secret she obviously doesn't want lover boy to know about. Interesting time line." For the first time since driving up to Summer's home on that Saturday morning, Adam felt a glimmer of hope. Finally, he might have the break he had been waiting for. "It's more than just a coincidence. Thought you might want to head on up to Boulder to pay her a visit."

"Telling me how to do my job?" Adam's chin dropped as his right brow raised. His expression and tone revealed his resentment toward a successful PI telling him, a seasoned detective, how to do his job.

"Not at all. I am simply concerned about Ms. Newman and her safety. In all of my years as a PI, I've seem too many love triangles become messy and downright deadly. That young woman sitting in the conference room with my bosses is the innocent victim in this, and she is also a special client to them."

"In what way, other than being her friends, is Summer special to them?"

With that question, Paul enlightened Adam about the difference in this case from the start when Nathan first called them. Adam was intrigued by how much effort everyone was putting into caring for Summer. He listened as the older man continued on, seemed to run out of steam for a moment, before adding, "As I said, she's special to them. So, as their PI, and with what I've learned, I am putting even more of an effort into my investigation. Get my drift?"

"Loud and clear." Adam took a sip of his cold coffee. Then he placed the cup on the desk and said, "Paul, you've done good work. The Blards are fortunate to have you working with them. Right now, I'm grateful to have you working on our side, and not against me."

"Well, thanks." Paul studied the man sitting across from him. "It is obvious that you also care about Ms. Newman. Take it from an older man who's had a few knocks over the years, right now as a cop, don't allow your feelings for Ms. Newman to cloud your judgment. I've checked up on you and your record as a detective. You're good at what you do. Get the job done. Find the one who is out to kill her, and then, if you still feel same way you do now, pursue your relationship with her." The older man allowed a knowing smile to appear in his seasoned eyes.

Adam affirmed the statement with a nod. He stood, and returned to the waiting room that was empty. Adam walked over to the receptionist's desk and inquired about the meeting Summer was attending in the conference room. Satisfied that Summer had not left the building, as she had promised, Adam took a seat to wait for her. He was glad to have a few minutes alone to sit, and think about the new information he had received about the case, as well as what Paul had said about his relationship with Summer. Adam allowed himself to relax in the chair, extending his legs out in front of him while crossing his ankles. Leaning back allowing his head to rest against the cool wall behind the chair, Adam began to process his new information and develop a plan.

—⚜—

"Well," Alex said after clearing his throat, "we have reviewed your motion for settlement with Summer and are ready to proceed."

"Good," Ms. Prime responded. "Mitchel wants to dissolve their marriage as soon as possible."

Summer had been looking at Ms. Prime. Her tone and words regarding Mitch's haste in wanting the marriage to end caused Summer to again turn her focus to her husband. Something was up with him. Summer knew that given the chance, Mitchel would do everything in his power to take revenge on her for throwing him out of their bedroom and then out of their home.

"As soon as possible? Mitchel, what did you do, get your girlfriend pregnant, and now you need to have a shotgun wedding?" Sarcasm and anger riddled Mitchel as Summer spoke. "Playing with the Mob boss's daughter is never a wise decision. Everyone knows that Octivani has a rep as bad as some of the old families in New York in days gone by. You better be careful her daddy doesn't do you in! Pow!" Summer had raised her hand and fingers as if they were a revolver. She spoke with vinegar in her voice. "The last thing I need is to have to bury you." With that said, Alex placed his hand on Summer's wrist. Summer saw Mitchel wince and the devastation that filled his eyes as he processed her words.

"Mitchel, I seem to have slumped to an all-time low. Even though you have been behaving like a slug for the past year, or so, you didn't deserve that." She turned her gaze away from him, as she sniffled.

"Ms. Newman," Ashley's voice was crisp. "Dr. Brown came here in good faith, to peacefully work with you toward the dissolving of your marriage. I would appreciate it if you would hold your bitter tongue toward my client, or I will be forced—"

"Ashley," Mitchel cut off his lawyer. "Right now I don't need for you to speak for me. Summer has every right to be angry with me. Summer, it is I who am sorry for every unkind, unloving things that I have done to you. To answer your question about my wanting to expedite our divorce, no—Jesslyn is not pregnant, at least"—concern formed on the creases of Mitchel's brow—"not to my knowledge. I can only say that I've made some decisions about my future. I only hope that my actions in the next few months will someday change your opinion of me for the better."

Summer was confused by Mitchel's mysterious words. His girlfriend wasn't pregnant as she had suspected. He's made decisions. Summer knew by the look in Mitchel's eyes that at that moment in time, he was being honest with her—well, as much as he was capable of being honest. Tension hung in the silence of the room.

"Summer has read over Mitchel's motion," Nikki said to Ms. Prime. She then turned to Mitchel, who was focused on his hands, which he had folded in front of him on the table. "Mitchel," Nikki's addressing him caused Mitch to look at her. He avoided eye contact with Summer. "We are questioning why all of a sudden you are willing to give Summer all of your marital property? Your home and contents that you purchased together, and your joint finances, what is left of them? As I am sure your attorney has discussed with you, property is normally divided between the two separating parties. We have yet to discuss alimony, which Summer is entitled to receive from you, Dr. Brown."

"Ms. Blards, my client is well aware of everything you have just stated. Judge Roberts is also well aware of Mitchel's need for the divorce to be finalized by the end of this month."

"End of this month?" Summer softly questioned as she looked over at Mitchel, who was focused on his lawyer. Neither one responded to Summer's question. She looked at Nikki, who shook her head, and then at Alex, who whispered in her ear. Summer nodded; however, she remained confused as she listened to Ms. Prime.

"Judge Roberts has agreed to expedite the divorce as long as we are all in agreement to the disposal of marital property. Having been in this judge's court for other divorce proceedings, this is good news for all of us."

"Ms. Prime, it is obvious that you know of your client's plans for his future, and most likely have brought this to the judge's attention. I noticed that neither you nor Dr. Brown made any comment regarding alimony."

"Mr. Blards, I assure you that now is not the time for us to discuss alimony. All I may say is that Ms. Newman will be well cared for in the future."

"Not good enough, counselor." It was Nikki who now spoke with sharpness. "As Summer's attorneys, we have a right to know what you and Dr. Brown are up to. You will step out into our other conference room with Alex and me, and you will enlighten us about Dr. Brown's plans." Nikki's expression dared the other woman to challenge her, as she added, "You know, counselor—no surprises."

Ashley nodded. She leaned over to quietly speak to Mitchel, then stood and quietly walked from the room. Her previous attitude of superiority no longer existed. Silence hung in the room with Summer still positioned in her seat, and Mitchel across from her. For a moment, they simply looked at each other, each lost in their own thoughts.

"Mitchel," Summer's voice was quiet filled with passion. "I thought I knew you as a person, the man whom I fell in love with—as my husband. I guess, since we are now sitting here hashing out the dissolving of our marriage, I never knew you as well as I thought. All those days and nights when you told me that you loved me, I now have to wonder if they were simply words you knew you were supposed to say to make me happy. I am not going to fight you anymore. I'm done. If this quick divorce is what you want, then I'll agree to it. Mitchel, I want you to know I don't see the need for you to give me alimony. Given the extent of your gambling debt, you need your money to pay your debtors."

"Summer, don't worry about my debts. For gosh sakes, woman," Mitchel snapped at her. "For once in your life, stop being considerate. Think about yourself, Summer. Frankly, I don't know how you can afford these two lawyers, much less will be able to maintain our home on your salary. Even though Ashley didn't say it, of course we'll work out financial support for you."

"You still care." Summer felt the wetness seeping into her eyes. She watched his eyes turn from the hardness, which had been there a while ago, to concern. "Mitch, in all honesty, I could not afford Nikki and Alex on my own. Despite my protests, Mom and Kevin, my stepdad, along with Uncle Andrew and Aunt Cassie have contributed to what they call their 'we love Summer fund.' Nate, you remember my friend Nate." Mitchel nodded. "He warned me to not attempt to repay any of them for their gift."

"That sounds like your mother, and her ability to rally the troops to come to your aid, and I remember Nathan. Now things are beginning to make sense. I bet he can't wait for you to be single again so he can move in and hump you."

"Mitchel, that snarly remark about my mother and your vulgarity toward Nate and me was uncalled-for," Summer snapped back. Once again, electrified silence hung between them like a downed power line dangling in a puddle of liquid.

"You're right, Summer." Mitchel closed his eyes and slowly shook his head. "I'm sorry," he breathed out.

"Accepted." Summer fought to keep her emotions in check as she spoke. "Before we digressed, I was going to say to you that I hope that in the future, you will not regret these hasty decisions you are making regarding our divorce, and that you are able to move on with your life and be happy."

"Summer," Mitchel's voice hitched. His eyes now shimmered with wetness. "Giving you what was our home and all that we shared will never undo the pain I have inflicted upon you. I too have hope for you. I hope that in time, when you know what I am doing, why I have done some things, that you will be able to forgive me."

At that moment, as the door opened, Summer was left with more questions and uncertainty. When the three lawyers reentered the room, they were silent. Their faces revealed nothing. Nikki and Alex sat back down in their chairs, with Summer once again wedged between them. Ashley took her seat next to Mitchel. With that, Mitchel leaned over and whispered to his lawyer. She whispered back and shook her head with an affirming no. The lawyers then hashed out a few of the remaining issues for the day. When all was said and done, and the papers to be submitted to Judge Roberts were signed, they all stood. Alex moved to the door and opened it. Summer remained close to Nikki as Mitchel and his lawyer headed for the door. She took a step and quietly spoke.

"Well, Mitchel"—tears were streaming down her cheeks as she looked at him—"I guess the next time we'll see each other will be in court. Take care."

"You too," his voice hitched as his hand gently stroked Summer's arm. Mitchel then stepped out into the hall.

16

Adam heard the door open, followed by the voices, before he saw the small group of bodies emerge through the doorway and into the hall. Focusing on the movement in the hall, Adam first saw Alex step out of the conference room. He was ushering the visiting attorney and Dr. Brown toward the waiting area. Looking past the three moving toward him, Adam saw Nikki move slowly through the doorway, with her arm placed protectively around Summer's shoulders. She was quietly speaking to Summer, who responded with affirming nods. As Adam watched them, the old private eye's words came back to him. Yes. Summer was someone special to the Blards. She was also someone special to him, and as soon as he gets her out of the office, he was going to do everything in his power to help her decompress and relax away her stress of the meeting. With that thought, Adam stood to wait for Summer.

When Ashley and Mitchel reached the waiting room, their eyes locked with Adam's. Both briskly spoke to him, as Mitchel opened the door for them to leave. Adam simply nodded his good-bye. He then turned to find Summer approaching with Nikki. Summer's weak smile informed him that her bravado was nearly gone.

"Adam, I apologize that our meeting ran a tad longer than expected. I hope we did not inconvenience you and keep you waiting for too long."

"Thanks, Alex, you all were fine. Honestly, I don't often get an opportunity for uninterrupted quiet time in the afternoon to reflect on a case, especially immediately after having an informative meeting with a private eye."

"So Paul's work has been beneficial for you?"

"Most assuredly." Adam's eyes shifted to allow his gaze to fall upon Summer. He smiled with ease. He stepped over and instinctively wrapped his arms around Summer, drawing her protectively to him. "Protecting this beautiful woman is of utmost importance to more people than she realizes. Summer, are you ready to go and get your Jeep?"

"Oh yes," Summer yawned.

"Adam, Summer." They both turned to Alex. "I suggest that for now, you and Summer head over to our place to relax until Nikki and I arrive home. Then the four of us can ride up to the park and pick up Summer's Jeep so she does not have to be driving alone on the highway."

"I like your suggestion, counselor. Summer, what do you think of Alex's suggestion?"

"That's why he's paid the big bucks," she said with a deadpan expression. Then her eyes began to shimmer with wetness. The stress of the day was quickly catching up with her. Alex softly chuckled. Nikki also found the humor in Summer's statement while knowing perfectly well that her husband did not make any more money than she did.

———

The conversation at dinner was upbeat, and just what Summer needed. Of course, sitting out by the pool with a nice cool breeze, the sun slipping in the western sky, dear friends, and an amazing caring man sitting by her side didn't hurt. Without realizing it, Summer released a long sigh filled with fatigue.

Adam reached over and took her hand into his. Summer did not resist his move. He cupped her palm and fingers while he stroked the back of her hand with his thumb pad.

"You're exhausted." His words were soft, as he quietly spoke into Summer's ear. She could feel Adam's warm breath on her ear. It tickled, while sending shards of warmth through her. Summer turned her head so that Adam's mouth was brushing her cheek. A smile appeared on her lips.

"How about I walk you home, get you settled in for the night, and then I'll head on home?"

"I'd like that." Summer stretched, then turned to her friends. "Nikki, Alex, thank you both for everything, and I mean"—she paused—"everything."

"Oh, Summer, it's our pleasure."

Summer looked from one friend to the other. It was obvious that Alex was in total agreement with Nikki's response. At that moment, Summer felt truly blessed to have such amazing friends, and one in particular back in Maryland, who had introduced them. Nate had truly taken care of her in her time of need, as promised. Now besides Nate, she had Adam taking care of her.

"Summer."

"Yes." Her eyes were unfocused. "Oh, Adam, I'm sorry."

"You don't need to be sorry." His fingers gently laced with hers as he spoke, "Wherever your thoughts have taken you just now, must have been mighty nice and comforting."

"It was. I was reflecting on how blessed I am to have wonderful people in my life."

"I hope I am one of them." His eyes shone with tenderness. At that moment, Summer heard something in his voice that informed her that he honestly meant every word.

"You, my dear detective, are at the top of my list of special people." Her eyes held his, as she tenderly smiled at him "So, how about making good on your offer, and walk me home."

"With pleasure."

Adam knew that the apartment was safe when they entered. After all, he had already been in the apartment twice that afternoon and once in the evening. Now, he was preparing to leave Summer for the night. Still, he was a cop, and he was going to protect Summer from any harm, if he could help it. "Okay, Sunflower. All clear," he said, as he walked back out of the bedroom into the kitchen/living area. "Sunflower," she exclaimed, as she entered the apartment, and took a step toward Adam. His smile just about melted her heart.

"Oh yes," Adam said with huskiness in his voice, as he eased Summer into his arms. "When my siblings and I were growing up, my mother always planted sunflowers in the spring. By late summer, the backyard was loaded with various shades of the flowers. I remember that they were so bright and just made you want to smile. You, my dear, make me want to smile even when we are not together. So, you are my Sunflower."

He leaned in so that his lips brushed hers. Summer felt the warmth and the moisture of his breath as his lips pressed against hers. Adam's hands moved to her back. He drew her close so that their bodies touched, just enough to entice. One, or both of them, moaned from the pleasure of their closeness. When their lips parted, Summer realized that her hands had somehow found their way to Adam's neck, and the bottom of his hairline. She knew as she looked into Adam's eyes and felt his body against hers that it was questionable as to who was more aroused. Summer sighed. One thing she knew for certain. It was going to be a long night for both of them. "So, when is your divorce going to be finalized?" Adam asked with unmasked desire in his eyes. Summer released a breath laced with her own unfulfilled desire.

"It won't be too much longer," she quietly breathed out, as her fingers toyed with the pieces of his hair near his ears. Summer's voice remained soft as she added, "and then, I guess we had best figure out where we're going."

"Sweetheart," Adam nibbled on her earlobe as he quietly spoke. The whole time he was gently stroking the side of her back with his index finger. His gaze held hers as he spoke. "I think we both know where we're going together."

"Yes, we do." Summer held her gaze on Adam, lost in the sweetness of the moment, until he spoke.

"For now, my Sunflower, as much as I am enjoying this moment, you need to get to bed, and I need to get over to my office to do some more work."

"More work?" Summer exclaimed. "Adam, why didn't you tell me earlier this evening that you needed to go to your office?"

"Hey now," he tenderly tucked a piece of her hair behind her ear. "No regrets for this evening. We needed tonight for us. Just so you know, I often return to my office in the evening to work on my cases." He kissed her forehead then added, "Summer, I want you to know that for the rest of this week, I might not be able to spend time as much with you as we both would like." She looked worried. He drew her into his embrace. "Take that fret from your eyes. I'm working on some leads, so hopefully before too long, you may return home. Remember that even though I'm not here, you will not be alone. Someone from the department will still be watching over you around the clock as always, and I will call you." Adam quietly added, "And, Sunflower, you know you can call me night or day. Actually, I'd like for you to call me more than you already do."

"Really?" Adam nodded with a grin that made Summer smile. "Okay then, as long as I can call you, and you'll call me." Summer grew quiet. Adam watched her and waited for her to add, "Just do me a favor."

"What's that, sweetheart?"

"Stay safe." She sniffled.

"Always for you, Sunflower." One more kiss to her lips, and Adam stepped from her warm arms to the door. Summer closed and locked the door, then moved to the window to watch Adam drive off into the darkness of night.

—————

Adam held true to his word he had given Summer. If he did not call her, he left a text message for her. Summer did the same with him. Sometimes she would send a simple

> Hi, I'm thinking of you. Stay safe and come back to me soon.

Before too long, Summer would receive a message back from Adam. She knew without a doubt that he genuinely cared for her. It felt good to once again feel that she was special to a man, and this one was a truly good man. One late-morning text message caused Summer to walk out of the ranger station to sit on a shaded bench. She sat down, rubbed her eyes of the wetness that had suddenly emerged, and reread her text.

> Could it be I'm falling in love with a beautiful Sunflower?

There it was, clear as day in writing—the *L* word. For sometime, Adam had been implying that he loved her. But now, he had said it. Summer already knew that while her marriage was dying, she too was falling in love with him. This in itself was causing an internal struggle for her. Although in a matter of days, the judge would sign the papers and she would be divorced and free to love any man she so chose to love, for now, she was married. A smile formed on her lips as she reflected on her life and the one man whom she had already chosen to love and care for: Adam. Summer sighed. Before returning a text to him, she felt a tugging at her heart. She needed to talk with someone. Yes, indeed! She needed someone who knew her and could help her process her thoughts, even those she had not yet identified for herself. Summer needed her mom.

"Oh my goodness, what a wonderful surprise to brighten my day!" Summer knew the joy she heard in her mother's voice was real. She smiled.

"Hi, Mom. Glad you like your surprise." She listened to another exclamation of happiness from her, then Summer playfully added, "I was worried that you might not like my post-honeymoon welcome-home gift for you." Summer's smile grew as she listened to her mother laugh and comment.

"My Summer Sunshine, you are a delight. So now, tell me all your latest news. What's going on in your life? Then, I'll tell you what's happening here, and we can compare notes."

"Oh boy, I know that tone. Do I detect trouble in paradise?" Amanda made a ghastly noise into the phone. Summer held her phone from her ear, looked at it while shaking her head, returned the phone to her ear, and said, "I'll take your 'whatever noise' as a yes, and I know, you're not ready to share. So, I'll start by telling you about what's been happening since we had our meeting with Mitch and his lawyer."

"I do hope it's good news! Do you have any idea when the divorce will be finalized?"

"Unfortunately, no. Both Alex and Nikki have assured me it won't be too much longer now that the judge has our petition."

"So, it's the waiting game that is driving you crazy."

"Gee, Mom. Sometimes it is scary with how well you know me."

"My dear child, I've known since I brought you home from the hospital that patience is not one of your virtues." Summer listened to her mother chuckle and provide further comments about her patience, or the lack thereof.

"You know, Mom, sometimes your blunt honesty is just what I need. You're right. I'm not patient. Neither Mitchel or his lawyer will tell us everything that is going on with these mysterious plans Mitchel is making for his life after the divorce. Well, I take that back. Nikki and Alex, as my lawyers, know some of what is happening, but apparently they also don't know everything, and of course, they won't tell me what they do know. Mom, it's so frustrating. You know I don't like being left in the dark."

"Oh, I know all too well how you are. Honey, I know I've already said how you are not known for your patience. Unfortunately, that's exactly how you have to be at this point. Patient, and don't bother with that pout of yours." Summer huffed and rolled her eyes. She figured her mother was probably shaking her head as she spoke. "So, Summer, I suggest that you find something to take your mind off of your troubles with Mitchel."

"Mom, someone—not *something*—is the second part of my need to talk with you." Summer listened. It sounded as if her mother was coughing, or perhaps choking. "Mom, are you all right?"

"Uh-huh," Amanda cleared her throat. Her voice was filled with surprise when she spoke. "Did you just say *someone*, as in perhaps a new man being in your life is the other reason for you calling me?"

"Oh yes." Summer felt her heart jump as she thought of Adam. "You heard correctly. I have a new man in my life."

"Summer, I know how high your standards are for yourself. You're still married."

"You're right. I do have high standards, and by law, I'm still married. However, we haven't—hey, wait a minute. You and Kevin didn't wait until his divorce was final to pursue your relationship."

"No, we didn't. Perhaps we should have."

"Oh no! Mom, I can tell by your voice and what you are not saying that something is wrong."

"I'm just surprised to hear you talking about a new man being in your life, when earlier this year, you had sworn off men. As your mother, I just hope you're not rushing into a new relationship before you are ready."

"Mom, I know what I said, and I am eating some of my words. Before I continue, please allow me to apologize for perhaps stepping out of line with my statement about you and Kevin."

"Apology accepted. Thank you, Summer."

"You're welcome. The last thing I want or need is for you to be upset with me. So, let me tell you about Adam." Summer talked. Amanda listened and asked the probing questions that helped Summer explore her true feelings. "You know, Mom, you always help me to see things more clearly. I guess I am truly falling in love and have something wonderful to look forward to in the future."

"That you do, Summer. By not rushing into something physical between you and Adam, you do have something very special to look forward to." Amanda drew in a breath. Summer knew by the silence that something was truly amiss in her mother's life.

"Mom," Summer hesitated, then forged on saying, "are you having regrets for giving yourself to Kevin early on in your relationship, and then marrying him?"

"No. Of course not."

"Then, Mom, what's troubling you? Do I need to call Kevin and chew him out for something that he did, or didn't do?"

With that, Amanda chuckled. Summer knew it wasn't the one in which her mother was truly amused by something. Her mother was trying to make light of a situation.

"You don't need to chew anyone out on my behalf. I'm just feeling very uncomfortable about a wedding that we have to attend in a month."

"Mom, you love to attend weddings. I know Dad isn't getting married, so, tell me what is stressing you out? Whose wedding is it, and why is this wedding making you uncomfortable?"

"With everything that's been going on in your life, Kevin's and my wedding, I didn't mention to you that Kevin's youngest son, Brian, is getting married."

"Oh. My. Gosh." Summer drew out every word for impact. "Oh. My. Gosh! Mom, this totally explains everything. You'll be attending the wedding as the second wife, the other woman, the stepmom. Eek! Oh. My. Gosh!"

"Will you stop with the 'oh my gosh'? I get it. You're in shock."

"I'm sorry, Mom. I just don't know what to say. You know, you're the one who always has the right words for any situation, not me." Summer paused only to hear silence, then added, "Does it help to know that I love you?"

A sniffling sound was heard, followed by, "It sure does, more than you will ever know, and I love you too, Summer. You know, Sunshine, right now I simply wish I could take a leave of absence and fly—no, make that drive out to Denver to be with you to help you through the end of your divorce, and whatever Mitchel is up to."

"I also wish that you could be here, but I also understand why it is impossible for you to come out here to be with me. You know, Dad has told me that he is willing to come out and stay with me for a week or two if I want him to."

"Really."

"You're smiling, aren't you."

"Yes. I am. Summer, honey, perhaps you should take your father up on his offer. I know I'd feel better knowing he was there with you." Summer smiled as she heard the tenderness and approval in her mother's voice.

"Well, Mom, I think you've helped me answer another one of my topics for consideration. It looks like I'll be calling Dad next."

"Glad I could help." She sighed. "Honey, as much as I'm enjoying talking with you—"

"I know. You need to get back to work." Now, Summer sighed. "Unfortunately, so do I. I love you, Mom. Thanks for being so awesome and helping me."

"I love you too, my Summer Sunshine. Before we go, I have one more question for you."

Summer knew that with her mother, the sky was the limit for what she might have on her mind. She waited, and then the question came—not at all what she was expecting. "Do you by chance have a picture of this hot detective of yours that you might share with me?"

Summer erupted into laughter. "I'll see what I can do." She was still laughing as she placed her phone back into her pocket. Her call to her dad would have to wait as duty calls.

17

Summer had awakened with a feeling of restlessness. Earlier in the week, she had spoken with her dad. Knowing that he was planning on coming out to see her had brightened her spirits immensely. While Summer had spent only one evening with Adam, she knew he was working hard and making slow progress on her case. Since the two most important men in her life were causing her to feel better about life, perhaps it was her recent conversation with her mother that had left her feeling unsettled on that late summer morning.

With coffee in hand, Summer walked over to the door, opened it, and made her ascent to the backyard to sit in the quiet of morning on the patio by the pool and think. Once settled in a chair at the end of the pool farthest from the patio door, Summer took a sip of coffee. While feeling the hot amber liquid slide down her throat, she took out her phone and hit one of her favorite speed dial numbers.

"Hello, beautiful!" Nathan's voice was filled with a smile, which in turn caused Summer to smile.

"Good morning, Nathan. Is this a good time for us to talk?"

"It sure is. I just left the judge's chambers at city court. My client opted to take the plea deal, so there will not be a trial."

"Oh wow. That's good news. I'm glad to know I'm not interrupting you from your work. I was afraid you might not have time to talk."

"Sum, of course I'd find time to talk with you. Actually, talking with you while I walk back to my car is perfect—no one to interrupt us on my end. I was going to call you later on today to check in on you and see how you're holding up."

"Aww. Thanks. Nate, I'm doing the only thing I can do. I'm hanging in there."

"Good to hear. Although from the sound of your voice, you're not as good as you want everyone to believe. So, my friend, talk with me."

"Nate, besides my divorce that seems to be taking forever—"

"It's really not that long," he quietly interjected.

"Easy for you to say, counselor, you're not going through the divorce."

"Noted."

"Sorry, Nate. You of all people did not deserve my snappiness." Summer took a sip of coffee. "Nate, you know from our conversations and our conference calls with Nikki and Alex that Mitchel is up to something."

"Right." Nathan could tell that Summer truly was a bundle of nerves. He only hoped that the mess would be resolved soon—rather than later—for Summer's sake. In his opinion, she was one of the most beautiful women—no, make that *people*—in the world. Kind. Compassionate. Intelligent. The perfect woman for him, if only he had romantic inclinations toward her, rather than considering her his ultimate best friend. His voice remained calm; however, it took on a quieter tone to cause her to listen more intently to him. "Summer, do you remember what I told you when we were sitting together on the porch of my parents' cabin?"

"Yes. You promised to be here for me."

"Exactly. Now, work with me through the events of this summer. How many phone conferences and private conversations have we had?"

"Too many to count." Summer sniffled, and as she did, she took a tissue from her pocket to dab her eyes and wipe her nose. Leave it to Nate to bring on the tears by reminding her of how her friend has been there for her. Nate had his own busy life both professionally and personally, and yet, he always managed to find time for her. Besides that, when they were conversing, he made her feel as though she was the only one in his life who mattered to him.

"Correct. Too many to count, not that I was keeping score with you, as you're in my *special persons club* and don't come with requirements, other than being my best friend." He heard Summer's sniffles and privately wished he could be there to give her a hug. At that moment in time, it was impossible. So Nathan simply continued talking and hoped that he would console his friend in her time of need. "Sum, I am already making plans to be out there with you for your final court appearance. Hopefully, within the next few days after your divorce is final, we'll find out what the weasel is up to. Now, if we have calculated the timing correctly, your divorce should be final right after Brian Wentzel's wedding."

"Kevin's son," she breathed out while her mind replayed some of her previous conversation with her mother.

"Right. His wedding is on the third Saturday of September. My parents and I have been invited to attend his wedding. My plan is to fly out on Sunday to be with you, as well as spend some much-needed vacation time away from work. I'm hoping the weather will still be nice enough to allow me time to lay out by the pool at Nikki and Alex's home."

"Vacation time!" she exclaimed. "Nate, how will going to court with me be vacation time?"

"Simple. I get to relax and enjoy watching Nikki and Alex do all of the work for you. My job will be to simply be your friend supporting you through your ordeal. Plus, I get to be your mother's spy and check out this detective of yours."

"Mom's spy! Oh great," Summer sighed. "Sounds like Mom's being a bloodhound again."

"Bloodhound, as in dog?"

"Right. Nate, it's nothing—really, just a private joke between my dad and me." Summer was suddenly concerned that Nathan might say something to her mother about her comment. Given how uptight she knew that her mother was, that was the last thing she needed to have happen. "Nate, you won't say—"

"Of course not. Although knowing your mother, I have a pretty good idea of what you were insinuating about her."

"Nate." There was pleading in Summer's voice.

"Relax, Sum. We're best friends, who know we need to keep our secrets from our nosy moms." They both laughed while Nate added, "And I, being an attorney, have an edge on both of our mothers."

"Oh really."

"Sure, Summer, I may use my attorney-client privilege for this call, or any of our calls that we want to keep private."

"Thank you, Nate." Summer took a sip of coffee. She heard what sounded like a door opening, or perhaps closing. "Nate, do you need to go?"

"No, not yet. I just got in my car and am starting the air-conditioning. It's ninety-six degrees."

"Oh yuck! I remember those hot late-summer, early-fall days all too well. That's too hot."

"It is. But I know you, Sum, and you don't want to hear about the weather here on the east coast. So, besides your divorce, which we've covered, what else is going on?"

"Earlier you mentioned Kevin's son's wedding."

"Yes."

"Okay, here it goes." She drew in a breath. "Since Mom wants you to spy on me, don't you think it's only fair for me to want you—no, make that, I *need* for you to be my spy and check up on her for me."

"Oh boy. First, Amanda, and now you. This is serious."

"Very." Summer's tone revealed just how serious it was for her. "Nathan, I am truly worried about Mom. I thought that if you had any pro bono work to do at the center for your mom, or my mom, that you could ease into a conversation about the upcoming wedding. You know, so that it would not make Mom suspicious of my concern for how she is handling all the preparation Kevin is involved in with his family and of course, Meg."

"You're sneaky."

"Very. I know my mother, and as I already have stated, I am very worried about her."

"Tell me what exactly is worrying you."

With that, Summer shared her concerns with Nathan. He asked questions, made comments, and Summer responded.

"Well now, Summer, I do see your reasons for concern. You know I love your mom, as if she were my aunt. Actually, I love her more than some of my aunts and often have wished I was related to her instead of them."

"Aww. That's really nice, Nate. Have you ever told Mom what you just shared with me?"

"No, I haven't."

"Well, I think she would appreciate hearing that, especially now with everything that is going on."

"If the time is right, I will. Hey, did I ever tell you about my childhood fantasy toward your mother?"

"No, you haven't. Do I want to hear about your fantasy?"

"It might give you something to laugh about."

"Why am I feeling fearful?" Summer drew in a breath while feeling unsure about hearing what Nathan had to say to her.

Nathan chuckled. "Because you know what I say will be the truth for how I felt toward your mom. So here it is. When I was...oh, between the ages of nine and twelve I guess, I fell in love with your mom. I proclaimed to my parents that when I grew up, I was going to ask her to marry me."

Summer burst in to laughter. Tears streamed down her cheeks. "Oh, Nathan, that's so sweet. You wanted to marry Mom. Aww." Summer sobered from her laughter. "But you know, it's also creepy."

"I know. When I hit thirteen, I discovered that you were becoming cute in a different way than when we were younger, and I thought age-wise, I might stand a better chance with you. Sum, you know, looking back on our lives of where we were and where we are now, I'm still in love with three amazing women."

"Three?" Summer asked, with curiosity in her voice, as to why Nathan was laughing. Then he spoke. "Did you expect me to leave my mother out of this?"

Now, Summer burst into laughter. Nathan had helped her to gain a place of calm by the time she hit End on her phone at the completion of their call. Her friend was going to be her eyes and ears keeping watch over her mother whenever possible. She didn't doubt that he'd somehow manage to elicit his parents' help as well. Releasing a slow breath, Summer closed her eyes and placed her head back on the chair to rest, to soak in the sun shining down on her. This was what she needed before heading in to work. Before too long, she felt a shadow come over her, momentarily blocking the sun. Summer opened her eyes and saw Alex sit down in the chair next to hers.

"Good morning, Alex." She smiled. "It's a beautiful day, don't you think?"

Alex allowed his gaze to pass over Summer before he spoke. "It is a beautiful day. You are obviously in a better mood than when you initially sat down out here."

"You saw me?"

He gently smiled and nodded. "I was going to come out for my early morning swim, but then I saw you come out here with your coffee and phone in hand. It was obvious that you needed your time, more than I needed my swim. So, I made breakfast for Nikki and me and got ready to head into the office with her. She's already been working since five this morning."

Guilt immediately took residence on Summer's face. "Wow, I'm sorry to have intruded on your morning routine. I guess I never realized that you swim in the morning, as well as at night."

"It's no problem, Summer. As it turns out, we received a call from Mitchel's lawyer."

"Oh."

"Yes. She, along with Mitchel, wants to meet with us next week to discuss how he wants to provide for you after the divorce is granted."

"Alex, I already told him that he didn't have to do anything for me." Summer felt the good mood Nate had helped her achieve, being swept away like the tide carrying her out to sea from the Chesapeake Bay. The restlessness was returning. There was a feeling of impending doom.

"Summer, I know what you said to Mitchel. In all fairness to him and to bring needed closure to your marriage, you need to hear him out."

"You know what he wants to do?" Summer looked intently into her friend's eyes. She saw his concern for her.

"Not everything." Alex kept his eyes on Summer, watching her process everything that had already been said between them. "However, Summer, I do know more of what is transpiring in Mitchel's life. At this point, all I may say to you is that you will be surprised. Mitchel is not the man whom we all thought him to be."

"That's both comforting and making me more uncomfortable at the same time. That man sure knows how to give me heartburn!" Summer glanced down at her watch. "Duty calls. Time to head to the park." She sighed. "On a day like today, with everything I have on my mind, I only wish I could get out on the trails instead of staying at the office."

"It won't be much longer."

"That's what everyone keeps telling me. You know, Alex, there's cabin fever—and then there's cabin fever." With that said,

Summer stood and listened to Alex's consoling words before disappearing into her apartment.

———

The warm summer day was progressing nicely for Summer and Cathy as they greeted visitors to the national park. Every opportunity to be outside was snatched up by both women. During the late morning, Bill stopped over to invite Cathy to attend a concert and barbeque in the park during the upcoming weekend as a benefit for the Wounded Warriors of Denver. Of course, while Bill was there, he filled Summer in on all of the news of the preserve. The beaver were being rascals and a headache for Wayne and everyone else by damming up the stream, which now flowed around the original tributary, which some years ago they had claimed as home. Laughter filled the porch of the rangers station. Bill went on to tell Summer that the doe and her fawn were thriving. An unexpected tear slid down Summer's cheek as she listened to Bill rave about how he would spot them on the range and in the thicket looking over toward the office.

"Summer, I have a feeling that when you are able to come to volunteer with us at the preserve, the deer will come up from the thicket to the fence to welcome you back."

Summer half smiled as sadness oozed from her moist eyes. She longed to have her life back, and the freedom to check on the deer as she pleased. "That would be nice. If you both will excuse me, I think I'll go over and see if I may help our visitors who are looking at the map of trails leading through the forest."

———

A while after Bill had left, Summer stood out on the porch of the office. She was gazing toward the area where visitors were warned not to venture because of the potentially dangerous bear family. Summer knew the unmarked car was in the parking lot with the officer somewhere in the woods keeping his surveillance. She had to wonder how much longer Adam was going to be able to justify her protection, and then have the officers pulled from her case to pursue other more important situations.

"Hey, Summer," Cathy's voice calling out to her through the screen door pulled Summer from her thoughts to the present. "Could you come here for a minute?"

"I'm on my way," Summer said, while taking one more long look toward the end of the parking lot.

"I still cannot get the camera on the north side of the building to come in clearly on the monitor. It's as if a bird did its business on the lens or something."

Summer had heard Cathy fussing about the monitor for the camera earlier in the day. Things like this happened with technology, and were to be expected, especially since the park's cameras were not the newest ones out there on the market.

"Have you looked at the film from last night?" Summer offered. "Maybe there was wind or squirrels on the roof that knocked the camera from its normal position. You know, Cathy, there could be a logical explanation besides birds as the reason for the camera not filming clearly."

Cathy continued to sputter about budgets and outdated equipment, while Summer walked over to view the monitor with her. Looking at the footage from the previous night, it was obvious that something had occurred up on the roof. But what?

"Well, since you don't care for height, and I'm younger than you, I guess I'm elected to go up on the roof and see what is going on." Summer noticed the grin that appeared on Cathy's face. "Smile all you want, my friend. Remember, there is such a thing as payback." Summer's twinkling smile in her eyes revealed she was teasing.

Summer walked around to the back of the building and headed for the storage shed that housed ladders, wood for fixing tables, and benches, as well as other supplies and tools that might be needed there at the station. As she passed by the west side of the rangers station, she looked for anything that might be out of the ordinary, both on the ground and up in the trees. Call her paranoid. Perhaps, thanks to spending time with Adam, she was simply more acutely aware of her surroundings.

Summer paused by the corner of the station. Something didn't look right with the aging bushes that had been planted many years ago. The small branches were broken, or intentionally pushed back with force to enable someone, or something, access to the side of the building. Remaining on the beaten path, Summer looked at the wall about a foot or so from the corner of the building. She had to wonder if those were scratch marks. Bear? Could be. But that didn't make sense. There was no reason for a bear to climb the building with so many trees in the area. Next choice for leaving the marks—human. Summer felt her lungs constrict. Her thoughts made her fearful for hers and Cathy's safety.

Cautiously studying the ground as she went, Summer made her way on to the shed to get the ladder out so that she could climb on to the roof. When she opened the door, she found a mess. Paint cans were knocked off the shelves. Wood that had been neatly piled against the wall was now knocked over and scattered onto the floor. Besides that, the ladder was not on the hooks on the wall, but carelessly thrown on top of the wood. Someone had vandalized the shed. She immediately stepped away from the shed, leaving everything as it was and began placing calls.

―――

George Davidson had not been pleased with the idea of Summer continuing to work after he heard of the attempt on her life. While the Denver police had assured him that they would protect her, he knew all too well that "where there's a will, there's a way." If someone truly wanted to kill Summer here at the park, he knew that they could do it. So far, they had been fortunate that no one had tried. Now, he had an act of vandalism to pursue. George hoped in the deepest muscle of his heart that the situation would turn out to be teenage pranksters. His gut told him otherwise.

When George got out of his official park pickup, he saw Cathy frantically pacing on the front porch. He did not immediately see Summer. George hoped that meant she had sense enough to be inside the building. However, knowing Summer, she had to be doing something to pursue answers to the break-in, and would not wait for the park police to arrive.

Gorge was making his way up the steps greeting Cathy, informing her of the time it would take for the park police to get to them, when they saw a vehicle speeding through the parking lot toward them. Dirt was kicked up forming a dust cloud behind the car, which was now slowing to a stop. George immediately recognized the man in a dark suit as Summer's protector, Detective Adam North. He stepped down off the steps to greet the officer. Granted, the detective did not have jurisdiction in the park, but George knew better than to not welcome another set of trained eyes. Plus, he also knew how much Summer needed the detective to be there—wherever she might be.

"Detective." George held out his hand to greet Adam, who did the same. While their hands were still clasped together, they both heard a noise on the roof.

"Oh, Adam, you're here." It was then that they saw Summer standing on the roof on the opposite side of the building from where she had seen the damage to the bushes. "Hey, George. Glad you could make it!"

"Summer," they both exclaimed. It was difficult to say who was more surprised to find her on the roof.

"I'm sure you have a good reason for being up there. So let me go ahead and ask, how did you get up there, and why are you up there?" Adam was concerned for her safety, a good twelve or so feet above the ground.

"Good questions, Adam, and I do have a logical explanation for you." She smiled sweetly at the two men who continued to watch her as she remained perched like a large beautiful bird on the edge of the slightly pitched roof ready to take flight at a moment's notice.

By now, Cathy had come down off the porch to stand with the men. She quietly chuckled. Her eyes sparkled as she called up to Summer, "Oh, there you are. Did you find anything interesting?"

"I have." Summer smiled down at her friend, then added, "Something very interesting. Detective I think this is more than a park issue. So you might want to join me."

"I will if you tell me what you used in place of the ladder to make your ascent onto the roof."

Summer's smile seemed to fill her whole body. "Easy," she said, as she stood and turned her gaze toward the large evergreen alongside of the cabin. "You see this big old tree?" Her eyes danced with joy as Adam responded. "Well, if you aren't concerned about soiling your clothes, or perhaps tearing them, you may climb up the branches and shimmy out on the limb to the roof, just as I did."

"You sure didn't see that one coming, did you?" Cathy quietly asked, as she watched Adam.

"Did you know that is how she got up there?" His gaze was zeroed in on Cathy, as if she had just been caught leaving the scene of a crime and was about to be interrogated by him.

Cathy was finding the whole scene a bit amusing. "I figured since I did not hear her go up onto the roof with the ladder, that she found another way. Our girl is smart. She knows how to use what nature provides us. Besides that, Summer knew to stay away from the other side of the building where someone had obviously made, or tried, to make their way onto the roof. Over here she could look at the other cameras as well as the roof, and hopefully not disturb any useful evidence."

Adam nodded. His expression softened about one degree before he returned his attention to the roof. "She sure is something," Adam breathed out. "All right, Summer, I'm coming up."

Summer moved from her squatting position near the edge of the roof to be closer to watch Adam make his ascent. From there, she was able to guide him to the best limbs for him to place his large feet, clad in his well-polished black shoes. Having left his suit coat in the capable hands of Cathy, Adam was not as constricted clothing-wise. Still, it was an arduous ascent given the smooth soles of his shoes, which caused him to slip on the branches, and his dress shirt that tightened against his back muscles as he climbed. More than once, Summer held her breath for fear Adam might fall.

"Adam, be careful. That limb I shimmied out on might not be strong enough for your weight. If you don't think it will hold you, go up to the next limb to your right. Whatever you do, please be careful."

Upon making his way successfully to the roof, Adam stood still to gain his balance. He drew in a calming breath. There was no way in heck that he would admit to Summer that he was deathly afraid of heights.

"Hi," she said, as she slid her arms around his waist. "Nice of you to join me."

"Nice of you to invite me." He drew her close. His eyes probed her eyes that seemed to be sparkling like diamonds in the sunlight and dancing with excitement. "So, what have you found up here?"

Summer noticed that Adam was not easing his hold on her. She also noticed something in his eyes for only a split second. Something was there that informed her he was hanging on to her for the duration. Realizing that they would probably be up there for a while, Summer suggested that they sit down on the roof.

"Feel better?" she quietly asked, while gently stroking his forearm with her fingers.

"I am," he said while drawing his arm around her, "and you, my dear, are a very perceptive woman. You figured it out that I have an issue with heights."

"I did. May I share a secret fear of mine with you?"

"Sure."

"I hate spiders. One of my biggest fears is getting bitten by a deadly one, and dying right there on the spot. Pretty stupid fear for someone working with nature, wouldn't you say?"

"Not at all. Your fear is as real as my fear of heights." He took her hand in his. "I'll make a deal with you. I'll protect you from spiders as long as you help me conquer my fear of heights."

"Deal." Summer breathed out a long slow breath, as she focused in on the reason for them sitting on the roof of the rangers station. "So, do you want to see what I've found and hear my theory?"

"Of course."

As the two sat on the roof, Summer pointed to the other side of the roof to the camera that had been in question earlier in the day by both her and Cathy. She went on to share what she had observed while on the ground and her suspicions about the roof.

"Look down there." Summer pointed out toward the far end of the parking lot where the old barricaded road was prohibiting people from journeying too close to the bear family. Adam studied the area Summer was pointing to. "The camera that is in question is the one that shows that area of the lot. Adam, I've been thinking about that area for a while, not just today. I've had this gnawing feeling that I can't seem to shake. What if—" Adam began to speak. She placed her hand on his leg. His muscles immediately tightened with her soft touch. "Please, let me finish." He nodded. "I know I have protection. But, I also have a theory. For some reason we've yet to learn, someone wants me dead. By now, they obviously know that you, as in you and the department, are protecting me while at work, and then at Nikki and Alex's home. So, they can't get as close to me as the first time when they tried to take me out." Adam nodded as he listened to Summer. "If someone was down in those trees with a high-powered rifle and scope, they could be sitting up in the tree even before we get here in the morning. The full limbs of the evergreens make a perfect shield to blind them from our sight. By taking out the camera, no movement or reflection of the metal of the gun would be seen on the monitor. Then, when I came out into the open—pow! No more Summer."

Adam sat perfectly still. He looked at the end of the lot and then into Summer's glistening eyes. "Summer, you are amazing. Everything you have said makes sense and bears looking into. You don't suppose there would be anyway I could lure you away from working here to working with me on solving crimes?"

"Thanks, but no thanks. I'll leave catching the bad people to you, and continue communing with nature."

Adam and Summer remained on the roof. She called Nikki and Alex while Adam called in to the precinct, giving Micah and his captain a heads-up about what had been found at the park. Given the fact that Summer was directly or indirectly involved in the situation, the captain, unbeknownst to Summer, placed a call to the FBI. The park police, unsure of whom had jurisdiction, had called in the sheriff to assist. The shed along with the side of the building were dusted for finger prints, and casts were made of footprints. Small pieces of fiber were removed from the bushes and placed in evidence bags. Before too long, FBI Special Agent Carp appeared. After talking with the Denver police and sheriff's deputies, he made his way over to the rangers station to talk with Adam. Removing his suit coat, revealing his weapon in his holster, he willingly climbed up the tree to join Summer and Adam on the roof. Summer was surprised to learn that he already knew of the previous murder attempt but would not provide further insight as to why the FBI was interested in her well-being. All Summer knew was that he agreed with her observations and commended her for being cognoscente of her need to protect herself from harm.

"Ms. Newman," Special Agent Carp said, while standing and watching the work being completed on the ground, "if you don't mind, I'd like to have a private word with Detective North. You're free to climb on down the tree."

"Of course." Summer turned to Adam. "Detective, I'll be waiting for you at the bottom of the tree." He nodded, while his eyes spoke words of concern and love. With that, Summer walked over to the branch and began to shimmy over to the trunk of the tree.

Summer had just come up from diving into the cool, refreshing water of Nikki and Alex's pool, when Alex informed her that they had company. She swam over to the edge of the pool and lifted her body out of the water. As she came to her feet, Nikki and Adam walked through the patio doors. She could tell by his smile and laughter that he was in a good mood. Toweling off, Summer slipped into her cotton cover-up, which barely covered her bottom. Slipping into Adam's arms, she knew he would soon feel the wetness of her suit and body. His lips found hers. At that moment, nothing else mattered for either of them.

Pop! The sound caused Summer to jump before they drew apart. Summer saw what Alex was doing, and then asked, "What is the champagne for?"

Adam's gaze was filled with love as he looked into her eyes. He gently stroked her cheek with his pointer finger. "The bubbly is for you."

"Me?"

"Yes, we're toasting you and your willingness to see your crises through to the bitter end with grace." Adam saw the color rising in her cheeks. He drew in her scent as well as the odor of chlorine on her skin. "It's over, honey."

"What? It's over, as in I can go home?"

"It sure is. Thanks to the break-in at the rangers station and evidence we found, connections were made, and the guilty parties are behind bars. Now, we are going to celebrate."

Filled glasses were passed around the circle, and everyone took a turn toasting each other. Needless to say, it did not take too long for the bottle to be empty. Then, Adam shared the news with them about how the pieces of the investigation had led them to the criminal.

As it turned out, the Denver and Boulder police had been working together, watching and suspecting Jesslyn Octivani as either the attempted assassin or the money source behind the scene. When they had questioned Mitchel and Jesslyn in the Boulder precinct, they had gotten her fingerprints, but nothing to match them to, that is, until she and her accomplice had gone to the rangers station the other night. Summer felt as if she was in a dream with everything she was hearing. While Jesslyn was in Alaska, she was scheming to get rid of Summer, whom she saw as hurting the man she loved and the father of her child.

"Oh my. Does Mitchel know about the baby—that he told me was nonexistent?"

"He does now. The poor man is in shock."

"Oh, how awful," Nikki added.

"It is. Ms. Octivani is now locked up in the county jail for breaking and entering at the National Park Rangers Station and conspiracy to commit murder, which includes her hiring a hit man. Word on the street is, Octivani is so angry with his daughter, that he has refused to pay her legal fees or her bail. The last I heard, Mitchel's lawyer is going to represent her."

"I don't believe it, it's over," Summer whispered, as she slumped into the chair. A tear fell. She looked from Adam to her friends who were all smiling. "Adam, you promised me that you would keep me safe and find the person who wanted me dead. You did that and more. Thank you." With that, Summer began to cry very real tears, which had been stored up inside of her for too long. Adam knelt down on the ground next to her and gently pulled her into his arms.

18

S ummer was up the crack of dawn loading her belongings into her Jeep. The workday was filled with joyful moments, as she impatiently waited for her shift to end, and return home. Finally her shift was over. As Summer slowly drove down her street, she looked at her neighbors' homes, and everything that was familiar to her. Moisture began to form in her eyes as she noticed everything that had changed, and not changed, in her neighborhood. She slowly pulled her Jeep loaded with her clothes and items she had purchased during her stay at Nikki and Alex's into her driveway. Summer felt her heart do a flip-flop. A renegade tear slid down her cheek.

The first thing Summer did upon standing in her driveway was to draw in a deep breath. Ah, not-so-refreshing familiar smells of suburban air. Home. Summer smiled, yes, she was finally home. Just as she was walking around the back of the vehicle, a familiar car slowed on the street in front of her home. The driver pulled up to the curb and stopped. Summer smiled and waved as she headed toward the car.

"Hey, beautiful. Welcome home," Adam called out.

"Oh, thank you, Adam," Summer said while nearly tumbling into his embrace. He drew his strong arms possessively around her. "Detective," she teasingly asked, "I'm wondering, do you greet all your female crime victims by calling them beautiful?"

"Most assuredly *not!*"

"Mmm. I like hearing that. Goodness, you smell and feel good. I bet I'm not smelling all that desirable right now since I was up on the trails for the whole day."

"The whole day?"

"Ye-up! The whole day! Oh, Adam, today was an awesome day for me. You have no idea of how wonderful it was, to be free to resume my normal daily work activities and go out on the trails." Her eyes sparkled as her smile grew. "It was as if the animals knew I had returned, and came out to greet me along the way."

"I'm glad for you, sweetheart." Adam's lips brushed hers. "Just so you know, you feel good in my arms, and you wear sweat nicely."

With that, Summer moved her lips possessively against Adam's lips. He playfully nibbled on her lower lip. Summer sighed, as Adam ended the kiss entirely too soon for her.

"Shall we head on in, so you can see the repairs and improvements that have been made to your home during your absence?"

"Sure," Summer's voice revealed she was still regaining her composure from their kiss. "I saw that my carport was no longer falling down, thank you very much. What else have you done around here during my absence?"

Adam smiled. His eyes had taken on a look of mischievousness as he gently tucked his arm around Summer, drawing her to his side. "Come with me, my beautiful Sunflower, and I'll show you." Summer stuck her hand into her pants pocket to pull out her keys as they made their way across the grass to the front walkway and steps. Adam smiled as he watched her from the corner of his eye. Then, he said with an edge of amusement in his voice, "Summer, you won't be needing those keys any longer for the locks on your house."

She abruptly stopped midstep and turned to Adam. Her brows were drawing close with concern. "Why not, pray tell?"

"Well, honey, while you were gone, we had a new alarm system installed, as well as new bulletproof windows and doors along with new locks installed." He reached into his pocket and pulled out a new set of keys. "These are for all of your doors."

Summer took the keys Adam was holding out to her. "Adam, you said *we*, as in more people than just you, did this for me. Who else do I have to thank for this kindness?"

"Nikki, Alex, and your friend Nathan."

"Nathan?" Adam nodded as he watched Summer process his words. "I can understand Nikki and Alex involved in this with you, but Nathan?"

"Oh yes. He's quite a character, and I look forward to meeting him."

"A character is one way to describe Nate." She was giving Adam her "I'm not sure I'm going to like this" look. Adam could see the concern in her bright wide-open eyes.

"Summer, honey, I want you to feel safe when you are here. Since I can't be here twenty-four–seven, I already had plans underway for installing a new security system for you. After consulting with your friends, and my colleagues at work who are also concerned for your safety," he couldn't help but smile, as he spoke. "You now have the same security system my colleagues and I use." He saw the tear drop from the edge of her eyelid onto her cheek and tumble downward. Reaching his thumb over to her cheek, Adam gently swiped the tear away. "Your friends—I guess I should say *our* friends—were glad to hear what I was doing for you and have readily assisted with the financial investment. It was Nathan who contacted Nikki and Alex and suggested the new bulletproof windows and doors. So if you're ready to accuse me of being overprotective, blame Nathan about your new windows and doors. If I remember correctly, Nathan said that as long as we are protecting you, we might as well go all the way."

"I can't believe you all did this for me." Summer now stood in the middle of her living room. She looked around, amazed by what she saw.

"Summer, do you want to see what else we did for you?"

"In a minute. Adam, before we begin the grand tour, I'd like for you to show me again how to turn off the alarm and then reprogram the system. Then, by all means, you may show me my other surprises."

After Adam showed Summer the new screen and other repairs on her porch, Summer made a small grocery list of items needed for dinner. She hastily reached into the freezer and pulled a package of venison steaks out, which they would thaw and grill later that evening. While Adam was away from the house, Summer had showered and changed into fresh clean clothes. Oh, it felt good to be back home in her bedroom with all of her familiar things around her. She was enjoying her quiet time alone and took her time moving through her home. Returning to the kitchen, Summer scrubbed a few large potatoes, put them in a small kettle, and on to cook along with the eggs that were hard-boiling for the salad she planned to make for dinner. Her bare feet made patting sounds as she moved across the floor. Midstep, Summer stopped. "Darn," she exclaimed to herself. "Dessert! What am I going to make with not much time to prepare anything? Besides that, what do I have to make?"

She scratched her head, and then had an aha moment. Of course. The berries she had frozen last year. On her way to the freezer in the mudroom, Summer lectured herself for not seeing or thinking about taking the berries out of the freezer when she had hastily removed the steaks. Upon pulling the quart bag from the freezer, Summer saw something in the back of the freezer on the bottom shelf. The package was unfamiliar to her and looked suspicious. After taking the berries into the kitchen and placing them on the counter, Summer called Adam.

"Sunflower, you did the right thing not touching the package and calling me. It may well be something Mitchel hid, and may not even belong to him."

"Oh, Adam. I really didn't want to hear that."

"I know, sweetheart. You and I both know that anything is possible where Mitchel is concerned."

"You're right." Summer sighed. "I just want this nightmare with him to be over."

"It will be very soon."

"How close are you to my house?"

"I'm two blocks away, Summer. I'll come to your side door and in through the mudroom. Don't turn off your alarm until you see me get out of the car." It was obvious to Summer that Adam was once again in full police detective mode.

"Yes, sir," she teasingly responded.

"Smart aleck," Adam responded. Of course, both of them were laughing as they ended their call.

———

Summer watched for Adam through her monitor in the kitchen. As she watched, she saw her next-door neighbor come home. A dog was running down the sidewalk with three kids about junior-high age chasing after it. Summer chuckled. Then, she saw Adam come into view slowing down his vehicle and turn into the driveway. When she saw him physically get out of the car, come around to the passenger side, and grab the two bags of groceries, she turned off the alarm and opened the door. Summer's eyes sparkled with joy like fireworks on the Fourth of July lighting up the sky.

"Oh, Adam, I felt so safe while I was here by myself. It was so nice to be able to watch for you to get here."

"I'm glad that you feel safe."

"You didn't by any chance see some kids from the neighborhood chasing a dog?"

"As a matter of fact, I did." He saw the concern in her eyes as he spoke. "As I was approaching them, one of the boys was making a tackle."

"Oh."

"I wouldn't be too concerned. The dog had surrendered and was licking the kid." He saw the concern disappear from her eyes. Relief took its place. One thing remained constant, and that was Summer Newman sure did care about all creatures, domestic or wild.

—⚬—

Adam listened to Summer tell him about the package she had found as they walked into the kitchen together. After placing the bags of groceries on the counter, Adam walked back out to the mudroom with Summer and opened the freezer door. He looked in and saw the package Summer was pointing to. His eyes met hers as he sighed and pulled his phone.

"That bad?" Summer asked while watching Adam's expression grow more serious as the seconds ticked away.

"It might be." He held up a finger. "Hey, Micah, I need you to take a drive over here to Summer's place. Yeah, she's finally back in town, safe and sound." He smiled and winked at her. Summer released a heavy breath as she watched him. "We have a mysterious package in the freezer. Right. Better give the DA a heads-up so she knows because we're pretty sure this belongs to Dr. Mitchel Brown. I'm also calling the captain so that he can notify the Feds. Right. Looks like we're probably sharing this with the FBI." Adam returned his phone to his belt clip. He noticed that Summer stood there shaking her head as she looked into the freezer.

"The FBI again? I thought they were finished with Jesslyn being caught." Worry lines formed on Summer's brow as she whispered out, "Oh, Mitchel, what have you done?"

Adam closed the door and pulled her close. "Summer, honey, we're just making sure we've included everyone who might have an interest in your husband, his associates, and his activities. For now, there is nothing we can do about the package. Let's go on into the kitchen and work on preparing dinner while we wait for Micah and the others to get here."

Summer nodded and walked back into her kitchen. The eggs were now very hard-boiled with only a skimming of water preventing the shells from burning, while the potatoes were just right. After saving the eggs and soaking them in cold water, Summer took a deep breath and unsuccessfully attempted to relax, while continuing to make dinner. She knew that Adam was right. Mitchel had placed that package in the freezer, but when? Why had she not seen it before today? There were too many questions in Summer's mind, and no immediate answers.

While Summer quietly chopped onion and green pepper for the salad, Adam quietly spoke on his phone. She glanced at him as he sat at her kitchen table. From what Summer overheard, Adam spoke with his captain and then someone from the FBI. His expression was serious as he spoke with one person and then another. Seeing him in action gave Summer a whole new appreciation for his passion for his work, his attention to detail. No wonder he had solved the case involving Jesslyn's attempt to murder her as quickly as he had. As she was the best at her job, Adam was the best on the Denver police force. Of course she was biased in her views of him. Summer smiled to herself and thought, *I have a right to consider my man is the best for the job.* Hearing a noise outside, Summer glanced at the security monitor.

"Adam, we have company. Micah is here. Wait. Looks like— ye-up! More black suits."

"Thanks, that will be Special Agent Carp," Adam said as he stood. His eyes held hers.

"Oh yes, I remember him. He kicked me off of the roof so you two could talk about this mess without me hearing what you had to say."

"Summer, honey, you know we were both doing our jobs, just as we are now working together to ultimately ensure you are safe." He moved over to her and slightly smiled. Having placed a soft yet possessive kiss on her lips, Adam then spoke with full command in his voice. "Summer, I need you to trust me to do my job, even if it means you are kept in the dark about some things." She nodded. "Thank you, honey. I'll show them in and handle the situation in the mudroom."

Summer knew fully well that Adam meant every word. She didn't need to worry about the removal of the mysterious package from the freezer. Adam had called in others from law enforcement to assist him. Just as she would not want him to get in her way as a park ranger, right now he didn't need her interfering in his work. So Summer resigned herself to the kitchen and kept herself busy with food preparation.

———————

With the mysterious package carefully removed from the freezer, and questions answered by Summer, Special Agent Carp, and Micah, walked outside with Adam to further discuss the case. When everyone had left, Adam returned to the kitchen. What he saw when he entered through the door amazed him. On the counter was a bowl of potato salad complete with garnish and looked like it should be photographed for one of the cooking magazines his mother was always leafing through. Two large venison steaks, nearly thawed, had been lightly rubbed with olive oil and herbs. The vegetables he had bought at the store were cleaned, cut, and skewed for the barbeque, and a sweet biscuit batter was being dropped onto cookie sheets to be baked as dessert, to go with the thawed berries placed in a ceramic bowl and drizzled on top of the biscuits. Adam felt and heard his stomach respond. Summer heard the noise as well. A chuckle erupted from her as she turned to smile at him.

———————

The evening ended too soon for Summer and Adam as they sat out on the porch. Dinner had been cleared up long ago. The sun had set in the western sky, while providing a beautiful array of colors for their enjoyment. Candles lit and positioned on the shelves along the wall of the house gave off a warm glow to the room. The smell of barbequed steak and vegetables lingered in the air, while the barbeque itself was positioned a safe distance from the house where it continued to cool. Adam placed his empty coffee cup on the small table. He stretched and glanced over at Summer. Her eyes were heavy, and with good reason, considering everything she had been through.

"Well, Sunflower, I need to get going," he said with regret, and promptly yawned. Summer also stood, then moved over to stand next to Adam.

"I understand."

Even in the subdued lighting, Summer's eyes sparkled with contentment. Adam's finger came up to her, where he found that one piece of hair that seemed to like to taunt him by hanging by her ear. He gently brushed the hair back, so it hooked behind her ear. Then, Adam tipped his head so his lips barely touched her.

"Summer," his voice was quiet, as if he was sharing a secret for only her to hear, "I'd like for you to go on inside before I leave, and set your alarm so I know you are safe."

Summer softly smiled. "Help me blow out the candles, and I will do it for tonight. However, Adam, after this, when you leave, I need for you to trust me that I am capable of setting the alarm on my own. You know there might be some evenings when you are not here—"

His finger drew over her lips. "Summer, honey, I understand. I know I'm being overprotective. I just can't help myself. I've never felt like this toward any other woman, and trust me, I've had my fair share of girlfriends through the years."

"I love you too, Adam." There, she had said it. She allowed herself to commit to the *L* word. His response made her smile. "But, Adam, if we're going to make this relationship work between us, you need to trust me to take care of myself, and not smother me." Summer leaned her body into his. She felt his maleness, and knew his desire for her. She wrapped her arms around his neck and placed a kiss on his lips, which about knocked him out of this world. This woman meant business, and she has staked her claim.

"Okay," Adam finally said, after recovering from the assault Summer had placed on his mouth. The hot energy that was surging through both of them seemed to fill the air around them. He drew in an unsteady breath while hanging on to Summer, afraid that if he let go of her, his legs might give way. "I will never again doubt your ability to handle a situation." Summer softly giggled as she continued to gently run her fingers over the back of Adam's neck and brush her lips over the stubble on his cheeks.

Summer had the remote in her hand so that as soon as Adam walked out the door, she could set the alarm. She did just that and smiled as she heard him say good-night through the door before walking to his car. Returning to the kitchen to finish tidying up for the night, and locking the inside door, she watched her monitor. Now, she was truly alone. Adam was slowly driving away, but only for tonight. He'd be back, that was for sure.

Wound up from the events of the day, Summer was not ready to settle down for the night. She looked up at the bird clock, a flea market find she had hanging over the sink. Eight thirty. Hmm. That meant it was ten thirty in Baltimore. "What to do, what to do," she said to herself as she turned on the night-light by the sink, then turned off the overhead light before she walked from the kitchen and into the hall. From the short hall, Summer walked into the living room, now lit by one lamp on the small table alongside the couch. She pulled her phone from her pocket and was already dialing her mother while plopping down onto the couch.

"Summer! Oh my goodness, my Sunshine, this is a wonderful surprise."

"Hi, Mom." Summer could not help but giggle. She suddenly did not feel quite as tired as when she had been sitting on the porch with Adam. Then, she had been totally relaxed. Now, she felt the energy from her mother surging through the phone. It was like a sugar rush; however, nonfattening. "I hope I haven't disturbed you and Kevin and didn't call you too late."

"Too late? Oh my goodness no, child. Even if I had been in bed, you know I would welcome your call." Summer skipped a giggle and went straight for laughter. "My goodness, you sound very happy. Obviously, there is good news that you couldn't wait until tomorrow to share with me. So, do tell!"

"Mom, you're right. I am exceedingly happy. As of tonight, I'm officially back in my home!"

"Oh, Summer. This is beyond good news. How wonderful for you!"

"It is, Mom." And with that, Summer regaled Amanda with all the adventures in returning home. Mom was pleased to hear about the new security system. But when Summer told her about the mysterious package and the FBI, her mother had much to say. Summer assured Mom that everything would be all right and that Adam had fully taken care of the situation.

"You know, Summer, I never cared for Mitchel. Out of respect for you and your choice in husbands, I tolerated him for you."

"I know, Mom, and I appreciate how you supported my choice and have not thrown my mistakes in my face."

"Honey, I love you too much to do that to you. Now," there was a smile in her voice as she spoke, "everything you tell me about Adam with how he makes you feel and how he cares for you makes me like him even more. I'm also glad to hear that you set boundaries with him, regarding the alarm system and your ability to set it, however—"

"Uh-oh. I know that tone in your voice."

"Well, sweetie, you need to listen to me. From what you've told me of your relationship with Adam thus far, I don't see any signs of him being an abuser."

"You don't." Summer was pleasantly surprised to hear her perceptive mother's impressions of Adam.

"No. I don't. He cares about you not only as your boyfriend, or whatever you choose to call him, and face it, he is significant." Summer giggled and responded, then listened to her mother continue. "He's also a police officer who, first and foremost, by nature of his training, wants to protect you."

"Mom, you are amazing. You listen. You hear me, and then you share with me your words of wisdom. Thank you, Mom." Summer yawned. "Sorry about that. Gee-whiz, it's almost eleven your time. You have to be exhausted and needing to get ready for bed."

"Sunshine, I'm tired from work. However, I'm not going to bed yet." Again, Summer heard the tone in her mother's voice. Time to investigate.

"But it's late. I just figured you'd want to quiet down for the night with Kevin."

"Kevin," she exclaimed. "Hah!"

"Oh boy," Summer released her breath through pursed lips, making the breath sound like air escaping from a deflating balloon. "Mom, do you by any chance want to vent to me?" She softly added, "I have time to listen to you."

"Sunshine, I didn't lie when I said I'm tired from work. But you know, other than the normal headaches, work really isn't my issue. In all honesty, this stupid wedding is going to be the emotional death of me—or my marriage."

"Mom, you can't be serious. Up until now, you and Kevin have been so happy. Is it truly that bad?"

"Trust me, Summer. It's bad."

"Tell me, Mom."

With that, Amanda shared with Summer the events that had taken place during the past two weeks, with Kevin's involvement in Brian and Lily Ann's wedding preparations. Summer was shocked by what her mother was saying about Kevin and his family. She asked questions and received uncensored answers.

Her mother's brutal honesty did not surprise Summer one bit as she listened to her. She was glad that they had such an honest relationship between them.

"Now that you have an idea of what I've been going through, do you know how many days since we returned from our honeymoon, that I've spent alone with my husband to do something enjoyable with him?" Summer remained quiet. She knew her mother needed to further vent, and she did. "None. Zero. Zilch! Am I angry? Oh, heck yes. Am I about ready to get in ex-wife Meg's face and tell her what she can do with her being the mother of the groom? I'd like nothing more than to slap and dropkick that conceited, obnoxious witch across the Atlantic Ocean." Summer gaped at her mother's words. "Don't worry, honey, I'm avoiding the woman like the plague for fear that if I see her, I may not keep my hands to myself. We both know that could be serious trouble." Summer could tell her mother was crying. She heard her sniffle, then quietly add, "Thank goodness we only have two weeks to go, and then the farce will be behind us."

Summer decided to allow a few seconds of silence to pass between them. Her mother needed a moment or two to calm down from her venting and crying. She too needed a moment to regroup and brush away her tears she was shedding in solidarity for her.

"Mom, I'm feeling your pain. Have you tried to talk with Kevin about how you are feeling about the wedding? Don't you think that in all fairness to him, you should at least try to let him know how you are feeling?"

"Talk with Kevin!" Amanda laughed her "did you seriously say that?" laugh. "Honey, when has there been time for me to talk with Kevin? I told you how busy he is at night, and on the weekends, he's either on the phone or out the door to be with his first family. Tonight he was so wrapped up in what he was going to do, he didn't even give me a kiss before he left." She paused long enough to draw in a deep breath, then continued,

"You know, Summer, it might not be so bad if once, just once, I had been invited to go along to be a part of the preparation. You know, during the car ride to and from the appointment, Kevin and I could at least have time to talk with each other. I'm sorry, honey. I shouldn't have dumped on you like this."

"Mom, I invited you to dump, and I'm glad you did. Honestly, I don't blame you for being upset with Kevin for not giving you a good-bye kiss. I too would have been peeved. Plus, you have a right to feel excluded. You are being excluded. I am curious though. If you had been invited to attend any one of the appointments, would you have gone?"

"Probably not. However, it would have felt good to have been invited. Do you realize that this past weekend marked Kevin's and my one month anniversary for being married?"

"I did realize that. Remember? I sent you a text. But from everything you have shared thus far in our conversation, I have a feeling Kevin failed to acknowledge it."

"Sunshine, you are correct. Saturday morning, he was out to play a round of golf with friends, then meet up with Brian for the rest of the day. By the time he got home, I was lying in bed in my nightgown I had worn on our wedding night and reading. He didn't even notice what I was wearing, as he asked me how my day was, while he got ready for bed. Summer, if my husband had actually listened and heard what I told him about my day, I might have been forgiving in his being gone for the whole day. He slid under the covers next to me, gave me a quick unromantic peck on the lips, yawned, told me he was tired and needed to be up early to go with Lily Ann's father someplace for something. He then rolled over and promptly went to sleep at nine o'clock on Saturday night."

"Oh boy." Summer fell silent.

"It gets better. I got up and went out into the living room. I took out the dartboard and darts I had purchased that week as an appropriate stress reliever, hung the board from the hook on the back of the apartment door, and proceeded to throw darts while I drank down a bottle of red wine I had chilled for us to share when Kevin got home."

"Mom, you drank a bottle of wine?"

"I sure did. I had purchased the wine to go with the dinner I had made for us."

"Let me guess," she paused, "dinner ended up in the garbage."

"No, Sunshine, it didn't. I am pleased to say that on Sunday morning, I got up an hour after Kevin had left for his 'fathers of the bridal party wedding prep' adventure, and I took the food to the shelter for our staff and the women and children staying there to have for lunch."

"Wow. That was really nice of you. So what did you and Kevin have for dinner?"

"Since I had eaten a large lunch with the women staying at the shelter, I made chef salads for dinner. Kevin was not pleased as he had seen the meal in the casserole dish in the refrigerator, and he expected me to have it heated and served for his dinner. Oh well."

"I take it you and Kevin had a fight."

"We had words, and before too long, the man is in for a rude awakening. Oh great. It looks like story time will have to be over for tonight."

"I take it, Kevin is home."

"Yes, he is."

Summer heard Kevin's voice. "Take a deep breath, Mom. Don't let him get to you. I love you."

"I love you too, Sunshine. Thank you so much for calling me, and still needing me in your life. I wish I could be out there with you to help you though the rest of your divorce."

"I do too, Mom. Remember, you are always welcome to come stay with me, should you need to get away."

"Thanks. I'll remember that." A few more words, and the conversation ended. Then Summer sat on her couch and cried for her mother.

19

Monday mornings were usually fairly quiet for Summer and Cathy as they eased into the week. Not on this Monday. Cathy came into the rangers station filled with news of the weekend. Bill had picked her up bright and early Saturday morning, then proceeded to take her out for breakfast before they headed for the park. When they got there, Cathy was surprised to discover that her cousin Thomas, who happened to be a disabled veteran, was participating in the day. A tear fell down her cheek as she shared his story with Summer, who also found herself needing a tissue to dab away the wetness in her eyes.

The conversation over coffee continued with Cathy telling Summer about the morning events, their afternoon spent at the flea market in a different park, and then returning to meet up with her family for the evening barbeque and fireworks. Summer noticed the subtle change in Cathy's expression as she told about sitting with her back resting against Bill' chest. His arms were snugly around her as they sat together on the blanket and watched the fireworks.

"Mmm. Sounds perfect. I'm really happy for you and Bill." Summer did not attempt to hide her smile. From what her friend had shared of her weekend, Summer had a strong suspicion that

Bill was going to become a regular visitor to the park, and not be there to commune with nature.

"Cathy, since you have spent most of the summer out monitoring the trails, and I was stuck here," Summer scrunched her lips to show Cathy how much she had not enjoyed being pinned down for her own safety. "Would you mind manning the office while I go out on the trails today?" Her eyes sparkled as she teasingly continued, "You know, I'd hate for you to be out at one of the primitive sites and have Bill show up to surprise you."

Cathy looked at her friend. She understood Summer's passion and need for the outdoors, and knew she was chomping at the bit to get out of there. So while having regaled Summer about her fun and exhausting weekend, and feeling she could use a quieter day, Cathy graciously accepted remaining in the office to meet and greet hikers and register campers. Summer didn't wait for another minute. She grabbed an extra bottle of water as she laid out her planned route for Cathy. Since she hadn't done major hiking for a while, Summer knew she needed to ease her body back into it. So, for today, she was going to hike up the trail where she had found the deer. She hoped the day's hike would not be as stressful as that day had been. One major animal rescue a season was more than enough excitement for Summer. Today, she needed time to be alone to hike, perhaps meet park visitors along the way, helping them if necessary, and allow her mind time to prepare for the days ahead.

<hr>

When Summer walked into Nikki and Alex's office for the next scheduled meeting between Mitchel and her, she was surprised to see that Mitchel was already there. He was sitting alone without his attorney. *Hmmm. That's a bit odd,* Summer thought as her eyes met Mitchel's. His expression was one of a man who appeared to have the weight of the world on his shoulders. Summer gave him a tentative smile and greeting, then walked over to the receptionist's desk. After a brief greeting to the woman, who would inform Nikki and Alex she was there, Summer walked over to Mitchel, who was now standing in front of the chair he had been sitting in.

"Mitchel, how are you?" Summer's voice was quieter than she had expected. She glanced around the room. "I don't see your lawyer." She left the statement open-ended to allow Mitch to answer as he so chose to.

"Ashley will be here in a few minutes. I came early with the hope that you and I could talk without having our lawyers hovering over us. Will you sit down here with me?"

Summer nodded and took the seat next to him. Both were quiet. It appeared that they both needed this moment to gather their thoughts, as the magnitude of the day's meeting hung between them.

"Mitch, before we sat down, you answered my second statement—question, but not my first direct question." Her eyes held him in her gaze. "Given everything that has played out thus far with our divorce proceedings, and now your girlfriend being charged with attempting to murder me," Summer paused. She saw the devastation in Mitchel's eyes. "Mitch, I don't blame you for what she did." Mitchel nodded in thanks. "How are you?" Her voice was filled with tenderness that surprised even her.

"I could be better. Summer," Mitchel sighed out a deflated breath. "It means the world to me to know that you are not holding Jesslyn's actions against me. I am truly sorry for what she did to you. When we returned from Alaska and the police questioned Jesslyn and me about our possible involvement in the attempt that was made on your life at our—I mean *your* home, I couldn't believe what they were accusing us of doing. I suspected her father." Mitchel grew silent, then added, "Summer, I had no idea she was capable of such a vindictive plot."

Summer focused in on Mitchel's expression. She felt in her heart that he was speaking the truth. At that moment sitting there conversing with him, Summer had a flashback to when they were first together. At that time, she could openly talk with him as they were doing now. She could trust Mitchel and what he told her as being the truth. That was so long ago. So much had happened and changed between them from yesterday to today.

"Mitchel, why did you suspect her father?"

"Because, Summer," his eyes conveyed his grief as he spoke. "While I was in Alaska, I received text messages from the old man. After his not-so-subtle reminder of my involvement with him—my gambling. He sent me a photo text of you with a comment attached."

"A photo of me," Summer exclaimed louder than she had intended. "Mitch, you mean to tell me that while you were in Alaska, he was following me?"

"Yes, but, Summer, you need to believe me when I say to you that I don't think he intended to hurt you, unless it was a last resort."

"That's not very comforting." Her expression and voice both informed Mitch of her seriousness.

"I'm so sorry. The old man following you, taking pictures of you and sending them to me was a means for him to threaten me to further conform to his ways." He sighed. "Summer, I'm ashamed to tell you that I was involved in some very bad stuff."

"Your new confession is shedding some light on my life with the Denver police and the FBI for me—I notice you used a past tense. So, does that mean you've managed to end your relationship with him?"

"Not completely. At least not yet." Mitchel drew in a breath. "Summer, I need for you to believe me that I never intended for you to be hurt, and if you had been hurt by Octivani, I could not have lived with myself."

Silence hung between them. Then Summer spoke, "Mitchel, despite everything that you've done, I do believe you. I also believe that deep down inside of you, the good man I once fell in love with still exists. Hopefully, some day, that man will reemerge, and another woman will fall madly in love with you, and you with her."

This caused Mitchel to smile. "Summer, you still are kind to me and wanting good for me. You don't know how I wish I could undo what I have done."

"Mitchel, rehashing the could-haves, should-haves won't change where we are. Because of your choices, we're both moving on." Summer paused, then asked, "So, what are your plans now that you and Jesslyn are no longer together, and you are apparently working on ceasing your relationship with the mob?"

"Summer, I've told you so many lies during the past two years. Right now, all I can do is ask you to not pry into my plans. I promise you that after our divorce is final, everything will come to light. I just need you to try to trust me one more time. Will you do that for me?" Summer saw the pleading in Mitchel's eyes. Then, he added, "Please."

A part of Summer sought to console him of the pain he was obviously going through. Another part of her cautioned her from being reeled in, like a fish caught on a hook, scaled, gutted, and filleted for dinner. Fortunately, and much to Summer's relief, she did not have to respond to Mitchel's request. At that moment, Nikki and Alex appeared from their offices down the hall, and Ashley walked in through the door. Summer noticed that all three of the attorneys were dressed in black. They looked so morbid. Granted her marriage had died, but did they have to play the parts? It reminded her of undertakers ready to plan, or conduct, a funeral with them!

—◆—

The final meeting for working out the last details before going to court the following Wednesday was underway. Once again, Summer was seated across from Mitchel, and sandwiched in her chair between Alex and Nikki.

"Ms. Newman, as you know, the package you found in your freezer contained the grand total of fifty thousand dollars. The money you stumbled upon was one of Dr. Brown's stash he had planted in what he saw as a safe place in case he had to disappear quickly while working for Mr. Octivani and his associates. As you know, on the Saturday morning when he moved out of the house, even though you were not there, both your lawyers and I were there to oversee his removal of his personal items from the home. With all of us watching him, there was no way he could go out to the mudroom and remove the package of money from the freezer. Unable to retrieve his money, Dr. Brown knew it was only a matter of time before you found it."

Summer had fully listened to the attorney. She was now intently watching Mitchel as she spoke. "Mitchel, you know how I feel about the money. I sincerely hope you plan to ask the judge for your money."

Mitchel's lawyer began to speak, only to be cut off by Mitchel. "Summer," he said with a tenderness she had not heard in a very long time. Emotions were swirling within her as she listened. "I'm not asking for the money. Declaring you don't want anything from me, you remind me of a mule stubbornly pushing your hooves into the ground unwilling to budge." She curled her lips at that. Mitchel softly smiled at her familiar response. "You know it's the truth." Summer nodded, and listened as Mitchel continued, "Summer, the bottom line is, whether you want the fifty thousand or not, the money is now yours for you to do whatever you want with it. If you won't keep it for yourself, then use it to help some nature conservation cause of yours. Give a donation to your mother's counseling center and shelter for battered women. Please, Summer. Please do this for me."

A tear fell from her moist eyes as she nodded and sniffled. She continued to look at Mitchel while remembering that she had been warned by Alex and Nikki that he was not the man whom she had thought him to be. The gentle words he had spoken while they sat together in the waiting room, and now his selfless act of kindness was proving in another small way that Mitchel had changed. But still, there was an itching feeling on Summer's skin like nagging chigger that wouldn't go way. Mitchel was still up to something, and she didn't like the itching feeling, or the unknown.

"Well, Mitchel, making your case for me keeping the money as you have, I guess it is now appropriate for me to say thank-you. I will gladly use the money to help both nature and humanity, just not for myself."

With that said, Mitchel smiled at Summer. She recognized the familiar smile of his that he had given her so many times in the past to say, "You're the best." Summer swallowed back her tears that were building inside of her. The reality of the day and its significance for both of them was hitting her like a category 5 hurricane. By this time next week, their marriage would no longer exist.

"Ms. Prime," Alex spoke up. "We have read over Dr. Brown's desires for the transfer of his offshore accounts to Summer. While not pleased about the money her husband had hidden from her, and is now leaving to her, Summer is in agreement to use one of the accounts amounting to one hundred thousand dollars to establish a foundation to work hand in hand with the Wounded Warriors Project of the state of Colorado and their families."

"Summer, that is a wonderful way to use the money!" Concern radiated in Mitchel's voice as he added, "But what about your future?"

"That is a good question, Dr. Brown." Nikki now joined in the conversation. "As per the agreement you have drawn up, Summer will be investing the money from the other account. You need not worry about the IRS. We are making sure all of the money will be properly reported, and appropriate taxes will be paid."

Mitchel sighed. He looked at Summer with moist eyes. "So then, Summer, you are going to be well taken care of." Mitchel's eyes held Summer's warm brown eyes that were also shimmering with wetness. "I'm glad to know that you are keeping some money for yourself to live on in the days ahead, and when you retire."

"Yes, Mitchel. Even though I don't want your money, I understand that I need to take this as a peace offering from you. So yes, I will be financially set for the future. Thank you."

With the final signatures placed on the necessary lines of the motions, the meeting came to an end. As they all stood and made their way for the door, Mitchel paused and waited for Summer to step closer to him. She saw that he was intentionally waiting for her and stopped. She then turned to address the three attorneys who were hovering by the door, like bats ready to come out in the twilight to swoop on insects. Their dark suits didn't help her overactive imagination at that moment.

She simply asked, "Would you all give us a moment of privacy? I believe there are a few things we still need to say to each other, without an audience."

Ms. Prime began to protest, only to be intercepted and promptly escorted out of the room by Alex. Nikki looked in at Summer. She nodded and smiled, then pulled the door so that it was only open ajar for the privacy Summer had requested. Now that they were alone, Summer drew in a breath. Her voice was barely a whisper. "Mitchel, you look so lost, like you desperately need a hug."

"Summer, I was thinking that you also look like you need a hug. I'd very much like to be able to remember this day with having held you in my arms for one last time," Mitchel whispered in return. He blinked away the tears forming in his eyes.

With that, the two drew into each other's embrace where they wept for themselves and for each other.

———⊶⊷———

Summer was sitting on her porch enjoying the late afternoon sun filtering through the newly installed screen and reading a mystery novel by one of her favorite authors. Now that she was in a relationship with Adam and learning more about the life of policemen and policewomen, Summer found she was enjoying the series about a state crime investigator even more than before. There were times when Summer read about the main character, she could almost envision Adam in the role. Well, except for the part where the character slept with another woman who came his way. A smile began to form on her lips as she thought of Adam. Someday he would sleep with a woman, and Summer was fairly confident that the woman would be her. Returning from her daydreaming to the story, Summer had read two more sentences when her phone rang. She quickly stuck her bookmark in the page and placed the book on her lap. Then she answered her call.

"Hello, Nate. I bet I know why you are calling me." Summer was now smiling.

He laughed. "Hey, Sum. You are correct. I just got off the phone with Alex, who told me you were planning to call me later this evening. So, since I want to talk with you about how things went, and need to talk with you about something else, I decided to go ahead and call you."

"I'm glad. With Adam working on a new homicide, I'm here alone, not that I mind given how safe I now feel thanks to him and my wonderful friends, especially you." Nate commented causing Summer to chuckle. "Well, I can't wait for you to get here and see just how safe my home is." Summer continued to regale Nathan about her home, then abruptly stopped, and said, "Nate, I've been rambling."

"Summer, I love hearing you ramble. That's a very positive indicator your life is getting back to normal for you." More laughter was exchanged besides a few teasing remarks. "Well, still it's good to hear that you are feeling safe. Now, I don't have to worry about you being alone. After I hear all your other news from you, we'll discuss my other reason for calling—your mother."

"Well then, we had best get started with our serious conversation. So, Nathan, tell me what Alex told you about our meeting with Mitchel?"

"Everything, except your private meeting with Mitchel when you kicked Alex, Nikki, and the other attorney out of the room."

"It was a sight. They reminded me of undertakers and bats!"

Nathan burst into laughter. Summer pulled her phone from her ear, looked at it, replaced the phone to her ear only to find Nathan still laughing.

"Honestly, Nate, it wasn't that funny."

"Sorry, Sum," he said while seeking to control his laughter. "I just love your descriptions of things."

"Well, I guess if I gave you a reason to laugh, then we're all good. Now, if you're ready to be serious, counselor." She waited to his response and then continued, "Honestly, I needed to have a private conversation with Mitchel. We both needed that time." She said no more.

"Summer, it sounds like you knew what your were doing, so I won't pry."

"Thank you."

"Anytime." Nathan paused to give them both a moment to collect themselves, before he continued. "Sum, I'm really glad to hear that you accepted Mitchel's financial gift. Your plans for the money are wonderful. I personally am grateful for you generosity toward our mothers' work. They both will be ecstatic to receive twenty-five thousand dollars for their not-for-profit."

"Did Alex tell you that it was Mitchel who suggested I give the money to our moms?" Summer listened to Nathan's response then added, "I know I didn't see that one coming. Honestly, it is a logical way for me to spend the money. But you know, Nate, at some point, my dad is sure to hear about my contribution to the Second Chance Crisis Center and Shelter for Women, and perhaps feel left out. So, I've also decided to give Dad and Uncle Wes ten thousand dollars for their expenses at the bait shop. The rest of the money will go to environmental causes I'm affiliated with at this time in my life."

"That is very generous of you. So, Summer, when do you plan on carrying out this philanthropic work of yours?"

She giggled. "I really don't see myself as a philanthropist. I'm simply getting rid of money that may have been gotten by illegal means, and turning it into something good to help people who are in need."

Nathan chuckled.

"What's so funny?"

"You, Summer. Do you realize that right now you sound just like your mother, and her passion to help care for others?"

"Oh my gosh!" Summer giggled. "You are right. Egad! Amanda lives in me. Send out the word via social media: Amanda has cloned herself in her daughter!" By now, Nathan was contributing his own take on Summer's revelation. "Goodness." Summer sighed. "It really feels good to laugh and joke around with you."

"Even if we are making fun of your mother?"

"Of course. Outside of my dad, only you can understand my joking around."

"I notice you never say anything about my mom in a joking manner. I wonder why that is? After all, we share a lifetime of memories of her as well."

"Yes, but if I said anything about your mother, that would be disrespectful."

"And you're not being disrespectful of your own mother?"

"Oh, holy nellie knitters! Did you have to go attorney on me and trip me up so that I hung myself by my own words?"

Again, Nathan roared with laughter. "Summer, my friend, you are fun to trip up."

"Gee, thanks."

"Anytime. So, when are you planning on presenting our mothers with your generous donation?"

"Well, considering everything that is still up in the air around here, work, and Dad coming out to be here with us for the court appearance—"

"Your dad's going to be there?" This was news to Nathan. He wondered how Amanda would handle that news.

"Yes, Dad will be here with us. I can't wait for you to meet Adam and him. Anyway, before you accuse me of rambling again, I plan on coming east in November to spend a few days in town with some of my favorite people, give our moms the money, and then fly up to New York, and spend Thanksgiving with Dad."

"That sounds nice. Well thought out," he added.

"I think that for this year, it will be good for me to spend Thanksgiving with my dad. With how tumultuous things are between Mom and Kevin, they don't need me underfoot for their first Thanksgiving."

Summer's voice dropped off. Nathan heard her concern, and with good reason. He knew that he needed to say something to draw her from her sadness and asked, "What about Adam? How does he fit into your plans?"

"Adam knows that Dad has invited me to spend the holiday with him and thinks I should go by myself to be with my family— that I've only met this year and am still getting acquainted with. Nate, I can't believe how supportive and considerate Adam is toward me. But, I do have to tell you, that he warned me not to accept any family invitations for Christmas."

"Oh?"

Summer smiled as she spoke and thought of Adam, and what his presence in her life meant to her. "Apparently he has something special planned, or is planning—I'm not sure which."

"A mystery, I like it! Sum, I'm sure that whatever Adam is planning, it is going to be wonderful."

The conversation continued between Summer and Nathan. While they talked, Summer made her way back into the kitchen. She turned her phone to speaker and placed it on the counter so she could begin to prepare dinner for herself and a meal that she would have ready for Adam to take with him when he stopped by later. As Summer worked, they chatted about life in Baltimore, including Nathan's new girlfriend, whom he might actually be breaking up with in the near future. Summer wasn't too surprised by his revelation. Then they reached the topic Summer was most interested in—her mother.

"Well, Summer, everything was going good with me keeping an eye on your mother."

"Oh dear. You said *was*, and that can only mean that Mom caught you."

"Right. Everything was going according to plan until today, when she caught me discussing your latest concerns with my mom."

"How bad was it?" Summer said, then held her breath, as if waiting to be submerged into a deep pool of water.

"Let's just say, at first she had some choice words to share with us."

Summer sucked in a breath, and then grimaced. "Ouch."

"Actually, after her initial display of annoyance, your mom sat in my Mom's office with us and cried. Summer, it about broke my heart to hear how Kevin has been treating her, all because Brian is getting married. What she shared with us is not the Kevin I've known my entire life. Yet, when I think back to when he was married to Meg, I see her intrusion written all over their problems. Sum, we both know that they've only been married a short time, and…well, their relationship is so fragile at this point. They should still be experiencing the joyful memories of their wedding and honeymoon."

"I know." Summer sniffled as she listened to her friend share his concern with her.

"I'm afraid Kevin is making a huge mistake. This may be a mistake that he just might not be able to repair anytime soon, if ever."

"Nate, you said *if ever*. Now, I am even more concerned for Mom, for them. Until now, I thought maybe Mom was just being jealous as the new wife. You know, competing with the established family and all that. Nate, do you honestly think that their marriage is in peril?"

"Summer, your mother is emotionally exhausted. I don't know about the marriage being in peril, but I do know that there are major issues for them to sort out in the near future."

Summer sighed. "I certainly don't like hearing this, but am really glad that you have given me a heads-up. Mom must feel all alone." Summer found unexpected tears welling in her eyes. She sniffled.

"Sum, I know how much you love and care for your mom. You two make an amazing mother-daughter team. Please hear me and trust me when I say to you that you need not worry about Amanda feeling all alone. She knows and appreciates what you and I have been up to, as well as knowing that Mom, Dad, and I will be watching out for her at the wedding. I actually got her to laugh at one point during our conversation."

"Really? How did you accomplish that?" Summer asked while chopping the mushrooms, which she would be adding to the diced onion she was sautéing to be added later on to the quinoa, and grilled salmon steak garnished with a wedge of fresh lemon.

"Well, I simply told her that I am going to be alone at the wedding and reception. I really am not looking forward to not having a date for the day. So I suggested that during the reception, when she was minus her husband, or became overly annoyed with Meg strutting around like top hen in the henhouse"— Summer giggled—"I always liked it when your mother used that expression when we were kids, and never before now had a reason to use it," Nathan added as a disclaimer, then continued on with his story. "Anyway, I told her that since she was a beautiful older woman, she could ditch Kevin whenever she felt like it, go cougar, and be my date." He paused to allow Summer time to laugh and comment. "Summer, I tell you, it was priceless to see her expression and hear her comments. Oh goodness, how I do love her and her ability to find the intended humor in the situation.

What's most important is that your mom knows I have her back. My mom, after recovering from hearing me call her best friend a cougar, is equally thankful for my solution for helping your mother to get through the day. Mom is also thankful because now your mom has no reason to be upset with her for plotting with us and spying on her."

"Nate, you are the best!" Summer sniffled; however, she had no control of the tears streaming down her cheeks. She dabbed her eyes. "Please give your mom a huge hug for me and tell her how grateful I am for her being there, yet again, for my mom. Also, my friend, when you get out here on Sunday, expect to get a huge hug and kiss from me."

"Won't Adam be jealous?"

"Aww, Nate, how considerate of you to think of Adam. He knows we're friends, and he expects us to be happy to see each other, hugs and all." Summer paused to allow herself to giggle. "Besides, I said nothing of kissing you on the mouth. Gross, ew! I love you, Nate, but not like that!"

The two laughed and wondered together down memory lane to reminisce of when they were teens and were exploring their feelings for each other. Everything was going along fairly fine with their budding romance, until the fateful day when Nate was visiting Summer at their apartment, and they were caught in a lip-lock by Amanda. They both admitted that they could have survived her mother's words, had it not been for the fact that two weeks earlier when they were together at Andrew and Cassie's, Nate was caught by Cassie with his hands on inappropriate places on Summer's body. Teenage hormones were ripening between them, to say the least. With their mother's watchful eyes and warnings, they soon decided that platonic friendship was probably best for them. After a few more minutes of laughter and conversation, the call ended. Summer continued to work on making her dinner. As she did, her thoughts returned to Baltimore, her mother, and her wonderful friends she had left behind.

20

Saturday—Baltimore, Maryland

Nathan was glad that the wedding ceremony was over and that they were now at the reception venue awaiting the arrival of the bride and groom. He was busy sending text messages to Summer with pictures of the bridal party, and a bonus shot of his parents. Upon receiving his latest response from Summer, he burst out in laughter.

"Nathan, honestly, what struck you?"

"Summer and I have been texting one another. She thinks you and Dad look terrific! But that's not what struck me funny. Take a look." He handed his mother his phone so she could see the picture and Summer's text.

Cassie gasped, and her eyes smiled and did her best to not laugh at Summer's response.

Well Laa—Dee—Dah! Aren't we Special!!

"Well, Nathan, we sure can tell that Summer is related to her mother."

With that said, Cassie handed the phone off to Andrew, who gazed at the picture, commented, shook his head, and sighed before handing the phone back to Nathan.

"I'd say Summer is a very perceptive young woman." Andrew added, "Sarcastic, but perceptive." At that moment, he allowed his gaze to pass over the reception hall, searching for Amanda. He found her standing next to Kevin, who was fully engaged in conversation with his brother, and apparently unaware that Amanda was near him. Andrew, well aware of Amanda's expressions and body language, was concerned for his friend. Knowing that there was nothing he could do at that moment for Amanda, he then returned his full attention to his family. "Son, while you are enlightening Summer about the day, perhaps you should censor your text, you know, to not cause her added distress for her mother."

"Wise observation," Cassie added, as she turned to Nathan. "There will be time for you to talk with Summer about the wedding and the reception when you are together. For now, we should find our places at our assigned table so we're ready for the arrival and introduction of the bride and groom."

—⁙⁙⁙—

The moment came for the wedding party to enter. Of course, Nate and his parents saw that Amanda was not introduced as the stepmother of the groom. Nathan had the feeling that Amanda's exclusion was to be an obvious intentional slap in the face orchestrated by Meg. He shared his thoughts with his parents, who were in agreement with him. Plus, they each made a comment about not seeing Amanda at the groom's family table with Kevin. In her place, already seated at the full family table next to Kevin was an elderly woman neither Cassie nor Andrew remembered seeing before today. Nathan had seen Amanda move away from the table after Kevin introduced her to the older woman and had exchanged words with her. He scanned the room and found

Amanda standing off to the side of the room. Something was terribly wrong. While everyone else had their eyes on the bridal party attendants, awaiting the grand entrance of Mr. and Mrs. Brian Wentzel, Nate was focused on Amanda. Then, it happened. No one else seemed to notice when she disappeared through the side exit leading to the bar. Nathan waited for the clapping to begin when Brian and Lily Ann came into the room. He then made his break and slipped out the same door Amanda had gone through.

Nate paused as he came in the doorway of the bar. He glanced around the dimly lit room and soon found Amanda sitting at a table in the corner. He figured she had intentionally chosen that spot for privacy and noticed she was already sipping what appeared to be a dark amber liquid from a glass. From the expression on her face, it was obvious Amanda was in a sour mood. Nathan knew he had not liked what he had seen in the reception hall. So he could only imagine what she must be feeling at that moment.

Nathan walked up to the bar, ordered his drink—scotch neat. Before leaving the bar with his drink, Nate asked for another scotch for himself, whatever the woman in the corner was drinking, and a copy of the bar menu to be brought to their table, as they would be ordering food to go with their drinks. With his drink in hand, Nathan walked over to the table and stood quietly while watching Amanda dab her eyes. Right at that moment, Nathan was so angry by how hurt she was, that he contemplated going back into the reception and having it out with Kevin. Allowing a cooler head to prevail, Nathan drew in a breath, then quietly spoke to Amanda. She looked up at him and gave him a very weak smile as tears trickled down her cheeks, streaking through her once perfect makeup.

"Coming to my rescue already?"

"No." She looked surprised by Nathan's answer. "Amanda, you don't need me to rescue you. What you need is for me to boycott the farce happening in the other room and sit out here with you in solidarity for the injustice you have been tolerating from your husband, and now everyone else."

Amanda sniffled and smiled a bit more as she raised her glass. "A toast, my friend."

"To what?" Nathan asked as he raised his glass with hers.

"First, to your parents, who raised you to be the outstanding man that you are today, and second to you for standing 'by your word' you gave to my daughter. Thank you, Nathan, for your friendship to both of us. You're an irreplaceable gem of a friend."

———

Nathan and Amanda both were in contact with Summer while they were waiting for another round of drinks and began eating the house cheeseburgers with a thick slice of onion and steak fries loaded with cheese and slices of jalapenos. Summer was very upset to hear how Amanda was treated at the beginning of the reception. Her once positive attitude toward her stepfather was rapidly deteriorating into something comparable to bear scat. She sent consoling words to her mother, then a text to Nate expressing her displeasure. Nathan had just taken another bite of his burger when a new text came in to his phone. He read it, then promptly shared it with Amanda.

> Food looks great. I'm jealous. Not really. Gotta go—steaks are ready! LOL!!

With that, Amanda sent her own text to Summer, and realized that for the first time all day—no, make that for the past two days, she was actually enjoying herself. Leave it to Summer and Nathan to make her smile. By now, the heat from the jalapenos was beginning to get to Amanda. Her mouth, esophagus, and stomach were all blazing into a five-alarm fire! She had drunk down her third JD neat that did nothing to squelch the heat, and decided that she had best take a break from the bourbon. With that, Amanda ordered a pitcher of seltzer with slices of lime.

Both Amanda and Nathan, who were out of direct view of the people entering the bar, enjoyed watching and commenting on the wedding guests coming to the bar for drinks while they ate their dinner. Just as Amanda was taking a bite of her burger, with juice oozing from her lips, she saw Andrew enter the room and begin looking around.

"Nate, your father is here, and obviously looking for us."

"I see him, and by his expression, I'd say Dad's not too happy."

At that moment, Andrew saw them and made his way through the noisy bar filled with people who were obviously in full party mode. When he got close to the table and saw they were eating bar food instead of the food being served inside the reception hall, he slowly shook his head. Andrew did not wait to be invited to join them. He pulled out a chair and sat down next to Amanda. The misery Amanda had been attempting to mask throughout the day was no longer being held at bay, as tears slid down her cheeks. Andrew reached his arm around her shoulders and drew her to him. She placed her head on his chest, as well as her arm around him, and wept. Nathan quietly filled his father in on the details as to why they were dining in the bar, and not at the reception. Andrew was livid. He continued to hold on to his friend, only now he held her tighter against him.

"Son, please go and quietly explain the situation to your mother. Ask her to join us, as we are now going to be dining in here with the two of you."

"Andrew, no." Amanda struggled to look up at him, while seeking to control her tears. "You and Cassie have known Brian since he was a child, and you should enjoy yourselves at the reception."

"Nope! Ont-ah—ain't gonna happen, my friend!"

Amanda blinked as she looked up at him. She couldn't believe it. Andrew said, *Nope, Ont-ah—ain't gonna happen!* Amanda knew that for Andrew to be using such atrocious grammar, things were most assuredly going to holy heck in a handbag.

"As of now, the Serenelli-Phillips family members who are currently residing in Baltimore are officially boycotting the Wentzel wedding reception."

"Andrew," Amanda continued to express her concern over him and Cassie not being at the reception. Andrew had not budged from his decision when Cassie and Nathan came into the bar. Cassie was smiling as she came to the table and waited for Nathan pull out her chair for her. "So, I hear cheeseburgers with onion and cheesy steak fries with jalapenos are the new in food for wedding receptions. Count me in," she said while easing into the chair.

Amanda looked around the table as Nate, standing next to his chair, began to move to go order for another round of food and drinks. She looked from one friend to another and saw the same expression. They each dared her to not accept their solidarity with her.

—⸺⸺—

After they finished their meal, the four who had initially boycotted the reception dinner decided to return to the reception under the pretense of having a cup of coffee, and perhaps a dance or two; when actually, they all were simply curious to see what Meg and Kevin were up to. Amanda sat at the table surrounded by her protective friends. She sipped her coffee that reminded her of coffee she had drunk while traveling on the New York State Thruway during the past year. Not a good memory for Amanda since it reminded her of Kevin and when they met at Cassie and Andrew's cabin. Amanda felt her eyes becoming moist as she watched Kevin move between his—*their* family table, Meg's family table, and the bride's family tables. Meg was at his side. Both Cassie and Andrew also noticed Kevin and Meg as they stood together fully engaged in companionable conversation with the guests. Cassie's quiet pointed words and her expression worried Amanda. She was concerned that before the day was over, Cassie and/or Andrew and Nathan might say something to Kevin that would harm their friendship. The last thing she wanted to do was to be the cause of dissension between Kevin and his friends, who had seen him through a tumultuous time in his life. As Amanda sat at Cassie and Andrew's assigned table with them and Nathan, her phone rang.

"Excuse me, it's Summer. I should take this."

"Hello, Summer," they all chimed in with Amanda. Laughter and friendly comments were made between them as they sat with Amanda.

"Yes, honey, they're all with me," Amanda said while smiling at her friends. "Summer wishes she could be partying with us." More comments were shared. "I agree, Sunshine. It does bring back good memories of times we all shared together. Yes, honey, I am blessed. Actually, Summer, we both are blessed. So, my dear, what may I do for you?" Amanda listened to her daughter. Her gaze passed among Cassie and Andrew and fixed itself on Nathan.

"Oh, no, I know that look," Nathan quietly responded. "Is Summer tattling on me?"

"Yes, and I appreciate your good intentions."

"Son," Andrew cleared his throat. "Didn't I warn you to not concern Summer?"

"Andrew, you, Cassie, and I could talk until we are blue in the face. You should know that with our children, they will listen to us to a point and then—"

"They think because they are now adults, they know everything," Cassie added, while Amanda nodded. Andrew saw the expressions on his wife and dear friend. He knew from years of experience with those two to not say any more about the subject.

"Mom," Summer's voice stopped Amanda from further commenting on her and Nathan. "You know we love you. I called for one reason, and that is to nurture the seed I had planted in your mind during one of our recent conversations."

Amanda cast her eyes down at the cup of nearly finished coffee and listened to her daughter. She knew the conversation at the table had grown quiet. She dabbed her eyes as she listened to Summer and glanced at her friends.

"Thank you, Sunshine. I do love you. Yes. I will consider your suggestion. Yes. I will call you later to let you know what I decide to do. Yes. I will give them all a hug for you." By now, Amanda simply rolled her eyes, which brought a chuckle from both Cassie and Andrew. "Yes, Sunshine. I will do that for you. I love you too. Bye."

Silence hung in the air as Amanda drew in a deep breath. Then she turned to Nathan. "Well, Nathan, along with other issues on my daughter's mind, it seems Summer is concerned that you will not hold true to your deal to be my date and dance with me." Her smile and eyes challenged Nathan to consider her words.

Before Nathan could respond, Andrew piped up, "Of course you will dance." He then looked lovingly at his wife. "Cassie, would you mind if I take Amanda for a spin around the dance floor before you and I seriously stretch our legs?"

"By all means, you and Amanda go ahead and dance. That will give me an opportunity to discuss an idea with our son."

"Cassie, Andrew," Amanda began to protest, only to have Cassie lift her hand, moving her fingers to shoo them away. She smiled and sighed as she knew better than to argue with Cassie. So Amanda turned her attention to Andrew. "Well, Andrew, if you're brave, I'll try not to step on your toes."

They were all laughing as Andrew stood and held out his hand for Amanda. She placed her hand in his and rose to her feet. Then they headed out to the partially filled dance floor. The music was perfect, upbeat classic rock. Amanda enjoyed having her dear friend guiding her around the dance floor. He knew perfectly well that she would not step on his toes, and would keep up with the quickstep and his own twist he added to the steps. Needless to say, heads were turning as people noticed them on the dance floor. Andrew leaned in and spoke to Amanda as the song came to an end. She smiled and nodded as the next song began. Once again, Andrew began leading her around the floor.

It was during the second song that Kevin realized Amanda was on the dance floor with Andrew. He watched. At first he was pleased to see she was obviously enjoying herself with him. As Kevin continued to watch them, it occurred to him that even though Amanda was smiling as she danced with Andrew, something was physically wrong with her.

As he stood and watched them, Kevin realized he had not seen his wife—his wife; a sudden stabbing pain seemed to sear through his heart. With everything happening at the reception, demanding his time and attention, Kevin had lost track of Amanda. He knew that he had to make things right with her, beginning with an apology for the debacle over seating arrangements for the meal. Kevin glanced around and found the table where Cassie was sitting and watching Andrew and Amanda move together on the dance floor. There was something about her expression that caused Kevin concern. An ominous feeling swept over him as he took a step toward Cassie. One thing Kevin felt certain of— Cassie's expression had something to do with Amanda, and the physical distress he saw in his wife.

—◦◦◦—

When the song ended, Amanda and Andrew, now thoroughly winded from dancing to two rather upbeat songs, came through the crowd to the table to find Kevin sitting with Cassie. As soon as Kevin saw Amanda flush faced from dancing, and her limp suggesting she may be in pain, he rose to greet her. Amanda's smile she had shared with Andrew immediately began to slip away when their eyes met. She couldn't pretend anymore that things were okay between them, when they most assuredly were not. Kevin reached his arm around her waist. Amanda closed her eyes to soak in the moment as she felt the gentle pressure of his hands on her hip. It should feel so good to have her husband finally paying attention to her. At that moment, all Amanda felt was the urge to cry. Having skipped her anxiety medication, so that she could drink, she was afraid that she might have a panic attack before the day was over. It could happen at any moment. She had to hold it together, especially when Kevin leaned over and brushed his lips against her jaw. Amanda drew in a calming breath, then turned to face him. His expression informed her that her breath must be rather obnoxious. Since she had eaten the same foods with Andrew and Cassie, their breath didn't bother her, so she hadn't given any thought that hers might possibly be smelling atrocious.

"My gosh Amanda, what have you been eating with all that onion?"

"I ate my dinner with—all that onion." At that moment, Amanda knew she was only hanging on to civility by a thread that could break without warning. She wanted nothing more than to blast Kevin with everything that had been bottled up inside of her. Her voice was tight as she continued, "They were delicious."

"I didn't see anything with onions when I passed through the buffet line."

"Well"—Amanda met his gaze with a look that warned him not to push it with her—"they were on my plate. I ate and enjoyed every slice. Too bad you obviously missed out."

"You had best have a mint," Kevin said, while holding out the breath mints to her that he had pulled from his pocket. Amanda heard him and wondered how such an intelligent man, whom she knew was compassionate and loving, could be so stupid! Seriously, he was concerned about her breath smelling like onions, but what about her feelings?

Both Andrew and Cassie quietly stood together and watched their friends. They knew that Amanda had just about reached her limit for what she would tolerate. As a precaution, Andrew had sent a text to Nathan, who was now on his way back over to the table to join them.

"No, thank you. You keep them," Amanda's voice quietly challenged Kevin, while she was touching his hand and pushing it back toward his body. "After all, you'll be needing them to ensure that your breath smells and tastes good, for all the kisses you will undoubtedly be giving to women throughout the remainder of the party."

"Amanda," Kevin was intently studying her as he spoke, "I've obviously missed something of importance."

"You think?" Sarcasm filled Amanda's question. Cassie mumbled under her breath in solidarity for her friend. Andrew was slowly shaking his head when his eyes met Kevin's eyes filled with bewilderment.

"Amanda, for now, I'll ignore that." Kevin drew in a breath. "Perhaps you and I should step away from here to have a private conversation so that you may reveal to me whatever it is that has been building up inside of you. Maybe then, we may get on with enjoying the rest of Brian and Lily's reception."

"Kevin, you don't need to worry about not enjoying the rest of your son's wedding reception. I will not do anything to embarrass you. In fact, I've made a decision."

"Oh," Kevin heard something in Amanda's voice that sent a warning through him. It was a feeling he often had in the trauma bay, when his patient was not responding to treatment and inevitably coded.

"That's right. Nathan has already told me that when I am ready to leave that he will be more than happy to give me a ride home so that I may go and cool off."

"You do seem uptight." Kevin was intently watching Amanda as he spoke. He saw her eyes rolling in disgust. "Perhaps"—he glanced over at Nathan, who was standing with Cassie and Andrew—"since Nathan has offered to provide you with a ride, it may be best for you to go home." Kevin did not like how quiet both Andrew and Cassie were being. He sensed that they all knew something of importance, yet no one was saying anything. Kevin fought to shrug off his ominous feeling as he turned to Nathan and said, "Thank you for attending to Amanda." Nathan nodded. Kevin then turned back to Amanda. He leaned over and brushed his lips against hers and said, "I'll see you later."

"No, you won't." Amanda breathed out, while she shook her head and fought back the tears.

"What?" Kevin hoped he had misheard Amanda.

"I told you. I'm leaving to cool off. That means I'm going away for a few days so I don't end up saying something to you that I will live to regret for the rest of my life. I need to clear my thoughts about us—you—me."

"Amanda, please." Kevin's eyes filled with moisture. "Don't walk away from me."

"As of now, I have no other choice. Good-bye."

<hr />

"Kevin, you need to respect Amanda's feelings and give her the space she needs." Andrew continued to speak with Kevin while Cassie walked outside with Nathan and Amanda. The obvious odor of onion on his breath opened the door for them to discuss the meal and seating arrangements. Until that moment, Kevin, who thought Amanda had given her seat to his aunt and then found another place at a vacant table, had not known that all the other tables were full of guests. Kevin had heard from his aunt that Meg contacted her and invited her to come if she felt up to it. He had originally thought Meg was simply attempting to show kindness to his eighty-seven-year-old aunt who had been recuperating from a total hip replacement. Now that he knew about Amanda not having a seat in the reception and Andrew, Cassie, and Nathan joining her in the bar to share a meal together, Kevin was livid. At that moment, he realized that Meg had manipulated the day to intentionally hurt Amanda and him.

—◁◁◁◁◁◁◁||||♒♒||||▷▷▷▷▷—

Cassie returned to the reception to find Andrew and Kevin still in conversation, only now they were seated at the table. She knew by the look on Andrew's face that he was laying everything out for Kevin about what Amanda had shared with them. Well, good. Kevin needed to wake up before it was too late. She too had an earful for Kevin. Her stop in the ladies' room, on the way back from seeing Amanda and Nathan off, had provided her with more fuel for the fire that burned in her. She quietly eased into the chair next to Andrew to not interrupt their conversation. Cassie slid her hand onto Andrew's forearm. He turned his gaze to meet her troubled eyes.

"Cassie, what's wrong?" Andrew asked.

Kevin also realized that something was troubling Cassie. "Did something happen with Amanda?"

"She's safely on her way home with Nathan at the wheel, then off for her cooling-off time. Kevin, you need to know this is not a spur-of-the-moment decision on Amanda's part. Over the past two weeks, we discussed her possibly taking a personal leave of absence."

"Two weeks." Kevin looked at Cassie but didn't fully see her. His mind was racing too fast to process her words. "I take it you know about the fight we had a few nights ago."

"I do." Cassie sighed. "Kevin, I have to tell you I am really disappointed in you. Do you realize that since you returned from your honeymoon with Amanda, you have chosen your ex-wife over your wife?" Kevin began to speak, only to have both Cassie and Andrew suggest he be quiet and listen. "I can tell you, as a woman, I fully support Amanda for how she is feeling right now. Our friend cautiously opened her heart to you."

"She trusted you to love her," Andrew added.

"Once again, Amanda feels betrayed. Frankly, I don't know if I can forgive you for what you've done to my best friend."

Kevin hung his head in shame. He sighed out words that were barely audible. Cassie and Andrew sat with him. After a few seconds of silence, Cassie quietly continued to speak.

"As long as we're laying out things for you to process, I might as well share this video with you. I recorded it while I was in the ladies' room." Cassie handed her phone to Kevin. Andrew watched the video with him. Both men were shocked by what they saw and heard. Lily and one of her bridal attendants, a.k.a. Kevin's daughter, Nicole, were having a conversation comparing Amanda and Meg. It became almost unbearable to watch as they commented about Amanda—making fun of her scars and her limp.

"I'm glad Amanda left with Nathan and didn't have to hear them."

"Kevin, don't be glad. While Amanda didn't hear that, she did hear them saying other things with Meg as we passed by them standing in the hall outside of the ladies' room."

21

Sunday morning, Kevin awakened to find that he was lying sprawled out on top of the bed. The tux he had intended to take off last night before was plastered to his body, as well as uncomfortable in rather important places. Moving his arm, Kevin caught a whiff of himself and realized that he was smelling of old sweat, stale liquor, and other reminders of the wedding. His head throbbed of pain. Everything that had transpired during the past twenty-four hours seemed surreal for him, as he yawned, stretched, and wiped the sleep from his eyes. The wedding was supposed to have been a joyful time for Amanda and him to share with Brian. Now, in the aftermath of the wedding, and all of the preparation that went into the day, Kevin felt like he had been watching a bad movie—a very bad movie. He sighed and moaned as he sat up and swung his legs over the side of the bed. It was time to face the day.

Moving through the apartment, Kevin was aware of everything that was wrong with his life. Most important is the fact that his wife was gone. Gone, as Amanda had informed him, "to cool off." Kevin reflected on Amanda's words as he moved into the kitchen to go through the ritual of making coffee. He knew her sarcasm had been one of her defenses to not allow him to see just how deeply she had been bruised by him. He remembered the shattered look in her eyes when they parted. Then, there was the information both Andrew and Cassie had shared with him. He shook his head, as if to release the inner turmoil, but to no avail. The headache he had awakened with had by now moved through his entire body. He ached for his wife, to hold her, confess his mistakes, and plead for her forgiveness. Kevin watched the coffee dripping into the carafe and blurted out, "I don't care about Meg, nor do I want her in my life. I love you, Amanda, wherever you are, and I want *you*," he emphasized the *you*, "and not Meg, in my life." The thought of Meg and how he had allowed her to worm her way into his mind and control him during the past few weeks made Kevin feel like—what would Amanda have called him? *Oh yes*, he thought, *she'd call me a slug or worse, which I am.*

After stirring the cream into his coffee, Kevin picked up his cup and walked into the living room. He sat down in the chair by the window and looked out into the Inner Harbor. Then, after taking a sip of coffee, Kevin said to himself, "I'm known for my skill and expertise in saving people who come into the trauma emergency room and are hanging on to life by a thread. I'm a physician—a healer. My greatest day as a doctor was when I used my gifts and resources that saved you, Amanda, after your motorcycle accident. Well, sweetheart, I'm thinking about us, as you told me to do." Kevin wished Amanda was there with him so he could tell her what he was feeling at that moment. She obviously wasn't, so Kevin continued on and told the empty apartment what he needed Amanda to hear. "If I can't find the solution and save our marriage, then I'm nothing. I will be nothing without you."

Upon finishing his second cup of coffee, Kevin had begun to develop a plan of action, which he was now calling his marriage trauma procedure. "Well, sweetheart, you said that I am not to contact you. However, you didn't say anything about me not calling your family." He picked up his phone and proceeded to make his first call.

"My goodness, this is a surprise to hear from you on Sunday morning, following your big day." Kevin could picture Amanda's grandmother sitting in her cabin nestled in the side of the lower Adirondack Mountains in upstate New York. The old woman coughed.

"Good morning, Mary, are you feeling all right?"

"This cough, why, it's nothing, just the change of seasons reminding me I'm getting older."

"As you said, you are getting older and your health is a concern for us. Speaking of us, Amanda didn't by chance make her way up there to check on you and your cough?" Mary coughed again and then quietly spoke, "Tsk-tsk-tsk! Now, I understand why you are calling me. My Amanda skedaddled someplace and didn't tell you."

"No, she didn't, Mary. Amanda told me she was going away for a few days, just not where."

"Well, she's not here, so you might as well go on and tell me what you did to get yourself like butter melting on a hot skillet with her."

The invitation had been extended. Kevin accepted and shared with Mary what had happened since they returned from the honeymoon. She listened to him speak, while adding grunting sounds, tsk-tsk-tsk, and humphs. Finally, Mary spoke.

"Well, young man, you plumb got yourself a mess. Mmm-mm-mm. Goodness, I don't know 'bout you children. My Amanda has to be mighty mad for her to get in her snit and run off to think. You call me as if I have all the answers. Well, this time, I don't. About the only thing I can do is talk to the Great Spirit and ask the Spirit to help you both find each other, if that is what the Great One wants for you."

"Thank you, Mary. That means the world to me coming from you. You're a good person."

"Well, I don't know how good I am anymore, but I 'preciate what you said." Just before they ended their call, Mary asked, "Did Amanda take all of her clothes with her?"

"No, she didn't."

"That's good. I know my girl. She has a powerful love for you. Kevin, you betrayed her, and I could string you up for bear bait for that, but you listen to me." And Kevin did. Her words were fierce with passion. "When my Amanda returns, you best listen to her. She will fight with you, not to defeat you but to save your marriage. You best prove your love for her and stand up and fight with her for your life together."

"Thank you, Mary. I do believe that next to your granddaughter, you are the smartest woman I know."

She laughed into his ear. As she did, Kevin thought of how her warm chocolate brown eyes danced with joy. This in turn caused him to think of Amanda and the last time he had seen her eyes. Her sadness. He had to find her and, hopefully before too long, see the joy return to her eyes.

When the call was completed, Kevin leaned his head against the back of the chair. He closed his eyes, while he reflected on the conversation he had just finished having with Mary. She had been encouraging. For now, Kevin had hope that all was not lost between him and Amanda.

The next call Kevin made was to Amanda's brother Jim, who promptly lit into him for hurting his sister. By the time their conversation ended, Kevin ended up feeling about as big as an ant.

———

Cassie opened the front door to find Kevin standing there. She gasped as she looked at his appearance. Apparently he had forgotten to shave or comb his hair.

"Kevin, please come in." Cassie stepped back. Kevin entered and gave her a hug. "Andrew and I were about to sit down for lunch. Have you eaten?"

"Thank you, Cassie. I'm not hungry. I came here because I need to ask you and Drew a few more questions about Amanda."

"I see." Cassie's gaze softened as she looked at her friend. She placed her hand on his arm and took a step leading him toward the back of the house. "Andrew is sitting out on the patio. You know the way, so go on ahead and join him. I'll be out in a minute."

Kevin quietly stepped out onto the patio and noticed that Cassie had added a couple planters of fall flowers to the decor. A wave of sadness swept through him as he thought of how Amanda would like what Cassie had done. Then again, with how distracted he had been as of late, Amanda probably already knew about the flowers.

Andrew looked up from reading the Sunday paper. He immediately visually scanned his friend. "So," Andrew cleared his throat. "You look like you're having a rough day. I'm not surprised. Have a seat." Andrew nodded toward the cushioned straight chair. "I gather since you are here, that you want to talk some more about your wife."

By now, Cassie had appeared with a tray of food, three plates, cutlery, and three glasses of iced tea. Without speaking, she prepared a plate of food, picked up a setting of cutlery, and handed both to Kevin. She knew perfectly well the man had not eaten, and once again, she would take care of him, as she had done when his life with Meg fell apart.

"Thank you, Cassie." He then returned his full attention to Andrew, who was encouraging him to share what was on his mind. Kevin gave a recap of his morning and didn't leave anything out.

"Kevin, do you hear what you are saying? Jim and Mary both told you that Amanda is not up in New York with them. I will say that I'm pleased to hear that you listened to Mary. She's a wise old woman who loves and knows our Amanda better than any of us. But then as soon as Jim mentioned to you that his friend Stephen was not in town, you jump to conclusions that Amanda has run off to be with him. My goodness, man, listen to yourself. You're not thinking straight."

"Kevin, Andrew is right." Cassie looked at Andrew. He nodded. "Amanda is not with Stephen, at least to our knowledge."

Kevin slowly turned his gaze from Cassie to Andrew, and then back to Cassie. The whole time he was considering their spoken and unspoken words. "Yesterday, when Amanda left the reception with Nathan, you both knew where she was going, didn't you?" They both nodded. "Well, since you obviously know where my wife is, I'd appreciate it if you would be so kind as to tell me so I may go to her."

"Kevin. We made a promise."

"Gall darn it, Cassie. I don't care what you promised." Kevin's voice had risen to cause Andrew to step in.

"Kev, yelling at my wife is not going to solve your problem. Take a deep breath to collect yourself." Andrew reached over to the coffee table and picked up Kevin's untouched glass of iced tea. He held it out to Kevin. "Now take a long sip of iced tea and cool off."

Much to Andrew and Cassie's relief, Kevin followed Andrew's instructions. He placed the glass on the table, then turned to meet their eyes. Concern radiated from both of his friends. "I'm sorry." He sighed. "The last thing I want to do is argue with the two of you."

"Kevin, speaking for Cassie and myself, we understand your frustration, your pain, and are pleased to know just how much you love Amanda."

"When I spoke with Mary, she said that when Amanda returns, I had best listen to her." Both nodded in agreement, and as a nudge for Kevin to continue to share his thoughts. "Amanda's grandmother is a wise woman. She said that Amanda will fight with me, not to defeat me but to save our marriage. I've thought about that. Mary knows how passionate my wife is about what matters most to her. Well, I'm passionate too. I'm not willing to wait for Amanda to come home. I'm beginning the fight, our fight, right now. I need for you both to tell me. Where do I have to go to find my wife so that I may begin to prove my love for her and stand up and fight with her for our life together?"

"Thank you, Mary," Cassie breathed out, as she began to weep for her friends.

"Well, Kevin, as you know, over the years, Amanda has shared things with me that I have not shared with Cassie. Trust is a big issue for Amanda. I've—actually, we've both proven to her that she may trust us." Andrew could see Kevin's eyes turning from the glimmer of hopefulness to disparity once again. "You have most assuredly laid out a good defense for yourself and your right to know where Amanda is. So, now I'm faced with a quandary. Betray Amanda's trust or help you fight for your marriage."

"Oh, good grief." Cassie huffed. "Andrew, enough with alluding to your doctor-patient privilege of keeping Amanda's secret, betraying her, and whatever else is on your mind. Kevin, I'll deal with Amanda and her being upset with us for telling you where she is. I am certain that in the end, she will forgive us." Cassie looked at her husband. "Yes, Andrew, eventually she will forgive you. Geez." Cassie rolled her eyes, then turned to look Kevin dead in the eyes. "So, here's the million-dollar answer to your question. Last night, Amanda and Nathan flew out to Chicago where they spent the night with Ryan and George."

"They went to Chicago to see your son and his partner?" This was not at all what Kevin expected to hear.

"Yes, they flew out to Chicago. With you totally upsetting Amanda, and her deciding to take a leave of absence, Nathan made a quick change in his plans and added a stop off to see his brother. It was perfect for both of them."

"You said Nathan changed his plans to go with Amanda?"

"Oh goodness." Cassie sucked in air as she looked helplessly at Andrew.

"Ah, Kev, I gather that you do not know about Nate going out to be with Summer."

Kevin sat looking at Andrew as if he had no idea of what he was talking about. When was the last time Amanda had shared anything with him about Summer? Actually, when was the last time he had asked her about her daughter? Kevin sighed.

"Is Nathan helping Summer deal with the attempt that was made on her life? I've been so distracted by the wedding that—" Kevin did not complete his thought. Instead, he released a deflated breath.

"Kevin," Cassie's voice was quiet, yet commanding. "Summer is okay, much to our relief. Adam caught the person who was plotting to kill her."

"That's good—Adam. Who's Adam?"

"The detective who came to investigate the attempt on Summer's life. After a rocky first meeting, the two have spent time together. From what Amanda says, they appear to have a budding relationship." Cassie paused then added for effect. "The selfie picture I've seen of Summer and Adam is adorable. They look happy together."

"Wait a minute. There are pictures of them together?" Kevin watched Cassie as she smiled and nodded with her look of approval. He should have known Amanda had at least one picture of Summer and a new man in her life. Now, Kevin had to wonder what else he had missed. "What about Summer's divorce? I thought she was still legally married, or did I somehow miss that too?"

"Well," Andrew had cleared his throat. "You didn't miss that. Summer and Mitchel's divorce will be finalized this week. Originally, Nate planned to fly out today. As you know, things changed."

Now, Amanda's cooling-off time was beginning to make perfect sense to Kevin. Of course, Amanda would not go to New York. She knew that she did not need to go north when she had her allies in Baltimore and Denver assisting her.

"So, you both are indirectly telling me that my wife is on her way to Denver with Nathan to be with her daughter while she goes through the end of her divorce."

"She is," Andrew responded quietly to match the mood in the room.

"And this wasn't a spur-of-the-moment decision—"

"No, Kevin, it wasn't. Summer discussed with Amanda the possibility of her joining Nathan awhile ago. I had also assured her that she could take a leave of absence if she felt overwhelmed and the need to get away. I'm sorry that we could not tell you where Amanda was going when she left the reception."

"I understand and appreciate your loyalty to her. She is fortunate to have you both as friends."

"Kevin, we're also your friend, and if you're interested, there's a three thirty-five flight with a change in St. Louis, three fifty-five changing in Chicago, four twenty-five changing in Houston. Flights out at four forty-five and five both have stops, but no changing flights, and the six oh five is nonstop."

"Thanks, Drew. As much as I'd like to drive to BWI right now, I can't. I will need to clear time off from the trauma department as well as my teaching responsibilities at the university. So the soonest I might be able to get out of here is tomorrow night." Kevin sighed. This time, it was one of relief. At least now he knew where to go to find Amanda. Now, his hope was renewed that they could, and would, reconcile their differences in their marriage.

Denver, Colorado

Summer could hardly contain her excitement as she stood with Adam at Denver International waiting for her father's flight to arrive. Together they stood and watched the board that showed the progress of incoming flights. Then, they saw it. The plane that he was a passenger on was making its final approach to land on the runway.

Adam ran his hand down Summer's back as he quietly spoke to her. "Well, Sunflower, shall we move closer to the arrival door to wait for your father?"

"Oh, yes, Adam. Let's. I'm so excited and glad you are here with me." Adam took advantage of the moment, slid his arms around her, and kissed her. Summer did not hesitate as she melted into his arms and placed a gentle kiss on his lips. The announcement of the arrival of Stephen's flight brought them apart. Summer moved closer to the door her dad would walk through at any moment. Adam was right by her side.

"Summer, it's nice to see you so excited, and after what this summer has been like, I'm personally enjoying seeing something this special happening for you. Having grown up in a family with both of my parents involved in my life, I honestly can't imagine what it must be like for you, after all these years to have your father in your life."

"You're right." Summer smiled. "You can't imagine. But I'll tell you, Adam, when you meet my dad, you'll understand why I'm crazy about him."

—⁓⦚⁓—

The wait didn't take too long for the flight to land and the passengers to disembark. Adam watched as Summer—dressed in jeans, a green tee shirt with her father's bait-and-tackle shop logo on it, hiking boots, her hair pulled back into a ponytail, and minimal makeup—excitedly await his arrival. Then, a rather large, older man Adam assumed to be near his parents' age, casually and surprisingly similarly dressed as Summer, step through the door. His blue eyes, which reminded Adam of the clear lakes up in the mountains, roamed the group gathered to welcome their loved ones and friends. The man had an air of confidence about him. Adam smiled as Summer tugged his hand and propelled him forward.

"Dad," she called out while moving through the crowd. "Excuse us. Dad!" she called out once more while moving through the last of the people.

"Princess!" the man called out to her and stepped toward them. Adam simply watched as Summer literally threw herself into the older man's arms. He wrapped his arms around Summer, as if he were her knight ready to shield her from the world. Adam smiled as he watched Summer being held in her father's arms. Her father. This initial observation of Summer and him warmed Adam's heart. After thirty years of not knowing the other existed, there they were—father and daughter together. Adam could only wonder how special it must be for both of them. This was their moment, and he would not intrude.

"Oh, Dad, I can't believe it, you're really here." Her father chuckled, hugged her back, and then released her just enough so that he could look down at her. It was a toss-up between which person's grin was wider.

"Believe it, Princess. I'm here in the flesh. Goodness, you're just as pretty as the first time we met."

"Dad," Summer giggled. "I think you're a bit biased in your opinion." Her warm brown eyes sparkled with joy to match his.

"I do believe I have a right to consider my daughter to be a beautiful woman." As Stephen completed his sentence, he heard a male voice next to them. With that, Stephen glanced over to see Adam standing close to them and agreeing that Summer was beautiful. Having been told about him by Summer during one of their many conversations and having seen a picture of him, Stephen was not surprised to see him standing there, or adding his thought to the conversation. "Pardon our rudeness in not making formal introductions, Stephen Johnson, and you must be Adam, the young man I've heard good things about." Stephen extended his hand, which Adam immediately took a hold of. Their grip and subtle nod laid out their pact as the two most important men in Summer's life.

"Yes, sir. Mr. Johnson, I am pleased to meet you and look forward to being able to spend time with you and Summer during your visit." There was a pause in their conversation, then Adam added, "I see you have a small carry-on. Do you have a bag that we need to get from baggage claim as well?"

"Yes, I do. Thank you for asking." Stephen liked this man's manners. He also could tell that Summer's detective was keenly aware of their surroundings. That pleased him even more, knowing that Adam would be as protective of Summer as she claimed he was. "There was a time in my life when I could have gotten by with a small carry-on. Not anymore." He sighed. "It's tough to admit that I'm getting older, and not able to live carefree."

Summer placed her hand on her father's arm, while she laced her fingers of her other hand with Adam's fingers. Her eyes twinkled as she spoke, "Dad, you're not that old. But, knowing firsthand from traveling across the country, what a killer the time changes are to the body, I know you're tired from your long trip. Let's go get your bag so we can go to my place, and then you can relax."

—⁂—

Traffic around the Denver metro area was busy on that Sunday afternoon. It was September, which meant football. Of course, there was a home game played at Mile High Stadium. Still, with all the football fans who were leaving the game, adding to congestion on the freeway, Adam moved through traffic with ease. They were almost to the exit for Summer's neighborhood when his phone rang. Adam and Summer looked at each other as he answered. She knew. Sure enough. Change in plans. When Adam ended his call, Stephen listened to them quietly talk about Adam having to go investigate a homicide. Adam took the exit at a speed that caused Stephen to reconsider his first impression of Summer's boyfriend. He sped down one street after another, causing Stephen to hold on to the door handle. They went so fast that Stephen lost count of the streets they turned onto and went down, before pulling abruptly into Summer's driveway.

Summer leaned over and kissed Adam. "Be careful. I love you." She smiled at him then turned to look at her father sitting in the backseat. "Come on, Dad. We need to hurry and get your stuff out of the trunk so Adam can go." By now, Summer was already in motion opening the door to get out. She quickly ran to the trunk of the car and grabbed out her father's luggage.

"Sunflower," Adam called to her. Summer looked back into his car. "Don't forget to reset the alarm." He smiled. She rolled her eyes, while smiling back. "I love you too." As soon as the words were out of his mouth, Adam sped off to the crime scene.

Summer sighed as she stood with her father and watched Adam drive away. His portable magnetic light had been placed on the hood of his unmarked vehicle, and his siren was blaring as he drove toward the crisis. Stephen raised his arm to encase her shoulder. Summer leaned into him. She then looked up at him. He had a scowl as he looked down the now empty and quiet street.

"He really is a good driver." Summer's expression was totally serious. When her eyes met his, she had a look, as if to dare him to contradict her. With that, Stephen burst into laughter and hugged her tight against him.

"If you want to feel like you're riding a roller coaster. I'm just glad I don't have to ride with him on a daily basis."

"Dad."

"Honestly, Summer, I have no doubt in my mind that Adam knows what he is doing behind the wheel. Princess, I understand why he was driving so fast. I'm teasing you."

"I know, Dad." Summer attempted to smile, while releasing a breath. "It's just not easy for me to watch him go off like that. Even though we know it is a homicide he's going to, there is a possibility that the perp is still in the area and might shoot at Adam."

Stephen eased his hold, while quietly speaking, "Summer, honey, it's obvious this guy means quite a lot to you. I hope Adam realizes what a lucky guy he is to have you here waiting for him—worrying for him and his safety."

"Thanks, Dad. I'm glad you're here to be a buffer."

"Me too." He yawned. "So, let's go on inside, and then you can show me this alarm you need to set to keep Adam happy."

Summer tipped her chin down as she stood there. Her look was eerily familiar to him. He shook his head and smiled. "Say no more." Then, as he released her and picked up his suitcase, he added under his breath, "Amanda."

"Dad," Summer giggled. "You can tease, but please no picking on Mom."

Stephen raised his hands as if in surrender, while his grin increased. "Hey, you're the one who gave me the same kind of look she would have. I was just making an observation."

His gentle teasing had helped to calm Summer's unrest, at least on the outside of her. Summer showed him the flowerbeds she had made out in the front yard with her mother, as they approached the front door. She pointed out the new door that had been installed during her stay at Nikki and Alex's home. Stephen asked countless questions, which Summer answered to the best of her ability. Any question that she did not have an adequate answer for, she deferred for him to ask Adam later on when he was finished with work.

When they were inside, Summer set the alarm for the zone in the front of the house. At that time, she left the alarm off in the rear of the house, since they would be in and out of the back of the house and on the patio. After showing Stephen the house, and leaving him in the den to unpack and get settled in, she went into the kitchen to prepare a snack for them.

———◄═══▸───

"Wow," Stephen said while walking into the kitchen and seeing his daughter standing at the counter by the sink with her back to him. "It smells delicious in here. What are you creating?" he asked while walking over to stand next to her.

"For now, I thought we could munch on button mushrooms stuffed with cheddar cheese and bacon." She noticed his expression was not one of sheer delight, so she added, "Or we could settle for nachos and cheese and a beer."

"Ah, a girl after my own heart, nachos and cheese and beer." He smiled. "But I do have to say those mushrooms sound interesting."

Summer smiled at him before walking over to the refrigerator and grabbing two cold beers from the door. She closed the door with her foot and walked back over to where her father remained standing. She smiled and handed him the two bottles.

"Please open these for us while I heat the cheese to pour over the nachos. The meat I'm searing will go into the slow cooker with the par boiled vegetables. Then, while dinner cooks, we can sit out on the patio and enjoy our snack. Dad, I hope you don't mind, but we will be having company besides Adam to join us for dinner. The mushrooms I teased you about actually will be heated and served when they arrive."

"You obviously like to entertain." He was answered with a wide smile and a nod. Stephen was impressed by his daughter's attention to detail and her creativity with food preparation. "So, does Adam like your mushrooms?" he asked with a slight lift of his lips and tease in his voice.

"He does, and more—"

Stephen chuckled as he saw the way Summer's eyes danced with joy. Then, he watched the smile appear on his daughter's face. Sheer happiness radiated from her.

"So, will Adam call you when he's heading over, or just show up?"

"He'll call to tell me he's safe, and on his way." Summer moved the ingredients around in the cooker. Then, when satisfied, she placed the lid and continued with the conversation. "This isn't the first time we've been through an abrupt change in plans. My lawyers, and now dear friends, Nikki and Alex, have helped me through the first couple of times when Adam needed to go speeding off. You'll get to meet them."

"Your lawyers, are they the people whom you spoke of coming over later?" Summer grew quiet deciding what to say next. Stephen saw the uncertainty in her eyes. "Is there something you're not telling me about them coming here?"

"It's not about Alex and Nikki and coming over." Summer drew in a breath. She had been putting off broaching this topic of conversation for as long as possible.

He reached out his hand to touch her chin and lift it so that he could look deep into her eyes. Her hesitant smile confirmed his suspicion that something was amiss. "All right, Princess, you're stalling. Right now you are reminding me of someone whom I won't name, but we both know." He sighed. "Go ahead and tell me what's going on."

"Okay, here it goes." She drew in a deep breath. As she did, her father tilted his chin down and scrunched the corner of his lips to indicate he was losing patience. Summer quietly began, "While you were settling in, I had a call from my friend Nathan. He is Cassie and—"

"The doctor's son. They have the cabin on the lake. I remember them." Stephen intently watched his daughter as she spoke.

"Yes, remember I told you Nate is a lawyer. He hooked me up with Nikki and Alex."

"Right." Stephen was getting an uneasy feeling in the pit of his stomach. "You said something about him coming out to be here with us on Wednesday, when we go to court for your divorce."

Summer nodded. "That's right." Summer drew in a breath, then continued. "Dad, you need to know that Nate is arriving by plane in about"—Summer glanced at her watch—"an hour."

"I'm confused. Why is his coming suddenly an issue?" Stephen watched Summer's expression that was about as turbulent as a midsummer storm in the mountains, and waited for her to continue.

"It's not an issue for Nate to be here. But, Dad, you need to know, Mom being here with him might be a problem."

Stephen was surprised, but pleased to hear that Amanda was coming to Denver. He knew in his heart that his daughter also needed her mother during this difficult time in her life. "Princess, please tell me why you think your mother and the Doc being here might be a problem?"

"That's just it, Dad. Kevin won't be here. Mom's coming alone." She could see the question in his eyes. Summer released a heavy sigh, then forged on. "There have been some things going on in Mom' life, but I'm not at liberty to say why Mom is coming here without Kevin. You'll need to ask her what is going on."

Amanda without Kevin? Stephen was confused. He saw something in Summer's eyes. Moisture. She was tearing up. Oh boy. This was bad. At that moment, Stephen was unsure that he wanted to be there, for the drama he was sure would unfold outside of the courtroom.

22

The front door bell rang while Summer and her dad sat on the porch together. Summer stood and walked with ease to the front door, with her father by her side. When Summer introduced him to Nikki and Alex, she was pleased to see how comfortable he was with her friends. She knew at that moment that the evening would be a memorable one for all of them. The small group made their way through the living room and hall to the kitchen. While Stephen and Alex continued on to the porch, Summer and Nikki stopped in the kitchen to attend to the food Nikki and Alex had brought to contribute to the evening's festivities. Summer's mouth watered as she gazed over the platters of fruit and cheese Nikki had prepared. The bottle of red wine they brought, along with the food, was placed in the refrigerator to chill. Summer had just walked out onto the patio with Nikki when she received a text message. Her soft smile did not go unnoticed by her father. He silently watched Summer move with grace back into her house. From where he sat, and she stood in the kitchen, he could see her with the remote in her hand. Ah. Stephen understood what was happening. Someone was arriving, and she was waiting to turn off her alarm system. He surmised that the text had probably come from Adam. It didn't take long for Stephen to hear from Summer's exclamation and know exactly who had arrived. He'd give them a moment alone.

"Nate, welcome." Summer hugged her friend and then whispered in his ear, "Thank you for keeping your promise and taking care of Mom for me."

Nathan hugged Summer close to him and whispered, "Anytime, Sum. Besides, it really wasn't that difficult, once I commandeered A and C to help me with Operation Rescue Amanda." Summer giggled. Nate smiled at Amanda, who stood by him and was quietly watching him interact with her daughter. Her weary eyes actually sparkled as she listened to his playfulness when he spoke aloud. "So, Sum, since I'm standing here holding you, a beautiful woman, and have an equally beautiful woman standing next to me, allow me to introduce you to my hot date I picked up at Brian's wedding." That comment caused both Summer and Amanda to burst into laughter. Amanda began to shake her head when Nate added, "She's my new cougar, and I'm the envy of the other single men who were at the wedding."

Summer looked from Nathan to Mom, who was continuing to shake her head and not quite laughing at the absurdity of it all. "Oh, you two!" Summer exclaimed. She then ripped herself from Nathan's hug to snuggle into her mother's embrace. "Mom, welcome welcome welcome. I'm so glad that you decided to come to be with me. I couldn't imagine going through this week without you being here. I just wish both of our lives weren't in crisis, and we had a happier reason for being together."

"Me too, my Summer Sunshine. Me too." Amanda sighed while snuggling her daughter closer to her chest.

Nathan smiled approvingly at what he saw unfolding with his friends. He knew that they needed this moment in time to be alone together. So, having been to Summer's home before, and knowing that his friends were already out on the porch, he made himself at home and quietly slipped away toward them.

Amanda sniffled back her tears as she held her daughter tight against her body. Their hearts beat strong in solidarity. Amanda whispered out, while fighting to hold back her tears, "Summer, I love you so much. Even though it would be nice for both of us to have everything going smoothly in our lives"—she sighed— "I'm so glad you still need me and want me to be here as you go through this rough time in your life."

"Oh, Mom, I love you too, and I will always need and want you to be with me. You, my terrific mom, are the reason I shine." Summer felt her mother's arms tighten, and she now sniffled with her. Since the beginning of the year, they both had been through so much turmoil. It grieved Summer's heart to see the pain and sadness in her mother's eyes. The familiar sparkle that Summer looked forward to seeing whenever they were together was gone. "Mom, you are welcome to stay as long as you need to be here. We'll talk, if that's what you want, or hike—whatever you need."

Amanda eased her hold on Summer so that she could look into her eyes. What she saw didn't surprise her. Summer's eyelashes glistened with wetness, the same as hers did. "Honey, thank you for your concern. I'm sure we will have our quiet time to talk." She softly smiled while touching a piece of hair hanging by Summer's ear and rubbing it between her thumb and pointer finger. "Honey, this week, I'm here for you, and I do not intend to impose on you. After all, your father—"

"Mom—" was all Summer got out of her mouth before Amanda placed her finger on her lips. Her eyes spoke before her lips moved.

"Summer, I'm glad that he is going to be staying here with you."

Summer nodded and then responded, "Dad's already here and out on the porch with Nate, Nikki, and Alex."

"I know." Amanda sighed. "He's not the quietest person I know, so I could not help but hear him talking and laughing with them." With that, Amanda shook her head and almost smiled. "Sunshine, you both have been looking forward to this time to be together. My precious child, I've had you to myself for thirty years. I will not intrude on all of your time with him throughout the course of this week." Summer was scrunching her lips. Amanda could not help but tenderly smile, while knowing full well what her daughter's facial expression meant. "You might as well let me finish." Now Summer's lips slowly began to form a pout. Amanda cleared her throat. "Summer Brooke, your pout won't work. I have already made a reservation at a hotel." Summer shook her head as sadness and moisture pooled in her eyes. "Hey now, we will have our time. But, Summer, honey, as you and your dad need your time, I also need some time alone to process everything that is going on in my life. Remember, my troubles with Kevin is the ultimate reason for my being here."

"I know, and of course I respect your need for quiet time for reflection. But, Mom, I just don't feel right about you needing to spend money on a hotel room when you may sleep in my bed. Dad's sleeping on the daybed in the den, and I can sleep on my couch."

Amanda sniffled. "Summer, there will be other times in our future when I will come stay with you. Right now, this is the way it needs to be for all of us. Besides, being at the hotel downtown, I will be able to check out the Molly Brown House, and other points of interest."

"Okay, you win," Summer spoke with resignation in her voice for the way things needed to be.

"Good." Amanda drew in a breath and slowly exhaled. "Now that we have sleeping arrangements resolved, let's go save Nathan and your other friends from your father."

Summer seized the moment and gave her mother one more hug, then with arms laced together, they walked out onto the porch. Laughter greeted them as they stepped through the door. This is what Amanda needed. Younger adults who reminded her of all that was good in the world. Nikki and Alex immediately stepped over to greet Amanda, who once again thanked them for participating in Summer's birthday surprise and for all they had done for Summer since that weekend.

When Stephen saw Amanda, his smile grew. He immediately stood and took a few quick steps toward her, while surveying her appearance. She was wearing a beige cotton pullover sweater with a simple gold chain laying on her chest, jeans and hiking boots on her feet. Her hair was gathered at the nape of her neck with a multicolored scarf. Stephen saw that her makeup was minimal, as he had expected to find; however, her eyes caused him to draw in a short breath, as he saw the unmasked pain through the smiles she shared with Nikki and Alex. He had seen that look once before, and he knew who had caused the pain the first time. Guilty where he stood for their past. But now in the present, Johnson decided he would do whatever he could to help her through her tumultuous time with Kevin.

"Nathan, have you ever seen two more beautiful women than these two standing with us?" Stephen asked, while keeping his gaze fixed on Amanda. He didn't wait for Nathan to respond. Stephen reached out and gathered Amanda's hand into his. "Calli, you look like you need a hug." Then Johnson saw the tear escape from her lid and race down her cheek like water tumbling over the falls on Goodman's ledge back home in New York.

Both Nikki and Alex moved slightly to open the space between them and Amanda. Without a word, Stephen closed the minimal space between them and eased his friend into his arms. Amanda lowered her head to his chest. The back of her head was tucked into his armpit. Her arms seemed to move by themselves as she slid them around Stephen's waist. He raised his hand to gently hold her head against him. Summer sniffled as she quietly watched her father tenderly care for her mother. Seeing them together, it was easy for her to imagine them being a little younger than her, madly in love with one another. All these years later, they still had a bond. In their own special way, they still needed each other. Summer quietly mouthed to Nikki, Alex, and Nathan that they should leave them alone.

Nathan had also been watching the interaction between Amanda and Stephen and understood their need. At that moment, as close as Nathan had always been to Kevin and his family, a part of Nathan almost wished Kevin could be there to see Stephen caring for Amanda. *Perhaps,* Nathan thought, *given what Kevin and Meg had put Amanda through, Kevin needed a taste of his own medicine.*

Amanda sniffled and began to stir while standing in Stephen's arms. "So, was it good for you?" she asked while looking up at him with a weary smile and shimmering, wet eyelashes.

"The best." He gave her his smile that almost seemed to wink at her. It was his special smile he had always reserved for Amanda, and only her.

She sniffled again. "I see you pulled out your secret weapon." Moisture was again seeping into her eyes. Tiny droplets sparkled on her wet lashes.

"You noticed." His eyes twinkled as he allowed a confident uplift of his lips to appear. "I kept it all these years in case of an emergency like this one."

"Oh really?" Amanda spoke with more bravado than she actually felt. She then drew in a breath.

"Oh, yes." Stephen stroked her back. "With a woman like you," he looked intently into her eyes as he continued, "a man has to be prepared."

"Hmm...prepared you say." Amanda paused, as if deep in thought. Then, with a totally sober expression while blinking back tears, she asked, "Afraid you can't handle me?" Amanda heard herself ask the question and wondered how their conversation, which she knew was intended to make her feel better, had gone so weird between them.

"Baby"—Stephen touched the tip of her nose and winked—"I learned a long time ago when to surrender to you. You're too hot for any man to handle." He drew her in to his hug as he added, "And I wouldn't want you to change." They quietly uttered words that neither Summer nor anyone else could hear. Summer, who was mesmerized by her parents' interaction, quietly watched and listened. Stephen then turned totally serious and spoke so Summer could also hear his words. "Calli, I do hope that in time, you will feel that you can trust me to be here for you. I hope you will tell me what's so terribly wrong in your life to make you decide to come out here without your husband."

That was all it took for Stephen to say for Amanda to meld into a puddle of tears. She wept, and Stephen held her. For how long they stood with Stephen comforting Amanda, neither one knew. It was the sound of more female and male voices in the house that finally drew them apart.

———

Stephen enjoyed watching his daughter meet and greet and flow through the evening with her guests. Adam had returned to join in the party atmosphere that had been created in Summer's home. A newcomer named Micah, another detective, Adam's partner, had also arrived. Stephen noticed that the detectives blended in well with Nathan and Alex. From what he saw in these men thus far, with how they spoke with Summer and treated Amanda with respect, Stephen approved of his daughter's choices in male relationships. While welcomed into the conversation with the younger men, he continued to keep an eye on Amanda.

Stephen noticed that shortly after Adam arrived and was introduced to Amanda by Summer, she disappeared into the kitchen. He went to investigate. There he found Amanda putting the finishing touches on the appetizers.

"Does our daughter know you're in here working on preparing the food while she is socializing with her guests?"

Amanda continued carefully removing a tray from the oven. Stephen recognized the stuffed mushrooms Summer had prepared earlier in the day to be heated at this point and then served. When Amanda had the tray on the top of the stove and the door closed, she finally looked at Stephen.

"She will, soon enough. I see the look in your eyes. Don't worry about Summer and me. She'll get on me later." Amanda softly smiled, as if she knew a secret. She then added, "Johnson, we have this unspoken agreement that when one of us is the hostess, and if the other is at the gathering, she steps up and works behind the scene to help out."

"Uh-huh." He rubbed his chin. "Not buying it. Looks to me like you're hiding out, keeping yourself busy in here so that you don't have to worry about what others might think about you being here alone, without your husband."

That comment caused Amanda to rear up like a startled animal, and she was ready to strike. Her eyes drew close, warning Johnson to not say any more. She breathed out through her nose—another sign she was feeling pushed too far.

"Finally, I got you to the place where you're going to let down your guard, stop hiding and hopefully talk to me."

"Stephen," Amanda sighed. "I'll talk when I'm ready, and I will talk with whom I choose. While I appreciate your concern for me, please don't be surprised if you are not on my list of confidants. Too many people are already involved in this mess, and while I love and appreciate everyone for caring for me and sympathizing with me, I need some quiet time to just process what has been happening. I need space so that I may come to terms with what is happening in my tattered life." Amanda then released another breath and raised her hand to stroke Johnson's jaw. "Please, Stephen, be the friend I need for you to be at this moment." She drew in a breath. "I know you're here for me, and that means more to me than you'll ever know. Be my shoulder to cry on, if that is what I need. Laugh with me and tease me. But please, don't pressure me to talk when I'm not ready."

Stephen raised his fingers to gently touch her hair as he had done countless times during their youth. His eyes held hers. Love and concern shone in them as she looked into his steady gaze. "Calli, I let you down once in your life when you needed me most. I will do my best to not let you down this time. I will be the friend you need me to be."

"Thank you." Amanda drew in a calming breath. Her emotions were all over the place. She was too vulnerable and needed to focus on something other than Johnson standing way too close. Picking up the spatula, she began moving the stuffed mushrooms from the warm tray to the platter that the appetizers would be served on. "Stephen, while I am finishing this, would you help me by getting a fruit tray and a cheese tray out of the refrigerator?"

Stephen and Amanda kept the conversation to a minimum as they walked out onto the porch. They placed the platters on the table Summer had arranged by the screen window. Summer came over and thanked both of them for helping her. With a kiss to each of her parents' cheeks, Summer glided away to Adam's side. Stephen once again found himself engaged in conversation with Wayne and George. He noticed that his daughter sure did have a slew of men in her life, and they all seemed to hold her in high regard. Pride surged through him as he listened to the two men talk about Summer's heroics in saving the doe and her fawn, as well as their successful outcome.

Stepping away from the picture-perfect table, Amanda immediately began speaking with an attractive woman whom Stephen figured was about the same age as Summer. A man, whom he had not yet been introduced to, leaned over and hugged Amanda. They shared in a laugh. Stephen smiled to himself. He had a perfect excuse to once again be near Amanda, without her accusing him of hovering over her.

"Ah, Johnson, you found me once again." Amanda smiled and gave him her look that informed him she was on to him. *Darn, that woman is good*, he thought, as she asked him, "Have you met Cathy and Bill?"

"No, I haven't, Mandy." He smiled.

"Well, then I'll fill in for Summer and do the honors. This is Cathy, one of Summer's good friends and colleague. Cathy and Summer working together make formidable park rangers, and this is Bill, Summer's friend who works at the wildlife refuge preserve where Summer volunteers. And now that he knows who the two of you are, allow me to introduce you both to Summer's father, Stephen Johnson from the Great Sacandaga Lake Community in upstate New York."

Cathy smiled. "Mr. Johnson, it is a pleasure to meet you. Summer has often spoken of you since you were united in May. It is good for family to be together, especially now." Cathy's eyes shifted along with everyone else to watch Summer, as she stood with Adam's arm protectively around her shoulder. "She needs both of her parents to be here with her, more than she knows, or would admit to any of us."

Stephen's gaze moved to fall on Amanda. He quietly breathed out into her ear for only her to hear, "And I wonder where she gets that from?"

"I wonder," she responded, then turned her gaze toward Summer. "Excuse me," she said and stepped away.

<hr />

Summer was exhausted by the end of the evening. She stood outside on the driveway with Adam watching Nate leave with Nikki and Alex to go to their home. Adam's arms came around her with his hands tenderly holding her against his taunt body filled with desire. Summer sighed as Adam seized the moment and leaned in to gently place his lips on Summer's moist, warm partially-open lips. Both felt the heat rising between them. It was Adam who reluctantly pulled away.

"I love you, Summer."

"I love you too, Adam." She sighed. "We better go in and see what my parents are up to."

"Maybe we shouldn't and allow—"

"Trust me. There won't be any 'and allow' with them. My parents are in my home together and are too quiet. By now, one of them could be dead, and that's what has me worried."

Adam, who was still learning about Summer's family, immediately grew concerned. "Do you honestly believe that your father would intentionally hurt or kill your mother?"

Summer burst into laughter. "Adam, honey, my dad is not the one you have to worry about."

"Oh?"

"Adam, it's time you hear more of the story about Mom, and the two men who until last year had gotten away with raping her thirty years ago."

By the time Summer finished her story about the previous winter, Adam simply shook his head in disbelief. "You're right, Summer. Your mother is quite a woman. Please remind me to never make her mad at me."

"Honey, Mom already likes you. Treat me right, and you won't have to worry about her." Summer leaned in and gently kissed him. "Honestly, Mom's really a gentle person, unless you mess with either of us." She cleared her throat for effect. "We had best go in."

Adam held open the door for Summer to enter her home. Quiet conversation was heard coming from the well-lit kitchen. Summer smiled, as they walked into the room, to find her mother at the sink with her hands in the dishpan washing dishes. Her father had a dish towel in his hand and was placing dried dishes and containers on the counter for her to put away.

"Wow! Thank you both." Summer was smiling as she walked over to stand by her parents. "You know, I should be upset with the two of you."

"Oh, here we go." Amanda rolled her eyes and sighed.

Stephen remembered days gone by and understood Amanda's expression. He then looked over at Summer and Adam as they stood together. "Princess, I do believe that right now might not be a good time to complain or tease with your mother."

Summer had caught a glimpse of her mother's expression. She nodded and stepped over to gently place her hands on her shoulders. Even before her hands were resting in place, she felt the downward movement of her shoulders sagging. "Mom, you look pretty beat. How about you quit for tonight and relax with us out on the porch for while?"

"Thank you, Summer." Amanda smiled as she dried her hands and turned to face her daughter. "I am tired, and I think that if you are willing to give me a ride to the hotel, I'm ready to turn in for the night."

"We'll all ride to the hotel with you," Adam added.

"Are you planning on driving?" Stephen asked.

"Yes."

"Dad," Summer piped up. "Adam's off duty, so you don't have to worry about his driving." With that comment, Summer regaled Adam and Amanda about Stephen's reaction to the ride to her house from the airport. The humor of the situation caused Amanda to laugh.

"Well, Adam, if my daughter trusts you, so do I." Without a word spoken between them, mother and daughter linked their arms in solidarity. Adam could not help but smile. At that moment, he knew his heart warmed. His admiration for Amanda, as a mother and as a survivor, was growing by the minute, and his love for Summer, for simply being who she was, was growing by the second.

Summer yawned as she unlocked the ranger station door. It was Monday morning. Nathan had already called to share his plans for the day with her. Of course, he would be stopping by her home that evening for a visit with her and whomever else was there. Summer found herself smiling, as she stepped inside the cool building and her booted feet clomped along the pine plank floor. After turning on the lights, she opened the windows to allow fresh air to pass through the space. As she turned to boot up the computer and prepared to look at the security monitors from the night before, her phone rang.

"Good morning, Mom." Summer could not help but smile. Not one, but both of her parents were in town. At that moment, life was good. Her soft smile quickly disappeared as she listened to her mother share her plans for the day. "Mom, are you serious?" Summer could not believe what her mother was telling her. "Yes, it does sound like an adventure. Mom, I honestly have never heard of that company conducting guided trips up in the mountains, so you can go prospecting. Yes, I'm sure you can take care of yourself." Summer sighed. "Mom, before you decide to spend money on something that might not be legit, please let me contact Adam and see if he knows about this prospecting company, or one that is more reputable."

Their conversation continued, then Amanda sighed. "Summer, the last thing I need is for you to be distracted from your work on account of me, so I will make a compromise. I will stay in or around Denver, and go to the Museum of Nature and Science, or perhaps Dinosaur Ridge, or something else that I find interesting."

"Mom, thank you." Summer sniffled. "I really appreciate you making this compromise."

"I know, honey. The last thing I want is for you to be worrying about me. Even though I am perfectly capable of taking care of myself."

"Mom, I hear you loud and clear, for the second time this morning, I might add."

"I'm sure you do."

"You know, Mom, prospecting does sound like fun. Perhaps we can research this together and then go do some prospecting together during one of your future trips out here."

Summer's suggestion was welcomed and led to more lighthearted conversation and laughter. Then the sound of Stephen's footsteps was heard on the steps as he made his way to the building from the parking lot. Summer was glad he had wanted to take his time walking around and give Summer a chance to get settled in for her day's work, as well as time to privately speak with her mother. She heard him walking on the porch, and stopping to read the information tacked on the bulletin boards.

"Mom, I need to get to work. Yes, Mom, I will be able to work with Dad here. No, he won't be underfoot." Summer chuckled at her mother clucking like an old hen. "Yes, Mom. I'm sure, he's going hiking up on the trail where I found the deer. Yes, Mom, I'll make sure that he has a map and extra water. Mom, you need not worry. I will do my best to make sure he gets back here safely. I know you are thinking of me, Uncle Phil, and Aunt Becky. I love you, Mom, and I know you won't admit you care and are worried about Dad's safety." Summer laughed at her response. "Enjoy your day, and call me later. Bye."

The door of the office opened, and Stephen stepped inside. His expression was priceless. Then he spoke with sheer delight. "Princess, you have no idea what today means to me—being here with you. I've waited my lifetime to get out here to hike in the Rocky Mountains."

Summer beamed. "Well, then let me get you a map of our park, highlight the best trails for you to explore, and give you a couple of extra bottles of water, and energy snack packs to go with your lunch we packed."

They hugged as they stood together at the registration log. With his day recorded in the log, Stephen began his day's journey out on the trails. Summer watched him begin his hike at an easy pace. Both of her parents were doing their own thing for the day, and she was part of both of their plans directly, or indirectly. Joy filled her heart for herself and her family.

23

It was now mid-Tuesday afternoon. The warm late summer sunshine shone down on the small suburban home. Summer glanced out the kitchen window to see the birds gathered in the backyard. A smile brushed her lips. She was glad that she had taken both Tuesday and Thursday off to bracket Wednesday, when she would be in court. The anticipation of the day had Summer a bundle of nerves. Having company was the distraction she needed to occupy her frazzled mind.

Earlier in the day, Summer and her father had gone together to the lumberyard and the hardware store to purchase the necessary supplies to make a bookcase. It had been an adventure for them, especially bringing the lumber home tied securely on the roof of her Jeep. While they were at the lumberyard, Stephen knew exactly what he wanted, and would not be deterred from his decision. As Summer listened to him speak with utter confidence, she realized that she had inherited some of her ability to visualize in her mind how something should be done, and then do it successfully, from him.

Now, her father was out under the carport, working on the final step of staining the bookcase he had made for her. Summer heard him muttering under his breath about driving his pickup truck the next time he came to visit so he could do home improvements around this place the right way. Summer fully smiled. His willingness to be there with her and to do for her caused Summer to pause and reflect on how blessed she was to have her father in her life. She felt a tear well up in her eyes and slide down her cheek. For so long, it had been only Mom and her, but now she really did have a family—her own family to love and moments like this to share together.

⎯⎯◦⎯⎯

It was break time around Summer's home, as per her father's orders. Summer sat on the patio sipping iced tea while quietly listening to him share stories about life in the Adirondacks. Summer never tired from hearing about his past and present, as she was finding that it helped her to feel more connected to him and her Johnson family. From what he shared, it sounded like her Uncle Phil had been something of a prankster when he was younger and in school with her mom.

"Dad, are you teasing me? Did this story really happen?" Summer had listened to the story that involved him, her mom, Uncle Jim, and Uncle Phil, but she just didn't know if she should fully believe her father. She knew that like her mom, he too was a storyteller.

"Princess," he said as he began laughing all over again, "if you truly do not believe me, call your Uncle Jim. He will tell you what they did. Then, you'll see. I'm telling you the truth."

Although Summer had decided to believe her father, there was a playful challenge thrown between them. So, to further their fun, she pulled out her phone and called her Uncle Jim. He was surprised and glad to hear from Summer, who quickly revealed the true reason for her call. She asked her questions. He answered. By the time the call ended, Summer's mouth was still hanging open in disbelief.

"Are you going to close your mouth anytime soon?" Stephen quietly asked and chuckled as he watched Summer processing what she had just heard.

She shook her head while closing her mouth, then looked at her father and repeated what she had heard. "They honestly stuffed Uncle Jim's and your hockey uniforms with straw, put them in a canoe, and placed it up on the edge of the roof of the school."

He was nodding and smiling. Summer saw something almost sparkle in his eyes. It was as if, for a brief moment, he had gone back in time and relived the scene in his mind. "That was mild for what your mother was known for doing."

"Okay, so I believe it happened. Now, tell me, did Mom and Uncle Phil get in trouble?"

"Those two? Huh! That would be the day!" His feigned scowl disappeared to form a grin. Again, he slowly shook his head. "Even though the principal and everyone else in the community knew that they both were guilty as sin, neither one would give the other up."

"What? You mean they were each other's alibis?"

"Oh, yes. They worked it out good. Your mother and uncle came off as innocent lambs who couldn't possibly have been at the school. They told everyone that they were only guilty of being at the cemetery, after dark, visiting your grandmother's grave. You see, your grandmother Callison had died two months before, so no one could argue with Calli's need to feel close to her mother and be at the cemetery to grieve over her passing." Summer's eyes were growing larger by the second as she listened. "My little brother and your mother did go to the cemetery, and they left flowers that they cut from my mother's flowerbed, for proof of their alibi. They just never admitted to anyone when they stopped by the school for their mischievousness."

Summer burst into laughter. After wiping her eyes, she asked, "So did Mom ever confess to you that she did it?"

"No," he shook his head and did that quirky thing with the side of his lips, while his eyes seemed to sparkle with humor. Then, he added, "And neither did your Uncle Phil. Through the years, after your mother left us, when we were all reminiscing about our youth, Jim or I would occasionally recall that prank, and Phil would simply get this look in his eyes. He'd smile and sometimes make a comment about how it was a tough break for us getting caught."

"Wait, Dad. You mean Uncle Jim was right. You and he did get punished for what Mom and Uncle Phil did?"

"Oh, yeah." He rolled his eyes. "Princess, we didn't get in trouble at school—no proof we did it. We got in trouble with my dad who was certain that someone from one or both of our families was guilty. Even though he had a good idea who was truly guilty, but having no proof, as spiritual leader of the community, he felt that he needed to punish someone for the prank. So, your uncle Jim and I were the ones to take the punishment."

"Oh, Dad, that must have been tough on you, being the minister's son and all. I'm so sorry to hear this." Summer was biting her lips to not laugh.

"Uh-huh. You sound it." He too was smiling. A sigh and a shake of his head followed. "Now, looking back on it, I do see the humor. Ah, those were the days. Your mother—she sure was something."

———————

Summer heard the sound of a car slowing down on the street in front of her home. She stood, quietly moved inside to look at her monitor, and watched the car come to a stop at the curb. Whomever was in the driver's seat sat there for a moment. Then, she saw the driver's door open. When the person stood, Summer immediately recognized him and gasped.

"Princess, what is it?" Stephen called out as he stepped through the patio door into the kitchen.

Summer felt her heart racing as her eyes met her father's. "Dad, I need you to promise me that you will not say or do anything that will upset Mom."

"Is your mother back?" His eyes questioned as his lips began to turn upward.

"No," Summer shook her head.

"Then, why do you think I'll upset your mother?" Stephen stepped closer to Summer. Concern radiated from his drawn eyes as he held his daughter's gaze. Then, he looked and clearly saw the person in the monitor. "Oh, great." He sighed out while running his fingers through his hair. "Princess, I will not promise you anything when it comes to that man. He's hurt your mother, and that does not sit well with me."

"Dad," she placed her hand on his arm. "I know for a fact that Mom has not shared what has happened between them with you, nor does she want to talk with you about what has happened." She saw the look of hurt in her father's eyes. Summer assumed it was probably because her mother had confided in her, and not him. She tried to be as soft as possible when she said, "Please try to understand. Mom appreciates your friendship. But, right now, she just really wants for you to be in the middle of my life, not hers." Summer's eyes conveyed her love and concern for both of her parents. "Now, I have more company to greet. Please," she paused, "for Mom—and me," she added for good measure.

With that said, Summer hastily made her way through her home to the front door, while clicking the buttons on her remote to turn off the alarm. She couldn't believe it. Dr. Kevin Wentzel, who should be in Baltimore, Maryland, was standing in front of her home. By the time Kevin reached the middle of the cheery, flower-bordered walkway, Summer was opening the front door. Taking a deep breath for courage, she stepped outside.

She had met her mother in the morning at the hotel for a very early breakfast so that they could talk in private. From their conversation, Summer had a strong suspicion that her mother was unaware of Kevin's plan to come out here. Oh boy! Not good—not good at all! Keeping her dad in check would be bad enough, but her mother—Summer was beyond worried at what might happen when Mom saw Kevin. As she watched Kevin approach, Summer immediately noticed everything about his appearance. This was not the same self-assured, confident man Summer has seen before. His clothes looked as though he had spent more than one day in them. She also noticed that he had at least one day's growth of facial hair on his face. Wow! The man was a sheer mess!

"Hello, Kevin," Summer attempted to sound welcoming, as she stood and watched him make his approach to her front door.

"Hello, Summer." His voice along with his bloodshot eyes further revealed the fatigue Summer had first noticed in his step. "I'm sure you were not expecting me to show up at your doorstep. I do apologize for this intrusion," he humbly added. Summer remained silent while watching him. There was something different about his voice. Strain. Perhaps remorse. She didn't know. He breathed out a heavy breath. "I'm looking for your mother."

"I gathered you were not here to visit me." Summer knew she sounded snarly, and that she needed to be polite; after all, the man was her mother's husband. Still, there was so much she wanted to say to him; however, it wasn't her place to ridicule him for what he had done. She hesitated for a moment as she thought about her dad, who had—much to her relief—remained inside. She had an uneasy feeling as she spoke. "Kevin, I regret to inform you that Mom's not here right now."

"Oh," he did not attempt to hide his disappointment. "I was under the impression that she had come to Denver and that she would be here with you."

"I gather that." Summer sighed. "You are correct that Mom is in Denver—she's just not here right now. When Mom and I spoke earlier today, she did not mention anything to me about you coming out here." He nodded, as if in defeat. At that moment, Summer felt a twinge of sadness for him. "Kevin, I'm sure Mom thinks you're still in Baltimore. She will most assuredly be shocked to find you here. Now, having said that, I feel that you need to know that since my house is so small, and not adequate for multiple sleeping arrangements, Mom is not staying here with me."

"She isn't?"

"No. Mom's staying in a hotel during this visit." She watched his eyes as he processed her words. "My dad is also visiting, and this is his time to be staying here with me. Mom knew that Dad would be here when she decided to accept my invitation and come. So, to avoid an awkward situation with them both being here, Mom, by her own choice, is staying at a hotel." Summer instantly decided that if her mom wanted him to know what hotel, she could tell him herself. "So, as I previously said, she's out for the day." She glanced at her watch. "I expect that she will be here in a little while. In the meantime, you are welcome to come in and wait with us for her to arrive."

"Thank you, Summer. As you said, your father is here with you. Since I came here directly from the airport in hopes of finding your mother, I'll go and get checked in to my room at the hotel where I am staying, and if it is all right with you, I'll return later." Summer nodded, as Kevin released another sigh. This was not a deflated one, as the others had been. "What time do you expect your mother, and when should I return?"

Summer glanced at her watch. She knew for certain that Mom would be there for dinner. "I expect her to be here by four, or four thirty. We will be eating around five thirty, or six o'clock, depending on when Adam and my other guests arrive. Kevin, you are welcome to join us." At that moment, Summer hoped that she had just done the right thing. She knew that her mother might not appreciate her extending hospitality to Kevin. But something was softening in Summer's heart as she stood there with him.

She felt as though she had to extend the olive branch for herself, perhaps even for her mother.

"Thank you, Summer. I appreciate this, even though it is obvious you are not pleased to see me, nor want me here."

"Kevin, that's not completely correct." Summer gently placed her hand on his arm.

"We can talk as I walk with you to your car." He nodded, as Summer withdrew her hand from his arm and began to walk with him. Her voice was quiet, forcing Kevin to intently listen to her as she spoke to him. "In case you don't know, Mom and I had many lengthy conversations before Brian's wedding. From what she shared with me, I'd say you really messed up." Kevin nodded. He sniffled, withdrew a tissue from his pocket, and wiped his nose as they continued to walk and Summer spoke. "If my life wasn't in such chaos of its own, I would have flown out on one of those weekends and told you exactly what I thought of you—what I think of you. But Mom being my mom warned me to not interfere and be one of her go-to people, her confidant. Out of respect and love for my mother, I did just that. Then came the wedding. Boy, did you ever mess up from the time you got up that morning until Mom left the reception." Summer was talking faster now, with an intensity that struck Kevin as being similar to Amanda. She was her mother's daughter through and through—filled with passion for those whom she loves. He knew in his heart that he needed to continue to listen to Summer, and he did. "Listening to Mom share her pain during these past few weeks, and then hearing from Nathan, Aunt Cassie, and Uncle Andrew, as well about the fiasco at the wedding, I've had time to reflect on the similarities I see in our lives."

"And what have you discovered?" Kevin quietly asked. He sniffed back more of his emotions. At least Summer was speaking to him; perhaps that was a start toward reconciliation with Amanda.

"Kevin, I know firsthand what it feels like to have my husband cheat on me, to lie to me, and to betray my trust." Kevin flinched at her words. He too knew what it felt like to have your spouse cheat on you; after all, Meg's affair had been the final straw that decimated their marriage. He listened to Summer pour out her feelings to him. "In some ways, while I suspect in the weeks leading up to the wedding you didn't physically cheat on Mom, I sense that prior to and at the wedding, you did emotionally cheat on her, and perhaps unknowingly, or unintentionally had an affair with your ex-wife, Meg." Summer paused. "I may be wrong and may have stepped out of line, but this is how I feel. Kevin, I love my mom, and it grieves me to see how deeply you have hurt her."

By now, they had reached the driver's side of Kevin's rental. He reached out and gently took a hold of Summer's hand. Raising her hand to his lips, Kevin placed a soft kiss on the back of her hand. "Thank you, Summer. I truly thank you for your honesty. You've given me more to consider before I see your mother."

Summer remained on the walkway in front of her home and watched Kevin slowly pull away. He would be back. When he returned, her mother and father would both be there. Summer suddenly had an ominous feeling run up her spine. She knew that with her parents directly involved in this encounter, anything could happen. With that, she pulled out her phone and sent a text to Adam to enlighten him about the change of events.

By the time Adam arrived at Summer's home, Nathan, Nikki, and Alex were already there. Summer was glad that he was now there with her to serve as a buffer for her when her mother and Kevin appeared. In the meantime, while waiting for their arrival, Summer busied herself with entertaining her other guests. Adam was well aware of Summer's apprehension of having her mother and Kevin at her home along with her father. He capitalized on the opportunity to have a private conversation with Summer when she returned to the kitchen for more chips and salsa.

"Honey, when you called your mom to warn her about her husband being in town, what time did she say she would be here?"

"Anytime now."

Summer took comfort with Adam standing there with his arms around her. He had already been her buffer through the chaos of the summer months. Now, on the precipice of her divorce being finalized, revelation about everything Mitchel had been up to and was going to do, Summer had to deal with her parents, and stepfather. Could her life get any more out of control? Summer didn't want to think about the possibilities. Instead, she sank into Adam's arms that encased her, enabled him to reach into the bowl of chips, take one out, and load it with salsa before placing it at Summer's lips. While his hand held the chip at Summer's mouth, he gently placed his lips against her earlobe. "Eat your chip, Summer," he whispered, as he began to gently nibble on her ear.

Summer moaned as she opened her mouth for Adam to place the chip on her tongue. She had no idea how she chewed and swallowed the chip, while he murmured words of love in her ear. At that moment, Summer forgot about the rest of her company. All that existed was Adam and her alone in her kitchen. Her mind was soaring to another place, a sensual place for only him and her. Heat was rising from her toes upward through her body. The salsa had nothing to do with it. Adam was the only heat she needed.

"Summer," the sound of Nikki's voice brought Summer and Adam back to the present. He continued to hold Summer as she steadied herself. She drew in a deep breath as Adam released his hold on her and stepped away. Nikki's eyes smiled as she took in what had been happening between them while they were alone in the kitchen. "Your mother has arrived."

"She has?" Summer felt her cheeks grow warm with color. She cleared her throat, while glancing up at Adam, and then began straightening her blouse. "I obviously didn't hear her come."

"We know. Your mom noticed you both as she came in through the kitchen door. She didn't want to interrupt you both from your—oh, how did she put it?" Nikki softly and approvingly smiled. "Oh yes, your private conversation."

"Busted again by Mom." Summer quietly chuckled. "She sure does have impeccable timing." Adam raised a questioning brow. "It's a long story going back to my teenage years. I'll tell you after things calm down around here, and we need a good laugh."

"I'll hold you to it." Adam leaned in and gave Summer a gentle kiss by her ear. "Since we've been busted by your mom, and Nikki, perhaps we should go out and join everyone else, who appear to be partying on the porch."

"Good idea." Summer beamed, then picked up the tray filled with food.

Nikki walked on ahead of them to the porch. As they passed the monitor, Summer glanced at the screen. She recognized the car pulling up in front of her house. "Adam, honey, please take this tray on out to the table for me." He saw the distress in her eyes as she handed him the tray and asked what was suddenly wrong. She responded with anxiety in her voice. "Kevin has just arrived. I'd like to go out and meet him, and hopefully be a buffer for when he meets Mom, if that's at all possible."

Adam quietly spoke words of encouragement; then, he took the tray and headed out to the patio. When Adam entered the porch, he found that Amanda and Stephen were no longer there with Summer's other guests. He gazed out and around the backyard. Concern consumed him as he saw them standing together by one of the new flower gardens that had been made in the east of the yard. They stood with their backs to the house and appeared to be unaware of what was happening behind them. Adam was fairly certain that Kevin would not like seeing them together. An ominous feeling swept over him as he quickly headed out the side door to meet Summer and Kevin as they approached the house.

"Adam." Summer warmly smiled. "I'd like for you to meet Mom's husband, Dr. Kevin Wentzel." Summer then paused in her step and looked at Kevin. By now, Adam had closed the distance and was standing next to Summer. "Kevin, allow me to introduce you to *the* man—my man, who is instrumental in saving my life, Detective Adam North."

Kevin noticed the silent interaction between them as he extended his hand to greet Adam. "It is nice to meet you, Adam. You certainly chose a special young woman to save."

"It is nice to meet you as well." His arm came protectively around Summer's shoulder. "I agree with your observation. Summer is *very* special."

"Well, thank you both for your accolades." Summer looked at Kevin, who was now more put together than when they met earlier in the day. While at the hotel, he had apparently showered, shaved, and dressed in different casual clothes. "Mom is…" Summer gazed around the group of people gathered on the patio. "Oh, I don't see Mom. She was here. Hmm." Summer felt Adam's hand gently squeeze her shoulder.

"Honey, the last time I saw your mother, she had walked out into the backyard and was standing by your flower garden. Summer, I believe your father was also out there." His eyes had connected with her. She saw his concern, and in a split second, her own expression went from one of concern to distress.

"Oh, I see." She drew in a breath as she turned her gaze to Kevin. She saw his expression when he heard that her parents were together. At that moment, Summer wished that Kevin had simply remained in Baltimore and waited for her mother to return, but he hadn't. So, she drew in another breath to muster up all the courage she could find, and breathed out, "Kevin, if you will come this way with me, I'll show you where Mom might be." Strained words were shared as the three began to walk together through the carport to the backyard. Just as Summer was ready to say something else, Kevin's gait increased. He stepped away from them. Summer gasped as she saw what Kevin had seen. "Oh, Adam," she exclaimed, "this is horrible." Summer did not wait for Adam to respond. She took off on a run after Kevin, who was now charging toward Stephen. Adam saw what the other two had also seen. Johnson was standing in the backyard, apparently in an intimate conversation with Amanda, and to make matters worse, he had his arm around Amanda's shoulder. *Great,* Adam sighed out, as he began to run toward them all. *Looks like I might now be back on duty—and my girlfriend's parents of all people!*

"Stephen," Kevin growled out like an angry dog, "I should have known you would be here, waiting like some vulture ready to swoop in, and claim Amanda and her wounded soul once again for your own."

Kevin's words, laced with anger, caused Stephen to drop his arm from Amanda's shoulder. Amanda gasped as she and Stephen swung around to face him. Tears were streaming down her cheeks, reddened from crying during her conversation with Johnson.

"Kevin, oh no—" Amanda stood there with a look of terror in her eyes. "You need to believe me. This is not what you think."

"Not what I think," he said with an accusatory tone in his voice. "Amanda, I came here to Denver looking for you, my wife. I was prepared to admit to you my sinful behavior toward you as of late, and hopefully work with you on reconciling our differences. Yet, when I arrive, I find you with your old lover's arms attentively wrapped around you. To add more salt to our open wounds, you are standing here with all of these witnesses, who apparently approve of your behavior. So you tell me, Amanda," his voice challenged, "you tell me what I should think finding you, my wife, here like this?" Hurt was now mingled with the anger on Kevin's face. "I obviously misjudged you. Before I leave, Amanda, I am curious and need to ask you one question. What makes you any better than me?"

"Kevin," Amanda didn't have a chance to say anything else before it happened.

"You fool," Stephen growled as his right fist came up and connected with Kevin's nose. Blood spattered from the impact onto his light-blue polo shirt. Kevin stumbled backward, lost his footing from the force of Stephen's fist against his face, and fell to the ground. Stephen advanced as if to continue to pummel Kevin.

"Johnson, no—oh no." Tears were once again streaming down Amanda's cheeks.

"Dad, stop!" Summer exclaimed. She then turned to Adam with pleading in her eyes and voice. "Adam, please do something."

"Mr. Johnson, sir, you need to move away from Dr. and Mrs. Wentzel. Take a deep breath and pull yourself together." Adam continued on explaining the ramifications of Stephen's actions. By now, Adam had managed to insert himself between Kevin, lying on the ground, and Stephen, standing there with fire in his eyes. Adam then glanced down to see Amanda kneeling on the ground next to her husband. "Dr. Wentzel may press charges against you. I hope for your sake it doesn't come to that."

"Thank you, Adam." Amanda's voice was raw with emotion as she looked up at him and then at Stephen. "Johnson, you idiot! You acting like a buck fighting to protect his doe was downright stupid. I'm not your doe! Get it! You had your chance to love and protect me thirty years ago. You blew it!" She knew her words hurt. At that moment, Amanda didn't care. "I don't want or need you to go meddling in my marriage. This is not your concern, so leave us alone." Amanda felt Kevin's hand ease onto her leg. She looked at his hand. His wedding ring glistened in the early evening sunlight. She slid her hand over his, while she turned her gaze to look at him and quietly spoke. "Kevin, for the record, Johnson was not taking advantage of me, or anything else you first thought when you saw us together. We were standing together because he was praying with me—for us and our marriage."

—◉—

The last rays of light disappeared over the mountains to the west. Summer walked alone in her backyard, while Adam and her father were in the living room watching a late-season baseball game on television. She needed this quiet time to reflect on everything that had happened during the day. Her mother had called not long ago to give an update on Kevin's condition. After going to the ER to have Kevin's broken nose set, they gathered his belongings, checked him out of his room, and relocated him to her hotel room. In the morning, they would be over to get Kevin's rental car, return it to the rental agency, and meet her at court. Summer breathed out a sigh as she looked up at the starlit sky.

"Thank you, God—Great Spirit, for not abandoning us." When she breathed out the last of her prayer, she turned and headed toward her house. "Home run!" she heard her father and Adam exclaim. Summer smiled and increased her pace toward the two men she treasured most in her life.

24

The alarm clock went off much too early for Summer. Her eyes remained shut as she rolled over and blindly reached for the alarm to shut it off. She moaned out a yawn as she felt her hand connect with the incessantly buzzing clock, and knocked it off the stand to the floor. "Great," Summer huffed with disgust. With her eyes now open, she focused on retrieving the alarm that was now making a dying buzzing sound. Picking up the clock, Summer discovered that it was still working properly. "Good. The last thing I need to add to my day is to go shopping for a new alarm clock."

Summer sat up and threw her legs over the side of the bed. Sitting there, she rubbed the sleep from her eyes and stretched. It was a ghastly sound. Summer glanced over at the door and listened. It was then that she heard the gentle tapping sound against the closed door.

"Summer, Princess, are you all right?"

"Yes, Dad, I'm all right. Thank you." Summer could not help but smile at his concern.

"All right then. I thought I heard a noise, and was concerned that you might have fallen."

"No," she softly giggled. "I didn't fall. I almost killed my alarm clock," she said while getting her terry robe on.

"Murdering your alarm clock, tsk-tsk-tsk. Here I thought my daughter was the gentler of the two Newman women." He chuckled, causing Summer to giggle again as she heard him say, "Coffee's on."

Stephen was beginning to turn to head back toward the kitchen when he heard the sound of the doorknob turning. He stepped back and waited for Summer to emerge from her room. The first thing he saw when she opened the door was her smile, which seemed to reach from her lips to her dark brown eyes. Her warm smile was like a ray of sunshine, reminding him of morning sunlight glistening on the lake back home. Now, he felt as if he could understand why Amanda had given their daughter the nickname of sunshine. She's beautiful—simply beautiful.

"Mmm, I smell it." Her smile grew as she leaned up to kiss him on the cheek. "Oh goodness, you smell pretty good too. Nice aftershave." Summer laughed out, as her father swept her into his embrace and teased with her. "Dad, even with everything that happened last night between you, Mom, and Kevin, I'm truly grateful that you're here with me."

"Princess, I'm grateful that you still want me here." He gave her a gentle squeeze, and then began to draw away from Summer. "How about we get that coffee?"

"Good idea. This morning, I don't have time to get sappy. Plus, I still have to hit the shower and get ready before Adam—" Summer stopped midsentence.

"What is it?" Stephen asked. He saw something in Summer's eyes.

"I forgot Mom said that she and Kevin would be stopping by this morning. They planned to get his rental car to return it before we go to court." Summer sighed.

"Don't worry," he said, while touching his finger to lift her chin. "They've already been here and are gone."

"They were here?" With that said, Summer finished peeling herself from her father's embrace and walked into the living room. Opening the curtains, she looked out toward the street. Sure enough. The street was empty. "I take it you saw, or at least heard them when they came to pick up the car?" Summer was now turning away from the window and heading back across the room toward the kitchen and her morning coffee.

"They were here at seven fifteen this morning." He fell into step with Summer, as they both headed toward the kitchen. "Your mother waved at the window before she got into her car to follow Kevin." He shook his head. "Gee, that woman still has eyes like a hawk. It must have been he—I mean, *heck* for you growing up in her home with that uncanny ability of hers to know what was happening around her."

"Ah." Summer smiled. Her eyes were lit up with a touch of playfulness as she spoke. "So you tried to be sneaky and watch her by pulling back the edge of the drapes, hoping to not be seen." She allowed a moment of silence to hang between them before continuing, "Only to be snagged by Mom. Tsk-tsk-tsk." She shook her head while continuing to smile. She softly patted his arm. "My poor dad." Her eyes were sparkling with mischievousness that said everything else she was thinking. "Busted by Mom. Mmm-mmm-mmm. I could have—perhaps should have—warned you. Nah. It is more fun to hear of you being busted." Summer was now giggling with delight.

"You're enjoying yourself, aren't you?" he asked, while pausing at the kitchen door to allow his daughter to enter the room before him.

"Ye-up, er do!" Summer continued to smile as she walked toward the cupboard. Her bare feet patted against the cool kitchen floor.

"Princess, I hate to burst your bubble but," he quietly said, while coming to stand next to her by the counter, "that wave from your mother was not one of her friendly waves."

"Oh," the frivolity of the moment was gone. Concern now filled Summer's voice as she spoke. "What makes you say that?"

"Her eyes." Stephen's serious, rough voice filled with emotion sent a shimmer of fear into Summer. She didn't finish filling her cup. Instead, she placed the pot back on the burner. At that moment, Summer turned her gaze to meet her father's troubled eyes. "Princess, your mother, as we both know, has very expressive eyes. Even from a distance, you can easily read her, that is, if she wants you to. This morning, she most assuredly wanted me to know just where we stood with each other. The look she gave me…" He swallowed the moisture forming in his mouth. Then, he sighed out, "I saw that look in her eyes one other time in my life."

"Dad." By now, Summer had placed her hand on her father's arm. Concern was beginning to consume her. "I can see and hear your distress. What aren't you telling me?"

"Honey, the last time your mother looked at me like that, she…" He sniffed back his emotions. Summer waited, unsure she wanted to hear what her father would say. "Princess, she looked that way just before she disappeared from my life for thirty years." He released a breath that reminded Summer of a tire on a vehicle going completely flat. "Thirty years she was gone. Then, I got her back. Now, when I thought I was doing the right thing because I love and care for her, I obviously blew it! Summer, look what I've done to all of us—to you." He slowly shook his head, as if in disgust with himself. "I should have listened to your mother's warning." He released another equally deflated breath. "I never should have clobbered the miserable son of a gun."

"Oh, Dad, please don't beat yourself up over this. You did what you thought was right at the time." Summer was now very concerned for him. "Dad, since Sunday afternoon, you have reached out to Mom, caring for her. I saw the way you two were together. Mom may not want to admit it to herself, or anyone else, but I'll tell you, she still has feelings for you. Then, Kevin shows up unexpectedly wanting to reconcile with Mom. It is obvious he loves Mom, and as upset as she was with both of you, Mom clearly has chosen to love and devote herself to Kevin and their marriage. Everything that happened yesterday in my backyard sounds to me like a page from a romance novel, or romantic movie scene." Her attempt to lighten his mood didn't work. "Dad, I guess what I'm trying to say is, Mom is in a precarious emotional state. Give her time to cool off and think things through. I have a feeling that in the end, when Mom has time to process everything that has happened, the two of you will remain friends."

"Cool off, you say." He sighed. "That's what I'm afraid of, Summer. Your mother is cooling off, and this time, I fear she is going to totally freeze me out of her life. With her, it will be an ice age of epic proportions."

"Dad." Summer looked into his eyes. Her expression was filled with compassion as she spoke. "I'm so sorry to hear you sound so defeated. I don't know any other way to say this. So, here it is. If Mom freezes you out of her life, as you believe she might, well, that's her choice. It will be her loss because I happen to know that you are a terrific person."

"Thanks, Princess." He swallowed his emotions as Summer slid into his embrace to hug him.

"You're very welcome, Dad. Please remember that no matter what should happen between the two of you, I still love you. You are my dad, and I need you to be in my life, just as much as I need Mom in my life."

"Ah, Princess, you sure are one in a million. I happen to love you too. Don't you ever forget it!"

—⁓⁓⁓—

On this morning, there was no time for leisure sipping of coffee at the table. Breakfast was eaten in haste. Then, with coffee mug in hand, Summer disappeared into her bedroom, showered, and dressed in what she thought was record time for her. For Summer's last appearance in court to hear the judge grant her and Mitchel's divorce, she chose to wear a hunter green dress with a scoop neckline, fitted bodice, A-line skirt, three-quarter sleeves, and a hemline just under her knees. A simple gold chain given to Summer by her mother hung around her neck, while on her feet she wore brown pumps with a one-inch heel. The shoes were Summer's least favorite part of her attire, as she'd much rather have bare feet or her hiking boots on her feet.

Adam arrived and was greeted at the front door by Stephen. He smiled as Summer called out her greeting to him from her bedroom. Adam remained standing in the living room with Stephen, where they quietly rehashed the events of the previous night. When Summer finally appeared from her bedroom to join the men waiting for her in her living room, they both took in her appearance. Stephen smiled and watched Adam as he immediately moved with a flowing yet possessive motion toward Summer.

"Wow, Summer. You look beautiful. I almost feel sorry for Mitchel, and what he gave up by turning away from you." Summer blushed as Adam moved in to brush his lips across hers. The kiss was simple, yet revealing of them being exclusively in a relationship with each other.

"Thank you, Adam." Summer looked deep into Adam's eyes as she continued to speak. "I actually do feel sorry for Mitchel."

"How so?" Adam asked.

"During the past couple of years, Mitchel made multiple unwise choices. Each choice has had a severe consequence for him." She paused to allow the wave of sadness pass through her. Summer drew in a deep breath for calming purposes. It was then that her gaze softened. "Adam, Dad, don't you see? Mitchel has not only given up his life with me. Because of his actions, he has lost his once good reputation as a scholar and as a scientist. He no longer has his teaching position at the university, or the future he thought he would have with Jesslyn. Need I continue?" Both men shook their heads. Summer nodded in agreement, released a heavy sigh, then said, "We better get going. With morning rush-hour traffic, I don't want to run the risk of being late for court."

"Who is driving?" Stephen asked with a straight face, while maintaining eye contact with Summer.

"I am," Adam said.

"Oh, well, Princess, there you go." His smile was now growing. "With Adam driving, you'll be there with plenty of time to spare. You may even have time to go get coffee before going into court." He winked at his daughter. "As for me, I'll have time to go to the men's room and hurl."

"Dad," Summer wailed. She then burst into laughter, while realizing that her father was teasing and had helped to lighten her mood.

—————

The drive from Summer's suburban home into the city was not all that bad. Rather than take the interstate, which was jammed from a "mid rush hour, three-car, and tractor trailer" accident, Adam wove through the web of city streets. When they neared the main entrance of the courthouse, Summer saw Nathan and pointed him out to Adam and Stephen. She noticed that he was smiling, conversing, and opening the door for Amanda and Kevin to enter the building with him. Adam slowed his car to a crawl as he was prepared to stop to drop off Summer and her father before parking in the adjacent parking garage.

"I'll let you both out," Adam began to say, only to have Summer speak up.

"Adam, in light of the altercation that occurred last night, I think that it will be best for all of us to stay together. Just now, I caught a glimpse of Mom. Even though she was smiling, as she entered the courthouse with Nate and Kevin, Dad doesn't need to encounter her without both of us there as a buffer."

"Point well taken." Adam slid his hand over to rest on Summer's hands, which she was wringing with anxiety. "We'll stay together." Adam glanced in his mirror to find Stephen watching him. "Is that all right with you, sir?"

Stephen nodded. "Princess, given the importance of this day for you, we'll do everything you ask of us."

"Thank you, both." Summer sniffled and drew in a breath as Adam continued on toward the parking garage.

Summer, Stephen, and Adam were surprised to find how quiet it was in the building when they came in the main entrance. Adam, much to Summer's amazement, knew the officers on duty at the security checkpoint. They shared greetings that helped to calm her nerves, as Summer and her father passed through the metal detectors with ease. She saw Adam place his revolver and badge in the basket before walking through the scanner. Suddenly, the alarm rang out as Adam walked through the metal detector. Summer gasped, only to have Adam console her as he walked on through the security checkpoint. He stepped aside with one of the officers, who were whispering and chuckling with Adam, as if they shared some inside police joke or secret. They all turned to Summer and immediately sobered when they saw her look of distress.

"Summer, honey, you need not worry. It was my concealed piece that set off the alarm. Everything is all right." Adam stepped over to Summer and slid his arm protectively around her shoulder. Summer then released a breath that she had not realized she had been holding. "I do want to introduce you to John Long. We went through the police academy together."

The officer allowed a slight smile to ease to his lips. "Hello, Summer. It is nice to see you again. You obviously don't remember meeting me—"

"Oh my gosh," she exclaimed. "John. I'm sorry for not recognizing you. Of course, you're Cathy's brother."

"Summer, no hard feelings—you obviously have a lot going on here today." He winked and smiled. "Cathy told me to keep an eye out for you and to take good care of you, or else."

Now, Summer chuckled. "And we both know that you better listen to your sister. It would appear that my small world has just expanded." She smiled while looking between Adam and John. Their conversation remained light, and included Summer introducing John to her father. Then, it was time to head upstairs in the elevator.

———

When the elevator door opened, Summer immediately caught sight of her three attorneys, and her mother and Kevin standing with them. Summer noticed that this morning, her mother wore dark dress pants, along with an aqua two-piece sweater set. Two silver chains dangled from around her neck. Although her mother was softly smiling, Summer saw the lines of worry in her eyes and jaws. She also noticed that she had her fingers laced with Kevin's fingers. Their bodies touched, as if to announce to the world that they had reconciled and were now inseparable. Both of Kevin's eyes were darkened, turning from red to black and blue. His nose was packed and covered with a soft protective splint to keep his bone in place. Summer glanced over at her father who was also taking in the scene before them.

"Dad, remember our conversation. Give them space," Summer quietly warned.

"I will, Princess." He gave her a quick squeeze on her shoulder. "Adam has already suggested to me that he sit between your mother and me as a buffer." He saw the worry immediately leave Summer's expression as he continued, "Adam is a good man. I like the way he anticipates, assesses and acts. Good police officer. Your Uncle Jim will like him."

Summer smiled as she recalled how her uncle had cared for her mother and her during the trial last May back in upstate New York. She chuckled. "There are similarities between them, aren't there?"

"More than you know." Stephen smiled as he drew his daughter into his arms for one more hug before settling in for court to begin.

—⚡⚡⚡⚡—

Summer was now seated with Nikki and Alex. She saw Mitchel's attorney, Ashley Prime, enter from the door leading to the judge's chambers. There was no sign of Mitchel. Then, she saw him. He was accompanied by two men who were wearing black suits and very serious expressions on their faces. Summer's mind was spinning with a multitude of questions as she looked at Mitchel. Their eyes met. He gave her a slight smile and mouthed, "I will always love you." Summer was stunned as she watched Mitchel take his seat next to his lawyer. The two men were seated in chairs to the other side of him. At that moment, Summer glanced around and noticed more people in dark suits were in court with them. Then, Judge Roberts entered, and Summer's life changed forever.

Judge Roberts reviewed with Summer's and Mitchel's legal teams the motion for divorce and the financial agreement that they had reached. Summer listened to the words that were spoken, almost as if she was in a tunnel and was hearing an echo. It felt as if she were dreaming until she heard, "As judge, I am going to be granting the divorce between Dr. Mitchel Brown and Summer Newman-Brown, effective as of this date and time. Now, having said that"—the judge looked directly at Summer— "before I give my final decree on the divorce, and adjourn this hearing, we have one more matter to address. Ms. Newman, you are obviously aware of our guests in court with us this morning." Summer nodded while swallowing her emotions and listened. "These guests are from the FBI and the US Marshal's Office." Summer's heart did a flip-flop as she listened. "They are here on Dr. Brown's behalf. After court is adjourned, you and Dr. Brown will be escorted out by the marshals, who will give you both a few moments to speak with each other. Ms. Newman, after this morning, not only will you and Dr. Brown be divorced, he will no longer exist. As part of Dr. Brown's agreement with the FBI, he is going to be a key witness against the Octivani crime family. During the trial, Dr. Brown will be in a safe house, and then he will enter the witness protection program."

FBI—US Marshals—witness protection program. Summer was beyond stunned by this revelation about Mitchel, and his plans for his life. She turned to Nikki, who mouthed for Summer to listen to the judge. Alex slid his hand over onto Summer's and gently squeezed for reassurance. Summer blinked her tears back as she gasped for air.

"Ms. Newman, Dr. Brown," Judge Roberts spoke with compassion and concern for both of them, and then said while signing the divorce decree, "this divorce is fully granted. Court is adjourned."

Everything seemed surreal for Summer. Mitchel and she were now divorced. In a matter of time, he would no longer exist in her world. She watched as the two marshals escorted Mitchel from the courtroom. Then, a marshal came over to her and escorted her out as well. When Summer entered the room and saw Mitchel, they immediately stepped into each other's arms and wept together. They whispered words for only the other to hear, and then they kissed their final bittersweet kiss. Theirs to remember for a lifetime. When they drew apart, the marshals stepped up next to Mitchel to escort him out. As Mitchel stepped through the door into the hall, he paused, gazed back at Summer, and quietly said, "I will always love you. Be happy, Summer. You deserve it." He then turned from Summer, who was blinking back her tears, and then he was gone.

Summer was glad to have a local sheriff deputy escort her to the elevators where everyone was waiting for her. Adam had been first to see her approach them, and immediately went to her side. He spoke quietly to the deputy while he held on to her, and she wept out tears. Then, a gentle hand touched her back. She recognized the touch and quietly spoke to Adam. In one fluid motion, Summer turned from Adam into her mother's arms and wept with heart-wrenching pain.

"Mom," Summer's words were barely audible, "I don't know if I could have made it through this without you being here."

"Sunshine, it warms me to know you need me. However, I do believe that Adam is longing to hold you. If your father and I were not here, he would have stepped up, and been all the support you needed. Am I correct, Adam?" Her tone dared him challenge.

"You are correct, ma'am. Summer, I love you, and am here for as long as you'll allow me to stay by your side."

"And I love you, Adam. It is nice to know I am entering into a new season of my life with you by my side." Summer found a smile was beginning to take form as she turned to her mother. "Mom, with everything that has happened, I do hope you and Kevin will come over to my place. Nate, Nikki, and Alex will be there with us."

Amanda tenderly smiled. "Sunshine, thank you, but no, thank you. Right now, we will be going back to the hotel. I have an injured husband and a marriage to take care of. Summer Brooke," she intentionally kept her voice quiet, but firm, "I see the pout forming. Put it away. You have Adam, your dad, and others to comfort you. How about I call you in a little while to let you know how we're doing?" Amanda gently touched Summer's cheek as she added, "Honey, we'll find time for us to be together before we return to Baltimore."

"Okay. But, Mom…"

"Yes, Summer?"

"I'm going to hold you to it." Summer sniffled. "I love you, Mom."

"I love you too." Amanda drew Summer into her embrace. She then whispered in Summer's ear, "Now, go to that cute detective who is waiting to take care of you." With that said, Amanda placed a gentle kiss on Summer's cheek before stepping away from her.

Summer and Adam watched her mother and Kevin leave. They both noticed who the couple spoke with and whom they omitted. Summer sighed as she realized her father had called this one correctly. Apparently, her mother had frozen him out of her life. She had to wonder how long the winter season would last for them this time around.

25

Summer had become accustomed to hearing the normal rhythm of her father as he moved through her house. In a few short hours, he would be gone, and her home would once again be too quiet.

"Princess," Stephen's quiet voice seemed to naturally coincide with her mood.

"Yes, Dad." Summer sniffled as she turned from the counter in the kitchen, where she was preparing their lunch meal.

"Since I'll be leaving in a little while, I went ahead and stripped my sheets from the bed and replaced the trundle under the daybed for you. Where would you like for me to put these sheets to be washed?"

By now, Summer had wiped her hands and was walking toward him. She softly smiled, while moisture began to form on her eyelashes. "Thank you, Dad. I'll take them."

When Summer reached out to take the linens from him, he gently clasped his hand around hers. At that moment, Stephen's eyes held Summer's, as if to memorize every part of her. "Am I detecting that you are saddened by my leaving?" Summer nodded. "Hey now, Princess, you know the holidays aren't all that far off. You're coming east to be with me and our family for Thanksgiving.

Plus, you'll get to see your mother's family as well. Come here, you." Stephen opened his arms, which Summer immediately stepped into. "Summer, I am proud of you and how you have carried yourself through these past days, weeks, and months. I am sorry for adding to your pain by my lashing out against Kevin the other night."

Summer tightened her hold on him. "Dad, thank you for your kind words. Honestly, when I first saw and heard everything, I was more concerned about how you were once again hurting Mom. Adam helped me realize that your actions toward Kevin was purely a guy thing."

"I know, Princess." He sighed. "I seem to have no trouble hurting Amanda, and am not surprised that she stayed away from here last night. Summer, you should know that we did text each other, and then briefly talked on the phone."

"I'm glad to know that. So—" She looked intently into his eyes. Her voice was filled with hope as she spoke, "Is everything okay between the two of you?"

"Well, Summer, she has accepted my apology." His expression revealed his regret for his actions.

"We're back to taking it one day at a time, to see if we can salvage our friendship."

"That sounds like how Mom has always been—move with caution, one day at a time." Summer sighed. "Dad, let's move on from talking about Mom to talking about us."

"All right, what's on your mind?" Stephen leaned against the counter as he watched and listened to Summer share her feelings with him.

"This summer with everything that has unfolded in my life, I've had plenty of time to reflect on the conversations we had last May when we were getting acquainted. I've been thinking about how you said…let's see if I get this right. 'Love is an amazing fragile gift that we are given by God to share with other people.'"

"Princess, you have an extraordinary memory. I'm glad you chose to remember what I said about love, because it is a gift, one that we're blessed to get to share at this time in our lives."

"I agree. Mitchel discarded our love, and look at how God is, as you say, blessing me. Last spring, who would have thought that Adam—not at all the type of man I would normally migrate to—would now be totally planted in my life to grow in love with?"

"Honey, God's love manifests itself in us through relationships—his with us, and ours with each other." Stephen paused to collect his thoughts. "Sometimes the storms of life challenge our love to abide. But in every situation we face, we can always trust that God, as the Prophet Jeremiah said to Israel, God has good plans for us. The God I know is not about destroying and hurting us. God is about giving us life, a future that is filled with hope and goodness, a life filled with love."

"Thus says the son of Reverend Johnson."

Stephen tilted his head as a smile grew on his lips. Summer giggled as he spoke with a chuckle in his voice. "Okay, smarty. I see where you're going. Just so you know, those words I just shared with you were paraphrased from one of my favorite passages from the Bible. It's from Jeremiah chapter twenty-nine, verse eleven."

"Thank you, Dad, for sharing that with me. I just might have to dig out my Bible and check it out for myself. Here's a thought. Maybe in the future when we talk on the phone, you can point me to some other good passages for me to read."

"I will be honored. You know, Summer, your mother also knows scripture."

"I know she does. But, Dad, I'd like for this to be something special for us to share together."

Stephen could not help but sniffle back his emotions. His smile revealed the depth of his love for her. "All right, Princess. You sure are full of surprises and keep me on my toes. For now, we best get our lunch and then head for the airport."

Summer felt the exhaustion sweeping over her as she returned to her home alone for the first time in days. Nate had said his good-bye to her last night, before heading to Colorado Springs with Nikki and Alex. Adam was at work, and her father was now on his way back to New York. Summer glanced at the clock hanging on the wall in her kitchen. She sighed while realizing she had time to relax on her porch with a cup of tea, before Mom and Kevin were expected to arrive.

The gentle breeze blowing the curtains, and the tea and quiet were all relaxing, causing Summer to doze off to sleep. She awakened to find her mother gently calling through the screen to wake her. Summer yawned, stretched, and stood.

"Hello," Summer sleepily said, while moving with haste to unlock the porch door. She yawned again while making a ghastly sound. Of course, her mother gave commentary, as they greeted one another and embraced.

"Sunshine, you looked so peaceful that we contemplated not waking you."

"You know if you had left without waking me, you—" Summer had drawn her brow to indicate her displeasure over her mom's words.

"I know. You don't need to elaborate on the trouble we would be in with you." With that, Amanda smiled tenderly at her daughter and held out a bag she was holding in her hand.

"What's this?" Summer reached for the bag and peeked in. "Oh my. Lobster tails, steak, fresh vegetables. Yum! Thank you, Mom."

"Don't thank me, thank Kevin. This feast was his idea. I thought discount hot dogs and generic chips would suffice." There was a hint of humor in her voice.

"Hot dogs, right." Summer could not help but smile as she turned her attention from her mother to Kevin. "Thank you, Kevin, for overriding Mom's idea. How are you feeling?" she asked as they all walked into the house.

"I'm definitely sore from having my nose broken, and set into place by an ER resident." Kevin looked at Amanda with tenderness. "Your mother is a natural nurse and has eased my pain more than the resident ever could." Summer noticed a slight tinge of color come to her mother's cheeks while Kevin spoke. She could see that things were much better between the two of them, as Mom doted over Kevin. "The whole experience has given me a new perspective regarding receiving treatment at the ER. My broken nose is bad enough. I can only imagine how painful some of the necessary treatment is for my trauma patients."

"You're right," Amanda quietly spoke. There was no anger in Mom's voice, as in the past few days and weeks. Summer watched and listened to their interaction. "Kevin, you don't have any idea of what it feels like to suffer from a major trauma. But I know firsthand that you are gentle and caring. Sometimes, my love, your gentle, caring spirit does more to alleviate fear, panic, and pain quicker than the medical treatment you provide."

"Mom's right. I'm glad that when we met in February, Mom reminded me that you were her trauma specialist. Even though I haven't been through anything as traumatic as Mom when she had her accident, I remember how you spoke with Uncle Andrew, Aunt Cassie, and me."

"Really. I'd like for you to tell me what you remember." Kevin listened as Summer shared her experience of the trauma. At that moment, Kevin realized that he had much to learn from her, and take back to the ER with him. When Summer completed her thoughts, Kevin discovered both women had tears in their eyes. He opened his arms. "This doctor prescribes a group hug." With that said, Amanda and Summer stepped into his embrace.

Summer was busy moving around the kitchen when Adam arrived. She smiled, wiped her hands, and headed outside to greet him.

"Hey, beautiful," Adam called out.

"Hey, yourself," she said as she slid into his arms. Their kiss was filled with love, yet restrained due to the company out back, and the nosy neighbors. "Kevin, just put the steaks on the grill. Perhaps you'd like to assist him."

"Trying to get rid of me already?"

"Not at all. I'm just hoping for some time to be alone to talk with Mom."

"Then talk with your mother, you shall," Adam said, as he glanced out the window. "I take it you'd like for me to suggest that she leaves Kevin's side and come in to help you?"

Summer smiled and nodded in approval at Adam's astuteness.

"Mom, I'm glad you came inside with me to help me finish preparing dinner."

"Me too." Amanda observed her daughter as she moved about. "Summer, I can tell you obviously have something of importance on your mind. Why don't you just say what is troubling you?"

"Okay." Summer drew in a breath for courage. "Are you going to forgive Dad for striking Kevin and meddling in your life?"

Amanda gently smiled. "Ah, I had a feeling we were on your mind. Honey, the other night, I said many things out of anger, frustration, and fear to both men whom I care about very deeply."

"Fear?"

"Yes, fear. Kevin is my husband. He was lying on the ground, injured—"

"And your love for him caused you to lash out at Dad."

"Yes. I was angry at him. Since then, I have obviously calmed down and talked with your father. Hmm, and what's that smile for?"

"Dad told me that the two of you had spoken and that you were back to taking it one day at a time."

"We are, and yes, once again, I've forgiven him." Amanda saw the concern lingering in her daughter's eyes. "Summer, honey, your father and me…well…we're complicated. We are not working on having a peaceful relationship solely for ourselves."

"Oh?"

"No. Your father and I are working at being friends because we love you, my Summer Sunshine. We don't want you to suffer, simply because we get bugs up our old fannies, lash out and mistreat each other."

Summer began to laugh. "Bugs up your old fannies. I like that—it works for you two!"

"Goodness, the laughter sounds great," Adam said as he came into the kitchen. Kevin stepped over to Amanda, who began to once again dote over him. Adam continued on over to embrace Summer. "We're ready for the lobster tails and kabobs."

"Great, I'll get them from the refrigerator. I do believe Mom and I are ready to come out and join you both."

The evening passed by too quickly for Summer. It was time for her mother and Kevin to leave. This was not only good-night, but also good–bye, for they had an early morning flight back east. She hugged Kevin and said her good-bye to him. Then turning to her mother, Summer saw that moisture was forming in her eyes as well as her own. She sniffled.

"Hey now, come here you." Mom opened her arms and drew Summer into her embrace. "No tears from you, or I'll start crying, and then we'll have a gosh-awful mess."

This caused Summer to smile and sniffle back her emotions. "It would be a ghastly sight, wouldn't it!"

"Uh-huh. So no tears until after I'm gone, and you can find comfort in Adam's arms."

"I'll do that. Mom, I'm glad that you and Kevin are back on track with each other."

Amanda released a breath and allowed herself to smile. "We're getting there. Kevin and I have begun analyzing how both of us acted and reacted in the weeks after our honeymoon, as well as the day of Brian's wedding. We both agree those weeks were like a category five hurricane for us. Our fragile new marriage was ravaged—almost decimated by the storm. However, Kevin and I are both committed to making our relationship work. Together we are digging through the debris of pain and misunderstanding, and already have found our cornerstone is intact."

"Your cornerstone?"

"Yes, Summer. Our marriage—our relationship stands on our love and commitment for one another. We have learned a vital lesson, and will never again take our love for granted. Each day we are working toward rebuilding our trust for one another."

"You mean your trust."

"Not totally, Sunshine. Trust is a two-way street in any relationship." With that, Mom shared with her about her own responsibility in the breakdown in her marriage. "So, Summer, now you see that Kevin and I have weathered our storm. We are ready to go home and begin a new season in our lives. We have the hope and confidence that our marital relationship will bloom and grow in the fertile soil of love. Of course, we will encounter more storms along the way, and we will get through them together. You my precious child, you also are now in a new season in your life. Attend to it with great care."

Friday at the rangers station was relatively quiet. Summer received a call from Mom after they had arrived safely in Baltimore. When the call ended, Summer walked outside into the warm sunshine beaming down from the clear blue sky. As Summer walked, in quiet solitude, she thought about everything that had transpired in her life during the past year. Her marriage to Mitchel reminded Summer of one of the plants in her garden—one that had been neglected and had withered away. Now, new growth was appearing in and around her. She had love and hope for a bright future with Adam, her parents, and her friends. At that moment, Summer turned her face toward the heavens and breathed out, "Both Mom and Dad have been right in their counsel. Thank you, Great Spirit—God, for this gift of love and new life that is yet to come."

> *For everything there is a season, and a time for every matter under heaven. (Ecclesiastes 3:1)*